HOUSE *of* BATHORY

ALSO BY LINDA LAFFERTY

The Bloodletter's Daughter

The Drowning Guard

HOUSE of BATHORY

A Novel

Linda Lafferty

LAKE UNION
PUBLISHING

Text copyright © 2013 by Linda Lafferty

Printed in the United States of America.

Published by Lake Union Publishing, Seattle

www.apub.com

ISBN-13: 9781477808641
ISBN-10: 1477808647

Cover design by theBookDesigners

Library of Congress Control Number: 2013914136

For my beloved sister
Nancy Lafferty Elisha
(because Daisy said I had to)

Prologue

SARVAR CASTLE

HOUSE OF THE NADASDY HORSEMASTER

WESTERN HUNGARY

OCTOBER 31, 1589

In the first minutes, the midwife Agota did not notice anything strange. Her purple-veined hands cradled his head, the baby slick and silent. She smiled at the infant as his eyes opened, blinking at the dim candlelight.

"He is a Magyar, sure enough," she said, admiring his eyes.

The mother groaned, her pelvic muscles still contracting.

"His eyes will be green as his grandfather's," the old midwife said, nodding in admiration.

Sarvar Castle would rejoice tonight, for at last a son was born to the Master of the Horse.

But as she prepared to sever the umbilical cord, the old midwife gasped. Her hands, still stained in warm blood, flew to her face.

The mother pulled herself up, sweat dripping into her eyes.

"What is wrong?" she groaned. "Speak, Agota!"

The old woman shook her head. A second later the babe bawled, a hearty bellow from his tiny lungs.

The mother held out her arms, begging for her baby.

The midwife swaddled the baby in a clean linen sheet, stopping once to drag her withered fingertips over her body in the sign of the cross. Then she thrust the baby into his mother's arms. He quieted immediately, staring silently into his mother's eyes.

"Look, Mistress!" Agota dug her wrinkled pinkie finger under the baby's tiny lips. He mewed in protest.

vii

The mother saw what had so disturbed the midwife. Under the lips was a full set of tiny white teeth, fully formed. "He is a Taltos," hissed the old woman. "One of the Ancients!"

Agota pried open the tightly balled fist of the infant's right hand. Her breathing resonated in the small room, still heavy with the scent of sweat and birth.

"Only five fingers, blessed mercy!" she said.

It was the baby's mother who tenderly loosened his left fist. It was she who discovered the sixth finger.

"It is the sign!" she cried. "What shall I do? What will become of him?"

The candle guttered, a draft crawling under the door. Rain pelted the thick leaded glass.

"Show no one your babe," said Agota. "If the Habsburgs learn, they will dash his brains out."

There was a knock on the door. The midwife and her patient exchanged looks.

"Send him away!" the mother whispered. "Let no one enter this chamber."

The midwife nodded. She opened the door only a crack. One of the stable boys stood outside.

He doffed his cap, revealing dark hair studded with bits of straw and oat chaff.

"The Horsemaster would like to meet his new—excuse me, is it a son or a daughter?"

Agota hesitated, her old tongue licking her cracked lips before she spoke.

"Tell the Master he is the proud father of a healthy baby boy. But the Mistress is still weak and begs he visit her later, when she is fit to receive him."

The door shut quietly. The midwife waited, listening to his retreating steps. Then she slid the bolt.

The mother clutched the baby close to her breast.

"No one shall learn this secret but my husband," she said. "Swear to me you will tell no one and carry this secret to the grave!"

"Mistress, I swear by all that is Holy," murmured the woman. "A Taltos is a divine power. I would be cursed should I bring any harm to this babe, for they are of powerful blessed magic."

The young mother swept back her sweaty hair, her eyes unfocused as she thought.

"I shall feign sickness and the baby's as well. I shall allow no one to visit."

"Still there will be talk. You must go away, far from this kingdom," said the midwife. "And I will cut off the sixth finger, this very day."

"My baby!"

"Hear me, mistress. Either the Church or the King will seek him out. Even the Bathorys themselves might fear him. The mistress Erzsebet who has married Master Ferenc is—strange."

"What do you mean?"

The old woman's face twitched.

"She has cruel ways—" Agota looked over her shoulder, whispering these last words. "There is more of Transylvania in her than Hungary. The Ecsed Bathorys would put this baby to death, for they fear the power of a true Hungarian Taltos."

"But he is innocent!"

The baby nestled against his mother's breast now, nursing gently. She felt only the gentle pull of the newborn's lips, like the sweep of a brook's current, sensing his tiny teeth only as the rocky bottom in a wave of sweet kisses.

"You must leave Sarvar until the babe is five. That is when the baby teeth are set in the jaw of a normal child."

"But the finger! The wound that is left?"

"Say the child tangled his hand in a well rope. Or the slip of a kitchen knife as he reached for a carrot piece."

"So much deception!"

"You must protect your son."

The mother nodded, her face etched in misery.

"And watch for the signs," said the midwife. "He will see things we mortals cannot. The Taltos are possessed in a waking dream, going between the human and spirit worlds. And they communicate with animals, especially horses."

The young mother closed her eyes. "At least his father will be thankful for that."

PART

-1-

Chapter 1

"Daisy."

Alone in her office, Dr. Elizabeth Path murmured the name of her patient, her chin propped in her cupped hand. Her mother hated it when she did that. "Sit up straight," she'd snap.

The oak office chair the psychologist had inherited from her father creaked as she hooked her ankles around the base. She gazed out her office window at the light dusting of snow on Mount Sopris.

The fingers of her left hand absently twirled her wavy brown hair into a thick rope stretching below her collarbone. Her mother hated that, too. "Fidgeting," she called it. Bad enough for a woman nearing forty to have hair past her shoulders, but then to play with it like a child! And such pretty blue eyes—wear some make-up. What are you saving yourself for?

Mom, thought Betsy. *What a piece of work.*

The digital clock transformed into a new minute, a ghostly parade of time dissolving into the black background. Betsy had exactly thirty-three minutes until her patient arrived. She had no answers for Daisy. No answers for Daisy's desperate mother, either.

Damn it. An image of her father crossed her mind, a look of disappointment in his sky-blue eyes. "Listen, Betsy. Hear what lingers in the air unspoken."

Unspoken, yes, Papa. I can hear "unspoken." But what can anyone hear in utter silence?

Betsy needed to find something, anything to break through the silence of Daisy Hart. The sullen girl refused to offer anything more than listless sighs and shrugs, her black fingernails rending larger and larger holes in her dark fishnet stockings.

She would cough occasionally, closing her kohl-rimmed eyes so tightly she smeared her cheekbones black. Betsy would see a flash of that one canine tooth that hadn't been corrected with braces, incongruous amid an otherwise perfect row of straight, white teeth.

Session after session, Daisy's strangled cough echoed in the little Victorian parlor Betsy's father had converted into an office for his own psychiatric practice years ago. The Viennese clock would chime the hour and her Goth patient would rise without saying a word and leave.

Silent as a ghost.

Daisy was an enigma, all wrapped up in a black crepe bow. And her psychologist had not managed to untie the convoluted ribbon.

Betsy shifted the copy of *A Jungian Analysis of Dreams* on her lap. Freshness, purity. Daisies symbolize illumination, enlightenment, a reflection of the sun.

That only told her about Daisy's parents' state of mind when she was born, but nothing about the girl herself.

Betsy pressed her thumbnail against her front teeth, thinking.

Freud tended to interpret dream symbols literally, but for Jung it was the personal feeling associated with the symbol that was the key.

Betsy leaned over to her laptop, in the autumn light that streamed in the south-facing windows. She typed "Daisy" in a dream analysis website, the kind that would leave fellow analysts sneering in disdain. It was like reading a horoscope in the local newspaper.

Still, when a patient presented a dilemma, it was a sinful pleasure to cast off her formal training and indulge in a quick chuckle.

Her computer screen filled with diet ads: grossly shrinking and swelling bodies beckoned on the right margin. Tarot card readings flashed in neon colors.

TO SEE A DAISY OUT OF SEASON IS TO BE ASSAILED BY EVIL IN SOME GUISE.

She looked out the window at snow-capped Mount Sopris. Almost imperceptibly, she shook her head.
She Googled again.

DREAM MOODS
TO DREAM OF WALKING IN A FIELD OF DAISIES REPRESENTS GOOD LUCK AND PROSPERITY. SOMEONE WILL BE THERE TO OFFER YOU A HELPING HAND AND SOME GUIDANCE FOR YOUR PROBLEMS.

Ha! Betsy thought. *Offer me guidance! That's a good one. Daisy couldn't guide herself out of a hall closet.*
Betsy's short fingernails clicked over the keyboard. One more try.

TATTOO SYMBOLOGY—WHAT'S BEHIND THE TAT?
DAISY IS THE SYMBOL OF SISTERHOOD.

Betsy snorted, the way her father loved to hear her laugh. The laughter was swallowed in the silence of the empty house.
Winter was near. A few remaining aspen leaves quivered in clusters of bright gold on the branches. Fallen leaves rustled dry and curled, chasing each other across Main Street, crushed to crackling bits under the occasional slow-moving car. Overnight all the remaining leaves could wither and the ground freeze rock hard.
Betsy was desperate to get outside. The warmth of autumn did not linger in the Colorado Rockies. Snow was in the five-day forecast.

There was just this one patient—Daisy—to see before she could close her laptop and head out into the last of the sunshine. Hurry up, damn it!

Still another quarter of an hour. She opened her e-mail and read her mother's brief message again.

BRATISLAVA AND THE SLOVAK COUNTRYSIDE NEVER CEASE TO ENCHANT ME. I GO TO VISIT CACHTICE CASTLE TOMORROW, HOME OF THE INFAMOUS COUNTESS BATHORY.

I WILL SEND YOU A POSTCARD, DARLING.

Betsy closed her eyes. She stifled a sob, biting her fist. How could her mother be so nonchalant, so callous? *Enchant* her? It was not a decade ago that Betsy's father had died in a car accident in Slovakia. How could her mother bear to go back?

Enchanting? What the fuck was wrong with her mother?

Betsy drew a breath. Her mother, a historian and professor, had loved Eastern Europe long before she married the handsome Slovak-born Jungian psychiatrist. No doubt the Bratislava she spoke of was the Bratislava of seventeenth-century Habsburg Hungary, the heart of her research. The death of Betsy's father had not stained that image. Dr. Grace Path's eyes and ears would not see her husband's blood streaking the rocky ground. His widow would see only the Court of Matthias II, Holy Roman Emperor.

Grace's research was what she had left. Who was Betsy to deny her that?

There was a knock on the door and then the sound of retreating steps. Through the window, Betsy could see a well-dressed, shapely woman in her midforties—only a few years older than Betsy herself. Jane Hart, Daisy's mother. And her coming to the door—even if only to knock—was a significant event. In the weeks Daisy had been coming to Carbondale, Jane had never visited the office, as if afraid of some kind of contamination. She would drop her daughter off, then pick her up again when the session was finished, never leaving her car. *She's afraid of infection,* thought Betsy. *As if she'd pick up a mental illness by crossing the threshold.*

Betsy quietly moved closer to the window to listen in as Jane argued fiercely with her daughter. Discourse between a mother and a patient was a powerful tool in analysis. Besides, this was the first time she had ever heard her patient speak more than monosyllables. Daisy fingered a gold cross around her neck as she shook her head stubbornly.

"I don't need to see a shrink," she said. "I'm not crazy. I'm tired of this shit!"

"I'm not saying you're crazy. But you have a problem, and it's damned lucky you didn't choke to death last weekend."

"Would that have made you happy?"

Jane ignored that. "And look how you're dressed! And that crap on your lips. It looks like smeared chocolate."

Daisy tossed her jet-black hair in defiance, the scowl on her matte-black lips setting deep creases in her white makeup.

"You think I should wear some kind of peachy-fake, come-fuck-me lipstick like yours?"

Jane's body went rigid, her hands curled into bony fists.

"I'm calling your father," she snapped. She pulled a ruby-red cell phone from her purse.

"Dad has *nothing* to do with this!"

Betsy noticed the crack in the girl's voice, registering a jolt of fear.

Her mother pressed speed dial. "I want him to know exactly how you are behaving."

Daisy snatched the phone from her mother's hand and threw it into the street. "Fuck it, Mother. I'll go, OK? Just leave Dad out of this!"

The girl stalked toward the front door, leaving her mother to scramble after the phone and then follow.

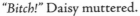

"*Bitch!*" Daisy muttered.

Betsy straightened the papers on her desk and prepared to greet her patient.

"Betsy," began Jane, brushing past her daughter into the little Victorian house, "things have gotten *worse*, not better since Daisy started with you!"

Betsy did not answer at once. She caught Daisy, still poised on the threshold—not in, not out, that was Daisy all right—watching from the corner of her eye. Now that her analyst was the object of Daisy's mother's anger, she was worthy of interest.

"How are you helping her?" Jane demanded. "And look at all the papers and clutter in your office! I don't get the impression you are professional—"

"How have things gotten worse?" Betsy finally said, answering Jane's question with one of her own.

Betsy watched mother and daughter stare at each other, fury in their eyes. Neither one of them blinked.

"What happened?" Betsy asked.

Again neither answered. The autumn air was suddenly filled with an animated conversation in Spanish from the Mexican grocery next door to the office.

"*¿Quiere algo más, Señora?*" said a singsong voice.

Betsy beckoned Daisy to step into the office, closing the door quietly behind her. The cheerful Mexican voices were shut out, the resulting silence ominous.

"Well? What do you think, Daisy? How have I failed?" Betsy asked.

Daisy shook her dark hair, obscuring her eyes.

The psychologist turned. "Jane?"

Jane began picking at her manicured nails. Betsy caught a whiff of expensive perfume.

"I don't know why she won't tell you," she said. "It happened *again*, damn it!"

"What happened?"

Jane looked at the door, as if contemplating a quick exit. Then she set her lips firmly deciding to answer.

"She almost choked to death over the weekend. She was strangling on her own spit—"

"That's NOT what the doctor said!" interrupted Daisy. "You always get everything so freaking wrong!"

Betsy kept her expression neutral. Something had finally provoked her patient to speak with true emotion. "Why didn't you call me?"

Jane looked at Betsy, exasperated, but with a flash of terror in her eyes. The psychologist interpreted it as real fear, not an affectation.

"I had to take her to the emergency room. They gave her a muscle relaxant so she would stop choking. She couldn't breathe!"

"What was the drug?"

"I don't remember. I can find out."

Betsy turned to Daisy.

"Did it work?"

The girl snorted in derision.

"And they found no obstruction in your throat?" Betsy wanted to provoke an answer. Anything. "Any irritant? Hot peppers or vinegar? Any cleaning fluids? Ammonia?"

Daisy just stared, playing ferociously with the charm bracelet on her wrist.

"Daisy—don't be rude. Answer her! There was nothing," said Jane. "You know that. That's what this is all about."

"So what did they decide was the cause?" Betsy asked.

Jane looked down at her nails again. This time she managed to chip off a fleck of the polish.

"Nerves, they said. A psychological problem. That's why we're here, isn't it?"

"Oh, bullshit Mother!" shouted Daisy, stomping her heavy boot on the wood floor. "The only reason we're here is because you think I'm weird. You hate me and you hate the Goth world."

This girl could *talk*, thought Betsy. *And what a mouth.*

Jane sucked in a breath and expelled it, her finely chiseled nostrils flaring. She glared at Daisy and turned to Betsy.

"Before we moved to Aspen, she was a perfectly normal child. She was an accomplished equestrian, red-cheeked and healthy. Absolutely normal. And lots of friends. Of her same . . . social class."

Betsy looked back at Daisy's mother. "Jane, what do you define as normal?"

"Not—not *this*! Look at her! The black lipstick, the shredded dress, the white makeup as if she's a corpse. She should have color from hiking in the mountains, be out with friends—normal friends."

"Mother!"

"She shouldn't look like a freaking vampire! There, I've said it!"

"I am NOT a freaking vampire. I'm Goth!"

"Whatever. Vampire, Goth . . . in Aspen, of all places. It's weird. And so—so *outré*!"

Daisy's eyes burned. Betsy heard the slight tinkle of the silver bracelet as the charms trembled on her wrist.

"Damn it, I should be able to take her out to lunch without *cringing*!"

"All right," Betsy took over. "We have established that Jane thinks you have a problem. And what about you, Daisy? This therapy is about you, no one else. What do you want to accomplish here?"

Daisy looked at her mother and then again at her analyst. She pushed her hair behind her ears.

Betsy was ready for Daisy to tell her that this was all a waste of time, that she didn't want to accomplish anything, that there was nothing to "accomplish," that she was happy the way she was, maybe tell her to go to hell. And after that, Betsy expected the girl never to utter another syllable in her presence.

But she was wrong.

Daisy's gaze settled on her analyst. The doctor and patient looked each other in the shifting, golden light of the low autumnal sun.

Then the girl closed her eyes tight and swallowed.

"The choking freaked me out."

The psychologist saw the one misaligned canine tooth glint and disappear as she spoke. The girl opened her eyes and looked down at her pale hands. When she raised her gaze again, there were long black smudges under her eyes. Betsy had to strain to hear what Daisy said next.

"I don't want to die," Daisy whispered. "Help me."

When the sound of Jane's Audi had faded away, Betsy noticed how Daisy's shoulders relaxed.

"I want you to get a notebook," Betsy said, "and keep it beside your bed. So you can write down your dreams." Her patient was talking, now it was time to move ahead.

"What for?"

"Dreams are the bridge to your unconscious mind. Your strongest urges, hopes, and fears often make an appearance while your conscious mind sleeps. I mentioned this at our first session, but . . ."

"But what?"

"You were so—nonresponsive. Now it's time to start working in earnest. The progress we make starts with your wanting to communicate. You're ready now."

The girl shrugged her bony shoulders and studied the toe of her boot.

"Whatever," she mumbled.

Betsy asked her to write down any previous dreams that she could remember. "And particularly epic dreams. The ones that seem to go on and on like a movie, rather than just short scenes."

"Why? Why are dreams so important?"

"Dream interpretation is a basic principle of Jungian psychology. Your dreams provide clues to your unconscious mind."

Daisy nodded her head. The canine tooth suddenly flashed in a smile.

"And nightmares?" she asked, her voice low. "You want me to write about those, too?"

"Especially nightmares, Daisy."

The girl ran her tongue under her lip. "This Jung guy sounds interesting. Dreams, nightmares? Creepy."

The psychologist nodded. "Dreams are an open portal to your unconscious mind."

"And—how about your soul?"

"Well, yes. Jung believed that. But my goal is to help you discover mental health."

"And what haunts me, right?"

"Your unconscious struggles, yes."

Daisy nodded slowly, her hair obscuring her face.

"Cool," she whispered.

Chapter 2

Only the palest wash of light seeped through the arrow loopholes in the stone fortress. Winding her way up the turret stairs, Zuzana carried a candle, lighting the torches along the icy walls. The sudden flames sent rats slinking into the dark, their mean chatter echoing in the frigid air.

A cat pounced, seizing a rat by its neck. Zuzana's startled gasp cast a cloud of vapor that slowly faded above her head. The cat gave a low growl, dragging its squeaking prey into the shadows.

Cats everywhere. A plague of cats! But all the cats the witch Darvulia brought could never rid the castle of vermin. What matter? Zuzana was late in the preparations for her mistress's morning toilette. The girl shivered in the cold Slovak dawn. She hugged her coarse wool shawl closer to her body, her fingers chilled raw and aching.

The servants' door to the Countess's dressing room opened grudgingly. Zuzana heard the stirring of the bedcovers and linens in the bedroom beyond. She cursed herself for falling back asleep after the horrid dream that had left her choking and gasping for breath like a carp on dry land. Even as her eyes snapped open, she still saw the castle walls awash in blood. She had struggled to regain her breath, the red gore slowly fading to gray stone once more.

She kissed the tiny crucifix around her neck. Her chapped lips moved silently in prayer.

Zuzana was the only handmaiden Countess Erzsebet Bathory had brought from Sarvar Castle in Lower Hungary, but she was never allowed to enter the inner bedchamber. She was obliged to keep to the frigid corridor and the dressing room. For Zuzana that was a blessing, God's intercession that spared her from crossing the evil threshold, and every night she whispered a prayer of thanks.

Some of the Slovak women teased her about her exclusion from the bedchamber with its plastered walls and silk tapestries. Zuzana could not enter, they said, because the Countess could not bear to see the handmaiden's scarred face upon waking.

"A *nocny* in the morning light, when the sun should chase away the demons of darkness!" mocked the big-bosomed Hedvika.

Nocny. Nightmare. The village handmaidens called her "nightmare" in their poor and heavily accented German. They spoke only Slovak, not a word of Hungarian, but the Countess suffered them. The ones who did not sleep on straw pallets in the castle made the long walk up from the village before dawn, their cloaks pulled tight against the winter snows, wary of the amber-eyed wolves that lurked in the darkness.

Čachtice Castle perched high on a rocky mountainside, surrounded by the wild borderlands of embattled Royal Habsburg Hungary, hard against the Ottoman territories to the east. Too often the acrid smell of gunpowder and scorched land scented the morning air, carried from the battlefields beyond.

Zuzana stirred the embers in the fireplace and added twigs to resurrect the flames. The warped panes of the windows distorted the light, casting irregular coins of pale brightness. A bird beat its wings, launching into the dawn from its roost. The maid raised her eyes to watch it flutter away.

She yelped, her fingers singed by the newborn flames.

Zuzana could hear the creak of the wooden bed and the rustle of sheets. A servant would be massaging the mistress's small white feet with ambergris oil and scenting them with lavender before she eased them into the kidskin slippers. And Darvulia would be giving the Countess a morning potion, chanting spells to protect her.

Zuzana hurried about her chores, knowing any moment Countess Bathory would demand her full attention.

The silver brushes, ivory combs, and filigreed hand mirror were laid out on starched linen. The perfume vials and tins of powders lined the vanity table. Zuzana pulled the stopper from the crystal flask of Hungarian water—aqua vitae, rosemary tops, and ambergris. Her pale lips curved up in pleasure, the smell was divine and she knew it would please her mistress. The handmaiden took satisfaction in Countess Bathory's legendary beauty, due in part to Zuzana's work in maintaining the creamy perfection of the Countess's porcelain-white skin. Zuzana created her own potions from the rendered fat of peacocks and minerals from the banks of the River Vah.

The Countess took a fierce pride in her complexion. She never exposed her skin to the rays of the sun. The stingy light that crept through the arrow slits and slipped around the velvet edges of the curtains was the only sun she could abide.

It was said that the Countess had a mortal dread of the sun.

That is where the foolish folklore lies, thought Zuzana. While the village people of Čachtice whispered legends of demons, Zuzana knew better. It was the Countess's vanity that made her hide from the light.

Night was Bathory's time for excursions in her black lacquered coach or for entertaining guests in the great hall of the castle. And just now, at this early hour, the exact parting of night and day, was when the Countess insisted on making her toilette, when daylight was the weakest and she could inspect her skin in the looking glass, without fear of the sun's harsh rays.

The Countess's voice murmured in her bedchamber, and Zuzana's chest tightened. She still had one chore to perform: the most difficult part of the morning, polishing the looking glass.

Clutching a soft rag, the maid's fists churned furious circles over her reflection, as if she could erase herself. The shining glass reflected the pale morning light, teasing the girl with her own image.

Zuzana frowned and blocked the heartless glass, playing hide-and-seek with her reflection. She finally closed her eyes, smarting with tears, and turned away.

Zuzana was not fair of face.

The pox had scarred her once-perfect skin, though she had slipped the malady's embrace with her life, unlike her handsome older brother, who had died in an earlier wave of the Hungarian scourge, years before she was born. The plague had carried him away, his skin blue, his rattling breath surrendering his soul into the other world. Even so, death had been kind—the peasant boy was in his winding cloth before the Bathorys fully understood his involvement with their adored daughter. Zuzana shuddered to think of what hideous torture would have befallen him had he survived the fever.

Indeed the pox had been a blessing in disguise for both brother and sister. Ladislav had died before he could be tortured; and Zuzana, who was born beautiful as the sunrise, was scarred so badly that the villagers turned away from the sight of her. Strangers scowled and made a sign to ward off evil if they encountered her along the road. The town idiot threw stones at her, jeering. But her affliction had captured the attention of the powerful Countess Bathory, who had taken mercy on the scarred girl, as one might take mercy on a mongrel puppy.

Still, the Slovak maids teased her mercilessly. When their mistress was not in earshot, Zuzana endured their taunts, especially the cruelest from Hedvika.

"Only the devil could sear thumbprints so deep in your skin."

Was she really so ugly? Her bright blue eyes still shone from under thick black lashes, her hair gleamed a flaxen yellow, but the pox scars on her skin were the only feature the maids noticed—and scorned.

Zuzana heard the creak of the hinges. She stuffed the cleaning rag into her apron pocket.

The entourage of handmaidens accompanied the Countess only as far as the doorway. They were forbidden to enter the dressing room and Zuzana knew why: Erzsebet Bathory could not abide the sight of a fair maiden beside her in the looking glass.

Only one trusted girl, the pretty dark-haired Vida, accompanied the Countess. She helped seat her mistress upon the cushion and then spread the heavy train of her red velvet dressing gown along the carpeted floor. The maiden kept her head bowed and did not lift her face.

The Countess glanced at the silver-backed brushes and flasks of oils and potions. Her bejeweled hand ran over the ivory comb, caressing the handheld mirror, the silver pot of lip stain. Her lips curved in satisfaction.

Zuzana watched as Vida kneeled to smooth the hem of the velvet train on the floor and then backed silently out the door.

The Countess settled back into the chair. Zuzana curtsied, her head low and tight in respect.

The Countess lifted Zuzana's chin with her cold, white hand and studied her maid's face. The girl trembled in her mistress's grasp.

The Countess laughed, her white teeth gleaming in the blazing light of the torches.

"My little monster," she murmured, still holding the girl's chin. "How delightfully ugly you are! Not like your charming friend, *Slecna* Vida."

"Yes, Madame," Zuzana replied, looking into her amber eyes. "I live to serve you, my Countess."

"Yes," the Countess said, pulling the girl beside her to gaze into the looking glass. Zuzana shut her eyes.

"Open your eyes, my pet."

The girl opened her eyes wide at her mistress's command and saw their reflections side by side in the silver glass.

"Do you think I am still beautiful?" the Countess asked, looking at her image in the mirror, her chin pointing left and then right. Bathory's gaze was childlike and wistful, black lashes framing her feline eyes.

Zuzana did not hesitate.

"Of course, Madame, your beauty takes the breath from anyone who gazes at you. You are the fairest woman in Hungary!"

The Countess cast a look of scorn, her arched brows diving together above her thin nose. More words tumbled from Zuzana's mouth. "—and of the Holy Roman Empire and beyond, Madame. More beautiful than the youngest maiden in Christendom, and far beyond to the Oriental kingdoms, I am certain."

The Countess's face softened and she gazed at herself again in the glass. Her blood-red lips broke into a smile, exposing her even white teeth. Zuzana felt a cold chill clutch her spine.

"But I am two and a half score," the Countess replied, studying her reflection.

"Ah, but Countess! Not in the looking glass. See the white skin and blazing eyes! How they beseech your admirers to embrace your beauty."

The girl took up the silver brush, gleaming in the torchlight. She softened the boar bristles in the palm of her hand, bending the stiff hairs back and forth until they were supple.

"With your permission, Countess."

Her mistress lifted her chin, almost imperceptibly. Zuzana stroked the long auburn hair, taking care not to tug at any errant tangle.

Erzsebet Bathory closed her eyes and moaned, her long, pale fingers twisting together in her lap.

"Ah, Zuzana," she whispered. "If you were only beautiful . . . like your brother."

Beautiful? Her words sent another shiver up the girl's spine. The Countess noticed a small tremor in the stroke of the brush and looked up at the girl's pox-scarred face.

Zuzana was no beauty now, God be praised.

Chapter 3

I'm looking forward to our session," Betsy said. "Did you bring your dream notebook?"

Daisy's eyes seemed glassy and unfocused. She said nothing.

The psychologist held her breath. *Not again*, she thought.

Daisy entered the office like a sleepwalker. Then she saw Ringo, the mongrel shepherd curled up on a hooked rug, warming himself by the stove. It was the first time in months that Betsy had brought him downstairs to the office.

The girl's body relaxed, light returned to her eyes, dimples creasing her white makeup.

"What a gorgeous dog!" she said, her hand extended for him to sniff. "May I pet him?"

"Of course," Betsy said, marveling at the transformation. "He's a big baby."

Ringo licked the girl's hand. Although sweet and gentle, he wasn't a licker, and Betsy's forehead puckered in astonishment.

He thumped his tail hard, as if he recognized Daisy.

Then he licked her white face. Betsy felt a stab of jealousy.

"He never licks anyone on the face. Not even me."

Daisy extended her neck as Ringo sat up, still intent on licking her.

"This is strange. It's almost as if he knows you," said Betsy.

17

Daisy buried her face in his fur. Betsy noticed tears glistening in her eyes, as she stroked Ringo's ears flat against his head.

They started the session talking about dogs and went on from there. It was by far the longest conversation patient and doctor had ever had.

"I had a German shepherd when we lived back in New York," Daisy said. "We had several dogs, but Rosco was mine. He slept in my bed and ran alongside my horse on trail rides."

"Tell me about riding."

"I used to ride. A lot. I rode competitively, three-day eventing, horse shows."

"But not now?"

"I don't have a horse here and I—I've lost interest. It's not my world now," she said, turning away. She looked longingly back at Ringo.

"What is your world now, Daisy?"

"Goth." She answered, her voice losing its softness. A pinched look took over the youthfulness that for a few minutes had shone through the white makeup.

Betsy called Ringo over. He laid his head in his mistress's lap and she stroked his ears.

"What is Goth exactly?"

Daisy moved in the armchair, shifting her weight. "It depends who's defining it."

"How about you? How do you define it?"

"There's the music. I'm not big into that, except Jim Morrison and the Doors, old stuff. The heavy metal, forget it. But it's a scene for Goths."

"What else?"

"Black clothes, edgy hair, makeup. All that. But the real thing is shunning the superficial world, trying to see past the surface. Embracing the shadow world, not shutting the portal like most humans do."

The psychologist held her pen poised in the air.

"The shadow world?"

Daisy wound a strand of dyed black hair tight around her finger, just the way Betsy often did.

"Shining a light into the past—" she replied, the sheer effort of speaking seeming to torture her. She coughed, but struggled to finish her sentence. "—into the black tunnel. The darkness beyond, who we truly are. Who we may have been before."

Betsy made herself look down at her notebook. She had expected to hear a tirade against the mainstream culture, a defense of an alternative lifestyle. Rebellion.

"Do you think you do it to annoy your mother?" Betsy asked.

Daisy smiled slowly, her tongue searching mischievously for that rebellious tooth. Ringo stood up and left his mistress for her patient's outstretched hand.

"Not really." Then she shrugged. "Well maybe, but that's not the point. I'm just trying to concentrate."

"Concentrate on what?"

Daisy dropped her hand from Ringo's chest. He groaned as he made three circles, finally lowering his body and curling up by her feet.

"On murmurs, voices that have lived before. To hear ripples of the past. And . . . ," she said, the muscles in her jaw straining, "the search for my soul."

Betsy nodded. Her heart was racing. Daisy sounded as if she were quoting Carl Jung himself.

Betsy made two cups of ginger tea with honey. Daisy drank quietly, looking around the room.

"Oh, I need to tell you that I have an upcoming trip. I'll miss a week's session with you, but we can try for two sessions the week before I leave or when I get back. I'll take a look at my schedule."

Daisy cast her an anxious look.

"You are going away?" she said, picking at her cuticles.

"Just for a few days," said Betsy, noticing the effect her words had on her patient.

Daisy nodded, her movements stiff. Her eyes fixed on the cream-colored bookshelves, from floor to ceiling.

"You have a lot of books. Have you read them all?"

"No, I haven't."

"They look really old," said Daisy. She stood up and ran her finger along the spines, inspecting the cracked leather with her fingernail.

Betsy winced, but didn't interfere.

"Leather. Really dusty. Like these are ancient. Where did you get them?"

"I inherited them," Betsy said, looking out the window at the trembling aspen branches.

Daisy tilted her head to the side to read the titles. She stopped at a slim, cloth-covered book. She began to pull it from the shelf and then stopped.

"Jung?"

Betsy nodded.

Daisy tried to read the title on the spine, but stumbled badly. "Synchronizitat . . . Akausalitat . . . What the fu—?"

"In English it translates to 'Synchronicity: An Acausal Connecting Principle.' We had a first edition of it once. But it disappeared."

"What does that mean?" Daisy asked, pushing the book back on the shelf.

Betsy knew she had to redirect the conversation, but she didn't want to risk having her patient shut down, reverting to moody silences.

"Synchronicity was a theory of Jung's. It is the idea of two or more events that are apparently unrelated occurring together in a meaningful manner."

The girl wrinkled her white-painted forehead. "What does *that* mean?"

"OK. Let's say you hear your cell phone ring four times in the morning, but no one is on the line when you answer. And then later in the day, you hit four stoplights, all turning green, right in a row, and that has never happened to you before. At school, there is a lottery and you pick the number 4444 and you win. There is no causal relation, but there may be a deeper meaning."

"Goth," Daisy said, rolling her kohl-lined eyes. "Totally."

"It is interesting you would say that—"

Daisy turned back to the shelves of books. "You inherited them? From who?"

"My father." Betsy swallowed hard. Why was *she* answering all the questions now?

Daisy's hand halted in midair. It fluttered down again to her side. She stared over her shoulder at Betsy.

"Your dad was a shrink too?"

Betsy touched her tongue to the roof of her mouth, making herself hesitate. She wanted to answer: *My father was a renowned psychiatrist. He was the real thing, a graduate of the CG Jung Institute in Zurich and a faculty member of the Jung Institute in Vienna. He treated some of the world's most prominent families. He worked with patients with serious psychosis, behind the locked doors of an asylum.*

He was a genius, she wanted to say.

"Yes, he worked in the field of psychology. Daisy, please. We need to talk about you."

"OK. OK."

Daisy collapsed in her chair, heaving a sigh. She picked up her cup of tea. She studied its depths and tipped it up to her mouth, obscuring her face. Betsy could see the gleam of white skin shining through the part of her dyed jet-black hair.

"What kind of relationship do you and your mother have?"

Daisy looked over the brim of her cup, her eyes hardening.

"What do you think? You've seen us. We fight like cats and dogs."

"Which is your mother? A cat or a dog?"

"Oh, definitely a cat," she said, nodding. "Oh, yes. A cat."

"Why a cat?"

"I don't know. You can trust a dog. Cats are . . . different. And my sister, Morgan—even more of a cat."

"So you don't think you can trust your mother or your sister?"

Daisy twisted her mouth. "I didn't say that, Betsy."

"And you? Are you a dog?"

"Absolutely," she said, rubbing Ringo's side with the toe of her boot. "I'm just a loyal dog."

The psychologist made a note, her pen gliding over the white sheet of paper.

A cell phone chimed.

"You forgot to turn off your cell phone," said Betsy.

"Yeah, sorry. I got to take this."

Daisy fished a black iPhone out of her purse. Then a ruby-red cell phone.

"Hello? . . . Dad, I can't talk. . . . Yes, I am. . . . I'll call you later."

Betsy noticed her patient wince.

" . . . I don't know . . . later." Daisy punched the END button hard, as if she was trying to kill it.

"Your father."

"Yeah, it won't happen again. I forgot to turn his phone off."

"His phone?"

Daisy hesitated.

"He wants me to have this one with me, all the time. It's got a GPS tracking device. Like he knows anything about where I go in the Roaring Fork Valley. Big deal. He gives me extra allowance if I take it with me everywhere."

"Doesn't he live back East?"

"Yeah, but like, he is *so* weird," she said. "It's part of the divorce arrangement. He wants to keep in contact with me."

She covered her mouth and coughed hard, phlegm rattling in her throat. Betsy handed her a box of tissues.

"Spit it out, Daisy. Really."

"That's gross," she said, struggling not to choke.

"It's healthy. Like an athlete does. Don't swallow, spit it out."

Ignoring her, Daisy swallowed hard.

Betsy watched her struggle to clear her throat. Then, when she thought the girl had recovered, she asked, "Why do you think your father—"

Daisy turned her face away.

"I don't want to talk about my dad now, all right?"

Betsy knew she was testing the ragged edge of Daisy's patience.

"OK. We'll talk about something else," she said, scanning her notes. "You said you listen to ripples of the past. Your past?"

"No. No, a long time ago. I dream of a castle. Jutting up into the sky from an outcrop of rock. Like something from a Dracula movie. Very Goth, right?"

"Go on."

"Red velvet drapes. Heavy dark furniture. Enormous chests with big iron hinges. And—a strange smell, like . . ."

"Like what?"

"Like a coin purse. Like pennies rubbed together. Metallic."

Betsy scribbled down Daisy's words.

"Anything else?"

"I see horses. Most times," she said.

"Are the horses comforting to you? Or are they menacing?"

"Mostly comforting. But sometimes they are terrified, rearing and whinnying, like they smell a fire."

"Do they strike out at you?"

"Oh, no. Never." She paused. "They warn me."

Chapter 4

The mud-splattered coach shuddered to a stop at the outskirts of the village of Čachtice. The crossroad led up the hill to the gray-and-ivory castle looming against the sky.

The carriage horses snorted in the cold, clouds of vapor rising into the frigid air. Their eyes were ringed in white as they pranced nervously, straining at their bits.

"Quiet now!" urged the driver. The brass lanterns on either side of the coach swung wildly, banging against the wood as the carriage lurched.

"Passenger Szilvasi, descend at once!" shouted the driver.

A flock of ravens exploded in flight from the castle walls. Their screaming call was answered by the ear-piercing whinny of the horses, rearing in unison, sharp hooves slicing the air.

"Get out!" shouted the driver, wrestling the reins.

Janos Szilvasi jumped down from the coach, throwing his sack into the snow beside the muddy road.

"Let me quiet them," he shouted up to the driver, as he approached the horses.

"Get away!" said the driver. "They will strike you! Stay away from the mare—"

24

Janos made a soft whistling sound, staying to the right of the rearing horses. The mare could not see the ravens now. She looked nervously at the human being who approached, her nostrils flaring.

"Easy, now, easy, easy, easy," Janos crooned in a singsong voice as if speaking to a child. And again came the strange whistle.

The mare reared again, her whinny echoing across the valley.

"Stay away!" shouted the driver.

Janos did not heed him. He steadily worked his way closer and closer to the horse's shoulder. He slowly placed a hand on the mare's neck, murmuring as he looked at her from the corner of his eye.

The skin on her neck quivered under his touch, rippling like a lake surface punctured by a barrage of stones. The harness slowed its jingling as the mare calmed. All the while Janos spoke to her, his breath small puffs of mist in the cold air.

The mare relaxed her tightly bunched neck, slowly lowering her ears closer to the man's mouth.

"What are you saying to my horses?" asked the driver, his voice full of suspicion. "Are you casting a spell on them? Come away from the horses."

"Let him, you fool!" shouted a thin passenger, craning his neck through the carriage window. "The horses will overturn the coach and kill the lot of us!"

Janos did not look away from the mare. He moved in front of her, risking a strike from her powerful foreleg—a blow that could easily break a man's leg. He could feel the warm breath of the second horse, a bay gelding, trying to reach his hand with its muzzle. He ran a hand over the chest of the gelding. He moved to the right of the coach and faced the steep road.

"A horse sorcerer," said a kerchiefed woman, looking out the window of the coach, She shoved her husband's head out of her way so she could see better.

"Thank you, sir," said the driver, blowing out his breath, as he felt the slack in the rein. "You have skill with horses." He wiped his nose on his ragged sleeve. "The Countess should be pleased to have you."

"I hope that is so," replied Janos. Then he nodded to the horses. "Was it the ravens that startled them?"

The driver shook his head, and motioned for Janos to come near. He whispered, "They always sweat and rear when we pass by Čachtice Castle, night or day."

Janos noticed the driver's hand tremble in its fingerless glove. He could smell the *slivovica*, the fiery plum brandy, on the man's breath. The driver drew a silver flask from his pocket, offering his passenger a draught.

"To steady your nerves for Čachtice Castle," said the driver.

Janos shook his head.

The driver shrugged and took the drink himself, his body relaxing as the harsh alcohol slid down his throat.

"We must make Beckov before nightfall. I bid you well, Passenger Szilvasi."

Janos backed away.

"Ya!" shouted the driver, slapping the reins lightly on the horses' backs. The wheels of the coach churned up frozen mud, leaving Janos at the side of the road.

The remaining passengers in the coach stared wild-eyed at the man who had shared their journey across the Hungarian flatlands to this remote outpost on the flanks of the Little Carpathians.

The kerchiefed woman made the sign of the cross, whispering a silent prayer. She kissed her fingers and extended them in the frosty air, back toward young Master Szilvasi.

Janos watched the coach disappear down the road. He picked up his sack and gazed at the fortress castle rising from the rocky hill above the treetops. The ravens still cawed overhead, circling the fortress in erratic loops.

"Do not let her catch you staring, Horse Sorcerer," warned an old man, appearing from below the road on a path leading from the dark pine forest. He carried a load of brush and twigs strapped to his bony back. The stranger spoke broken German.

"I beg your pardon?"

"She will cast a spell on you, the evil witch," the woodcutter said. He spat. "That Hungarian sorceress is the devil incarnate."

Janos placed a wool-wrapped hand on the old one's shoulder. "Pray tell me, sir, what do you know of the Countess?"

The old man grunted and shifted the load on his back. "How do I know you're not a Hungarian spy, sent by the Bathorys?"

"You are right, I am Hungarian. Is it so obvious in my German?"

The old Slovak laughed.

Janos slid the sack off his shoulder and drew out a flask of wine.

"Here, Grandfather. It is the last I have, but I will share it with you. Will you speak to me of the Countess? I swear I will tell no one, by my family's honor."

The old man shifted his heavy load of wood. His dirty face was streaked with sweat despite the cold.

"My bones could do with a rest. Let me taste your wine."

Janos could smell the tang of the old man's body as he tipped the flask up toward the sky to drink. The woodcutter belched as he pulled the flask away from his lips. He smiled, watery eyed.

The old man was the first Slovak Janos had met who would dare speak of the Countess. He had tried to pry information from his traveling companions, but they only looked at him pop-eyed and silent. At the very mention of Bathory, the stout matron would cross her fingers to ward off the evil eye. She would not let her husband utter a word about the mysterious woman.

This old man was ready to talk.

"There are women—young girls—who go to serve her and never come back," he whispered. His tongue poked out and touched around his lips, searching for any remaining wine. Then he wiped his mouth with his sleeve.

"Good girls, they were. When they were babes, I would pinch

their cheeks and watch them play on the village square. Now they are gone," he sighed. "I shall never dance at their weddings."

"What do you mean, 'gone'?"

"Gone. Disappeared. But no one dares whisper a word—except for our village preacher, a good Lutheran, with God's own pure fury in his soul. All the villagers are scared to speak, even the desperate mothers who cry themselves to sleep at night. The Countess makes up stories, tales that the girls have gone to serve at her other castles or at her house in Vienna."

"How do you know they are not?"

"No one ever hears from them again."

The sentries spotted Janos long before he reached the ramparts of the castle.

"Who goes there?" a guard shouted in German.

"Janos Szilvasi, horsemaster from Sarvar Castle of Nadasdy. I am here to serve Countess Bathory."

The guards had been expecting Szilvasi for a fortnight. They let down the plank used for foot traffic.

"Master Szilvasi—welcome to Čachtice Castle," said the head guard, straightening his hat over his gray hair. He was immaculately dressed: a red jacket skimming over his hips, a black wool hat, a sword at his side. His boots were of fine leather, with not a trace of manure or straw and no dark stains of horse sweat. Janos frowned at the gleaming footwear.

"My name is Erno Kovach," continued the man. "I command the Countess's castle guards." He did not extend his hand. "You look too young to be a horsemaster."

Janos saw the man studying him, gray eyes flicking from Janos's worn boots to his well-traveled cap.

"When my father was sent to fight in the Ottoman wars and train our King Rudolf's cavalry, I took over his position at Sarvar Castle. I am skilled enough, Guard Kovach," Janos said, his tone of voice challenging the guard. "I was called away from my duties at Sarvar to serve the Countess by her mandate."

Erno Kovach regarded the blond young man, the red blossom of youth still coloring his cheeks. He wondered if this boy truly had the command of horses his legendary father possessed, or whether the Countess had summoned him for his handsome countenance, and especially his youth.

"And your father now?"

"He trains the white Spanish stallions in Vienna for King Matthias."

Kovach grunted. "Follow me, Szilvasi. I will accompany you to the stables. Jiri—send notice to the Countess that her horsemaster has arrived."

"Yes, Captain."

A cobweb of frost clung to the granite blocks of the castle wall. As they emerged from the archway into the busy courtyard, Janos's eyes took in a whirl of activity. Flocks of chickens pecked the cobblestones for grubs. Butchers stripped entrails from hanging pigs and handed the buckets of guts to the sausage maker who selected the choice bits for his grinder, hurling the slop in the drainage ditch for the dogs and ravens to devour. Knives flashed as farmers trimmed huge heads of cabbage, sharp blades hacking away the tough outer leaves and stalks. The dairyman pulled his wares from a wooden cart, offering them to a stout cook who stood with her hands on her wide hips as he boasted of the quality of his product, pulling back the linen cloth so she could inspect the crocks of butter and wheels of fresh cheese.

Children chased flocks of geese about the cobblestones, only to run shrieking when a gander turned on them, hissing through his sharp yellow beak and flapping his powerful wings.

A mutton carcass roasted on an enormous spit, the fat sizzling and sparking the coals into flames. The fire licked the meat, spreading the rich aroma through the air. A blacksmith pounded on his anvil, the sound ringing over the courtyard. Bits of molten iron flew, glowing yellow-orange, leaving scorch marks on the worn stones of the courtyard.

Janos followed the guard to the stables. A team of ragged boys assembled in a line in front of the arched entry. Despite the cold, fat lazy flies buzzed from piles of warm manure and the stench of aged horse piss stung Janos's nose.

"Welcome to your domain, horsemaster," announced the guard captain, sweeping his arm wide.

Janos wrinkled his nose and his jaw clenched, muscles working taut under his skin.

"What conditions are these for Bathory horses!" he said, his voice rising in anger. He whirled around. "Who is responsible for this?"

One of the older boys came forward, his face smeared with dirt.

"I am, sir. My uncle was in charge until he took ill with the plague. He died a fortnight ago," said the boy. He ran his dirty sleeve under his runny nose.

Janos trembled with fury, his hands clenched in tight fists at his side.

"Bring out the horses. At once!"

One after another, the horses of Čachtice Castle were brought out into the courtyard, which was paved in end-cut wooden blocks. There were twenty-seven horses in all, and every one showed evidence of neglect. There were boils on the backs of several, proud flesh festering over wounds, cracked hooves. Several were lame with blistered coronets from standing in old urine-soaked straw. Two bay mares were crippled with thrush. When Janos picked up their hooves, he saw the soggy flesh and smelled the stench of rot.

The last horse, three boys brought out together.

The white stallion reared, his front hooves flashing. His eyes were ringed in white and his piercing neigh was a threat that ricocheted around the castle walls. The boys held him by ropes trying to keep him on the ground.

He, like all the others, was thin despite the band of muscle that still clung to his powerful neck.

"These wretched horses are starving!" said Janos. From the corner of his eye, he saw a movement in one of the windows of the castle. But his attention returned quickly to the horses.

"We feed them, but the horses have no appetite," said the head boy. Janos looked closer at the boy's eyes. They were shining with fever.

"They nose aside the grass and choose to starve," said the boy. Janos saw the beads of sweat on his face. His cheeks burned bright red, his eyes glassy.

"What is your name?"

"Aloyz, sir."

"Aloyz, you are ill."

"Yes, Master Janos," he said, shuffling his rag-tied feet. "But do not send me away, I beg of you. I need to work for our family, else we will starve."

Janos nodded. "Where is the hay?"

Aloyz beckoned him to a leaky wooden-shingled hayshed. The grass was wet and mottled with black, white cobwebs lacing the mildewed interior.

"The Countess is lucky she has any horses left!"

The head guard approached Janos. "The Countess said to give you this."

In the Kovach's hands was a braided leather horsewhip, glistening black in the sunlight. Janos wrinkled his brow.

"What is this? I shall not strike these miserable horses."

Kovach looked over his shoulder toward the castle.

"Take it!" he said, shoving the whip into the horsemaster's hands.

Janos let the whip drop into the mildewed hay. He glared scornfully at the head guard and turned to the stallion which still raged and reared, lathered now with sweat.

"Easy, boy," said Janos, approaching him. The horse reared again, and the three boys pulled hard on their ropes.

"Stand back, Szilvasi! That horse is mad," shouted Guard Kovach.

"Easy, boy, calm down, now, easy, easy," said Janos. He looked down at the horse's lightning-fast hooves, not meeting the animal's eyes.

Janos stretched out a hand, slowly. The stallion snorted, but did not rear. He snorted again, bunching his long neck muscles in a tight arch, then he turned his muzzle toward Szilvasi's outstretched hand.

Janos reached out and stroked the stallion's neck.

The horse slowly released the knotted muscles and lowered his head, his nostrils flaring as he pulled in the scent of the man. He snorted and stamped his front foot, not fully convinced to trust a human.

"How long since this horse has been ridden?" Janos asked.

The boys looked at each other and then to the ground.

"No one rides him, sir," said the leader. "He cannot be handled. He was bred as Count Nadasdy's mount, but the noble gentleman died before the dam foaled."

Janos slowly worked his hand up the horse's neck, toward his head. The horse lifted his head slightly, his skin quivering spasmodically as if covered with flies. The beast's nostrils flared, showing red, and his eyes remained ringed in white.

But he allowed Szilvasi to touch his broad chest.

Szilvasi turned toward the guard. "Please tell the Countess that the horsewhip will not be necessary," said Janos, his hand moving toward the horse's withers.

Keeping a wary eye on the stallion, the guard approached Janos and whispered in his ear. "The whip is not for the horses. It is to be used on the stable boys."

Janos dropped his hand from the horse's withers and the stallion jumped back, dragging the boys with him.

Janos looked the guard in the eye. Then he turned toward the window where he had seen movement a few minutes before. He stared at the castle and lifted his chin in the cold air.

"Send back the whip to the Countess," Janos said, his words steady and calm. "Tell her I shall have no need of it for boy or beast."

Chapter 5

And you might want to be a little more professional about your office," Jane had said again, picking Daisy up from yesterday's session.

"Get yourself a good maid. Maybe one of those Mexican women next door? Pick up all the clutter. When was the last time you dusted?"

Betsy sighed.

Jane was right. I am the world's worst housekeeper.

Betsy cast her eye about the little Victorian house, hands on her hips. The small of her back ached just thinking about cleaning up.

Periodicals—*Quadrant, Jung Journal, The Journal of Analytical Psychology*—lay scattered across every horizontal space in the house. Towers of Jungian textbooks teetered, their balance precarious, especially when Ringo wagged his tail.

Betsy spent a day organizing, occasionally looking out at the fat snowflakes that fell outside her window, obscuring the view of Mount Sopris. *A heavy dump,* she thought. *Big wet packing snow, perfect for an early base on the ski mountains.*

The bookshelves were already jammed tight. She could at least split the book towers and stow half of them behind the couch where they weren't so obvious. Betsy dusted the fronts of the leather-bound books on the shelves, not daring to pull them out—she might not be able to wedge them back in again.

She cleaned out the old mahogany bar, one of her father's favorite possessions. She wiped down the bottles of *slivovica*, the potent plum brandy her father always served his guests.

And she remembered the first Christmas after her father died. That awful holiday her mother spent with her, getting totally smashed on Slovakian plum brandy.

It had been snowing hard on Christmas Eve. Snow crystals rattled against the windows, the harbinger of an approaching blizzard, the kind that kids prayed for—the schools closed for a snow day.

Grace had arrived the day before. Her face was haggard, carved to the bone with grief. When they hugged, Betsy felt her mother's ribs sharp against her arms.

"Take a semester off, Mom," she said. "Come home and take care of yourself. Let me take care of you—"

Grace had pulled back, rigid, lifting her chin.

"I am fine, Betsy. Work is the best therapy for me."

Grace poured herself a glass of *slivovica*. She stood glaring at the twinkling lights of the Christmas tree. "Your father always loved Christmas," she said.

"Mom, sit down. Let's talk."

"I don't want to talk," muttered Grace. She knocked back a gulp of the brandy, grimacing as the alcohol burned its way down her throat.

Oh, shit! Betsy thought. *Here it comes.*

Betsy knew the look on her mother's face—a harbinger of a coming storm. Grace's eyes squinted belligerently as she peered over her glasses, studying Betsy as if she were a curious antiquity in a museum.

"You are too much like your father," her mother said finally, slurring her words. She slumped back against the wing chair.

Grace had never been fond of *slivovica*. She took another gulp.

"What do you mean, too much like Dad?" said Betsy.

"Why did you go into psychotherapy? Such a sloppy field. No boundaries, not a proper science. And why did you divorce that great guy you had?"

"Mom! You were livid when you found out we had gotten married. Don't you remember?" Maybe she'd been right, but Betsy wasn't going to mention that now.

"John Stonework would have shaped you into something, given you some limits, a clear focus. Not living in this backwater little town—"

"I love Carbondale. Mom, I was brought up here!"

"Over my objections. I would have raised you in Chicago. Given you more polish, more ambition. It was your father's doing, keeping you here."

"Well, it's not like you stuck around much after I was in middle school."

"I told Ceslav I would go back to the university teaching after you were old enough. He led me to believe he'd do the same."

"It would have been nice if you'd been around more, not just weekends and summers."

Why was she doing this? Why have a fight now? Her mother needed her help. But Betsy couldn't stop. "You could have been there to answer some questions, help me through—"

"Why? Adolescence is a ridiculous time in a person's life. All we would do is fight. That's what mothers and daughters do at that age."

"You weren't here enough to—"

"Your father mollycoddled you. Damped down the fire in you."

Betsy swallowed hard. "What? What do you mean, 'damped down the fire'?"

"Low expectations," her mother mumbled, staring through the crystal-clear liquid in her glass. "You turned out to be too meek for my taste."

Betsy knew it was the *slivovica* talking, but she felt as if she had been punched in the stomach.

"But that John," said Grace. "If you had stayed with him you would be at MIT."

"MIT doesn't have a graduate psychotherapy program, Mother."

"Teaching at Boston University then," said Grace, stretching her arm out for the *slivovica* bottle. She sloshed the liquor into her glass. Sticky liquid spilled over the rim, onto the hooked rug.

"Mom. That's over fifty percent alcohol—"

"Maybe Harvard. You are smart enough. It's not smarts you're lacking."

"I never wanted to teach at a university—"

"Doing empirical research. Publishing! Making a name for yourself."

"I help people, Mom. Isn't that a good thing?"

"Like your father. Humpf!" Grace said. Her tongue stuck to the roof of her mouth. She made clicking sounds. *Like a dolphin*, Betsy couldn't help thinking.

"Helping people!" Grace repeated, her tongue finally unsticking. "Like they were little broken toys that he could fix. Glue them here, glue them there. He never wanted to publish his work. Do you know how well respected he was in Vienna, before we married? Then all of a sudden, it was like he wanted to hide under a rug. Disappear."

"What's wrong with helping people with their problems?"

"Helping people! That's for social workers and school teachers! School crossing guards, boy scouts—"

"You know what, Mom? I think you've had too much *slivovica*. And you're really acting out here because you're heartbroken over Dad."

"Don't you psychoanalyze me, Missy!" Grace said, shaking a bony finger at her daughter. "I don't need your advice."

Grace's face crumpled with grief. She began to cry.

"We could talk about Dad without it being a fight," said Betsy, softly. "You need to talk to somebody."

Grace closed her eyes tight, shaking her head, trying to rid herself of the words.

"I want to talk about *you*, not your father!" she said, tightening her grip around the stem of her glass. Betsy saw the outline of her finger bones, clutching like a perched bird.

"If you had stayed with John, he would have straightened you out. He was a practical young man. No nonsense. He would have been a damn good father, a good provider. I would have had grandchildren by now."

Betsy suddenly couldn't breathe. She tried to answer her mother, but no sounds came out of her mouth. She got up, grabbing her parka off the peg. She wrapped her burgundy wool scarf three times around her throat, pulled on her tasseled ski cap and gloves.

"Where are you going?" snapped Grace, leaning forward in her chair. She nearly lost her balance and toppled to the floor. "Betsy! It's a goddamn blizzard out there!"

"I'd prefer the storm out there than the one here, Mom."

Betsy slammed the door shut, blinking hot tears. Snowflakes melted against her eyelashes, blinding her.

Chapter 6

After Janos had inspected the horses, he asked if he could be presented to the mistress of the castle.

"The Countess does not hold audience until dusk," said Guard Kovach. "She will see you after sunset."

Janos stared back at the gloomy castle where he had seen the shadowy movement.

"I think I may have caught a glimpse of her," he said. "When I was working with the stallion."

The guard looked at him, his brow arched.

"I doubt that, Horsemaster Szilvasi. Not in the light of day."

The guard raised his gloved hand. He beckoned Szilvasi to follow him to the barracks, where guards and stable hands took their rest.

The heavy door creaked open to a common area. A warm breath of cabbage soup greeted the traveler, its sulfurous scent obliterating any other odor, except an occasional whiff of the guards' unwashed bodies.

"You can lay your blanket near the hearth," said the guard. "The kitchen boys keep the fire burning throughout the night."

"You the new horsemaster?" piped a high voice. "It is about time someone cared properly for those miserable animals. They are almost meat for my stewpot."

The cook was a thin man whose skin stretched tight across his skull. Janos could see the workings of the muscles in his neck and jawbone as he spoke. The only meat on his body was the muscle in his forearms, forged from stirring the massive iron pot. For a cook, his meager flesh did not bode well for the food he prepared, thought Janos.

Janos turned halfway to the guard.

"I would like to get to work on the stables and treating the horses as soon as possible. Cook, do you have some sugar?"

"Ach!" he responded, shaking his skeletal head at Janos. "You think a barracks cook would have sugar? The castle kitchen keeps sugar locked in the pantry under Brona the cook's shrewd eye. It is imported from Venice and costly—"

"I will need as much as five spoonfuls. Please procure it at once for the horses' welfare. Better than in the belly of a sweet-toothed nobleman."

Guard Kovach and the cook eyed each other. They were not certain how to respond to the impudent young horsemaster.

"Guard Kovach, do you use lime in the privy?" asked Janos.

The guard's forehead creased in anger. "We run a clean barracks here—what are you implying?"

"Good, I will need at least a half bucket of lye. And straw, like the straw used to cover night soil. I want enough clean, fresh straw to fill the stables a foot deep."

By nightfall, Guard Kovach saw the new horsemaster hard at work, flanked by his ragged crew of stable boys, though Janos had made the feverish Aloyz rest by the fire, covering him with a blanket.

Janos held a bay mare's back leg on his knee and cocked the stinking flesh of her hoof toward his face.

"See—the triangular part of the hoof is the most sensitive," he said to the boys. "Never cut it, unless the flesh is dead and hanging. It is live and vulnerable to pain, the same as your finger or toe."

With a sharp knife, he carved out the muck and embedded stones around the island of soft flesh. Then one of the stable boys sprinkled lye into the rotting hoof. Fingers protected by a rag, Janos pressed the chalky powder deep into the rot.

"Every day you must do this until the flesh is dry and healed," he said, still holding the mare's hoof in his hand. He straightened his knee and let go of the hoof. The horse snorted and the stable boys nodded as they accepted the horsemaster's instruction.

Guard Kovach walked toward the mare and saw white glistening on a festered wound. As he approached, he could see the shiny granules of sugar.

"What is this?" he said. "You have used the Countess's fine white sugar on horseflesh?"

Szilvasi smiled at the guard, whose face was still contorted in astonishment.

"You will see, Guard Kovach, how quickly the wounds heal with a regular dusting."

He ran a hand around the mare's withers, his fingers skipping over the wound. She twitched under his touch.

Guard Kovach scratched his head. "I have come to tell you that the Countess will grant you audience. She sends word to come when the moon has risen."

Janos arched his eyebrow. "Such strange habits the Countess has in welcoming a faithful servant from Sarvar Castle," he said, stretching his arms wide over head, hands balled in fists as he yawned. "I am so tired. Perhaps the Countess will agree to see me in the morning, since she has kept me all day awaiting an audience."

"You will sleep after meeting the Countess." The guard stood, arms crossed on his chest, taking in Szilvasi's appearance. "Go see the cook and ask for a bucket of water and a rag to bathe. The Countess is fastidious about cleanliness. She abhors the smell of a man's sweat or the stench of beast."

Janos snorted and turned away, massaging his own sore back; he had spent hours bent over horses' hooves, bearing their weight in his hands.

The guard grabbed the young man's shoulder, spinning him back around. "Do not take the Countess's wishes so cavalierly, Horsemaster. She does not endure informality."

"And I do not endure brutality!" said Janos, shaking free of Guard Kovach's grasp. "What the devil did she mean sending me that horsewhip?"

Guard Kovach started to answer and then clamped his mouth shut, looking over his shoulder. He saw the stable boys' eyes grow large with fear as they listened.

"Go bathe, Szilvasi. You stink of horse piss," said the guard. He turned and walked out of the pool of light cast by the lanterns into the dark of the cobbled courtyard. "You have yet to grasp the ways of Čachtice Castle."

Chapter 7

It's a few weeks late for Halloween," Jane said, looking up from her *Vogue* magazine. She threw a contemptuous look at Daisy's shredded crepe dress and white Goth makeup.

"Ha, ha," Daisy said. "That kills, Mother. You should be on Comedy Central."

"You'll scare the neighbors," snapped Jane. "And they'll think I'm a bad mother, letting my daughter traipse around in a torn dress in a howling blizzard."

"Screw the neighbors," Daisy said, fastening the buckles of her boots. "You think too much about other people's opinions, Mother."

"And maybe you should think more about what people think. Just a little."

"Why? Besides I'm not going to walk around this neighborhood anyway. What's to see but big stupid mansions and greedy men with wives younger than their own daughters. They are disgusting."

Jane glowered at her daughter.

"What?" Daisy said.

"You know, Daisy, you have gotten awfully bitchy lately," she said. "I might just call your father to let him know what a pain in the ass you are."

Daisy's breath caught, and she coughed.

"Are you all right?" said Jane, anger vanishing from her face. "You shouldn't be going out—"

Daisy threw on the long black wool coat she had bought at the thrift shop.

"Where are you going?" Jane asked, her hand on her hip.

"Wherever I want."

Daisy slammed the door, making the snow slide off the porch roof.

She drove the BMW down Red Mountain, sliding around the first corner and nearly crashing into the guardrail. The car stalled and when she got it started again, she crept down the hill in first gear.

She parked at a pull-out at the bottom of Red Mountain Road along the Roaring Fork River. She set off along the river on the Rio Grande trail, earbuds wedged tight in her ears. She smiled, listening to a Doors' song, over and over again.

People are strange when you're a stranger . . .

It was snowing hard, as if it were January. Snow gathered thick on every branch, shaking loose the last yellow leaves from the aspens. She trudged down the snowy path, looking at the river. There was ice along the shore but then the water broke out, running fast and dark between the snow-blanketed rocks.

The snow was falling heavily now, coating her eyelashes, blinding her, despite her hood. Jim Morrison and the Doors were blasting through the earphones.

Faces come out of the rain

When you're strange . . .

Oof!

She hadn't heard him racing down the path. She sprawled on the ground, cursing in the snow. Her legs were tangled up with a sweaty, cross-country skier who had slammed into her.

T.N.T. oi oi oi!

T.N.T. oi oi oi!

His earphones dangled from his neck, blasting out AC/DC.

I'm Dy-na-mite!

"Oh, shit! Are you OK? I didn't expect anyone," he said.

"Couldn't you *see* me?"

"It's a freakin' blizzard. You were in the middle of the trail."

"What an idiot!"

"Are you hurt?"

"Get off me!"

The crash had knocked the wool hat off the skier's curly blond hair.

Daisy recognized him from school. He was a snowboarder. *One of those extreme guys who competes in the X-Games*, she thought. *I had to go to pep rallies for him.* There was nothing a Goth despised more than a pep rally.

He crawled off and pulled her up, despite the fact he was still on his skis.

"God damn it!" she said. "Now I've lost my earbuds."

Daisy could still hear his music blasting from his earphones, a final insult. Hard rock. Booming.

"Here they are," he said, digging them up out the snow. He gave her a crooked smile. "Wow, you are sassy, Goth girl."

"Go to hell, asshole!"

He wrinkled his nose, laughing at her.

"What's so funny?"

"Enough with the drama, OK? Jeez."

He handed her the wet earbuds and pressed the PAUSE button on his iPod.

"Look, I'm really sorry."

A hard gust of wind blew the snow sideways. He had to almost shout. Daisy could smell some kind of fruity gum on his breath. A whiff of the tropics in the middle of a snowstorm.

"It's OK," she said, mumbling.

"You were hard to see, you know," he said into her ear.

"What? Because I'm not dressed up in garish colors like some cheerleader?"

"Hey! I didn't say that. Wear what you want, that's cool. I just didn't see you, you know."

Daisy brushed the snow from her coat, shaking out her hood.

"You want me to walk you to your car or house or something?" he offered. "It's snowing kinda hard."

"No, I'm going down to the Slaughterhouse Bridge to catch the bus back to the trailhead. I've got my car parked there at the pull-out."

He looked at her dubiously, swatting the bottoms of his skis with his pole to knock off the ice that had accumulated.

"Sure you're OK?"

"Yeah, yeah, really."

Shit, she thought. She didn't want him to think she was a wuss, just because she wasn't skiing or doing some kind of hardcore snow sport.

"Look, I used to ride horses and take lots of crashes," she said. "I've cracked ribs, broken my arm twice, and dislocated my shoulder. This is nothing."

"Yeah?" he said, his face creasing up in a smile. "I know all about bad wipeouts," he said, cleaning the snow from his goggles. "OK, I'll see you in Spanish class."

Was he in her Spanish class?

He waved a pole at her and skied off, disappearing into the swirl of snow.

A long, wet half hour later, she crossed the river and started trudging up the steep Cemetery Lane hill toward town. It was a long hill, but at the top she could catch the bus the rest of the way into town. The street was silent, the houses shut tight against the storm. The only person she saw was a woman sweeping the snow off her car with a broom. She stopped working and stared at Daisy as she walked past.

Daisy could feel the woman's eyes on her back as she trudged on, stumbling over chunks of ice the snowplow had thrown on the side of the road.

Women seem wicked when you're unwanted
Streets are uneven when you're down . . .

Cemetery Lane. She came to the black wrought-iron fence around the cemetery, ringing the graves and the massive century-old cottonwoods.

A good Goth never passes a cemetery without paying respects. Even in a blinding snowstorm.

It was peaceful under the branches of the cottonwoods, the trunks of the trees packed white with blowing snow. She wound her way through the cemetery, gazing at the stones, reading the inscriptions. The oldest graves dated back to the 1880s.

She always looked for the children. Sometimes she bought carnations or roses at half off at City Market and placed them on the graves.

She stopped to read a newer stone, speckled with flecks of burnt-orange lichens. Ceslav Path. Loving husband of Grace and father of Elizabeth.

My shrink had a father named Ceslav?

Daisy stood shivering in the snow, feeling a strange vibe. Jim Morrison shouted in her ear.

When you're strange

No one remembers your name . . .

Daisy pulled out the earbuds and pressed the PAUSE button. She kneeled in the snow, touching the tombstone with her gloved hand in the silence.

And she wondered: *What kind of name was Ceslav?*

Chapter 8

At dusk, the courtyard of Čachtice Castle slipped into silence. The butchers who stained the cobblestones red with their slaughters had gone home, the geese were locked away in their coops, the clang of the smith's hammer was silenced. The dairyman's wagon had creaked down the long rutted road to the village. The sausage maker's cast-offs had long been consumed by the ravens and dogs, and the last of the blood licked clean by the cats. The soap-maker's shavings had been mixed with water to make a lather and rinse off the remains of the day, leaving the stones wet and polished, the moon's reflection dappling the gleaming courtyard. The torches cast shifting waves of brightness across the walls of the castle, and sentries stood watch in the moonlight.

A thin servant with nervous eyes came to summon Horsemaster Szilvasi to the castle.

Janos wore an open-neck white linen tunic over his dark breeches. It was the kind of shirt a wealthy farmer might wear to a horse fair or tavern. He wore no coat, only a boiled-wool riding jacket, threadbare with age.

The servant surveyed him, moistening his dry lips.

"Sir, forgive me. Do you have anything more suitable to wear before the Countess?"

Janos narrowed his eyes at the servant, clad in black velvet, the silver hooks of his fine cloak gleaming in the torchlight. The horsemaster dropped his eyes to scan his own clean white shirt.

"No, this will do," he said, testily. "I am a horseman, not a castle servant."

"Very good, sir. It is just that—"

"What?"

"The Countess is . . . fastidious."

"I wish she were more fastidious with the care of her horses," answered Janos. "And in welcoming a weary traveler from Sarvar Castle."

The servant took a step back. His eyes were ringed in white, much as the horses' had been.

"I beg you, sir!" he whispered, his voice hoarse. "Do not criticize the Countess in my presence." The servant looked about the empty courtyard, searching the shadows for spies.

"You are scared of your own shadow, man! Take me to the Countess," said Janos, dismissing his concerns with a wave of his hand. "I am losing patience. And I am weary for my bed."

The courtyard was treacherous, the water on the cobblestones already beginning to freeze. The servant worked his way around the edge of the yard, placing his feet carefully. Janos followed, the click of his riding boots sounding a steady beat on the stone.

The guards opened the massive door of the castle, hinges creaking despite regular coats of pork grease. A servant took Janos aside and patted him roughly, searching for weapons.

"There are enemies of the Bathorys," he said as way of explanation.

The tapestry-hung halls were illuminated by wrought-iron candelabras. Ornately carved furniture—chairs, chests, and long tables—shone darkly with thick coats of beeswax. The walls—where not covered by tapestries—were hung with oil portraits of Nadasdy and Bathory ancestors, men in gleaming armor, their hands on bejeweled swords, ready to kill the Islamic invaders. One portrait showed the Countess's husband, Ferenc Nadasdy, triumphantly seated atop a pile of slain Ottoman warriors, their blood coating his boots.

Ferenc had been dead for five years, killed by a wound received in battle—though in the taverns of Nadasdy, it was whispered that the mortal injury was inflicted by a disgruntled harlot whom he neglected to pay.

The air was rich with kitchen odors, wild boar roasting in the open hearth. Janos knew the savory smell, soured by the stink of singed hair where stray bristles had remained in the flesh. The bitter smell of burning hair was chased by the sweet aroma of autumn apples.

Outside an oaken door on the first floor flocked a half dozen young maidens in court finery. Their long silk skirts, laced velvet bodices, and finely beaded headpieces must have been fetched from Vienna, thought Janos, for there was certainly nothing as refined to be found in the wilds of Upper Hungary.

The ladies-in-waiting curtsied and lowered their heads as the horsemaster approached, though he could see them sneaking looks. He heard one stifle a gasp, and a muffled giggle.

"There is no need to bow, maidens," said Janos in German. "I am a servant, just as you serve the Countess."

The Slovak women giggled at his fine manners and Hungarian accent. A couple of bolder girls made eyes at him.

The manservant rapped gently on the door, and it opened a crack to expose the mouth and nose of a pretty—though painfully thin—servant girl. They exchanged murmured words and then the door was quietly opened. Janos was ushered into a vast chamber, illuminated by chandeliers with hundreds of flickering candles.

The room was square and sparse. At the far end sat a black-veiled woman.

"Approach, Master Szilvasi," called the woman. Her starched lace collar stood straight out from her neck like a square banner, quivering slightly as she spoke.

Janos's face twitched with impatience, but he wisely chose to compose himself before he reached her shrouded presence.

He stood a few feet from what appeared to be a throne—and bowed deeply. He stared at the Countess's red-slippered feet, peeking out of the stiff folds of silver and gold brocade.

Janos wrinkled his nose. A strong smell of copper coins wafted through the air, metallic and acrid. His eye surreptitiously hunted for its source.

"Countess Bathory, it is an honor," he said.

"Is it?" she said. "I have heard that you were impatient for your bed."

Janos swallowed, marveling at how quickly gossip traveled in this castle. Then he collected his thoughts, thinking of the conditions in which he had found the horses.

"You heard correctly. Your—what would you call them, spies?—have served you well. Yes, Countess. I am tired after two days of hard travel and a grueling day in the stables."

"Spies? You are impertinent, *Pan* Szilvasi! They are loyal servants who report the truth and warn me of ill conduct."

"What do you consider ill conduct, Madame? I come from the Sarvar Castle—your own property. At your request, Madame."

"You needn't remind me, as if I am too aged and addled to remember!" she snapped.

Janos decided to take another approach, muting his anger.

"I am devoted to the horses and will see that they thrive and are trained to the utmost of my ability. Your stable shall be worthy of the Bathory name."

Janos could see the black veil tremble. He wondered what lay behind the curtain of black mesh.

"I understand my stable boys have disappointed you."

"The horses are in bad condition, Countess," said Janos. "I will work hard the next few weeks to bring them back to health."

"My stable master died and his nephew is an idiot," said the countess, lifting the veil from her face, and folding it over her dark auburn hair.

"I—"

Janos stopped speaking. He stared at the white face, skin as smooth as fine marble, the color of Venetian porcelain. Burning amber eyes, unlike any he had ever seen, stared at him under delicately arched brows.

The woman looked inhuman, a perfect statue created by the most skillful sculptor. Except the eyes. The eyes were feral, catlike. She was stunningly beautiful. He could not look away. His eyes ran over her features, again and again, hunting for imperfection.

He found none, despite her age.

She nodded to the footman, who handed her the braided leather horsewhip.

"You returned this to me," she said. "I sent it to you with a purpose."

Janos made himself look at the horsewhip and not the woman's face.

"It was not necessary. The horses do not need whipping and the stable boys are simply ignorant."

"The sting of the whip can quickly correct ignorance."

"I find other methods more effective, Countess."

There was a little gasp among the throng of handmaidens.

The Countess gave them a sharp look. A sudden silence settled into even the most remote corners of the room.

"They say you inherited your father's—nay, your grandfather's—uncanny dominion over horses. I remember him from my childhood at Sarvar Castle. I was fifteen when I was brought as a bride there."

"I understand horses. It is not dominion."

"Do you believe you can ride my white stallion?"

"I know I can."

The marble face broke into a smile that was somehow hideous, as if the sculptor who had created her had never meant for such an emotional betrayal to cross that visage. The sculpted features, haughty and perfect, looked as if they would shatter, casting jagged white shards on the floor.

Then the face regained its marble composure, no expression marring the milky smoothness.

"Is there something lacking in my performance, Countess?"

"Yes," answered the perfect face. "Bozek, show Horsemaster Szilvasi back to his quarters."

The manservant appeared out of the shadows, at Janos's elbow.

"There is one thing you lack, young horsemaster," said the Countess, lowering her veil once more.

"And what might that be?"

"Humility," she said. "But you shall learn it here at Čachtice Castle."

She snapped her fingers, the sound echoing through the great hall.

Two guards seized Janos, their strong fingers biting into his arm. He was whisked back into the hall. The torch flames leapt, fed by the gust of wind as the massive door slammed shut behind him.

Chapter 9

Betsy heard footsteps outside on the porch. She opened the door. "Dr. Path?"

Framed by the blue trim of the door was the most striking young woman Betsy had ever seen.

She had long dark red hair—a natural auburn. Strands whipped about her face in the wind. Her skin was startlingly white, like a porcelain figurine. It was an outdated look, especially in contrast with the outdoorsy Colorado style to which Betsy was accustomed. Then she realized she was staring at the girl's green, amber-flecked eyes.

"You are Dr. Path, aren't you?"

"Yes—I'm sorry," Betsy said, forcing herself to stop examining the girl's eyes. "Do we know each other?"

She looked so familiar. Betsy was sure she had seen those features before.

"I am Daisy Hart's sister, Morgan. May I come in?"

"Of course, I'm sorry. I guess I should have seen the family resemblance."

Betsy knew she was staring at the young woman, but she couldn't help it.

"Underneath all that Goth make-up she wears, how could you?" said Morgan.

She frowned, lowering her chin. Her long hair swung down in her face. Then she tossed her glorious mane back behind her ears. Her eyes glittered. Her lips formed a word, but no syllable was uttered.

Betsy stepped aside and let the tall elegant creature enter her office.

"Please sit down, Morgan. So. Daisy's sister?"

"I am sorry to drop in on you like this, but I've come to check up on Daisy. My . . . dad gave me your contact information."

"You are from New York, right?"

"Yes, though we live most of the time in Florida now."

"We?"

The young woman hesitated.

"Dad and I. After the divorce, I chose to stay with my father and Daisy went with my mother."

"I see."

Morgan looked around the room. Betsy noticed she focused on the leather-bound books.

"And . . . ?" Betsy let the unspoken question hang. Morgan had come to see her, uninvited; Morgan was going to have to carry this conversation.

"Yes," she said, reluctant to stop inspecting the house and book-shelves. "Dad and I are really worried about Daisy. I heard she had another choking episode and went to the ER."

"That was a while ago."

"Did she say why it happened?"

"Excuse me?"

"I mean, in therapy, did she say anything that might have trig-gered the choking? What did she say exactly?"

Betsy sat back in the chair and her fingers sought the end of the armrest. She grasped hard as if she were on a carnival ride.

"You know, I really can't talk about your sister's therapy with you. It is confidential."

The catlike eyes narrowed almost imperceptibly. "You are trying to help her, right? I mean, she must tell you everything, right? Has she told you the nightmare about the vampire?"

Betsy opened her mouth to answer, but the reply was stillborn in her mouth. It was none of this girl's business what Daisy said to her in a therapy session.

"We are working together toward discovering the causes of her distress."

"Distress?" Morgan scoffed. "Is that what she calls it?"

Betsy's fingernails dug deeper into the fabric. "No, that is what I call it."

"Well, she's a spoiled brat," said Morgan, spitting out the words. Her green eyes narrowed, glinting. "She has been spoiled rotten since the day she was born. I'm sure that the only reason that she is doing this choking thing is to draw more attention to herself."

Betsy didn't respond directly. Instead, she asked, "Morgan, are you staying with Jane and Daisy?"

The visitor sniffed and rolled her eyes. "Yeah, *right.*"

"Do they even know you're here?"

"No. I'm just passing through. I leave this afternoon. My father wanted me to check up on Daisy's . . . progress. And to meet you."

Morgan fiddled with her starched white collar. Then she dug in the pocket of her suede jacket, producing a white business card from a tooled leather wallet. "Here. This is her dad's number."

"*Her* dad?" Betsy asked.

Morgan glared at her. "He's her biological father. I am Jane's daughter from her first marriage. Anyway, he says that if there are any questions or breakthroughs, call him first. Not Jane."

"Your mother? You are asking me not to call Jane?"

"Yes. Call him first."

"I've never met your father. I have met Jane. She signed the papers and writes the checks. Daisy lives with her, not with her father."

"Roger pays you. He's the one with the money. He can pull her from therapy any time he wants."

Betsy turned the card over in her hand. "Tell him to call me. I feel uncomfortable with the situation and I feel I should adhere to protocol."

Morgan's eyes widened. "Protocol? Wait! You can't tell Jane I've been here."

"Why?"

"Just don't. It will—upset her, and really confuse Daisy. I swear it will."

Betsy's mouth tasted sour. She realized she had taken an instant disliking to this attractive young woman. What was it about Morgan that set her on edge?

"You understand that I am under no obligation to do anything you say. My only concern is Daisy."

Morgan hesitated. The green eyes stared at Betsy, cold and glittering.

"You don't like me," she said slowly. "I can sense that. But I have an important question for you. And it might be helpful for Daisy. I wish you would give me an honest answer—"

"What is it? If it's about your sister, the answer is no. I will not discuss her."

"No, Dr. Path. You've already made that abundantly clear," said Morgan waving away Betsy's response. "Just a simple question, nothing to do with Daisy."

"Go ahead."

"Is it possible to—I don't know—inherit or borrow a dream from someone?"

"What are you referring to? I don't understand the question."

"Let's say someone dreams about—say, vampires. Like my sister does. Is it possible for me, say, to pick up that dream?"

Betsy said, "What, catch it like a flu?"

"That's not what I mean. What if the dream world she has at night is the same as mine. Exactly the same."

Betsy studied Morgan's amber-flecked green eyes and recognized an emotion.

Fear.

Betsy hesitated, then nodded.

"People who are close, or who are connected somehow to similar emotional feelings, can have similar dreams as a manifestation of a burden they share, especially if they are exposed to the very same experience."

Morgan shook her head adamantly. "You don't understand, Dr. Path. What if the nightmare is the same, exactly the same—a castle—identical characters—ghouls with white faces—"

"You may have heard Daisy describe her dreams and unconsciously picked up the detail and emotion—contaminating, if you will, your own dreams." Betsy felt as if she had gone too far. She shouldn't be talking about Daisy even this much.

"If you will excuse me," said Betsy, rising from her chair, "I am expecting a patient."

Morgan rose from her chair, following Betsy to the door. Betsy swung it open. A few dead leaves blew in circles on the porch, refugees from the earlier snowstorm.

Morgan frowned, making her way out into the unsettled weather.

"There is one more possibility," said Betsy, called after her. She wasn't sure what prompted her to continue this conversation, especially as Morgan was a few steps into the wind. "There is a phenomenon called shared dreaming. A sort of astral traveling, an out-of-body experience. Carl Jung himself believed in synchronous dreaming as part of the collective unconscious."

Morgan nodded, deep in thought. She jingled the car keys in her hand.

"Roger will be in contact soon," she said. "Good-bye, Dr. Path." Then Morgan turned and walked back to her car, patches of snow-packed ice crunching under her boots.

Chapter 10

Dr. Grace Path wanted to scream, but the hood covered her mouth and she knew screaming would do no good anyway. No one could possibly hear her. She was in a car, hurtling over a road she couldn't see.

She had struggled, but it was useless. And now, little by little, her mind began to work again, began to think, began to analyze.

The smooth ride made her certain they were on a motorway. It was a luxury car, she could tell by the purring motor, the leather seats. A heater blasted her with warm air, carrying the scent of a new, expensive automobile.

She could see the flash of headlights occasionally as they filtered through the thin material of the cloth that had been thrown over her head.

The two men in the front seat spoke a language she did not understand. It was not Slovak.

The hood smelled of an old-fashioned scent. What was it? Clean smelling, freshly laundered. Had they used this same hood to kidnap other people?

What could they want with her? She wasn't rich. There was no chance of ransom.

Lavender. The scent on the hood was lavender. And, even now, even here, her mind noted that "lavender" was the root of "laundry"— the flower was used in the Middle Ages to camouflage odors, protecting precious cloth from mildew. Fresh-washed linen left in the sun, strewn with the flower. From the French. Late fourteenth century.

She felt the sting of tears in her eyes. Damn it! What could they possibly want with her?

As the hours passed, they ignored her, except to ask if she wanted water. They spoke in heavily accented English.

"Yes, water please," Grace finally said. She hated to give them the satisfaction, but she was thirsty.

She heard the crackle of a plastic water bottle being opened, and the sloshing of water into some sort of glass.

The car's overhead light snapped on just for a minute and she felt the presence of a man stretching back toward her from the front seat. Pale translucent fingers pulled the hood a little way off her face, shoving a thin tube toward her mouth.

"Is straw," said a young man's voice. "Hood stays over eyes, lady. Drink."

The fingers pushing the straw into her mouth were ghastly pale— white bones against the black cloth of the hood. They smelled metallic, inhuman. She shuddered, trying to pull her head away from the fingers.

"You not like water? It comes from the springs deep under castle. Healthy, mountain mineral cures all sickness—"

The driver cursed angrily in the unintelligible language. The man giving her the water said nothing for a few seconds.

"Here. Drink, lady. Drink."

Chapter 11

Wet snow sluiced under the tires of the taxi pulling up to the curb at 150 West Seventeenth Street.

Betsy paid the Pakistani cabbie, tipping far too much. She chalked it up to her excitement, she was actually about to see Jung's *Red Book*—she wanted the entire world to share her excitement, the joy of anticipation.

Forget the analyzing, Path, she told herself. *You are on vacation this weekend.*

She marched through the sidewalk's dirty slush, her cheeks burning from the wind gusts rocketing down the city canyons. Betsy was always amazed by how sharp Manhattan's wind could feel, comparable to the sting of blizzard gusts in the Rockies.

She pushed the glass door open and was embraced by warmth and yellow light. She sighed with delight.

The Rubin Museum exuded the scent of the sacrosanct. Betsy had visited it before, to see the Buddhist mandalas and Tibetan art. When she was at Jungian conferences or visiting friends in New York in the winter, she would often duck into the little private museum for a cup of chai or a curry soup to chase the city chill away.

She often thought of her father here, though he died years before it opened. He would have loved it.

Tonight's program, however, was the only reason she had flown to New York for the weekend. Carl Jung's *The Red Book*—Jung's illustrated chronicle of his journey of the soul and battle with madness—was on display at the Rubin. This original manuscript had been locked in a Swiss bank vault for fifty years. This was the first time it had ever been seen in public. Along with the book itself, the museum was presenting an extraordinary series of discussions that were virtually public Jungian analyses of prominent artists, writers, intellectuals, and mystics.

Jung, a protégé of Sigmund Freud, had moved further and further away from Freud's principles. He eschewed his mentor's rigid adherence to sexual trauma as the root of most mental illness. Jung believed in the collective unconscious, that all humans shared a common pool of ancient knowledge and experience that they were not aware of, but which affected every moment of their lives. Dreams and intuition were valuable tools to not only the psyche but to the soul.

At the age of thirty-eight, in the year 1913, Jung was haunted by his own demons, foreseeing the death and destruction of World War I. His visions tortured him further until he labeled them a "psychosis" or "schizophrenia," but instead of trying to cure himself, he explored his visions in what he termed "active imagination." He illustrated his dreams and began keeping a series of notebooks, which were later transcribed into a big red leather bound book, *The Red Book*.

Each evening discussion in "The Red Book Dialogues" paired a Jungian psychoanalyst with one of the notable guests. The celebrity would be shown an illustration from *The Red Book*, seeing it for the first time right there on stage, and then the psychoanalyst would ask questions about the viewer's feelings and interpretations of the drawing.

This particular night the celebrity was a tarot card reader named Rikki Gillette, to be interviewed by Dr. Jane Kilpatrick from the C.G. Jung Institute.

Betsy's mother was originally going to meet her for this event, but Grace was still engrossed in historical research in Slovakia. Besides, thought Betsy, her mother never "got" Jung. This would be far beyond her comfort zone.

She thought of her father. If only he had lived to see *The Red Book* tonight.

There were plenty of familiar faces in the crowd. To see the manuscript, written and illustrated by Carl Jung himself, was a psychoanalyst's version of making the pilgrimage to Mecca.

Betsy waited her turn to peer down at the enormous tome, encased in bulletproof glass. Every few days the pages were turned. She gazed in awe at the twisting colors and bizarre forms on the two selected pages.

Superimposed on a labyrinth of river blue and beige lines was a figure of a—turbaned man?—outlined in red and black. He fell back, staggering from a golden ray of light piercing—his heart? But if it was his heart, why did it look like a club, as on a playing card? His face showed no fear—surprise, perhaps—and . . .

Betsy leaned closer.

Ecstasy. The man was being touched by the divine.

Others crowded around her, she could smell curry on someone's breath, perhaps the woman behind her in line. Betsy only then realized that the man was standing on a snake, an angry snake ready to strike.

"Excuse me—may I have a look if you are finished?"

Betsy nodded, but it was agonizing to step away from Jung's original work. She was thankful that her mother had given her a first edition copy of the book for her birthday a few weeks before.

Betsy joined the slow-moving line into the auditorium. An usher asked her to pick a tarot card from the fanned deck in his hand.

"It's part of the shtick for tonight," he said, winking at her. "Hold onto it."

Betsy turned the card over in her hand. Her breath caught in her throat.

On the card was an illustration of a girl, sitting upright in bed. Her face was cupped in her hands—she was clearly crying or terrified. Above her were nine swords, dangling in the air. The bedspread was covered with zodiac symbols and roses.

Betsy made her way to an empty seat. She pulled out her iPhone and did a quick search:

THE NINE OF SWORDS COMMUNICATES AN INSTANT MESSAGE OF GRIEF, ANGUISH, AND EVEN TERROR.

The lights darkened and the English curator introduced the two guests, analyst and analysand—the fortune-teller who would share her interpretation of one of Jung's illustrations.

Betsy read on, her eyes glued to the iPhone screen.

IT IS CONSIDERED TO BE UPSETTING AND DISTURBING AS AN OMEN IN A DIVINATORY TAROT READING.

"And would you all be so kind as to turn off your pagers and cell phones? Thank you," announced the curator.

The man next to her glared at her. She clicked off her phone.

Dr. Kilpatrick presented Rikki Gillette with the illustration. It was the same one that Betsy had studied so intently a few minutes earlier. The audience was shown a projection on the wall: the red and black turbaned man and the maze background.

"Tell me your immediate reaction to seeing this illustration, please."

"My first reaction is that I want to cry," Gillette said. She thought a moment longer. "The maze is reminiscent of Van Gogh, his struggle for a way to go . . . the intercept of madness and of the Heart Chakra."

"Heart Chakra!" muttered the man next to Betsy. "Yeah, right! New Age—"

"Shh!" hissed a young woman. Betsy noticed her long red hair and its glorious sheen, even in the dark.

Gillette continued. "But I don't see anguish in the figure's face. No, I see St. Anthony, a dark walk of the soul. And the piercing light is illuminating, raising the man up."

"And the snake?" asked Dr. Kilpatrick.

"He is not afraid of it. It is the light that captures him absolutely. If he focuses on the light, the snake is powerless. He is walking a razor line between rational and irrational. His spirit is speaking to him."

"As a psychic, do you feel a spirit speak to us?" asked Kilpatrick.

"All the time. But you must go to a place of silence to hear it. Not the jabberwocky of language, of social commitments, of things to do. The spirit is giving you clues constantly, if you can just *see* them, just *hear* them . . ."

She looked up from the illustration.

"Each member of the audience was given a tarot card when you came in," said the fortune-teller. " Look at your card please. Who has the Nine of Swords?"

Betsy turned her card over in her hand.

"I do," she said, waving it. She stood up. "What does it mean?"

"The tarot is a collection of symbols, deeply mythological and indicative of archetypes," said Gillette.

Betsy nodded. She knew that, as any Jungian would. But what about this particular illustration? What did it mean? Why did she find it so frightening?

"The Nine of Swords is also called the Lord of Cruelty," said Gillette. "It means you are or soon will be dealing with family secrets. Secrets you may have sensed. But you have not realized the depth and darkness of what was being withheld from you."

Betsy's face began to burn. She felt hundreds of eyes on her.

"There is a lot of pain here."

Betsy started to speak, but the tarot reader shook her head, continuing. "The content is getting in touch with your overwhelming sense of fear. Is there a Scorpio in your life?" Betsy tried to think. *A Scorpio?*

"Talk about nightmares!" laughed Gillette, and everyone joined her laughter. "Keep a dream journal," said Gillette. "And good luck."

In the question-and-answer session that followed, a distinguished white-haired man stood up across the aisle from Betsy. He was leaning on an elegant walking stick with a silver handle.

"Could you speak to Jung's theory of synchronicity and its implication in tarot cards, Ms. Gillette?"

There was a murmur of approval from the analysts in the audience. Betsy noted the foreign accent of the man—Eastern European? She wondered if he had studied in Vienna as her father had.

"Synchronicity? The entire universe vibrates to synchronicity, if only we can hear the rich symphony. The first strains of music, created at our beginnings, the notes wafting through space and time, gathering momentum. But it is only the attuned ear that can detect the chorus."

Betsy listened. She thought of her father. *The third ear, you must develop the third ear,* he would tell her.

She shuddered in the dark so violently that the man next to her shifted his gaze to her.

"It is chilly in here," she muttered, fixing her stare at the two women on stage.

"I am so sorry to conclude this fascinating discussion," said the curator. "But our time is up. Thank you all so much for attending tonight's 'Red Book Dialogue.'"

The audience clapped, and the lights came up fully. Some people rushed forward to ask the psychic questions.

Who did she know who was a Scorpio . . . other than herself?

She hailed a cab to her hotel. In the dark, her fingers fumbled over the tarot card deep in her jacket pocket.

Betsy shivered in the darkness of the cab. She felt a strong urge to be back in Colorado, back to work. She knew she wouldn't sleep that night, not until she was back in her own rumpled bed in Carbondale.

Chapter 12

Before she left, Betsy had spoken with her neighbor at Marta's Market—a Mexican food and clothing store—who had eagerly promised to take care of Ringo anytime Betsy had to be away from home.

"This is just a quick trip," Betsy promised. "A few days in New York."

"*No hay problema*," said Marta, and her two teenage boys had nodded their heads, smiling from their work stacking crates of fresh vegetables. A waft of fresh roasted chiles came in from the back alley, green chiles blistering in a metal drum over a propane flame.

"We take Ringo for walks, give food, water. Doctora no worry," said Luis, the eldest. He put his bear-like arm around Betsy.

Luis was the biggest—but gentlest—young man Betsy had ever known. The Latina kids in the neighborhood called him "Arbolon" or "Big Tree."

Then Marta shooed him away and gave Betsy a kiss on the cheek and a generous *abrazo* herself. She smelled of sweet corn masa from making tamales.

"Luis and Carlos, they take good care of your doggy."

Betsy left them the key to the house, a bag of dogfood, Ringo's leash, and the number of the vet only a half block away.

And her cell phone number, just in case.

Several times a day and once a night, Carlos or Luis walked to the town park with Ringo on a leash, occasionally letting him run loose when they knew a police officer wasn't around to ticket.

One evening, just after sunset, a girl with jet-black hair and a black wool coat and boots stopped Luis on the sidewalk.

"Where did you get that dog?" she asked. "He's not yours."

"It's Doctora Betsy's," said Luis, eyeing her up and down. "Hey, where is the funeral?"

"What?"

"Where is the funeral, girl? You all dressed in black."

"Funny," Daisy said.

Luis shrugged, his heavy shoulders lifting and falling with a seismic shift.

"You know Doc Betsy?" he asked.

"Yes, I am a . . . friend. I was just going to visit her."

He eyed her silently. Friend, he thought. No, she must be one of the Doctora's *locos*. No matter. Underneath all that black-and-white makeup, the girl was *bastante guapa*. Even with the wild *colmillo*, a crazy tooth like a *lobo*.

"Good. La Doctora's friends are my friends," he said, winking. "Come have a beer with me, *amiga*. Doc is out of town for a couple of days."

Luis noticed the creases in her brow, plastered in white makeup. "You and me and a Tecate, *bruja*."

"I can't. I'm—underage."

"Yeah? Cool, me too. Come on, funeral girl. Cheer up with some *cerveza*."

"I can't, really. Hey, just let me pet the dog, OK?"

"Sure. Sure. Girls always go for the pups."

Ringo pushed close to Daisy, licking her bare hand as she scratched his ears. Luis watched as Ringo twisted his body, wagging his tail frantically at the girl.

"He likes you," said Luis.

"Yeah. I like him, too."

"Why don't you come with me? I've got to feed him."

Daisy straightened up from petting the dog. "You have a key to the office, I mean, her house?"

"Yeah, man. She trusts me with the dog, the house. Everything," he said, puffing out his chest.

Daisy hesitated for just a moment, then, "Sure, yeah why not?"

They walked back along Main Street just as the streetlights flickered on. A gust of cold wind from the mountains barreled down the road, biting at their skin. Daisy put on a pair of black wool gloves.

"Whew! This is when I wish I was back in Veracruz, man. Drinking a *cerveza*, eating ceviche. Watching the girls in their bikinis. Everyone sweating, drinking, having a good time. Mariachis—"

Luis dug a house key out of his front pocket as they started up the walk. But as they approached the house, Ringo gave a low growl. Luis grabbed his muzzle, silencing him.

Daisy saw movement in the office window, beyond the aspen trees. She put a hand on Luis's arm. "Someone's in there!"

Luis's body turned stone hard. He pulled a switchblade out of his pocket and snapped it open.

"You wait here and hold the dog."

"The hell I will. I'm coming."

They crept closer to the window.

A man in black stood hunched over Betsy's desk.

"What's he doing?" said Luis.

Daisy squinted in the darkness.

"He's going through her papers," said Daisy.

Ringo growled again. Luis tried to hold his muzzle, but the dog tore away and began to bark frantically. He leapt at the window, snarling.

Luis raced to the door, struggling with the key in the lock, leaving Daisy with the dog, which lunged at the glass, still barking.

The intruder looked up at the snarling dog. His eyes were the palest blue, the shade of a washed-out sky. His skin was ashen, with a bluish cast—the color of dead flesh.

He looked straight into Daisy's eyes, as if he could see her perfectly in the darkness. And then he smiled.

She screamed so loud all Main Street heard her.

Chapter 13

*A*fter I saw the burglar, I was so freaked out all I wanted to do was talk to Betsy.

But she isn't here. When I need her most. When she needs me the most, damn it! I got an eerie sense. Someone is out to hurt her bad.

That dude rifling through her drawers had looned-out blue eyes, the color of glacial lakes. A sinister blue. He was looking for something—I bet it wasn't money.

I'm doing some research, trying to get a fix on Dr. Betsy, where she is taking me with all this journaling. I've been Googling Jung. He is wicked intense—like he was surfing the darkness when they were just inventing cars and stuff.

But I totally get it. I'm thinking of starting a blog, especially for Goths. Dreams, especially.

Ever since I started with Betsy, my dreams have become more . . . disturbing. I used to remember just bits of a night's dream, weird fragments—a checkered tile floor or stones in the battlement of a castle. Red shoes.

Now the dreams are intense. The colors scream, and every detail sizzles.

There is one dream I will not share with anybody.

I dream of blood. vats of blood. Human blood. A woman made of white marble slides into a shiny brass tub with wide bands of copper. A tub of blood.

Her body submerges shoulder deep and she sighs with satisfaction. Ahhh! she says. Ahhhhh!

Like she was in a freaking bubble bath.

She cups her hands and splashes her stony face, the red liquid clotting in her cuticles, coloring her fingertips.

It is so freaking Goth, but it totally creeps me out. I wake up bolt upright in bed, screaming my head off.

My mother runs in, shouting, "Wake up, darling, wake up!"

But I can't forget the last image in the dream: the rock woman smiling, slowly gliding down into the bath until she submerges completely, disappearing into the blood.

Chapter 14

race felt a cold draft from an open door and heard the hollow echo of footsteps. Blinded by the hood, she focused her other senses and her wits. The echoing footsteps. The cold draft, despite the warm fire she could feel and hear crackling somewhere nearby. She must be in a large building—too cavernous to heat effectively. There was a smell, musty and rich—and cold. Beeswax, cedar, the tangy odor of ancient carpets and mildewing tapestries, damp from the humidity of constant rains. The scents of a castle.

"Are you ready to talk now, Dr. Path?" asked a man in fluent, if accented, English. Someone drew off the hood, making her gray hair stand on end.

She looked around the room. Three emaciated women stood, staring at her, their eyes sunk deep into their sockets. They looked pathetically unhealthy—starving and pallid.

She blinked, trying to focus her eyes. The women were wearing white face paint. There was a hunger in their eyes—starving beasts watching something to feast upon.

She turned to the speaker—and recoiled in surprise. It was the man who had bought her champagne for no apparent reason in Piestany an hour before she was kidnapped. The stranger, a tall man with white hair, had skin as pale as a corpse, except for his purplish lips.

"Why am I here? What do you want from me?" she asked, narrowing her eyes.

"I only want to meet your daughter," said the man, folding his hands in front of him. "I believe she has something that rightfully belongs to me."

"Who are you?"

"You may address me as Count."

Grace blinked her eyes, trying to focus. The man was a blur of white skin and sensuous lips.

"Would you like your spectacles?" he asked.

Spectacles, she thought, not glasses. His accent is possibly Hungarian. He must have been schooled in England, or had an English tutor as a child.

"Yes. Please," she forced herself to say.

One of the stick-thin women clicked open Grace's leather briefcase. She took a pair of glasses from a case, handing them to the historian.

The woman lingered there, breathing deeply. Grace could hear an audible sniff, as if the woman was smelling her.

"Not those," snapped Grace. "In my purse," she said. "The ones you have there are just for reading."

The woman looked at the Count. He gave a curt nod. From the shadows, a fuchsia-haired woman pulled out Grace's purse.

"Yes, the ones in the beaded case."

Grace held still while the skeletal hands adjusted them on her face. As the woman drew away, Grace looked at her arms. Purple and yellow bruises, withered skin.

"Where am I?" she asked. She glanced about, taking in her surroundings. The fireplace was fifteenth-century granite with a marble mantel, smooth from centuries of wear. A muted fresco of Roman emperors and Habsburg rulers was recessed in the coffered ceiling above her head. A Venetian artist, she decided. Fifteen, sixteenth century at the latest.

"You are in my home. In Slovakia. Welcome, Dr. Path."

"Welcome? How dare you! You kidnapped me!"

"Kidnap? That seems such a hostile term. I have invited you to sojourn in my castle."

"Why? What do you want with me? I am a historian, what could I—?"

"Again, I ask only what we can do to persuade your daughter to come and pay me a visit."

Grace pretended she didn't hear. "Why are you holding me prisoner?"

The Count arched his brow.

"Because you might be useful to me. Your husband was not, I am afraid."

Useful. The word rang in Grace's ears. A throbbing sound—her heart?—pounded, deafening her.

"My husband died in a car accident ten years ago!"

"Yes. We thought that might bring your daughter here again. Unfortunate death, but necessary."

Grace's mouth went dry. She made a clicking sound when she tried to talk. She swallowed hard.

"What do you mean, again?"

"Ah, you have forgotten. Years ago, when she was a child of—what, five or six?—you brought her in tow to a research congress in Bratislava. It was a congress on the reign of Matthias II."

Grace's memory raced. There had been so many researchers and experts there. Hundreds of people. There had been a moment of panic when she couldn't find Betsy—the little girl had disappeared.

Then she remembered, the moment from decades ago suddenly perfectly clear in her mind. The tall, elegant man with a silver-topped cane who held her daughter on his knee, gazing into her eyes. *Who is that man?* she had thought. As she rushed forward to reclaim her daughter, a tinkling voice drifted through the air. "Ah, Count Bathory. Is it not enough you have captured all the women's hearts in Czechoslovakia and Hungary? Must you cast your spell on American hearts so young and tender?"

"Count Bathory," Grace whispered now as she looked at the man who held her prisoner. "I remember—you had my daughter—"

"Ah, good. So you do remember me. I was quite offended when your husband pretended he could not. Especially after all our—time—together."

A stab of pain struck her chest and she closed her eyes.

"I have heard you are researching my illustrious ancestor, Countess Bathory. You realize that we are approaching a very special anniversary in the next few days?"

Grace stared at her captor.

"Of course you know—"

"What do you want with my daughter?" she interrupted.

"That is my own personal business," he said. "But let's just say she might possess something I need."

A shadow crossed his face. The light in his eyes turned flat.

Then he forced a smile, drawing back the vivid lips, exposing long white teeth.

Chapter 15

Zuzana spied on the new horsemaster from the arrow slits of the keep. She had known him as a youth from Sarvar Castle in the flatlands of Lower Hungary, but it had been thirteen long years since she had seen his boyish face.

He had grown—in physique and in confidence. Her first recollection of Janos had been as a silent boy sipping beer in the corner as their fathers exchanged stories, clapping each other on the back.

But that was before he became her best—and most loyal—childhood friend. The boy who had taught her to ride.

Now she watched him speak to the head guard, self-assured in his stance, despite his beardless face.

Janos's father, Anastatius Szilvasi—horsemaster to Count Nadasdy—was a close friend of her father, Ales Bende. Ales was the castle smithy and his skill in shoeing Count Nadasdy's vast stable of horses was appreciated most by the horsemaster himself. Szilvasi and Zuzana's father had ridden many campaigns together against the Ottomans. Bende ensured that the horses were expertly shod, keeping Nadasdy and his cavalry well-mounted.

The horsemaster was known to dip a ladle into their ale barrel on occasion, breaking coarse bread with the family. Zuzana's brother

Ladislav had worked in the stables during his short life and had been a favorite stable hand.

"Your brother had a way with horses," said the elder Szilvasi. He chucked little Zuzana under the chin, ignoring her pocked skin and deep scars. He lifted her up on his knee, jogging it under her as if she were on a pony ride. She squealed with delight. She loved nothing more than horses.

"I think my own son, Janos, has the gift as well, but time will tell."

Horsemaster Szilvasi would bring Janos in tow, a small boy who remained quiet and serious, listening as the two men, blacksmith and horsemaster, exchanged news about horse breeding, the encroaching Ottomans, Habsburg politics, and the Bathory-Nadasdy involvement in the Austrian-Ottoman War.

Zuzana, only five years old at the time, stared across the room at the boy. He ignored her for she was only a baby, a baby with a scarred face.

"Did you fall into a fire pit?" he asked her one day.

"No," she said, bewildered. "What fire?"

The boy reached out his left hand. For the first time, she saw the long white scar on the edge of his hand.

He stroked the rim of a deep pock on her face, solemnly tracing the scar. Zuzana snatched at his wrist, flinging his hand away from her face.

Zuzana touched her skin with her baby fingertips, ducking her chin down like a scalded swan. "Mama says it was the pox. The angels saved me."

"Angels? No, you must have had the wink of a witch to save you from death. You are born lucky."

Janos Szilvasi was the only soul to ever call her lucky.

The next morning, Zuzana woke with a terrible cold. Her throat burned when she swallowed, her nose ran constantly, soaking her linen rag.

How can I attend the Countess in this condition?

Zuzana powdered her nose, to conceal the red swelling and chafed skin. She stuffed the linen rag in her apron, trying hard not to sniffle.

The Countess settled into her high-back chair for her morning toilette. She looked up at her attendant in mirror.

Zuzana sneezed convulsively, her hands flying to cover her face.

"What? Zuzana, you are ill! How dare you approach me in this condition!"

"I am sorry, Countess."

"I will not have you attend me with your sniffling nose and rheumy eyes," said the Countess, her finger jabbing toward the door. "Out, immediately! Work in the kitchen toting water, fetching wood for the fire. Whatever Brona the cook orders you to do."

"Yes, Countess."

"Only return when you are well again. Not a moment before."

"But who shall attend to your toilette?"

The Countess hesitated. She dragged her fingertips across her complexion, inspecting her skin in the mirror.

"Send in Vida. She may attend me until you are healthy once more."

Zuzana ran to fetch Vida from the cold corridor, where she still lay on her palette, straw woven into her long black hair.

"Wake at once! Comb your hair—you are expected in the vanity to perform the Countess's toilette this morning."

Zuzana saw the horror cross the girl's face as she scrambled to her feet.

"Me! Attend the Countess's skin? But she commanded me never to accompany her again—"

"I have all the unguents and powders laid out. I can teach you. First you clean her skin with ambergris oil, using the white lamb's wool—"

"Zuzana! I have heard how she attacks those who do not please her. She bloodied the face of the girl who tugged at a tangle in her hair."

"You must not tug. You must compliment her ceaselessly, entertain her by indulging her before her looking glass. After the ambergris oil—do use it sparingly, it is dear—apply the special clay I have prepared in the crimson glass jar. It whitens her complexion. Leave it to work its wonders for a quarter of an hour. Then remove it with rosemary water. That is in the blue flask. Next . . ."

Vida composed herself at the door, her heart thumping in her throat.

"Countess. I have the pleasure to—"

"What has taken you so much time! The fire in the grate has gone out. I am chilled and will most likely take ill, like the wretched pox-faced girl who left me here."

"Madame, I came as soon as I understood the ways of Zuzana's toilette methods," said Vida, turning white. She hurried to the grate, feeding the faint embers with dried twigs.

"I will have the fire ablaze in no time," she said, coaxing flames with her breath.

"Bring me the ermine furs, girl!" said the Countess, shivering.

Vida glanced at the embers, still dull and stubborn. The little twigs only smoked. The Countess coughed, waving the smoke from her face.

"You are really quite useless. My furs, at once—"

"Yes, Countess."

Vida opened the cedar chest, pulling out the sleek fur cloak. She draped it over the Countess's shoulders.

The Countess saw Vida's soft white hands in the mirror as the girl adjusted the cloak. Vida's hands grazed the Countess's.

Small, pale hands, supple with youth. As white a porcelain. As perfect as a doll's.

The Countess looked down at her own hands, which, unlike her face, showed the march of time. Thick ropey veins meandered across the backs, punctuated by the white boney knuckles, wrinkled with age.

She snatched her hands away, hiding them under the ermine cloak.

"Clumsy girl! How dare you touch me with your peasant hands."

"I am sorry—"

"Fetch me a hot mulled wine, boiled and steaming. At once!"

"Yes, Countess."

Countess Bathory searched out the girl's face in the mirror.

Vida's skin was flawless and moist, like so many of the Slovak maidens. Her cheeks were flushed from her efforts at the fire. Her young bosom heaved, like an injured bird the Countess had once held in her hand as a little girl. The small bird flew against the leaded glass of the castle in Ecsed, her childhood home.

She had gathered the bird up in her hands, examining it. The dazed bird opened his beak, gasping for air. After a few moments it had regained its wits, breathing hard with fright. She squeezed it, smiling as she felt the tiny heart palpate under her fingers.

The Countess's eyes turned cold, their amber color frightening the handmaiden.

She had squeezed it until the tiny heart stopped.

"Did I not urge you to stir the fire to flame? Did I not tell you I was chilled to the bone? What is the matter with you, stupid, stupid girl?" she hissed. "You shall be punished. I shall tell Brona the cook to withhold your food. You look too fat and lazy to me."

"Yes, Countess. I shall make the flame blaze and call for hot *mendovino* to chase away the chill."

The girl knelt at the fire, blowing with all her might. The twigs caught flame. She fed it small branches, one by one. Then she ran to the door.

She caught Zuzana in the hall.

"She detests me!" cried Vida. "She will tell Cook to starve me."

"I heard what transpired," said Zuzana, wiping at her nose with her soggy handkerchief. "I had my ear pressed to the door the whole time."

"Then fetch the *mendovino*, hurry!" said Vida. "I must return before the fire burns out."

"Ambergris oil first," called Zuzana over her shoulder as she ran down the corridor. "Mind whatever you do, and do not drip anything on her ermine cape or you will be done for!"

Chapter 16

So what are you doing for the solstice?" Kyle said, stopping by Daisy's locker. "What do Goths do on their special holiday?"

Daisy had been avoiding him since he crashed into her that day on the Rio Grande trail.

"Kyle? Right?"

He shook his head.

"You *know* it is. We've been in the same class since August. Come on!"

Daisy raised her chin defensively. How was she supposed to keep track of his name? They had nothing in common, right? He was a jock, she was a Goth. Period.

"Anyway, you didn't answer my question. What do you do?"

"The solstice? Dude, that's not for a couple weeks."

"But what do you Goths do?"

"Not much," she said, banging her locker closed. "Listen to music, hang with a few Goth friends, maybe. Stay at home and channel energy."

He looked disappointed. Daisy didn't know why it bothered her.

"And visit the cemetery at midnight," she offered.

His face lit up. *Like a freakin' Christmas tree*, she thought.

"Hey, can I come with you?"

Daisy threw him a what-the-fuck look.

"Why? You aren't into the Goth scene."

"Maybe . . . I'm curious. And I read your blog about Goth stuff."

Daisy dropped her jaw, making her white makeup crease. What did this guy know about her? Why was he interested?

Daisy glanced to see if anyone was listening to the conversation. There were a couple of popular girls giving them the eye, but they weren't close enough to hear.

"And what is that crazy book with all the zoned-out pix you download?" he whispered, close enough to her she could smell his tropical fruit chewing gum.

"*The Red Book.*"

"It's sick—those crazy illustrations. Wild colors. Like, was he on drugs or what?"

"He may have been 'crazy' when he drew them. He was exploring his psyche and his soul."

Kyle didn't say anything. He looked into her kohl-rimmed eyes. "I want to spend the solstice with you."

"With me? Are you sure?"

"Yep. I'm sure."

"Why not?" she said. Her tooth hooked over her lip, and she was trying to keep herself from smiling.

Betsy stifled a yawn. Her flight from New York had been delayed four hours due to another heavy snowstorm.

As she waited for Daisy to arrive for her session, Betsy pulled the Nine of Swords from her jacket pocket, setting it up on her desk. The image of the sobbing girl sent a shiver down her spine.

"What's that?" said Daisy, entering silently through the door.

Betsy jumped. She snatched the card from her desk, shoving it into a drawer.

"Nothing, just . . ."

"It's a tarot card, right? The Nine of Swords. Whew, watch your back, Betsy! Especially after that creepy dude broke into your house—"

"Let's not bring that unforturnate occurrence into your therapy session," said Betsy. "It had nothing to do with you." She saw a beige book in her patient's hand.

"What do you have there?"

"It's the I-Ching," Daisy said. "It's like a Goth bestseller. Anyway, I read the foreword. Did you know it was written by your guy? Carl Jung?"

Betsy straightened her back.

"No. Yes! I mean, I had forgotten he wrote that."

"I was thinking about my dreams and Jung's theory of synchronicity," said Daisy. "I've been doing a lot of research on the internet. I had no idea that Jung was so—freaking awesome."

"So why did you bring the I-Ching?" Betsy asked. "This is your therapy hour, Daisy. Sit down."

An enigmatic smile crossed Daisy's face, exposing her crooked tooth. She remained standing.

"Ah, but you didn't really tell me all there is to know about Dr. Jung," she said. Her open palm thumped the book. "He was a fervent believer in coincidence."

"Synchronicity," Betsy said. "His theory of acausal connecting principles."

"Yeah, right. That part you told me, remember?"

Had she told her?

"You told me synchronicity is like a coincidence. Like the coins and dice falling in a certain way that has almost zero probability. Or a roulette wheel hitting the same number over and over. Or the principle behind tarot cards. Meaningful coincidences. Woo-woo-woo-woo," she said, making a comical haunted sound as she arched her black-penciled eyebrows up and down.

The conversation was unsettling. But the funny look on Daisy's face made her psychologist laugh.

"What does any of this have to do with your therapy, Daisy?"

"You didn't explain that this Jung guy was such a cool dude. Like he was into the occult, mandalas and Buddhism. And former lives."

Betsy hesitated. Why did Daisy's sudden interest in Carl Jung make her uneasy?

"He believed in exploring the unconscious, Daisy. That by examining your unconscious world, you can discover reasons for your behavior, your beliefs and fears. Jungian analysis—"

"No, he was—*Goth*. He believed in the spiritual world. Ghosts. Murmurs of the past . . . and how we are all connected."

Betsy thought of the tarot card. She shook her head.

"Carl Jung did not believe in ghosts and he certainly was not Goth." She straightened her posture. "He believed in the collective unconscious of the universe—"

Daisy flicked her ebony hair behind her shoulder, shaking her head vehemently. She opened the I-Ching, thrusting her finger at Jung's foreword.

"Oh, yeah, he did, Betsy. Believe in ghosts, I mean. And collective unconscious? *Hello!* Totally Goth. And the wild visions—"

"Jung experienced the 'menace of psychosis,' as he termed it," Betsy said carefully. "This was a very dark time for him, when he lost his grasp on reality."

"What's reality?" asked Daisy. "Hearing ghosts or me choking on my own spit for no reason?"

Betsy shifted in her chair, making the old floorboards creak.

"He is *so* freakin' awesome. I'm telling all my Goth friends about him."

Daisy closed the book with a definitive thud that resounded throughout the room. Ringo looked up at her, his brown eyes questioning.

Obsessive, thought Betsy. Her patient had perseverated on Jung.

"OK. You've made your point, Daisy," Betsy said, the tone of her voice rising in annoyance. "I am impressed with your research and the time you have spent learning about Carl Jung. Now, it is time for your session."

"OK, Betsy," said Daisy, collapsing into a wing chair, a victorious smile on her white-powdered face. "Ask me anything you want."

Betsy nodded. *Who was this stranger who sat across from her now, so affable and open?*

Chapter 17

It's time to come back, says the voice from the shadows. A sweep of heavy cloth—taffeta? A waft of perfume, hints of rosemary.

A cold hand touches me, a finger under my chin. I am paralyzed.

Answer my call.

Betsy woke up from her dream to the persistent ringing of the telephone.

"Hello?"

"Hello, is this Dr. Path?"

"Yes."

"I apologize for calling so early. This is Stephen Cox. I'm Dean of History at the University of Chicago. I have your number as an emergency contact for your mother, Dr. Grace Path."

Betsy sat up quickly, untangling her legs from the sheets.

"Is something wrong? Has something happened to my mother?"

"Well, that's why I'm calling. She was supposed to be back to teach a class yesterday, but she didn't show up. I was only informed of it this morning or I would have called you earlier."

"She's not there?"

"No, the last we heard from her was when she submitted a monograph by e-mail for proofreading, and that was several weeks ago."

Betsy's pulse began to pound in her head. She forced herself to breathe deeply. The voice on the phone went on.

"We hoped she might have been in contact with you."

"I had an e-mail from her a few days ago. Let me get it."

She stumbled out of bed, clutching the phone, and opened her laptop.

The computer whirred to life. She clicked on her in-box.

"OK, here it is. It's dated—December fourth, so six days ago."

SORRY I CAN'T BE WITH YOU AT THE RED BOOK DIALOGUES—I KNOW YOU WILL ENJOY IT THOROUGHLY. I AM GOING BACK ONCE MORE TO VISIT CACHTICE CASTLE AND BECKOV CASTLE TOMORROW, HOMES OF COUNTESS BATHORY.

There was dead silence on the phone.

"Is that all?" the dean finally asked. "No mention of returning to Chicago?"

"No, nothing. She just ends, 'I will send you a postcard, darling.'"

Again a silence. The dean filled it at last. "She was doing research in Slovakia and Hungary. She has a deadline for the book in mid-January."

"I knew she was doing research, but didn't know what she was working on."

"She didn't tell you? Yes, she has a publisher lined up and a title. *Countess Bathory: A Study of a Madwoman.*"

Betsy blinked in the early light filtering in through Japanese paper blinds. The bedroom was awash in an eerie rosy pink. "Study of a madwoman? What kind of historical treatise is that? She's no psychologist, she's a historian."

"She told me the publishers came up with the title. The point is that she was in Eastern Europe researching Countess Bathory. She had a special week-long seminar on the Habsburg Dynasty to teach this week. I can't imagine why she hasn't written or called. She had a hundred and twenty students waiting for her to appear."

"That's not like my mother. She would never miss a class without—"

The heat clicked on and the floorboards creaked. A branch rasped against the windowpane.

Betsy realized she had stopped talking midsentence. She could hear a faint buzzing on the line.

"Yes," the dean said at last. "That's why I am so concerned."

Betsy sat down at her computer and began to hunt through her e-mails. The pink glow of the rising sun reflected on her screen.

Shit, Mom. What have you gotten yourself into now?

Her mother was never good about itineraries, so the e-mail mentioning Countess Bathory was the only clue to where she had gone.

When Betsy looked on the internet, she found hundreds of entries for Countess Bathory, some spelling her Christian name as Elizabeth, some as Alzabeta or Erzsebet—English, Slovak, and Hungarian spellings. The countess had at least a half a dozen castles in the lands that were now Austria, Hungary, and Slovakia, but were then part of the Habsburg-ruled Holy Roman Empire. But Royal Habsburg Hungary was just a meager crescent, a stingy slice of territory. More than two-thirds of the once mighty Hungarian Empire was either part of Transylvania or had fallen to the Ottoman invaders.

In what remained of Royal Hungary, Countess Bathory owned more lands than the House of Habsburg itself.

Betsy checked the two castles her mother had mentioned in the e-mail: Čachtice and Beckov, both reduced to ruins. They were less than fifty kilometers from Bratislava and about fifteen kilometers from each other.

Why hadn't she mentioned that she was researching Bathory, when she normally stuck to the Habsburg kings? Rudolf II and his younger brother Matthias, in their fraternal struggle for the crown, were usually her focus. Why, suddenly, this Bathory woman?

Betsy clicked on travel articles and excerpts of books. Most of the write-ups described the ruins of Čachtice, at the foot of the Little Carpathian Mountains.

Then she read:

BLOODY LIZ WAS RUMORED TO HAVE TORTURED AND KILLED PEASANT GIRLS DURING HER MURDEROUS REIGN. SHE IS ACCUSED OF BATHING IN THE BLOOD OF BEAUTIFUL YOUNG VIRGINS IN ORDER TO KEEP HER YOUTHFUL APPEARANCE ETERNAL. COUNTESS BATHORY, ALONG WITH HER ANCESTOR, VLAD THE IMPALER, WAS THE BASIS OF BRAM STOKER'S *DRACULA*.

Betsy realized she had stopped breathing. She drew a deep breath, filling her lungs to capacity, and tried to quiet her mind.

What twisted psychological condition did this woman have? Preying on girls, obsessed with their blood! Was it a genetic predisposition for psychosis, passed down through generations of inbreeding among the aristocracy?

A dog barked in the neighborhood. Ringo growled. She glanced up at the windows, but the paper shades were lowered. No one could see her. She turned back to the glow of the computer screen.

There were no hotels near Čachtice, not even a bed-and-breakfast. This was a tiny village at the foot of the mountains. The closest hotels were about thirteen kilometers away in the spa town of Piestany. Betsy couldn't picture her mother staying anywhere fancy, so she began e-mailing every small hotel and B & B she could find in the Piestany area. She couldn't think of what else to do. And the repetitive act of copying and pasting the same brief query about a sixty-five-year-old university professor, traveling alone, gave her something to occupy her mind. Command-V, command-V—paste, paste, paste.

Why would her mother be interested in a murderous psycho-pathic countess?

Betsy searched through her file cabinet. She had gone through the *P*s three times already, each time more carefully.

She stopped, thinking. *Of course!*

Under M, for Mom.

Betsy found the file. Her mother had granted one session with her daughter, and one session only. It was a kind of graduation present to Betsy, to share the one dream Grace had ever remembered.

It was a dream Grace had had the night Betsy was born.

"Don't you dare analyze me, Betsy. I'm only sharing this because I never, ever dream. It must have been provoked by indigestion or the first spasms of childbirth."

It was clear that she wanted her daughter to hear this dream. Grace was such a left-brained academic, systematic and almost scien-tific in her meticulous research in history. She was so unlike Betsy or her husband, their Jungian world of dream interpretation dismissed as "malarkey."

Once Grace started talking, her words flowed.

I dream I am floating through a dense cloudbank that hugs mountain walls. The air clears and it is a winter day in a river valley.

There is a village below me. A fairytale village, dusted with snow. I see a tall church steeple and wooden cottages with straw-thatched roofs. Rosy-cheeked children play in the streets, though I can't hear them. They wear rustic clothes of long ago: the boys in wool caps and breeches, the girls with white kerchiefs and long aprons.

I feel that it is Eastern Europe, but I hear no voices, no accents to con-firm this. It is a soundless dream.

I veer away to a pond. White steam rises from the water and ice clings to the bare branches of the weeping willows. Frost outlines the bark eyes of the birch trees, staring solemnly.

Everything glitters as the sun's rays filter through the fog coming off the water in gentle waves, ghosts gliding over the pond.

A brittle shelf of ice lines the shore, a jagged silver plane on the dark water. Ducks float peacefully beyond, occasionally plunging to pull at strands of grass below the surface. They seem oblivious to the cold, their fat bottoms tipped up to the winter sky.

I feel at peace in a world of winter beauty.

Then I see her: a girl, submerged, coated in ice, her eyes open, blue and clear. She stares blindly, her long hair sparkling with frost. I have the impression she has tried to tear off her clothes, there is a rip in her bodice. A rose-colored mark blooms just above her breast, contrasting sharply with her flawless white skin.

Everything about her is beautiful. Except that she is dead.

Betsy shuddered and closed her eyes.

Where are you now, Mom?

Chapter 18

Betsy called the American Embassy in Bratislava, asking how to locate a missing person.

"Has she registered with the embassy?" asked a bored male voice. She heard the ping of an incoming e-mail in the background.

"No, but she entered Slovakia on her American passport."

"Name, please?" he droned.

Betsy could tell this man was not going to help her. She knew the type, the tone of voice, the desire to be rid of her quickly so he could update his Facebook.

She gave him her mother's name, age, description.

"She was doing research in the Bratislava area, possibly also in Čachtice and Beckov."

"I have no record of her registering with the embassy. Was she planning to stay more than a month?"

"Six weeks. I think."

"She should have registered with the embassy if she was staying that long," said the voice, with an admonishing tone. "I have no record of her."

"Can you tell me how to go about locating her? Can you contact the police department in Bratislava, or the areas around Čachtice or Beckov?"

"No, that is not a service we offer. Besides, it might infringe on her civil rights."

Betsy's hand tightened around the phone receiver.

"Her *what?*"

"Dr. Path may have decided she wanted to remain in Slovakia without contacting anyone. We have to protect our American citizens' rights."

"You are a complete idiot, do you know that?"

"Excuse me?"

"No, I won't!" Betsy said, punching the END-CALL button on her phone.

She held her head in her hands.

What should she do now? There wasn't anyone else in her family to call for help. Betsy was an only child.

Her fingers reached for the old, worn address book. She dialed a phone number that had been blurred long ago with tears.

"Hello?"

"John? It's Betsy."

There was an awkward pause.

"Betsy? Are you all right?"

Oh shit. Why was she calling her ex?

"No! No, I'm not all right. Mom's missing in Slovakia, she didn't show up for her first class after her sabbatical. The dean called me. He hasn't heard from her—"

"Slow down, Betsy. Your mom is missing in Slovakia?"

"That's what I said."

A pause. Those pauses she always hated because she could feel him thinking, processing information. Being so rational, damn him!

"Maybe there is a reason."

A reason! A reason for what? Suddenly all the poisonous currents that had flowed through her during their divorce came flooding back.

"John! There is no *reason*, except that something bad has happened to her."

Another pause.

"Betsy, pull yourself together. Let's think. What communication did she leave?"

Deep breath. "Not much. I have an e-mail saying she was going to see Countess Bathory's castle, outside Bratislava."

"Countess who?"

"Bathory—she was some kind of sadistic freak during the early seventeenth century."

"Historical research. OK, that sounds right."

So typical of John. His mathematical mind filtering out everything but the facts. Betsy could almost hear the whirring of his brain, a computer starting up from sleep mode.

"She was writing a book—she never told me about it. She's always stuck to Habsburgs and the Hungarian-Ottoman wars. Why would she write about some psychopathic monster?"

"Psychopathic monster?"

"This Bathory woman killed hundreds of young women. Tortured many more."

He gave a low whistle.

"Doesn't sound like your mom's cup of tea."

"And now—she's disappeared."

"Have you called the American Embassy?"

"They were useless."

Another silence.

"You want me to come out there?"

"To do what?"

"To—to be with you, Bets. You sound like you're losing it."

"I've got to do something."

"What? What are you going to do?"

"I—Oh, shit, John. I don't know."

"Give it a day or two. And—"

"And what?"

"Let me come out and see you."

Betsy went through the appointment calendar on her computer and began cancelling everything for the next two weeks. While she was waiting for someone to answer or listening to an answering machine, waiting to leave a message, her fingers flew over the keyboard, searching for a flight to Bratislava.

It made more sense to fly to Vienna and take the train—it ran every hour and took only fifty minutes to cross the Austrian border into the capital of Slovakia—

When Betsy reached Daisy's name in the appointment calendar, she hesitated.

I'll call her mother last, she thought.

Betsy's mind worked frantically, worrying about her mother. The last thing she wanted to do was see patients today, but she reminded herself that they had their own troubles and it was her duty to work with them. The day was filled with back-to-back appointments.

By the afternoon, she was exhausted. She had checked her e-mail every thirty seconds between appointments.

Nothing. She slumped over her computer and began to cry.

"Betsy! Hey, are you OK?"

Daisy had appeared silently. Betsy hadn't heard the door and Ringo hadn't barked or moved. Now he began to thump his tail.

Betsy looked up, and frantically tried to put on her professional face. A patient should know as little as possible about her therapist's private life.

"Oh, I am so sorry, Daisy. I didn't hear you come in—aren't you early?"

Betsy wiped her eyes on her shirtsleeve. John was right, she thought. She was losing it.

The next thing she knew, there was a silky black sleeve draping over her shoulder. It was like being hugged by Morticia of the Addams Family. Betsy smelled a perfume, something old like her grandmother wore . . . White Shoulders? Bellodgia?

Daisy set something down beside her on the table. Then she hugged her psychologist close again.

"It's all right, Betsy. I don't know what it is, but it will be all right."

Was this the same girl who had scowled at her in stony silence just a few weeks ago?

"Is it because you are freaked out about the burglar? I'm sorry we let him get away. He, like, just disappeared after I screamed."

"Thank you," said Betsy. "You could have been hurt. And, no, nothing was missing as far as I could tell. But it took a long time to put everything back together."

Betsy tried desperately to pull together her professional demeanor. *Damn, damn, damn.* A sobbing therapist. What a colossal failure she was! Her mind flashed on her father's sober face, reproaching her.

Never interject your persona into therapy. You are a blank screen through which the patient focuses on himself.

Daisy stroked Betsy's cheek, dabbing her tears with her fingertips. The psychologist pulled away from her, humiliated.

"Daisy, I think I may be getting the flu. I'm sorry. I think—I think I'm going to have to cancel our session."

"Oh."

Betsy watched as the girl pulled back, rigid. She looked frightened.

"I'm sorry. Really. But I—I think I'm getting a fever."

"Oh. Can I—can I get you some soup? I can run down to the Village Smithy and get your some of their homemade—"

"That's sweet. I don't. No, I don't think so. I'll call you later, when I feel better. OK?"

"Right. OK," Daisy said, nodding her head like a wooden puppet. "If you're sick, I can run errands for you."

"No. No. I'll call you. It's probably just a twenty-four-hour bug."

"Sure," said Daisy, not moving.

"Let me walk you out," said Betsy, rising from her chair.

As soon as she closed the door, Betsy rummaged through her desk. The tarot card with the sobbing girl lay in the shadows of the drawer.

Chapter 19

The Countess did not summon the horsemaster again for many days. Janos Szilvasi spent his days focused on his work, waking before dawn when the kitchen boys dragged in dry logs and kindling from the woodshed and stoked the fire to prepare the morning breakfast.

Often the predawn meal consisted of leftover root-vegetable soup and doughy dumplings from the smoke-black cauldron. Broken loaves of stale bread accompanied the meal, smeared with fat drippings: tasty or rancid, it did not matter to the cook. It was stodgy food to fill a workingman's belly. At least the morning beer was good: dark, bitter ale, surprisingly better than the breweries in Sarvar produced.

The Countess's horses thrived under Janos's hand. Their wounds healed, their lameness diminished as new flesh grew in the deep hollow of their hooves. Szilvasi procured grain for the most starved and, with the help of the stable boys, filed the horses' teeth smooth to help them chew and digest their feed.

The boys learned to rub the horses with coarse sacks until their coats shone. They collected pine resin from the forest and dabbed it into the cracks in the horses' hooves. Their backs ached with carrying fresh water in buckets from the courtyard well.

Janos took a deep breath. After a fortnight and half, the smell of the stables had changed entirely. He drew in a lungful of the essence of sweet straw, pinesap, and the intoxicating scent of warm horse— healthy and content. Wholesome.

The next challenge would be to ride the white stallion.

Zuzana spied from the tower on the strong young Hungarian, the friend of her childhood, now a man. She pressed her cheek against the rough stone, and blinked until her eyes teared with the blustery cold that threaded through the narrow opening in the castle wall. She remained immobile for long minutes, her gaze focused below, an ear listening for the tinkling bell of her mistress.

When she pulled her face away from the stone, there was an imprint of the rough granite on her poxed face.

She rubbed her cheek to return the blood to her skin. She knew she could stare all day at Janos and never tire of him.

His manner was efficient but kind, and he quickly won the confidence of not only the horses, but of the stable boys and guards as well. And he had earned the grudging respect of Erno Kovach, who put an arm around the young horsemaster's shoulder one day, drawing Szilvasi near as he shared a joke. It had been many months since Zuzana had seen the head guard—or any of the men—laugh; she considered the sight a minor miracle.

Zuzana was not the only pair of eyes spying on Janos Szilvasi. Small groups of handmaidens and scullery maids clustered around the edges of curtained windows throughout the castle, whispering and laughing.

"He will be mine by New Year's!" swore Hedvika.

The other girls tittered and the whispering began again.

"Perhaps he prefers black tresses strewn across his chest," challenged Zora, her fingers playing with her long black braid. "After all, he means to tame the wild stallion—he has dark passion pulsing in his veins."

"Ack, with your flat bosom, what could you offer a man like that?" said Hedvika.

Zuzana had often overheard the women, their pecking and clucking no different from the speckled hens that squawked in the castle courtyard. The horsemaster was no more than a tasty grub wedged between the paving stones to them.

She had a bitter taste in her mouth, and swallowed, remembering. This was the boy who had called her lucky. She had never forgotten him.

Chapter 20

Betsy knew she had one more patient appointment to cancel. She had procrastinated long enough.

"Hello?"

"Hello, Daisy?"

"Betsy? Hi, what's up?"

"I'm going to have to cancel our session tomorrow. In fact, I have to cancel our sessions for the next two weeks. An emergency has come up."

She could hear a constricted whistling and a muted gagging sound.

"Daisy? Are you there?"

"Yeah," her voice thin and high-pitched. "What's the emergency?"

"It's a personal family matter. I'm sorry, I wouldn't cancel if it weren't absolutely necessary."

There was a pause.

"There is some danger," said Daisy, her voice monotone. "I can sense it."

Just stop *that,* Betsy thought. *Stay out of my business.* "No, just—I have to travel to help out my mother."

"Travel where? Is this like a Christmas break or something?"

No more details about her private life, Betsy told herself. Absolutely none. "Daisy, is your mother home?"

"She's out shopping."

"Would you tell her I called?"

"Yeah. But why won't you tell me more about the emergency? I can feel something is wrong, I just know it."

"I've got to go. Good-bye, Daisy."

"Wait! What's your e-mail?"

"Why do you want my e-mail?"

"To stay in touch. Maybe I can help."

This was ridiculous, but Betsy did maintain a professional e-mail account for clients who wanted to verbalize their problems when she wasn't there to hear them. Sometimes it helped them to write out their fears, and then Betsy would have a journal of their emotional state when she returned to her practice.

Betsy gave her the address but added, "I may not have e-mail access every day while I am away. We will discuss your concerns in therapy when I return."

"Take care of yourself, Betsy. 'Cause I've got a weird feeling."

As Betsy got off the phone, she heard the wind whistling through the wooden shutters. What was she going to do with this patient who had so clearly transferred her fears to her therapist?

Chapter 21

For weeks now, Cook Brona had given Vida only the weakest broth. Occasionally the big-boned cook took pity and included a bit of boiled turnip, though this elicited a scowl from the ever-watchful Hedvika, her plump lips greasy with meat from her own full plate.

Vida pleaded for more, her stomach grumbling. Brona's eyes, set like raisins pressed deep in dough, glistened in sympathy. Food was all there was to Brona, and it tortured her to see a starving soul. But the Countess's orders were clear and disobedience was unthinkable. The cook turned her back to the girl.

"But Cook, look at me!" Vida cried. She held out a bony hand, her fingers like winter twigs.

Brona blinked her heavy-lidded eyes. Vida had been a beauty when she had arrived in June, the rose blooming on her plump cheeks, her hair shining like a raven's wing. The Countess had selected her personally to carry the train of her gown from the dressing room to the vanity, where the pox-faced Zuzana performed her sorcery with lotions and unguents.

Now Vida looked as if someone had sucked the very lifeblood from her. Her breasts had withered flat against her chest, her face was gaunt, cheekbones pushing through her translucent skin. In the hollows of her eye sockets, her cornflower eyes, once so merry with spirit, had receded in the plummy darkness. Never very big, she seemed to have shrunk to the size of a child.

The other girls had secretly given her scraps from their own meager portions. A bit of meat or a piece of coarse bread would travel from lap to lap under the table until it reached starving Vida, hidden from the eyes of Hedvika, who would have stung their faces with a slap, and, far worse, informed the Countess of their treachery.

One day, when Hedvika lingered with the Countess in her chambers, hunger forced Vida to leave the table. The other handmaidens spoke not a word as she rose and walked to the cold larder at the kitchen's portal. It was stocked with hanging fowl, smoked bacon, fresh eggs, cheeses, and wooden buckets of cream and churns of fresh butter. But most tantalizing of all was a large clay crock, filled with yellow goose fat, slick with translucent grease, creamier but more substantial than butter.

Her starving body shuddered with desire. Her thin hands flew toward the crock like birds to a perch.

"If you touch that, you will be severely punished," said a gravelly voice.

Vida whirled around to see Brona watching her, in her hand a soup ladle, steaming in the cold air of the room. A few rich drops fell from the ladle to the granite floor and Vida dropped to her knees, her fingers sweeping up the meaty broth and plunging knuckle-deep into her mouth.

"I am starving," Vida cried. Her shoulders began to shake and tears sprung to her sunken eyes.

"It is not my choice," said the cook. "Come away from my larder."

Brona extended her hand, scented with the smells of rich food, and pulled the starving girl to her feet. The cook's fingers immediately met bone, the flesh on the girl's arm emaciated. The old woman's heart skipped a beat.

Brona led Vida into the kitchen where the pungent smells of cooking made her knees buckle.

"Sit there, by the fire," she said. "It will warm your thin bones."

Vida slumped onto a three-legged stool by the hearth. Her face crumpled, tears stained her reddening cheeks.

"But why would the Countess starve me?" she cried. "I have served her faithfully."

The cook lifted a wooden spoon and beat it hard against the iron cauldron of soup.

"Your allegiance has nothing to do with this," said the stout woman, shaking her head so the greasy wattles on her neck quivered. She leaned close and lowered her voice. "It's your beauty that she hates. That is your curse." Her meaty breath was torture to the starving girl.

"My beauty?"

"She chose you for it and now she will destroy it. And if you die, that is no concern of hers."

"What can I do?"

Old Brona looked around and even up to the rafters, as if a spy might be perched above them.

"Flee, *Slecna* Vida. Leave Čachtice Castle and never look back," she whispered quickly.

Vida's eyes filled with tears.

"My mother is sick. The pennies I bring back keep her alive. There is no work for me in Čachtice, except as a prostitute."

"Better to starve or sell your body than face the anger of the Countess."

Hedvika strode in, demanding an extra rasher of bacon. She saw Vida and her face soured.

"What are you doing? Begging for food?"

"She has been given nothing," said the cook. "What concern is it of yours, Hedvika? You eat more than a force-fed goose."

"The Countess likes me plump," said Hedvika, glowering. "But this one—I know what the Countess has prescribed for her. She has no business here."

"This is my domain, harlot," growled Cook. She shook the spoon in Hedvika's face. "You think I do not know what goes on at night. Now get out!"

"Vida comes with me," snapped Hedvika.

The cook thrust out her lower lip like a ledge and pulled Vida to her so quickly the weak girl almost fell.

"Heed my words," the cook whispered.

"The Countess will hear of your treachery, Cook," said Hedvika.

The cook lost her scowl, a look of cold fear crawling over her face.

Hedvika's hand, slick with bacon grease, clutched Vida's bony arm, pulling her away from the kitchen. The girl almost fainted from the rich pork aroma. She would lick the grease off her sleeve as soon as she had a private moment.

Vida spent most nights on the cold stone floor of the castle outside the Countess's door, curled up like a dog on a mat woven of coarse wool. Bits of dried grass and burrs embedded in the yarn poked at her tender skin, and woke her to the muffled wail of cold drafts, winding their way through the dark corridors of the castle.

Often she would wake to see Darvulia holding a torch overhead, guiding the Countess down into the lower levels of the castle, toward the dungeon. "Sleep," the witch would command, her breath a ring of vapor. "This errand does not concern you."

Only in the broad daylight could Vida leave the castle, when the Countess did not require her services. She walked home, unsteady on her thin legs and worn leather shoes, to her mother's hovel in the village of Čachtice. Her few pennies bought soup bones and root vegetables and a few lumps of hard coal to keep a small fire burning for her sick mother, paying a neighbor child a portion of soup to stay with the ailing woman at night. And for all her bitter hunger, Vida knew she could not take even a drop of that soup for herself without endangering her mother's flickering life.

Then one night Vida was awakened by a murmuring in the Countess's chamber. Perhaps the Countess was dreaming. What would she dream of? Her many lovers, her dead husband? Her coffers of gold and her castles? Her palatial home in Vienna, near the great Cathedral of St. Stephan?

Then Vida saw the fine leather boots just in front of her head. A tall man stood above her, all in black, with a wide traveling cape around his shoulders.

How could such a man have climbed the stairs without waking her?

Without knocking, he opened the Countess's door, gliding through soundlessly.

Vida shivered. She recalled the village tales of a tall stranger, dressed in black, who frequented Čachtice Castle years ago, before Ferenc Nadasdy's death. It was said that the Countess had run away with the mysterious stranger for months. One day she returned to her husband. The servants sucked in their breath, waiting for the beatings, for Count Nadasdy was known for his wrath and cruel ways.

But the Countess had not been beaten or chastened in any way. Ferenc Nadasdy had taken her back and nothing was ever said. No bruise appeared on her face. The village people were shocked.

Was this the same stranger in black, come back to reclaim her?

Vida's stomach pinched up in a spasm. It felt as if her stomach was eating away at itself, folding over its emptiness, searching for nourishment.

She remembered the crock of goose fat and licked her lips.

Chapter 22

John's plane was delayed in Denver.

It had been snowing hard since just after midnight. The big wet flakes would make an excellent early snowpack on the ski slopes but obscured visibility and made it nearly impossible to land on Aspen's notoriously difficult runway, which was short and hemmed in by high mountains.

Waiting at the airport, Betsy looked out at the falling snow. Fat flakes swirled, playing tag in the wind. She wandered toward the small airport café to have a cup of coffee.

Why had she finally said yes to him? They had worked hard since their divorce to stay away from each other, to admit that it was a youthful folly, marrying while they were still undergraduates. Now he was an associate professor at MIT with research grants. Betsy had her own practice.

They had come so far.

Damn it! Betsy gritted her teeth, wondering what had possessed her.

The divorce had taken such a toll on her, she could barely stand to visit Boulder anymore. She couldn't walk across the campus without thinking of their college days, when they would lie beneath the towering oak trees on a blanket in the springtime, drunk on young love.

At weak moments, Betsy still remembered the touch of his fingertips as he traced the line of her jaw, the contours of her shoulders. She felt his warm breath lingering on her neck, intoxicating. He smelled of pine needles and warm, sunny hikes in the mountains.

They kissed tenderly as only the young can, staring candidly into each other's eyes. Athletic students in cut-offs threw Frisbees and bandana-collared dogs raced to catch them. In the distance rose the Flatiron crags, red rock against a bluebird Colorado sky. When they rolled and faced the other direction to shade their eyes from the bright sun, they looked at the sandstone façade of Norlin Library. Kids with backpacks full of books entered through the turnstile, turning their back on sunshine, Frisbees, and young love.

In towering letters Cicero's words were engraved over the library entrance. *Who knows only his own generation remains always a child.* Now those words haunted Betsy.

We were just children, she thought, waiting for John's plane to arrive. *And foolish ones at that.*

"May I help you?" said the café clerk.

"A cappuccino, two percent milk," she said.

The local paper, *The Aspen Times,* lay rumpled and open on the café table. The last person had scrawled a telephone number in the margin and her eyes focused on an item right below:

HARD ROCK, GOTHS, AND DIE-HARD PUNKS. GET IT ON TONIGHT AT THE BELLY UP. BLACK METAL BAND VENOM PLAYS A TRIBUTE TO BATHORY.

Bathory?

Her heart thumped and she stared at the ad.

"There you are!"

John set down his bag and scooped her up in his arms, his skin smelling of piney soap despite his long plane ride. He held Betsy for longer than was comfortable, and she was sure he could feel the sudden stiffening in her back.

He released her and stared at her face.

"You've lost some weight. I can feel your ribs."

Betsy shrugged and looked down at his old beat-up duffel bag. She knew it from their college days. "I always do when it starts turning cold."

"Hmmm," he said, holding her at arm's length in order to study her better. "Not usually until mid-January after you've had a few weeks of skiing under your belt."

Betsy looked away. She wanted to straighten the collar on her flannel shirt, but she knew that would indicate she had something to hide. During their marriage, she had taught him a lot about psychology. What she was studying, but also what her father had taught her over the years. She didn't want to give him clues to interpret.

"What was so engrossing in the local rag?" he said, jerking his chin at the paper. "You looked like you had just read your own death notice."

Betsy shrugged.

John looked down at the paper.

"Bathory?"

"A punk band. Goth, maybe. I don't know."

"Huh. I've heard of those guys—Bathory. Back in the eighties, I think. Come on, let's grab a bite to eat. I couldn't eat the crap they served in those snack packs."

Typical John, thought Betsy. It didn't rattle him that the name Bathory would appear in the newspaper, or that the paper was flipped to the exact page where the ad was.

Coincidence, he would say if she pressed him.

After their marriage broke up, he had earned a PhD in Advanced Mathematics and Statistics from MIT. He did not believe in meaningful coincidence, only numerical patterns. Coincidences were merely a matter of probability, little p in statistics. Wipe the slate clean and start a new problem, a coincidence wasn't worth examining. Not statistically important.

An outlier.

A wave of bitter memories swept over Betsy—the uber-rational mind of her ex-husband clashing with her intuitive Jungian training. She thought back to their last argument, the one that would end their marriage.

"My father! My father is in danger, I can sense it."

"Nonsense," he had said. *"You're nervous and tired, studying for your exams. There is nothing wrong with your father. Your mother would have called us if there were."*

"But John—"

"What's wrong with you? Get over yourself and your premonitions. You are completely irrational, Betsy. And self-indulgent! The world doesn't spin just because you dream it so."

"Me? What about you? Not everything is logical in life, John. There are outliers on a scatterplot, phenomena you can't predict. You never look beyond the world of reason and probability. I know something is wrong."

"You are hysterical," he said. *"You let your emotions rule you. How can you practice psychiatry when you think like this?"*

"Why won't you ever venture beyond the rational? Maybe you should do some self-exploration yourself."

"What total horseshit!"

And when they learned of Betsy's father's death, John turned away. He did not know how to console Betsy. It was the beginning of the end for them.

They drove down the valley and stopped at the Woody Creek Tavern for burgers and a beer. It was empty, except for a table of tourists and a crowd of local yahoos at the bar, their baseball hats on backward, watching football on TV.

"Not the same crowd," said John, looking around. The old photos tacked on the wall had faded now, a lot were gone. Someplace there were photos of the two of them nearly two decades ago—two college ski bums, raccoon-eyed from days on the slope, in full party mode.

"It's a weekday, people are working. But you're right, since it changed hands, the crowd isn't the same."

John tipped back his draft beer—Flying Dog Doggy Style, brewed locally. He didn't recognize anyone behind the bar, though Betsy could tell he was searching for a familiar face.

"Tell me what you have found out about your mom."

"Nothing. The embassy was useless. She was last in Bratislava on Sunday. She was going to one of the castles that Countess Bathory owned at the turn of the seventeenth century."

"Castles?"

"She had half a dozen of them. Mom mentioned Beckov and Čachtice. But Čachtice seems more likely."

"Why?"

"Because that is where the Countess did most of her killings."

"Are you still planning on going there?"

"Yes. I've been online looking for last-minute fares. They are astronomical."

"I'm going with you."

"What? No, you can't. You—"

"Thank you. Come back and see us again," interrupted the waitress, dropping their check on the table. "And have a good day!"

The two exchanged looks—their meals were still in front of them. John snorted a laugh. "Definitely not the same Woody Creek Tavern. Hunter Thompson probably would have shot her."

"John, really. How could you miss work?"

"I have vacation time. I've just submitted another grant and actually the timing is good."

Betsy bit a french fry in half, chewing in contemplation. She heard a roar from the crowd at the bar as the Broncos scored a touchdown.

John took the other half of the fry gently from his ex-wife's fingers and put it into his mouth. He chewed it, still looking at her.

"Let me help, Betsy."

She closed her eyes tight to keep from crying. She nodded, her body trembling with emotion.

"Come on," he said. "Let's get out of here."

When they got back to the office, Betsy could see movement inside.

Was the intruder back?

Betsy took a deep breath and opened the door quickly. Her heart beat hard against her chest.

Daisy sat on the floor of the office, with an enormous book spread in front of her. Betsy saw a colorful image filling the page.

"Oh, my God," said Betsy, her hand flying to her chest. "Daisy, what are you doing here? I cancelled our session."

Daisy looked up.

"I just wanted to see you again. Hey, you should lock your doors, Betsy. Especially after that burglar ransacked the place."

She shifted her eyes to John. "Who's the guy? Your boyfriend?"

Stop intruding on my private life, Betsy thought. *You are totally screwing up the patient-therapist relationship.*

"He—he's an old friend. John, this is Daisy Hart."

John approached, twisting his head to see the image on the floor.

"Is that a mandala?"

"Yeah, I guess. It's something Jung drew. He was discovering his soul," she pronounced ghoulishly.

Betsy suddenly realized exactly what Daisy had on her office floor. *The Red Book.*

"I saw it was inscribed to you from your mom, Betsy," said Daisy, as if reading her mind. "Your birthday was just a few weeks ago— that makes you a Scorpio. Me, too!"

Betsy swallowed hard. The tarot reader's voice rang in her ears.

Talk about nightmares!

Betsy shook her head, dismissing the thought.

"Why did you—what are you doing?"

John made a funny face at Betsy. *Are you all right?*

"I saw it on your shelf," said Daisy. "And I was like, 'Wow! What a coincidence.' My sister just sent me a copy a couple of days ago. Like synchronicity—"

"Your sister?" Betsy said.

"I told her how cool Jung is. She went to this show in the city, where these celebrities are analyzed on stage, looking at Jung's art."

"The Red Book Dialogues . . ." Betsy murmured.

John squatted next to Daisy and his finger traced the image of a jewel-colored mandala.

"Jung was quite an artist," he said. "I had no idea. It's like a medieval illuminated manuscript."

"Exactly!" said Daisy looking up into his eyes, beaming. "This is really the first time Morgan and I have ever had any common interest. And I mean *ever.*"

Betsy saw the white makeup buckle as her patient emphasized the last word.

"So Gothic looking," said John, staring down at the page. "It reminds me of the ancient *Book of Kells*—"

"Right? He should be crowned King of the Goth world," said Daisy. "Look—"

She turned the page gently.

Another illustration appeared, this one of a boat with a colossal golden orb and a man at the tiller. Below the boat was a giant fish or sea monster with bulldog teeth.

"Wow," whispered John. "Will you look at that!"

Betsy swallowed, watching her old lover—her ex-husband, the man who was mesmerized only by numbers and mathematical formulas—stroke his open palm over the image.

"What do you see?" Betsy said, kneeling down beside them.

"A huge gold gong and sea monster," began John.

"He's not a monster," said Daisy, offended. She twisted her crucifix cord around her fingers.

"What are you talking about? Look at those fangs," said John.

"It's an underbite—the opposite of fangs. The fish has a benevolent look in its eye. It's not attacking the boat—it's protecting the voyager."

"And what do you make of the shipwreck underneath?" asked John.

"What shipwreck?" Betsy said.

"Look, in the depths. There's a boat that hit the rocks and sank."

Betsy blinked. Until he said it, she had seen nothing. There it was. A sunken boat. And suddenly a thought shot through her mind as she looked at John and Daisy, their heads close together.

If we had a child when we were first married, she would be Daisy's age by now.

"Wow, John. You are right, the wreckage of a ship!" said Daisy, tracing the dark green swirls. She looked up at her analyst.

"Come on, Betsy. What do you see?"

Betsy hesitated. She thought of the visit Morgan had paid her. She thought of her mother lost in Slovakia.

And from the hundreds of books on the crowded shelves, Daisy had pulled down *The Red Book*, the birthday present her mother had sent just last month.

Fuck the patient-therapist relationship.

"I see eyes. Eyes in the sea, eyes in the sky. Watching," Betsy said.

Daisy nodded her head slowly.

"Yeah. I see them, too."

Chapter 23

Vida dreamed of eyes, glowing cats' eyes, watching from the darkness.

Everywhere she turned, the eyes followed, unblinking.

She woke with a start, a sudden cold draft curling under her throat. The door had been opened to the dungeon.

Vida buried her hands deep inside the woolen cloak she wore as a blanket. Her fingertips traced the outline of her ribs, skin stretched tight over bones.

She sensed an absence, a silence in the corridor. Sometimes the other girls, including the favorite Hedvika, left their servant chambers to accompany the Countess in what was referred to in whispers as "night games." Tonight must be one of those nights.

Her stomach groaned. She could stand it no longer.

Vida pulled herself slowly to her feet, taking care not to make a sound. Her soft leather shoes made little noise on the stone floor and even less on the thick Turkish carpets, looted from Ottoman war camps.

She descended the winding stairway, not daring to light a torch. In the dark, she might step on a skulking rat. But she was too hungry to care.

Before she reached the door of the larder, she could smell the pungent aromas of the treasures within. Brona set rat traps next to the clay-lidded bowls, ringed around the vessels like a standing infantry.

Vida pushed aside the beeswax-sealed pots of preserved fruits, the small kegs of honey. She stood on a wooden cask, her hands searching for the goose fat.

At last, behind a crate of bacon packed in coarse grains of salt, she saw it. Brown crockery beaded with cold grease. For a moment her head spun. She gasped for breath to keep from fainting.

One hand seized the small pot, the other sunk knuckle-deep into the yellow fat. She plunged her hand into her mouth, sucking and licking at her fingers.

Then she heard the buzz of flies and she turned her head.

A pale-skinned man stared at her. He was dressed all in black velvets and satins, appearing from nowhere. He held an ivory cane aloft and with a sudden sharp movement brought it down and smashed the crock in her hands into bits.

Her scream echoed through the stony corridors of Čachtice.

He looked at her hands, embedded with shards of crockery, speckled with blood.

He met her eyes and smiled, his teeth gleaming in the candlelight.

Chapter 24

You shouldn't be here," Betsy said. "It's getting late and your mother must be wondering where you are."

"It's not that late. And she doesn't care."

"You still have to go, Daisy," Betsy said.

Daisy closed the book and pulled herself to her feet. She made a couple of attempts to speak, but no words came. Only a hoarse rasping rattle. Her hand flew to her throat, her eyes widening like a frightened animal.

Betsy dropped her arms.

"It's all right, Daisy. Look at me," she said, her hands cupping the girl's shoulders. "Look at me! Stay calm. Follow your breath in and out of your nose, like you were tracing it with a bright light. See it move in, move out."

John pulled out a chair for the choking girl to sit. He put his hand on her arm, guiding her down into the seat.

Betsy took her hand, coaching. "Stay with it, Daisy. Pull in, breathe out. Think of nothing else. In . . . out. In . . . out."

The girl's mouth sucked at the air, desperate to breathe. Her eyes sought her psychologist's, looking to be rescued. Betsy had seen a child nearly drown in a swimming pool years ago, and when she plunged into the water to save the struggling girl, the eyes, wide in terror, had been identical to Daisy's.

Betsy moved her face closer to Daisy's, locking eyes.

John brought water in a paper cup, offering it to Daisy.

Betsy shook her head. "Not yet."

Betsy looked down at *The Red Book*, still open on the floor.

Five minutes later, Daisy was breathing freely, her chest moving rhythmically.

"It has passed, hasn't it?" said Betsy. "Do you feel better?"

Daisy nodded, still concentrating on her breath.

"We should get you home," said Betsy. "We'll drive you."

"NO!" gasped Daisy. "Not yet! No!"

"OK, OK." Betsy took the girl's hand again. "Not yet. Keep calm. Daisy, did you want to talk to me about something?"

"Yes. Yes."

"OK. When you feel up to it, we'll go into the—"

"Betsy, it's a bad time for you to stop seeing me. The dreams are super intense—"

"Intensity is good, Daisy. Write them down, everything. We'll discuss them when I get back—"

"You can't leave me now!" she screamed. "You just can't!"

Betsy sighed. She could feel the girl's hand sweating in her own, feel the panic in her ragged breath.

Of course, patients think everything is always about them because analysts convince them it is. All they experience, dream, or think is fodder for analysis.

Then Betsy allowed herself a selfish thought.

Now it's about me. Not about my patients. It's my mother, who disappeared in Slovakia. This is my nightmare.

Betsy had to disengage herself from her patient, but gently.

"I am going to be leaving town for a few weeks. But I'll be back, I promise—"

"A few weeks? Wait. You said two weeks. That was bad enough," she gasped.

"Daisy. It's a family emergency."

"What is it?"

"It's something I must take care of," Betsy said, gently. "I have no choice in the matter. I have to go."

"Maybe we should throw an I-Ching just in case. I have this awful feeling," Daisy said. "There is danger, I'm sure of it."

Chapter 25

The addled dwarf brought the coins. As he approached, the spittle on his open mouth glistened in the flickering torchlight. He breathed noisily, a grounded fish.

To Darvulia, the witch, he was exactly that: a fish. His eyes registered only movement, not sentiments. There was no compassion, joy, or sadness that touched him as he did the Countess's bidding. Yet that was no fault of his own. Unlike the dark hooded stranger who taught the Countess new "games" in the dungeon below, Fizko was born what he was, a fool.

The Countess chose three silver thalers.

"Ilona Joo—put these into the fire," she commanded. "Dorka and Hedvika, fetch the thief. She shall receive her punishment before she steals again."

Ilona Joo, wet nurse to the Countess's children—all grown and married now—did as she was bidden. The orange coals sputtered as the three coins eclipsed their glow.

Dorka brought the soot-faced skeleton of a girl toward the Countess. Vida had been locked in a dungeon in the depths of the castle. She had been given a few sticks of wood charcoal, more to drive away the rats than to provide heat. She had kept her pale face next to the heat, blistering her lips.

As she was escorted past the pressing crowd of servants, Zuzana grasped her hand, kissing her fingers. "May God bless you, Vida!"

Dorka yanked Vida away and shoved her hard, sending her sprawling on the ground at the Countess's feet.

"You have been accused of stealing," said Countess Bathory, eyeing the girl on the floor. "What do you say?"

"It is true. I tasted the goose fat—but I am starving, good mistress."

"I have given you food, shelter, and money to take to your mother, and you repay me with your thievery."

"I am dying of hunger!"

The Countess nodded to the nursemaid by the fire. "Bring me money, coins for our little thief."

Vida spun around to see Ilona Joo take the tongs from the hearth, pick the thalers out of the coals, and drop them on a metal tray.

Fizko pulled the girl to her feet.

"Give me your hand, thief," commanded the Countess.

Vida's eyes flew open in horror. "No, Countess! No!"

Darvulia stepped forward to wrestle the girl's hand open, calling to the idiot Fizko to help restrain her. Ilona Joo approached with the tray.

"You are lucky she does not burn your mouth," whispered Darvulia in the girl's ear. "Take your punishment well or she may invent another."

One by one, Ilona Joo lifted the coins with the tongs and pressed them into Vida's right hand.

The girl howled and then fainted with pain. The coins clattered to the floor and Ilona Joo picked them up, smoking, from the stones. The room smelled of seared flesh.

The dwarf idiot licked his lips, thinking it was venison on Brona's spit that brought the aroma to the air.

Chapter 26

The stallion reared when the cinch was tightened. The stable boy jumped away and fell backward into the straw. The horse pulled hard at the rope, black hooves slashing.

The boy scrambled away from the murderous forelegs, hands and knees in the scattered straw.

"I will handle him," said Janos.

The white stallion snorted, his nostrils flaring red-pink. He roared, an outraged neigh, a murderous high note that made the stable boys tremble.

"Easy, boy, easy," Janos began.

Again the screaming neigh, ringing through the air. The other horses jumped back, tugging at the common line tying them the length of the stable.

Aloyz brought a leather bridle, a heavy iron bit suspended from the two thick leather cheek pieces.

Janos touched his fingers to the cold, curved metal of the bit.

"No," he said. "Bring me a bitless bridle. I will ride him with just the reins so he feels my hands instead of the taste of metal."

Aloyz ducked his head and ran back to the locked tack chest—a precaution against the gnawing rats—to find a hackamore.

By the time Aloyz had returned to the stall, Janos had managed to calm the horse enough to rest his hand on the thick muscle of his upper leg and chest.

It would be another two hours of patience and coaxing before the horsemaster could slip the hackamore over the stallion's ears and nose.

Vida stumbled, reeling in pain, from the Countess's chamber. Her servant friends dared not help, though they interlaced their fingers in prayer, so tight their knuckles shone white in the dim light of the corridors.

"God bless you, Vida," one whispered as the girl rushed forward, her charred hands stretched open to the cold air like a blind woman.

"Run to the well and soak your wounds," screamed Zuzana, watching her only friend's torture. "Plunge them into the snow until the fire is quenched!"

"Silence!" hissed Darvulia, following Vida down the hall. "She should suffer in full, the dirty thief! If you console her, may you suffer the same, *Slecna* Zuzana."

Darvulia made certain that Vida did not stop at the well.

"You have been shown mercy," she said, shoving the girl through the gate of the castle. "The Countess's punishment could have been far worse."

Vida's mouth twisted in a howl as she ran from the shrouded darkness of Čachtice Castle into the light of day. She knew Darvulia was right. Muffled cries of tortured pain had reached her ears many nights as she lay curled on the rough mat outside the Countess's door.

The stallion reared, despite the calming words and gentle hands of Janos Szilvasi. The young horsemaster's legs were strong and his balance keen, but still he strung his fingers through the long mane of his mount to keep his seat.

"Open the gates," he shouted, the leather reins chafing his hands.

The stable boys ran across the courtyard, breathlessly reaching the guards.

"Unbolt the main gate, let down the drawbridge!" cried Aloyz. "Master Szilvasi takes out the stallion!"

The guards waited for the confirmation from Erno Kovach, who nodded. "Open!"

The horse reared back on its haunches as the gates opened, revealing the steep hill and winding road down toward the village.

"Stand away," shouted Janos, "I cannot hold him back!"

The rider knotted one hand into the horse's mane and drove his heels into the steed's belly. If he was going to bolt, it was better the horse sensed the rider's will driving him.

The slick paving stones leading to the castle gate made the horse slip, but he was sure-footed and quickly gained his balance. As rider and stallion emerged into the cold wind blowing from the peaks of the Little Carpathians, the village of Čachtice came into view, a toy miniature of thatched-roof houses below them. The road was wet and thick spatters of mud from the horse's churning hooves soon covered the boots of his rider. Janos narrowed his eyes, stinging with tears, against the biting mountain wind.

The stallion pinned back his ears, racing down into the barren fields below, where Janos knew the flat plain would allow him to gallop the horse in ever-decreasing circles.

At first the stallion ignored the rider's signals—the hackamore was not strong enough to restrain the beast. His legs wrapped around the barrel of the horse like tight bands, Janos rode without exerting his will, his body accepting the surging wave of motion under him.

The mud sucked at the horse's hoofs, and the hard gallop brought a lather of briny foam that worked down the stallion's flanks and legs.

Janos felt the horse's lungs heaving, the labored rhythm of breath in time to the three-count beat of the gallop.

As the horse slowed, if only a little, Janos put subtle pressure on the reins, a suggestion rather than a command. The stallion turned his head as Janos guided the rein, slowly working the horse into a wide circle, still at a gallop.

An hour later, Janos had slowed the stallion to a walk. He patted the horse's slick wet neck, grainy with salt. A smile came to his lips as he sniffed in the good scent of cold air and hot horse.

Then the smile vanished.

Stumbling down the castle road was a small figure, hands outstretched. A blind child?

The wind delivered her howling cries. A girl. No, a young woman, her face twisted in anguish.

Janos urged the horse closer with his legs.

"Who goes there? Maiden, what is your trouble?"

Vida thrust her hands out to the drizzling sleet. Janos saw the blistered hands, charred black and oozing.

"My God!" he cried. He dismounted the exhausted horse and held the girl's wrists. "How?"

"The Countess," sobbed the girl. "I stole a taste of goose fat."

Janos looked at the thin whisper of a girl, her oozing wounds. His eyes scanned the horizon where the towering castle loomed, blocking the weak sunlight. The horse whinnied shrilly, the high-pitched cry filling the air.

"We must get you help," Janos said. "I will take you home. Are you from Čachtice?"

"Yes," whimpered the girl. "A woman in the village makes healing balms."

Janos mounted and steadied the horse. He grabbed the girl by her bony forearm, swinging her light body in front of him on the saddle. The horse broke into a trot down the road, carrying the two riders toward the village of Čachtice.

Janos rode through the muddy streets of Čachtice. The sewers ran along the sides of the road, clogged with stinking waste. A woman flung open her shutter and emptied her clay chamber pot.

Janos raised his eyes at the sound.

"Agh!" he shouted, the filth just missing him, Vida, and the stallion.

The woman drew back into the house, slamming her shutters in consternation.

Vida was barely conscious, but she directed him in whispers and moans to a simple hovel with gray straw thatch and bundles of herbs and roots dangling on pegs in the cold winter air.

"Cunning woman," she gasped. "Care for me."

Janos helped her to the ground. She sagged against him.

Several of the townspeople gathered around, their mouths open in astonishment.

"Help her!" said Janos. "Take her to the witch!'

"I am not flattered to be called a witch," said a voice, aged and stern. "I am a cunning woman, a healer."

The woman inspected Vida's injured hands, nodding her head grimly.

"The Countess?"

The girl nodded her head.

"Take her inside. I will see what I can do."

Two men carried the girl over the threshold, disappearing into the cottage.

"And thank you, stranger," said the cunning woman.

"Janos Szilvasi. Horsemaster at Bathory Castle."

"May God defend you then. And do not mention you have given succor to this poor girl or you will suffer the worse. The Countess does not tolerate interference in her affairs."

Then the old woman disappeared into the darkness of her hovel, shutting the door on the stranger from Čachtice Castle.

Chapter 27

ČACHTICE LUTHERAN CHURCH
DECEMBER 19, 1610

The Lutheran minister Jakub Ponikenusz laid his Bible on the rough-hewn table by the hearth. He took care to put it far from the inkwell, for when he wrote his sermons he often took on a feverish intensity and his arms flailed, as if he were fighting the demons he had denounced.

His letters to the King had not been acknowledged until last Sunday, when an elegant man, dressed in silk and a finely tailored wool coat, had entered the Protestant church in Čachtice, standing at the back of the congregation.

The pews were packed full, as usual, and there was nowhere to sit in the little stone church. Still, seeing the finely dressed stranger standing by the baptismal font, Pastor Ponikenusz suspected he had not come to worship.

From the pulpit, the minister thundered, "The Countess feeds on our innocence, devouring our children, sisters, and even young mothers. How long will we wait in numbed silence as this witch snatches our loved daughters, tortures them, and ushers them to an early, unmarked grave?"

"You, sir, slander the name of Bathory!" answered the voice of the stranger at the back of the church.

All heads, young and old, twisted to see the nobleman.

"I speak the truth!" said Pastor Ponikenusz, his voice resonating. "And in the House of the Lord, the truth will be spoken in the name of Jesus Christ, Prince of Peace and Mercy!"

The wooden pulpit shook. Ponikenusz felt the power of a righteous God guiding his words.

The nobleman scowled. The thick-skinned peasants stared at the stone floor of the church rather than look so powerful a lord in the eye.

"I will speak to you after the service," he growled, pinching his aquiline nose against the smell of wet wool, boiled cabbage, and sour beer in the cramped church. "He is a Bathory for sure," hissed the cooper. "He will string up our good parson for blasphemy."

"I know the man," said a midwife, whistling through the gap in her remaining teeth. "He is the Count Thurzo, the Countess's cousin."

"The Palatine? Surely he has come to execute our pastor."

But the minister stood even straighter, his chin lifting with conviction.

"God respects the word of truth, and protects those of faith!"

Count Thurzo waited by his carriage. His face wrinkled in disgust as he watched the peasant congregation pour out of the church door.

When the minister had finished bidding each worshipper a good afternoon, he walked over to the Count, looking sternly at the nobleman. "How dare you interrupt my sermon, sir!"

Count Thurzo's mouth dropped open in amazement. "Your sermon? You fool! Your words could end your miserable life."

"I speak the truth, with God as my witness."

"You have chosen a powerful adversary," said the Count, flicking his eyes to a cluster of ragged peasants who stood watching from the careful distance, and back again to the minister's face. "Does that not occur to you?"

"I guide my flock and confront evil wherever it may be. I have no fear of men's politics or gold. Do you come here to imprison me?"

"No, though if your allegations prove wrong, that will be the case. I will see to it personally."

"I am not afraid of the dungeons," said the minister. "God knows the truth and so shall the King."

Count Thurzo straightened his posture and pressed his lips tightly together. "I come as an emissary of our King Matthias. He has sent me to hear your complaint against the Countess."

The minister paused for a moment. "I believe you are her cousin. Does this not present a conflict for you?"

The Count's gloved hand clenched. *You wretched little churchworm*, he thought. *How dare you!*

"We are related through marriage, on my wife's side. I serve my Habsburg king faithfully."

"Despite the Bathory name?"

The Count drew a quick breath, his face souring. *What impudence!* "Speak, sir. What evidence do you have against the Countess?"

The minister looked around the churchyard. Knots of his congregation stood nearby, their necks swiveling toward the Count and their minister.

"Perhaps you would like to take a walk in our cemetery, Count Thurzo," suggested the minister. "We can talk with more privacy among the dead."

Chapter 28

Grace studied the anemic jailers—with wild colored hair—who attended her day and night. Their heads drooped from their scrawny necks. They stared at her with feral eyes.

For days she pleaded for help. They remained silent, unblinking. Inhuman.

Their wolfish looks wore on her nerves. She turned on them finally, in a rage, tendons standing out on her thin neck.

"What is wrong with you? Have you no manners? Stop staring at me!"

The women exchanged looks and dropped their eyes to the carpet.

"Really. Pasty white faces and neon-colored hair hanging in your eyes. Go out in the fresh air, get some color into your cheeks. Eat some goose and dumplings. Drink a beer, for God's sake."

A shadow crept over their faces as the women exchanged looks. They did not meet their captive's eyes.

Grace pursed her lips and settled back in her chair. She was accustomed to young men and women of precisely this age in her lectures at the university. Her lectures were filled with serious historical detail of the Holy Roman Empire, but she was not above scolding a student for slovenly appearance or a disrespectful attitude.

"Surely you have something better to do than to skulk around here like a bunch of vampires," she snapped.

Their eyes flew open and the women breathed noisily, almost grunting.

"Oh, sweet Jesus," Grace said. "Is that the Count's game? *Really?* Vampires?" She gave a bitter laugh.

The girls' thin hands raked their wild hair—all but the youngest of the trio, a girl with blue hair, no more than fourteen, whose eyes had looked as if she could see the savory goose and steaming dumplings on a plate in front of her. She looked on in terror.

Grace played a hunch. "So the crazy Count has convinced you that you are vampires. He's starving you to death, isn't he? Well, you truly are a pack of fools."

The two women growled and hissed.

"What? Vampires?" she said, teasing them with the word. "You can't believe that, can you? That you are creatures of the night? Really! Do you feast on human blood? Really, I—"

The women snapped at each other, like a pair of frenzied pit bulls. The fuchsia-haired woman growled, catching the emerald-haired woman by the wrist.

She drew her lips back, exposing her ugly, yellowed teeth. As her mouth darted down to fasten on the skin of her prey, her eyes rolled back in ecstasy.

A howling scream pierced the air as her bite drew blood.

Grace recoiled in her chair, horrified, as the attacker sucked at the bloody wound and her victim growled.

"You are all mad!" she whispered.

She locked eyes with the blue-haired girl, who looked as terrified as Grace and who ran down the corridor screaming for the Count.

The Count bounded in with an energy that belied his apparent age. His lips were red and moist.

"Get back, Ona!" he commanded the fuchsia-haired demon. He struck her hard across the cheek, sending her reeling, her face streaked with the blood of her victim.

The green-haired girl cowered in the corner, licking the wound on her arm like a dog.

"What kind of lunatic asylum is this?" screamed Grace, still tied to the chair. "Don't you dare leave me alone with these psychopaths again!"

The Count gathered his composure, still heaving with exertion.

"How dare you disobey me?" he said to the groveling girl, her mouth stained red with blood.

"But, Master—she knows the secret!"

The Count's eyes widened, a graying brow arching. "What?"

"She called us—our name."

The Count whirled around. He stared at his prisoner.

"What did you say to them?"

Grace swallowed hard. She closed her eyes and when they reopened, ferocity glimmered there.

"I told them they needed to go eat a decent meal. They are crazy with hunger, can't you see that?"

"I will decide when it is time for a feeding."

"A *feeding?*"

"What did you say to them?"

"That they should eat, take in the sun. Young people shouldn't look like they do. They are patently unhealthy."

The Count laughed and cut it off with a snarl. His lips twisted cruelly. "What concern is that of yours, Dr. Path?"

"Don't you dare leave them with me. If the girl hadn't run to find you, they both could have turned on me."

The Count's face twitched with fury.

"OUT!" he roared at the young women. "Do not enter this room again." He pointed a long, shaking finger at the fuchsia-haired woman. "And Ona, I shall deal with you later."

The women flattened their thin backs to the wall, feeling their way toward the door without taking their eyes off the Count.

The Count's long fingers dipped into a vest pocket. He pulled out a knife and unfolded a thin blade.

Grace straightened in the chair. "You can torture me all you want, you psychopath, but I am not telling you anything about my daughter."

The Count smiled slowly. He waved the gleaming blade near her eyes, and traced a line down her neck with its point. He let the knife trail lower, across her shoulder, down her arm—when he reached her wrists, he made a violent thrust.

Grace closed her eyes tight, wincing.

Then she felt the blood return to her wrists and the sensation of cool air on her skin. He had cut her ropes.

"I will try to offer you the courtesy due a professor of Eastern European history. Come, peruse my library. You may find something worth reading."

The Count walked to his desk, tucked away in a far corner of the room. He pressed an intercom by the computer.

"Send in Almos," he said into the intercom. "I am going to try to find a way to keep you occupied, Dr. Path."

A boy, perhaps eighteen, came in. He bobbed a greeting and adjusted his glasses on his nose. Almos was clearly the Slovakian version of a teenage techie nerd.

"*Dobre den,*" he said, his voice courteous.

"Forgive him, he doesn't speak a word of English," said the Count. "I find that useful." He smiled and went on, "Before you were exposed to such a despicable display by my servant girls, I was planning to give you a surprise."

He nodded to Almos, who flicked on the computer. It hummed to life, blinking blue shadows across the boy's face.

"Naturally you will not be able to use the internet—Almos is disabling it now—but you will see that I have downloaded many educational programs. History, psychology, physics. Courses and lectures I have selected from various institutions. I thought they might keep you engaged while you are here with us."

"Thank you," Grace whispered, still shaking. *How do you feign gratitude to a madman?*

"And please, help yourself to the books in my library here. You may find some interesting reading while we wait."

"Wait for what?" she asked.

The Count didn't answer, staring straight ahead.

Chapter 29

The rattling of the wagon drew the gravedigger's attention.

"Here comes another," he called down to the man below, who heaved another shovel of earth up to the surface.

"*Ne*, Havel! Cannot be," the man in the open grave shouted back. "We have not finished this one."

The gravedigger above shook his shaggy head, scratching his neck. "'Tis truth," he insisted. "They've come to dump another."

He set down his shovel and wiped the dirty sweat from his face. Despite the cold air, his body was warm from the hard work of digging in the freezing ground.

Ales scowled up from below. "Does the carriage bear the emblem of the Countess?"

The first gravedigger squinted. "The damned teeth of the wolf." He spat viciously, his spittle soaking into the freshly turned soil.

Havel watched as the driver stopped and waited for the footman to fetch the pastor.

"Will you look at that?" he said, leaning against his shovel, watching, open-mouthed. Pastor Jakub Ponikenusz strode from the church, followed by another man, clearly a noble. The pastor stopped, arms folded, legs set wide, immoveable, and shook his head vehemently as the footman gestured toward the spiked iron gate of the cemetery. Standing beside him the gentleman listened, staring at the wagon's load.

"The pastor is not letting them in!" said the gravedigger, throwing down his shovel. "He stands against the Countess!"

"You take me for a fool," said the man in the hole. "Help me out!"

Havel reached down into the newly dug grave and hauled up his muddy-faced partner. "Look for yourself!" he said.

The driver had descended now and together with the footman gestured insistently at their covered load. The two gravediggers edged closer, so they could hear.

"No more of her evil shall find its way into sanctified land of the Church!" the pastor declared.

The driver protested. "But the girls are innocent! Surely they should have the blessings and comfort of the Church! They were baptized in the Church by Reverend Berthoni himself, God bless his soul."

"Yes, and it was Andras Berthoni who warned me of the Countess before his death! His letters are filled with damning evidence against that monster."

The driver and footman hung their heads.

"Come, Lord Thurzo," said the pastor. "See what innocent souls our Countess sends us day after day!"

The nobleman approached the wagon, his gait stiff and reluctant. Ponikenusz threw back the coarse blanket with a violent tug.

"Behold!" he said.

Thurzo gasped and raised a gloved hand to his face as he looked into the wagon.

A young woman lay on the bare boards of the wagon. Her face was contorted in agony, dark blood stains soiling her dress. There were small puncture wounds on her neck.

"What is this?" murmured Count Thurzo. The dried leaves crunched under his boot heel as he turned away from the sight.

"The Countess reports a rabid dog attacked her," said the driver. He, too, glanced away from the girl, his right hand making the sign of the cross.

Thurzo looked again at the girl's body. Then he stared at the pastor, saying nothing.

"I will bless those unfortunate girls, with all power instilled in me by the Church," Ponikenusz said, his voice softening. "Wherever their bodies are buried, God has already taken their innocent souls to his bosom."

The gravediggers looked at each other in disbelief.

"In the name of the Father, the Son, and the Holy Ghost," the pastor began, bowing his head.

The gravediggers pulled off their sweat-stained caps, loose dirt tumbling to the ground.

"So you see the graves—thirty-two in all. Graves of girls who had 'accidents' at the castle," said the pastor, his tone acid. "When the ground freezes too hard in the winter months, we stack the bodies in a root cellar to bury in the spring."

He led Count Thurzo through the graveyard to a row of fresh mounds of dirt.

"This one. Albina Holub. Born here in Čachtice. A knife slipped and cut her wrist when she was slicing vegetables. Cut it so badly that she bled to death. Clumsy girl, it seems. Serves her right, they said, for mishandling the Countess's fine cutlery."

Thurzo tightened his lips, pale as slivers of cheese.

"And this one, Barbora Mokry. It seems she slipped and knocked her head against the well, only a week after Albina had her mishap with the knife. An unfortunate coincidence. Gashed her head so badly that she bled to death. Nothing, it seems, could be done."

"And over here is the first maiden who brought me fresh bread and butter when I arrived at the parish. She called me Sir, and bowed as if I were a king. She was devoted to the scriptures, and would sit in rapt attention in Mass. Of course the poor girl could not read, but God's holy word resonated in her soul."

"What happened to her?" asked Thurzo.

"It seems that she attended to the Countess's bath when her regular attendant was ill with a fever. The water was too cool, sending the Countess into a rage. The Countess screamed at the girl, and beat her about the head and shoulders until she bled."

"And then what?"

"We do not know. There was a cut on her neck where the Countess scratched her in fury. And a savage bite, ripping the flesh from her breast. She—" the pastor's voice cracked. He clenched his eyes shut, his face pinched with emotion.

Then he looked into the Count's eyes. "The Countess simply wrote she bled to death."

Chapter 30

Winter seized Vienna on the eve of the solstice. Hard frosts choked the earth. Brittle leaves clung to branches coated in ice.

King Matthias II, ruler of Hungary, Austria, and Moravia complained first of the unseasonable cold and then the oppressive heat from the colossal ceramic furnace of the Hofburg Palace.

His peevish humor was aggravated by thwarted ambition. The summer had seen his army's bloody advance on Prague. The Brother's War, it was called, as Matthias's forces marched toward the Hrad, to wrest power from his brother Emperor Rudolf II.

Matthias had won control of the lower kingdoms, leaving Rudolf with little more than Bohemia, a scrap of his former empire, a flimsy mantle of dignity to wrap around the once all-powerful ruler of the Holy Roman Empire.

Then Matthias had felt the surge of power, like young blood flowing in his veins. Now as he cast an eye beyond the frosted glass windows, the dead, frozen gardens and winter silence gnawed at his heart.

The tributes to the new king were not sufficient to finance his struggle against the Ottomans, who waged ever-encroaching war on the Hungarian and Austrian fronts. If they took Vienna, all of Christendom could fall to the infidels.

For years, Matthias had served as commander-in-chief of the Royal Habsburg Troops, serving his brother and his kingdom. Rudolf II had squandered the riches of the empire on alchemy, astrology, art, and costly curiosities, while the troops had survived with meager wages and scant rations. The soldiers looted whenever possible in victories against the Turks, but those victories were too few as the Habsburg armies saw their lands conquered by the enemy. The fall of Estergom, ancient seat of Hungary, still haunted Matthias. The old Hungarian capital had been lost under his watch, for he had not the troops to match the Ottomans.

Now, he held another petition from the Countess Bathory. She demanded repayment of a debt—a debt he could not begin to pay—that had financed years of war against the Infidels.

Matthias flung the letter to ground. A bowing servant scuttled by, plucking the velum missive from the carpeted floor. "As if I even possessed the gold to repay the Bathory bitch. She owns more land than I!"

"Yes," said his trusted confessor Melchior Klesl, nodding. "And more castles."

King Matthias scowled, looking out the window at his frozen kingdom. "Send in Count Thurzo."

Melchior Klesl motioned to the sentries to admit the visitor.

Count Thurzo—who had been waiting for hours for an audience with the King—bowed deeply to Matthias.

"What news do you bring?"

Thurzo cast a glance around the room. "Might I ask for a private audience with Your Majesty?"

Matthias glanced to his confessor, who raised an eyebrow and nodded slowly.

The King waved a hand. All but Melchior Klesl left the room, silently closing the door.

"Speak, Count."

"The Countess Bathory is a murderess, my Lord. I have proof."

The King narrowed his eyes. "The accounts of the parish priest are true?"

"True and more. The church cemetery is filled with the bodies of young women, all of whom have served the Countess. Their bodies were mangled and devoid of blood. I have seen them with my own eyes. They say the Countess bathes in their blood to preserve her youth."

"What tidings are these? Is she a witch, Thurzo? I will have her burned!"

"Forgive me, my Lord. If she is a witch and burned at the stake, the Church will receive her lands," said Thurzo, daring to raise his head and look steadily into the King's eyes.

"He is right, Your Majesty," said Klesl. "Heresy and witchcraft are the Church's domain. It will seize all possessions."

"I cannot let such a woman terrorize my kingdom! Have we not seen enough mayhem and death by the heathen Turks?" said Matthias. "We will bring the Countess to trial. Have you any witnesses?"

"With good time I believe I can procure all the witnesses we need. The pastor is willing to testify."

"But punishment of her servants, even to the death—all this is within the limits of the law," said Klesl. "We could not bring a noblewoman of Bathory's standing to trial for abusing her own peasants. She has broken no law."

"There is one servant girl who escaped from the Countess with her life," said Thurzo. "She may be persuaded to testify. And she has information that is damning, even to a woman as powerful as Erzsebet Bathory."

The bishop raised an eyebrow. "Who is this girl?"

"I met her in the village, a maiden whose hands were scorched for stealing food. The local healer brought her to me as Palatine. The girl exposed her wounded hands to me. They both begged me to stop the torture in Čachtice Castle. The healer said that there are no local girls who will work again in the castle, that the Countess is a monster."

"Again, we cannot prosecute a noblewoman for what she does to her own servants," said Bishop Klesl.

"Yes," said the Count, "but this particular maiden was privy to conversations between the Countess and a witch named Darvulia. The Countess insisted the blood of peasants was not pure enough, that she was aging once more. She wanted to attract young maidens of impoverished nobility to lodge in Čachtice Castle, with the lure of teaching them the manners of upper nobility."

The Count took a step closer to the King and lowered his voice. "If she dares to harm them in any way, Your Majesty could take action against her."

The King moved to the edge of his chair in rapt attention. He sought the bishop's eye.

Melchior Klesl nodded. "Yes. Such a crime could be prosecuted under law. If Bathory were convicted, all her property would be confiscated and revert to the Crown. And of course just rewards to the Palatine who brings proof of her crimes."

Count Thurzo bent low to the King, obscuring his smile at Melchior's words.

Chapter 31

The azure-haired girl poured Grace a cup of Earl Grey tea from a teapot of museum-quality porcelain. The historian's eye studied the inverted trumpet-flower spout, the precision of the Isnik Turkish blue flowers on white background.

Soft-paste. Medici porcelain. White clay from Vincenza mixed with glass, copied from the Chinese porcelains, design borrowed from the Turkish invaders. The end of the sixteenth century.

Priceless.

This could be from Rudolf II's collection at the Kunstkammer. At the very least it belonged to a house of highest nobility.

Grace closed her eyes and forced herself to breathe deeply. She was kidnapped, subjected to blood-drinking madwomen, and then served tea from an art treasure. Who was this count, this madman who held her captive?

At least the blue-haired girl was the only person who now came close to her. The psychotic vampire women had been banished since their meltdown.

"Sugar?" the girl asked, her Slovak accent soft and lilting.

"No, just milk, please."

How bizarre, thought Grace, *that I should be shown such manners in the household of my captor, my husband's murderer. Sugar indeed!*

"Tell me your name," said Grace, accepting the cup.

The girl glanced at the locked door.

"Draska."

"Draska?" said Grace, remembering. A sob rose in her throat, but she checked it. It was the name her husband had called her in moments of tenderness.

"It means 'loved one' in Slovakian," said the girl.

Grace fluttered her eyelids, blinking back tears.

"Yes, Draska," said Grace, composing herself again. "How could you ever wind up serving the Count?"

"Excuse me. My English no good. Repeat please."

"Why do you work for the Count?"

"My mother, she cook. She and grandmother cook for he family, family Bathory, many years."

"*His* family, *his* is the possessive pronoun. Not *he* family."

Draska smiled brightly, thought better of it, and looked at the carpeted floor.

"You know I am a prisoner?" said Grace, stirring her tea.

Draska hesitated.

"Yes, you guest. Count needs you."

Grace flung the silver spoon on the carpet.

"Damn it! I am not a guest! I was kidnapped."

The girl's eyes flashed open, startled. She bent down to pick up the teaspoon.

"No understand."

Grace fought for control. Screaming would be too easy and too wrong.

"Why does the Count need me? Why does he want my daughter?"

"I no know."

"I *don't* know."

Draska smiled at the correction. "Yes, I don't know. Good teacher. You teach me English."

"My daughter will be worried about me. Just like your mother would be worried about you."

Draska ducked her head. "Yes," she mumbled.

Grace saw the girl's pity. She seized upon it. "Maybe if I could get word to my daughter somehow."

"Send e-mail."

Grace stared at the girl.

"I can't e-mail. There is no internet on that computer."

"Oh."

Grace drank her tea, wondering what the girl knew and didn't know. "Do you have e-mail?"

Draska smiled. "I have e-mail. I have text message. I have cell phone. I Twitter."

"You could e-mail my daughter and tell her I am alive and well. You don't have to tell her your name."

Draska shifted her weight on her feet and shook her head vehemently. "Count not like. Count knows everything."

Of course, thought Grace. *He is probably monitoring Betsy's e-mail somehow. Maybe the techie nerd has tapped into her account.* Bathory then would read any communication that aroused suspicion, especially one sent from Slovakia.

"What if you were to send an e-mail to another friend, in another country?" Grace whispered, looking around the room for a hidden camera. "Do you have friends in other countries?"

Draska hesitated. "Here, good lady," she said. "Help me correct my English on the computer."

"Correct your English?" said Grace.

"See my homework in English. I have grammar questions. You correct, yes?"

Draska sat down at the computer, leaning her body close to the monitor. She opened a Word document and typed in:

My cousin live in London.

Grace began to smile, and then checked her emotion. She said, "The first person singular of 'live' is 'lives.' You must remember to add the 's'. Let me give you a few examples."

She, too, moved close to the monitor, her back obscuring any hidden camera that might be focused on them. She set down her cup of tea.

GOOD. YOUR COUSIN SENDS A MESSAGE TO MY DAUGHTER. IT DOESN'T MENTION YOU OR ME. ABSOLUTELY NOTHING. BUT SHE WILL KNOW IT IS FROM ME.

"Now see. I have written three sentences with errors. Can you re-write them correctly?" said Grace, pointing at the screen.
Draska nodded, taking her place at the computer.

COUNT KNOW EVERYTHING. VERY DANGEROUS.

"Good, but not good enough. Look, you made a mistake here. I'll correct it and we'll try some negative third-person singular. Those are harder."

WRITE TO YOUR COUSIN. USE A FRIEND'S COMPUTER AND AT THE END, INCLUDE MY MESSAGE. TELL HER TO CUT AND PASTE AND SEND IT ON TO MY DAUGHTER. IT COMES FROM .UK INSTEAD OF .SK. I WILL GIVE YOU TWO LETTERS. TELL YOUR COUSIN TO SEND THEM A FEW DAYS APART SO THERE IS NO SUSPICION.

"OK. Put the sentences in negative, third person singular." Grace shifted position, always careful to block the computer screen.

MUST THINK. COUNT KNOWS EVERYTHING!

Draska closed the document, no changes saved.
"Thank you for lesson. Good teacher. Finish tea?"
Grace looked at the interior of her empty cup. Ancient white porcelain. Kings, queens, or other nobility had pressed their lips to the

same gold rim. She stared into the young woman's eyes, searching for some sign of agreement, some reassurance.

"I bring you dinner at six o'clock, Madam. Thank you for English lesson."

Draska gathered up the teacup, saucer, and ornate silver spoon, placing them on a tray. Grace listened to the bright clink of the porcelain as it rattled away toward the door. She couldn't help but wince, thinking of such an objet d'art being treated as common crockery.

She heard the click of the lock as Draska left. Then the hollow click of heels down the hall.

Chapter 32

John made the plane reservations online to leave the next morning. He alerted the American Embassy he and Betsy were arriving and rented a car in Bratislava.

All the traits that had contributed to their divorce—his concrete, black-and-white approach to resolving conflicts, breaking down a situation to a mathematical problem—now comforted Betsy. When they were married, she had accused him of handling their relationship with cold calculation, never allowing things to flow naturally, no room for spontaneity or a last-minute hunch.

"Come on, Betsy! I always leave a margin of error," he said one night, defending himself in the middle of an argument.

Margin of error. For John instinct, intuition—the element of humanity and surprise—boiled down to nothing but a margin for error. Betsy had wanted to smother him with a pillow.

Now, as she watched him print out their boarding passes, hotel reservation, and train schedules and then put their passports and her mother's e-mails into a travel folder, she sighed with relief.

"Relax a little, Betsy," he said, gentleness in his smile. "Get some sleep."

"I will," she said, gratitude washing over her. "Do you need anything in the guest bathroom?"

"I'm all set, Bets. Everything's fine."

"OK," she said. She looked up at him and managed a smile. "And, John—thank you."

"No problem."

She brushed her teeth, her mind reviewing last minute details for the early departure. Toothbrush still in her mouth, she walked out into the den and checked her e-mail one more time.

"Always multi-tasking, Dr. Path," John said, yawning. "Some things never change."

But Betsy didn't hear him. She stood frozen, staring at the e-mail she had just opened.

DEAR DR. PATH,

THE REVIEW BOARD OF *PSYCHOLOGY TODAY* IS INTERESTED IN YOUR PROPOSED ARTICLE ON THE USE OF CARL JUNG'S *THE RED BOOK* AS A METHOD OF TREATMENT WITH BORDERLINE SCHIZOPHRENICS. WE FIND THE WORK YOU HAVE DONE IN JUNGIAN ANALYSIS QUITE PROVOCATIVE. (WE CITE SPECIFI-CALLY THE INTERPRETATION OF THE JEWELED MANDALA. TRUE, PER YOUR SUGGESTION, THE SECOND MANDALA OF HARD, FLINTY STONE—THE MORE GOTHIC REPRESENTATION— WOULD SEEM TO BE MORE SUITABLE AS A STIMULUS PRESENTED TO A DELUSIONAL PATIENT, ESPECIALLY ONE WHO HAS AGGRES-SIVE OR EVEN MURDEROUS TENDENCIES.)

WE ARE MOST IMPRESSED WITH YOUR TREATISE VIS-À-VIS JUNG'S ILLUSTRATION OF A SNAKE CLIMBING TOWARD HEAVEN, AS IF IT IS SCALING A WALL TO BESEECH THE GODS FOR HELP. A CLUE TO THE MENTAL STATE OF THE PATIENT? RETURNING TO THE FATHER'S HOMELAND?

PERHAPS YOU MIGHT CONTINUE TO SEND US UPDATES ON YOUR WORK. WE ARE LEANING TOWARD PUBLICATION BUT MUST REVIEW YOUR FINAL RESULTS AND CONCLUSION. WE WANT TO MAKE SURE WE UNDERSTAND ONE ANOTHER (YOUR THIRD EAR, AS IT WERE) AND THAT YOUR THERAPY IS HEAD-ING IN THE RIGHT DIRECTION.

We look forward to hearing from you soon. We encourage your work, though you should be aware that if we do not write consistently it is because we have been intercepted by publishing demands here at the magazine.

It was hard to get us all on board to compose this letter, though we admire your groundbreaking work!

Edmund S.K. Dangerfield, PhD
Jane Highwall, MD
Morris S.W. Castle, PhD

Betsy sat down at the computer, foaming toothpaste leaking from the corners of her mouth.

"Ohmgow—" she mouthed, spewing the keyboard with white pasty gobs.

John looked up. "What is it?"

Betsy ran to the sink to spit.

"Read this e-mail."

John looked down at the screen and scanned it.

"Congratulations. But since when do you treat schizophrenic patients?"

"I don't! My father did. That's just it. And I haven't written a treatise."

"Huh?"

Betsy typed a search on Google.

"So what's this all about? A hoax?"

"Look. None of those names are on the masthead of *Psychology Today*. Who are these people? Dangerfield, Castle, or Highwall. Someone is trying to give me information. In a way that wouldn't alert a hacker! A hacker, John, who would be on the look out for communication from my mother. John, someone is hacking my e-mail, I know it!"

"Calm down, Betsy. You are not making a lot of sense."

"My mother sent me *The Red Book* for my birthday. This message is code. Someone is trying to lead me to Mom!"

Chapter 33

Countess Bathory stared at the young horsemaster, a cat watching a bird.

The white stallion had entered the castle gates at a walk, as calm as a king's horse. Excited by the activity of the crowded courtyard, the steed raised its head and began to trot, but Janos reined him in, commanding obedience. The horse ceased its prancing, walking by the blazing fires, hawking vendors, scattered livestock, and laughing children.

The Countess dropped her gaze and looked at her white hands cuffed in lace, her delicate fingers clasped in her lap. Then she turned her hands palms down and studied the blue veins of age that drew their tributaries across her skin.

She remembered another skilled rider, long since dead. A shiver coursed through her body. He was a stable boy and she was already betrothed to Ferenc Nadasdy. She—the daughter of both the Ecsed and Somlyo Bathorys, an incestuous inbreeding—was a valuable pawn in the union of the most powerful and the most wealthy families of Eastern Europe. Her cousin ruled Transylvania, her uncle was the king of Poland.

A marriage to the Nadasdy clan—not the highest nobility but immensely wealthy—was a propitious alliance. The Countess was betrothed at the age of nine and sent to her future mother-in-law's castle in the southernmost reaches of Hungary.

So far from home, in the castle of her future in-laws, she had sought comfort with a peasant boy, a stable hand by the name of Ladislav Bende from the village of Sarvar.

Promiscuous and willful, she was also a victim of the falling disease. Her future mother-in-law complained that the Ecsed Bathorys of Transylvania had not warned the Nadasdy family of the brain fevers that seized the young Countess, causing the girl's eyes to roll back in her head and making her soil herself. The fits were preceded by rage— rage that neither the Bathorys nor the Nadasdy family could control. She slapped and scratched her servants, screamed obscenities, and tore at her clothes, leaving them in shreds.

Then came the pregnancy. But the mistress of Nadasdy would not let her potential daughter-in-law's defects spoil the union, and neither would her Bathory mother. The alliance was too valuable to the two families.

She was sequestered in a remote Bathory castle to wait out her shame. The squalling newborn that issued from the Countess's fourteen-year-old body was banished forever.

The baby was taken away immediately. Her mother, Anna, could not allow a Bathory's noble blood to be spilled—even a bastard Bathory. So she gave the red-faced infant girl, wrapped in a woolen shawl, to a peasant woman.

"Never let us hear of this child again," she said. "Take her far away and raise her as your own. We will provide money to raise her in comfort, for she is of Bathory blood."

The young Countess heard of her lover's death a month later. Her father had traveled to Sarvar to kill him, but the plague had already carried the young man away.

The following year she married Ferenc Nadasdy as planned.

The Countess looked from the young rider to her hands. She reached for her silver mirror and studied her face, the flesh of her eyelids drooping despite Zuzana's tending.

Her mind drifted to the night games, and the girls' young, flushed skin.

Chapter 34

It was weeks after arriving at the castle that Janos first caught a glimpse of Zuzana. He rode the white stallion through the meadows below the castle and on beyond Čachtice Village to the edge of the dark forest.

Zuzana was digging in the banks of the stream, looking for the special gray clay she used in one of her potions for the Countess's skin. Her straw-colored hair was covered by a kerchief, but as soon as he saw the pocked skin, he knew who she was.

"Zuzana," he called, a smile spreading across his face. "Is that you?"

Startled, she screamed, her hand flying to her mouth. The stallion shied, taking a series of jumps sideways. Janos was a superb rider, but the horse was too quick for him and he tumbled to the ground, still holding a rein.

"You devil!" he cursed the horse, groaning as he scrambled to his feet.

"Are you all right?" said Zuzana. "I am sorry. I didn't mean to frighten your horse."

The horse, sensing his advantage, reared and pulled at the rein in Janos's hand.

"Quiet, now!" urged Janos, grabbing the other reins. "Quiet."

The stallion snorted at the girl with muddy hands, eyeing her warily. Instead of retreating in fear, she turned her palm up to his muzzle.

"Easy now, boy. Easy."

She stood her ground, speaking to the horse in a singsong voice. Janos rubbed his sore ribs.

"It's not your fault. He is not accustomed to unfamiliar sights and sounds. I am trying to train him, but it's not an easy task."

"The Countess thinks it a miracle you can ride him."

Janos's face tightened. "She does, does she?"

Zuzana flushed. The mention of the Countess had poisoned the moment.

"Your father told me you were her handmaiden. I was to look for you to give you your family's love."

"You could have asked for me," said Zuzana, looking down at the river.

"If I had asked, everyone would know there was a connection between us. The castle is a nest of spies." Zuzana looked away, biting her lip. "And I do not trust the Countess with any information."

Zuzana looked up at him sharply. "You must never speak ill of the Countess!"

"Why?"

"Because—she is too dangerous, too powerful. You must know that!"

"How can you bear to work with such a cruel mistress?"

Zuzana frowned, rubbing her muddy fingertips together.

"I have no choice," she said, her blue eyes glittering. "She picked me years ago to serve her."

"Are rumors true about her? Does she torture innocent girls?"

Zuzana stared at him, her eyes filling with tears.

"Does she murder them?" Janos was insistent.

Zuzana closed her eyes. She clapped her hands over her ears. Janos stretched his hand around her shoulders.

"Is it true?" said Janos, shaking her hard.

"Yes," she whispered. "I have never seen it, but I hear screams in the night."

Chapter 35

The Count's voice resonated in the library. He spoke as if he were addressing a large audience.

"Over the years, we have weeded out the illegitimate descendants of the Bathory line, isolating them. Those bastards of peasant stock who sullied the lineage have been, shall we say, dealt with. In some cases, there have been those so bold as to lay claim to the Bathory fortunes. While they were bothersome, they stood no chance of inheriting. Everything was nicely taken care of—until your husband started meddling."

Grace's face creased in defiance.

"My husband?"

"He was tracing the descendants of families whose daughters had been eliminated during the Countess's reign—and he planned to pay retribution. He had to be stopped."

Grace looked down at her left hand, at her gold wedding band.

"Ceslav was admitted to the Hungarian State Archives in Budapest. He argued that his Slovak heritage gave him a right to view papers taken from Slovak lands, and his mother was Hungarian. And—"

"And what?"

"And he was presented with hundreds of pages of documents

from the early seventeenth century. Record keeping was fastidious in the Nadasdy households. Weekly entries of purchases, salaries, debts."

"Why would any of that interest him?"

"Apparently among the stacks was a ledger the Countess kept in her own hand—a sort of diary. A diary that allegedly documented her . . . activities. I think your husband stole that ledger from the Archives. On those pages were the names of six hundred women. Six hundred twelve to be exact. Depositions were also written."

"Six hundred twelve women. Women that she murdered? My God!"

The Count's eyes focused coldly on the gray-haired woman.

"Your husband," said the Count, his nostrils pinched up as if there were an evil smell in the air, "took it upon himself to start the Bathory Reparation Project—to track down the descendants of the families of the women who were . . . dispatched."

"I never knew—"

"Of course you did not. You lived in blissful ignorance. Ceslav was ashamed. Instead of being proud of his Hungarian heritage, of having noble blood in his veins from a family that once ruled Eastern Europe for almost a thousand years, he disguised his roots."

"Ceslav? What 'noble blood'?"

"Dr. Path—your name should rightly be Dr. Bathory. Even the great Ferenc Nadasdy changed his name to Nadasdy-Bathory when he married the Countess."

"Bathory? No!"

"Your husband was a direct descendant of the first child of the fourteen-year-old countess. She was a bastard child, but still a true Bathory. Your husband's grandfather changed the family name from Bathory to Path when he moved from Budapest to Bratislava."

"I don't believe you. You are inventing things, just like this insane nonsense of the vampires. You are delusional!"

"The Bathory name is still revered in Hungary and Poland—the surname of kings, palatines, and conquerors. But Slovaks—Slovaks detest the name."

Grace shook her head vehemently.

"My husband was a psychiatrist in the asylum. He practiced in Vienna before moving to America. Why would he involve himself in this?"

The Count stared at her, a sudden darkness obscuring the light his eyes. She could feel the chill emanating from him.

Just as suddenly, the shadow lifted, as he regained his composure.

"Yes, well, that question is moot. The Bathory Reparations would require all descendants of Erzsebet Bathory to pay retribution to her victims' families' descendants. Perhaps ten percent of his income— he called it a 'tithe'—pledged for five years would not amount to much."

"What are you talking about? Ten percent of our income?"

"Perhaps it was peanuts, as you Americans say, to someone with the income of a mere psychiatrist. But to those of us with properties— real wealth—it was intolerable. He wished to scrub clean what he was so presumptuous as to consider the stain of blood on the Bathory name. As if that great name needed his help."

"My husband would have told me if he were involved in anything like you describe. We were—"

The Count held up his hand, brushing her objections aside. "Of course, none of us were obliged to join your husband in his project. But the word spread throughout Slovakia, Hungary, even Austria. It drew attention to those of us who refused to have anything to do with his project.

"And I despise having attention focused on me. I have my own projects that I prefer to keep private," he said. The cold shadow had returned. "Your husband knew that all too well."

His eyes flickered in anger—a change that made Grace shiver. She remembered what her husband had told her about the symptoms of psychosis: the swift, radical change in mood, the focused intensity in the eye of a madman.

"I intend to bring back the magic of my ancestors' reign, returning the once glorious power—and fear."

The Count looked off through the window at the mountains beyond the walls of the castle. He grimaced.

"Your husband was well aware of that. And the time has come."

Chapter 36

Darvulia breathed in the burning sulfur bitterness of the potion. A yellow cat jumped from its perch next to her, hissing and spitting at the smoking powder.

The witch wanted the Countess to sleep tonight, dead to the world. The black-clad stranger had ruined their night games, calling them little girls toying with mice. He had smothered all joy between Darvulia and her mistress, admonishing their "crude, imperfect" pursuits of pleasure.

It was he who had convinced Countess Bathory that the blood would rejuvenate her beauty.

It happened when Zuzana was away collecting special herbs for the Countess's skin. Another handmaiden was assigned to the Countess's vanity. The girl—nervous to be so intimate with her mistress—brushed through a tangle in the Countess's hair, provoking her to scream in rage. She seized the silver brush and struck the girl's face, opening a wound in her lip.

Drops of blood speckled the Countess's hand and face. She wiped away the red droplets and stared at her skin.

"You see," he said, suddenly appearing behind her. She closed her eyes at his voice, her body trembling at his touch. "Do you see the youth restored to your skin?"

His long pale fingers stroked her neck, and she trembled, swooning at his cold touch.

Then he walked out the servants' door, disappearing into the turret. The click of his heels echoed in the descending tunnel of stone steps.

The Countess felt the warmth of the blood on her face. Her eyes shimmered with astonishment.

The handmaiden trembled in the corner, covering the gash at the corner of her mouth.

"Look, Darvulia! I am transformed!" the Countess cried. She turned her face this way and that, examining her complexion in the looking glass. "My skin is as youthful as a young maiden's!"

Darvulia bit her tongue. She approached Erzsebet, studying her skin so closely that the Countess felt the brush of the witch's eyelashes.

The witch stepped back, shaking her head. "No, Countess. I see no difference in your skin."

Darvulia could see no change in her mistress, except the willingness to believe a new lover's lie. Jealousy bit deep in Darvulia's breast, seeing her lover drift away, a fool for the stranger's twisted hatred.

"You are blind," spat the Countess. "Look, look!"

Darvulia bowed her head, saying nothing more.

In the hours past midnight, the stranger's coach arrived in the pouring rain. His footman and driver struggled in the deluge, untying a wrapped package with the vague contours of a human body, but larger by two, even three times. They carried the burden down the stairs into the bowels of the castle, to the dungeon.

"What is that?" asked Darvulia, turning cold at the sight.

The stranger scowled at the witch from beneath the folds of his hood. "Begone, sorceress! You are no longer in the Countess's favor. It is a man's seed she hungers for, not the breast of a virgin witch."

"The Countess loves me. She loves women."

"Not now, witch. She does not love you or any other woman. She has learnt the ecstasy of a man's love, of domination."

The witch murmured a curse, more a growl than a human voice.

The stranger laughed. "You think your curses could affect me? You cannot guess of my power."

Darvulia retreated, silenced. Since the appearance of the man in the black cape, she had been chased from the Countess's bed.

"No better than a chambermaid," she thought. "I sleep in a pallet instead of my head resting on a goose down pillow, sharing Erzsebet's sweet breath as she dreams. Now her breath smells of blood."

The stranger had taken her place. When the witch approached the bed to perform the morning incantations, she could smell his sweat and semen—the fetid stink of a man—on the linen sheets. Linens that had only known the scent of women since the death of Ferenc Nadasdy. Lavender and rosemary, and the aroma of the Slovakian winds.

"Who is this man?" she wondered for the hundredth time. "And how does he wield such power over our Countess?"

From the moment of his arrival, the stranger was greeted as a god. The Countess ran to his arms and wept the first night he appeared in the great hall. Darvulia noticed that his dark eyes remained dry, his face smiling in satisfaction at the Countess's emotional outburst. A cruel pull—a twist—of his crimson lips betrayed triumph more than contentment.

"Who is he?" Darvulia whispered to Ilona Joo.

"I know him not," she said. "But there is something familiar. I have only seen glimpses of his face. He chastened me when he caught me staring."

Could he be her lover? Why does he pull his cloak tight, obscuring his countenance?"

"I don't know. His looks are more Transylvanian than Slovak."

Darvulia drew in her breath. She could not understand the Hungarian the two spoke. It had no semblance to Polish or Russian or dialects of Bohemia and Moravia. It occurred to Darvulia that the only ones who might understand them were Zuzana and the Hungarian horsemaster.

Ilona Joo whispered to Darvulia. "He wears the crest of the Bathory on his ring. The Countess must have made him a gift."

Darvulia had not noticed. Her eyes were too weak to see such a detail. Soon they would turn white as milk, rendering her blind.

Who was this stranger who made Erzsebet weep with joy? What power did he possess?

Chapter 37

Zuzana ducked her head, her chin tucked against her starched linen collar. The wind was bitter, and the fabric chafed against her skin.

"You know we have to do it," said Janos, his hand clasped on her shoulder. "You have to help me. We cannot let her continue."

She felt the weight of his rough hand, a hand that could work miracles with a horse. His skin was chapped and calloused, but warmth and strength emanated from his fingers.

"The Countess once aided women in the village. It was she who opened the home for the sick and injured widows of soldiers, fighting on the Ottoman front. Her good works were known throughout Hungary."

"Since the death of her husband, she is not that woman anymore," said Janos. "Wake from your dream! The Countess preys on women. She takes her pleasure in their agony."

"Will Vida recover?" Zuzana whispered, not daring to look up.

"I took her to a healing woman in the village," he said. "She gathered Vida into her care, treating her wounds with red oil. It was she who told me about the women's suffering, about the curse of Countess Bathory. And the pastor of the church came to bless Vida. He told me of the dozens of girls buried in the churchyard. He is prepared to stand in testimony against the Countess."

Janos spat bitterly on the ground. Zuzana watched his spittle melt into the muddy, pocked snow. She could feel his gaze on her. She knew he was judging her. How could she work for a murderess?

Zuzana had asked herself the same question. How could she have remained at Čachtice Castle, with the suspicions she had? At first she had felt blessed to have been taken in by the Countess, despite her deformity. Countess Bathory had showed her charity. Zuzana was honored to be chosen as handmaiden to Ferenc Nadasdy's wife.

But now Zuzana realized—she owed nothing more to a murderess.

"The girls who tried to flee," she whispered. "They—never made it to safety. They are dragged bound and gagged to the dungeon. I never see them again."

Janos closed his eyes tightly. When he opened them again, a steely glare blazed.

"We need proof. My father, Master of the Horse, has the King's ear."

Zuzana shook her head. "Not even the King can bring a Bathory to trial. As a noblewoman, she can punish her servants as she chooses."

Standing alongside his horse, Janos tightened his fist on the reins. The stallion sensed the tension. He sidestepped, snorting.

Zuzana stopped. The silence drew out and then, in spite of herself, she told him something she didn't want to say. She knew that there would be no turning back once she said it.

"Janos, I . . ." She forced herself to go on. "I overheard a conversation between the Countess and the dark stranger, through the door of the alcove."

"What dark stranger?"

"A tall man who visits her, always at night. All the servants fear him and he never shows his face. She was saying that the blood of Slovak peasants has not the purity to perfect her complexion. Three noblewomen from impoverished families are to arrive in the next few months, one is already on her way. They have been invited to learn the manners of high nobility from the Countess herself."

Janos stared at Zuzana, his jaw slack. "Would she dare to kill nobility?"

"She is mad, Janos!" she shouted, now able to say it at last. The wind snatched her voice. "Do you not understand?"

Janos pulled her close, looking over his shoulder. His warm breath whispered in her ear. "If she harms a member of a titled family, the King could proceed against her."

Zuzana drew back, her spine rigid.

"The first young countess will arrive any day. The Countess Zichy of Ecsed. She is of ancient noble blood from the Countess's homeland, but her family is impoverished. The Countess chose Vida to be her handmaiden."

Janos nodded grimly. A gust coming off the river lifted his sandy hair.

"Vida will be avenged. They will all be avenged, I swear before God."

Chapter 38

It snowed hard on the solstice. The wind roared up the valley, ripping the remaining leaves from the aspen trees, leaving groves of white skeletons behind.

Main Street was a blur of swirling white. Peering through the windshield of his car, Kyle crept along, looking out for drunken tourists. He slalomed around a staggering man with his skis over his shoulder, clearly a casualty of too much *après ski* activity, screaming at his pretty, much younger woman companion mincing behind him in furry snowboots.

At the stoplight on Cemetery Lane there was an accident involving three cars. Nothing more than damaged sheet metal—and maybe a couple of DUIs in the offing. Kyle maneuvered slowly around the mess.

"Park here," said Daisy, a block before the cemetery. "Pull way off the road."

"Why here?"

"The cops will get suspicious if we park too close."

"It looks like they have their hands full with traffic accidents. I doubt they can spare anyone to go looking for kids in the dark."

"Come on. Just do it."

They parked and Daisy showed him a break in the wrought-iron fence.

"Wow!" he said shining his flashlight on the tall cottonwoods.

Daisy smiled at him in the darkness.

"Normally there would be dozens of Goths here for the solstice. I guess the snowstorm is keeping everyone home."

They wandered through the quiet of the falling snow. It was snowing more gently under the tangle of branches.

Daisy knelt by a gravestone, brushing off the snow so that Kyle could read the inscription.

"'Dena May Moyers, born 1882, died 1884.' God, how sad," Kyle whispered.

Daisy withdrew a carnation from under her coat. The plastic floral sleeve crackled, breaking the stillness.

"May you rest in peace," she said quietly.

Kyle shone the flashlight at her for a second. Tears streaked her cheeks. "Hey. Are you OK?"

"So many children. So many died. Defenseless."

"What do you mean, defenseless?"

The sound of scraping startled them. They heard voices.

"Shh!" said Daisy.

Kyle knelt behind the tombstone.

"Shut off your flashlight."

In the snowfall, it was difficult to see. But they could hear picks and shovels clang against the frozen ground.

"Someone's digging," said Kyle.

"A grave robber!" whispered Daisy.

They crept closer, shuffling along the snowy path in a crouch.

They hid behind an enormous cottonwood just close enough to see three men. Two digging and one standing in a black coat and black hat, watching.

He uttered an order in a foreign language.

Daisy saw exactly the spot they were digging. She had knelt at the tombstone only days before, reading the inscription.

The men grunted. One of them cursed as he tried to dig the frozen ground. The pick handle ricocheted out of his hand.

"I know that grave!" whispered Daisy. "That's Betsy's father."

Chapter 39

Somewhere in Slovakia
December 21, 2010

Grace stared out the window as the rain blew hard against the warped panes. She adjusted her glasses on her nose, focusing on the black wrought-iron gate and stone guard station in the distance.

A shiny black Mercedes pulled up to the gate. After a quick discussion, the gate swung open and the car moved onto the gravel driveway. Instead of approaching the front entrance of the castle, the car stopped just below her window.

Two men dragged out a thin, pale-faced girl with scraggly blond hair. She was limp but conscious, looking over her shoulder at the surroundings but apparently unable to walk on her own.

They disappeared from view, most likely through a door and into the castle.

Grace heard footsteps in the hall and quickly sat down in an armchair near the window. She grabbed a book and opened it to a random page.

A clinking of crockery preceded the sound of the key unlocking the door.

Draska, thought Grace. *Maybe she'll let me know she sent the e-mail. Betsy will know something is wrong and—*

But it was a tall male servant who entered, carrying a breakfast tray laden with a variety of breads, a teapot, gold-topped jars of jams and jellies, and a container of yogurt. His skin was sallow. He wore no makeup, unlike the women who had watched her the first day, but he had the same starved expression.

"Where is Draska?" asked Grace.

The servant shrugged. "Not come."

"What do you mean, she didn't come? Where is she?"

"Not know. I bring food."

His eyes studied her with the same gleam and hunger as the women's.

"So are you a psychopath too? Another inbred Bathory nutcase?"

"Not understand," he said, his lip pulling up in a sneer.

"Forget it," Grace said. "Go—you are finished. Go away!"

He bobbed his head sullenly and retreated out the door, locking it behind him.

Grace left her breakfast untouched, tiny beads of moisture glistening on the butter, a thick skin forming on the little pitcher of hot milk. She walked wearily to the window, streaked with rivulets of water. Wind and rain lashed at the tiny clumps of grass growing stubbornly in the high stone wall that encircled the castle.

"Draska," she whispered. "Please don't disappear."

Chapter 40

ČACHTICE CASTLE
DECEMBER 21, 1610

The seventeen-year-old Countess Zichy of Ecsed was not well. Her head drooped out of the curtains of the coach. The carriage rattled into the courtyard, the horses' hooves clattering on the cobblestones.

Pulling aside the edge of the velvet curtain, Countess Bathory, still groggy from the sleeping potion, peered down from the drawing room of the castle. She watched the tired girl as the footman helped her from the coach.

"She is pale," said the Countess, her perfect complexion creasing in a frown. "Bloodless and thin. This will not do." She turned from the window. "Fetch Zuzana," she snapped at Hedvika. The servant returned almost immediately, accompanied by the pox-faced girl.

"The Countess Zichy of Ecsed is of noble blood," pronounced the Countess, lifting her chin. "The Zichy family has crossed with the Bathory lineage more than once."

Zuzana nodded.

"She will not tolerate the clumsy attentions of these Slovakian cows."

Hedvika blanched but said nothing.

"Go, Zuzana. Show her the Hungarian care she deserves as nobility. See that she dines properly and have the servants draw a hot bath for her. Tuck lavender sachets into her sheets and serve her mulled wine. Warm her bed with a pan of hot coals so she does not sicken."

Zuzana curtsied, but as she bowed her head, her eyes were open in amazement. She studied the brocade of the Countess's dress, her head lingering low.

Would she sacrifice one of her own relatives?

Hedvika brought Zuzana to the chamber door. The big-hipped Slovak maid beamed in satisfaction when the Countess of Zichy muffled a scream, seeing Zuzana's pocked face.

"Your face!"

"Do not be frightened of my appearance," Zuzana said in Hungarian. "You will soon be used to it. I shall care for you as no one else in this castle can. I serve my mistress the Countess faithfully and have for years."

"Thank God there is a civilized tongue spoken in this savage wilderness!" the young Countess answered with relief. "These savage Slovaks all bark at me in unintelligible German."

"I was raised in Sarvar Castle. I am here to serve you, madam. I am the Countess's personal handmaiden."

Hedvika's lips pulled down, a bitter taste in her mouth. She could not understand Hungarian but she sensed the visitor's acceptance of the ugly handmaiden.

"Oh, Countess Bathory is so good, so generous!" said Countess Zichy, clasping her hands. "Her own personal servant!"

The handmaiden bowed her head, saying nothing.

Zuzana prepared Countess Zichy a bath scented with rosemary. She sent the girl's dress and underclothes to the laundress. The Slovak maids brought the soaps, perfumes, and unguents that Zuzana used for Countess Bathory's own toilette. Zuzana could smell the traveling sickness on the noblewoman's body and clothes.

"Is she as beautiful as they say?" asked Countess Zichy. She was dressed in a robe for bathing—white linen that enhanced the pallor of her skin.

She looked to Zuzana like a white lamb for the sacrifice.

Zuzana steered the conversation away. "Drink some wine. It is good for your blood, Countess."

The girl's nostrils pinched in agitation. "Answer my question, servant."

"Yes, madam. The Countess Bathory is the fairest beauty in the Kingdom of Hungary. I have traveled with her to Vienna and compared her to the finest ladies of the court. There is no one more beautiful."

The Countess drew a deep breath. She took a sip of the wine, a wan smile warming her face.

"Her beauty must be matched with her goodness and generosity to allow me to learn the social graces of a Bathory."

Zuzana nodded and swallowed. "As you say, Countess."

"I could not believe my good fortune when my mother received the letter with the Bathory seal. An invitation to visit the illustrious Countess Erzsebet! My mother and father would move heaven and earth to give me such an opportunity. And—"

"I beg of you, Your Countess. The water will cool. Please, come."

"I do not want to catch a chill," said the girl, looking frightened now. "These Slovakian climes are cold, barbaric. The coach driver said there are hundreds of hungry wolves in the woods."

"Yes. You will hear them at night, howling."

The young Countess opened her eyes wide. She allowed Zuzana to lead her to the brass bath.

The messenger from Vienna arrived, his face and clothes splattered with mud. He had ridden nonstop from Hofburg Palace carrying a letter in his leather pouch. "Messenger from the King!" he shouted in response to the sentry's challenge.

Guard Kovach recognized the horse and rider as he looked down from the castle's battlements.

"Let him enter," he bellowed.

The rider dismounted, rubbing his aching back.

"Sentry Damek," said Kovach, "fetch the royal messenger a draught from the well. Order food be prepared in the barracks."

The messenger bowed in gratitude to the head guard. He took the wooden cup from the sentry and drank deeply.

"Come, I will accompany you to deliver the correspondence to the Countess," said Kovach.

The rider wiped his mouth, leaving a dark smear of grit and mud on his jacket sleeve.

"The letter I carry is not destined for the Countess."

Kovach wrinkled his brow.

The messenger continued. "Will you take me to Horsemaster Szilvasi, if you please?"

Chapter 41

Zuzana remembered the ledger.

She could still feel the young horsemaster's firm grip on her shoulder. It made her skin tingle to remember the weight of his hand resting there.

You know we have to do it.

Word had come that two other young noblewomen would arrive within the next two fortnights. Already the handmaidens were busy, cleaning and preparing the guest rooms, snapping freshly laundered linens in the air and floating them down on the feather mattresses, beating the rugs, finding flasks for water and wine for the bedside tables.

Brona the cook prepared sweetmeats and wine cakes, worrying that her cooking must compare favorably to all other kitchens in the kingdom of Hungary.

Zuzana thought about the ledger. Would a new name soon be entered there? Would the Countess dare to write the name of the Countess Zichy of Ecsed in her curling handwriting, evidence of her murder?

Did the ledger still exist?

Since the appearance of the dark stranger, Countess Bathory no longer lingered in the dressing room, writing names, inclining her head only slightly as the quill scratched the vellum, the ink soaking into the thirsty page.

The scratching of the quill had made Zuzana shudder, and only once had she been able to steal a glance at the names listed there.

Perhaps the dark stranger had persuaded Erzsebet to be more cautious. The ledger was probably locked in one of her drawers or in a coffer.

You know we have to do it.

She heard Janos's words again and knew he was right. She had to do what she could.

Long after the other maidens had drifted asleep, Zuzana crept from her straw pallet. As she entered the turret staircase with its cold rush of air, she shuffled her feet to scare away the rats in the darkness.

She opened the servant's door to the dressing room slowly, avoiding a sudden draft that might be felt in the Countess's bedroom. She stepped carefully, knowing her way so well she could avoid even the faintest creak from the floorboards.

But there was noise from the adjoining room. The bed creaked, and the Countess moaned and howled. Squeals of what could have been pain as easily as delight filled the air, the thrashing of limbs and stiff bedclothes brocaded in gold thread and pearls. The smacking wet sounds of lovemaking, sucking, panting, and groaning reached a crescendo.

Then there was silence.

Zuzana waited until she heard the hinges whine on the chamber door, and the shuffle and tap of footsteps as the Countess and her dark companion descended to the dungeon for the night games.

The moonlight shone at the edges of the heavy velvet curtain. Zuzana moved toward the writing desk near the west window. Surely this was the desk to which Vida had referred. Zuzana had never been in the bedchamber before.

Her finger grasped the drawer pull. It resisted stubbornly.

"It's locked," came a voice from the corner of the room.

Zuzana whirled around, gasping. From the shadows long white fingers extended toward her and grasped her shoulder.

"What are you doing in this room, *Nocny?*" It was the witch Darvulia. She peered closely at Zuzana's face. "You are forbidden to cross the threshold of the Countess's chamber."

Zuzana began shaking uncontrollably.

"The ledger," Darvulia said. "Of course. You fool. Don't you think the Countess takes the precaution of locking up her valuables?"

Zuzana looked at the witch's eyes.

"Please do not tell her I have entered the room, I beg of you!" said Zuzana, her voice a hoarse whisper.

Darvulia lit a candle, tipping the flame up near her face. Zuzana could see words forming on her lips as she composed a reply.

"Do you know the Countess shuns me?" said Darvulia. "She keeps company now with a man years younger than she."

"I know nothing about the stranger, only gossip from the handmaidens. I have never seen him."

"The others were toys to her," said Darvulia, apparently not hearing Zuzana's answer. "They meant nothing. But this one is different. To let such an evil man, so foul a man, into her bed." She made a noise deep in her throat, a combination of disgust and despair.

Zuzana looked on, terrified.

"See that she is damned, handmaiden. See that she is damned!"

Darvulia, weeping, made her way to the alcove. Zuzana heard the turret door creak open and listened to the retreating steps of the witch descending the winding staircase.

Chapter 42

The black-clad stranger disappeared the same night Darvulia vanished from Čachtice Castle. The witch was never seen again. Some said her heart was broken, and she wandered the forests mourning.

But others said The Dark One had murdered her so she would never share the Countess's bed again.

Brona, the cook, muttered a prayer. Hers was a different belief. "See, Zuzana. The two evil ones have left. There must be a Taltos amongst us—"

"A Taltos?"

Brona pulled the girl closer, whispering. "Witches sense when a Taltos is near. The Ancient Ones drive away evil spirits. If they are strong enough."

Zuzana stared at the wrinkled lips of the old cook, smelling the garlic and bacon grease in her gray-streaked hair. Another wild superstition, thought Zuzana. Vampires and Taltos in eternal battles, ghosts and witches floating through the air. To the Slovaks, every moment could be supernatural, the world filled with spirits and sorcerers.

Zuzana knew she was the last one to see Darvulia, in the Countess's bedroom, and she knew well the reasons for Davulia's leaving Čachtice Castle—the witch had been cast aside for another lover.

Zuzana did not say anything to Brona to dissuade her from her hope for a beneficent Taltos. Any helpful spirits were welcome. The true evil one was still right there, her bloodlust insatiable. The castle still smelled of blood and carnage, despite the strong perfumes the Countess wore and the frankincense she burned.

That evening, Countess Bathory, suddenly without either of her lovers and confidantes, was unapproachable. Her black mood terrified everyone in the castle.

"Your creams and potions do nothing for my complexion!" the Countess screamed at Zuzana. "Look at me! I am wrinkled and haggard as an old peasant."

Zuzana folded her hands, as if in prayer, beseeching her mistress.

"Madam, you are beautiful. Look again in the mirror, I beg of you."

"You ugly charlatan! Why did I ever show you mercy, you poxed curse!"

The Countess threw a silver hand-mirror at the girl, who dodged the flying weapon. It shattered with a tinkle of splintering glass.

"There is only one cure to restore my youth," said the Countess, gathering her skirts as she rose from the vanity chair. "And it cannot come from a lowly peasant!"

The Countess swept out of the antechamber, her stiff gown swishing. She slammed the bedroom door, leaving Zuzana kneeling on the floor, picking up the slivers of glass.

Janos was summoned.

"The Countess commands your company at dinner," said a tall manservant. "She expresses deep concern over her horses."

Janos opened his eyes wide. "Her horses? Her horses have never been in better condition. It is true that a few still have traces of thrush, but they—"

The messenger curled his lip, as if tasting something sour. "You are expected to dine with the Countess this evening, two hours after sunset. Present yourself at the castle—the Countess says you are to use the principal entrance, not the servants' doorway."

He turned on his heel, not waiting for Janos's reply.

Guard Kovach, who had been listening intently from the corner of the stable, puckered his lips in a low whistle.

"You are in trouble now, Horsemaster."

"What do you mean?"

Kovach approached, motioning with his hand for Janos to incline his ear. "She has taken a liking to you."

"What?" said Janos. "She asked to learn about the horses' condition!"

"She does not care about her horses. The word is that the dark stranger has disappeared again. There is never any telling when he will return. She is mad with lust."

"I heard she prefers young maidens to men," said Janos, his back stiffening.

"The Countess is not particular, as long as her lover is beautiful. And young."

Janos scowled. He looked over his shoulder and saw no one.

"I have no desire for the widow of Ferenc Nadasdy," he said, gritting his teeth. "I was born into the Nadasdy household—I was honored to have served them at Sarvar Castle and fought alongside them on the Ottoman front. I have never been a Bathory servant."

"Oh, no, Horsemaster. That is where you are wrong. You are a vassal to Countess Erzsebet Bathory for the rest of your life. How long that life lasts depends on the Countess's whims."

The Countess Zichy of Ecsed was also invited to dine with the Countess Bathory that evening

"I shall finally meet the Countess!" the young woman exclaimed as Zuzana brought the handwritten note.

"The Countess Bathory has been waiting for you to make a full recovery from your journey, madam. I have informed her you are now well enough to sup with her tonight."

Countess Zichy's face brightened, a smile bringing roses to her pale cheeks.

"I am also to inform you that the castle horsemaster will be joining the Countess for dinner this evening."

The smile dropped from Countess Zichy's face.

"The horsemaster? A servant?"

"Yes," said Zuzana. "A talented horsemaster from Sarvar Castle. His father serves King Matthias, training the Royal Spanish Stallions at Hofburg Palace in Vienna."

The young countess picked at her fingernails, frowning. "Still, he is hardly a noble. How can he possibly sit at the Countess's table?"

Zuzana chose her words carefully. "Because Countess Bathory wills it so."

Chapter 43

The train from Vienna took an hour. As the minutes passed, the landscape became more mountainous, the colors more vivid, the rock raw and craggy. Betsy felt as if they were traveling back in time. When they got off the train, the sounds of Slovak being spoken around them brought back unsettling memories of her father's death.

John and Betsy hailed a cab outside the station. The driver was listening intently to a soccer game on the radio. Then a voice broke in, giving what sounded like a newscast in a rapid-fire Slovak. The driver tightened his grip on the steering wheel. Betsy heard him mumble under his breath. He rolled down his window and spat viciously on the road.

Betsy tried her rudimentary Slovak with the driver as he wiped his mouth with his sleeve.

"*Co je to?*" she asked, pointing up on the hill.

He switched off the radio and looked at her, a bemused smile on his face. "*Vlavo? To je Bratislavsky Hrad.*"

"That's Bratislava Castle," Betsy translated for John. "My God, it's beautiful."

The castle on the hill overlooked the city, its walls rising steeply against the sky.

John gave a low whistle. "I wouldn't want to tackle those battlements if I were a Mongol invader."

The taxi driver sought Betsy's eye in his rearview mirror.

"*Ste Americanka?*"

"*Ano.*" Yes, she was an American.

"Obama *dobre*," he said, his smile spreading as he met her eyes in the rearview mirror. "Obama good president. You welcome in my country."

The taxi made its way through the warren of narrow cobblestone streets in the heart of Stare Mesto, the Old Town of Bratislava. The Hotel Arcadia was a thirteenth-century building, with arched hallways, a stained glass atrium, and a single olive tree in the lobby.

As John checked them in, Betsy sat exhausted and glassy-eyed in a tiny bar off the lobby staring at the TV, which was showing a news program. A beautiful blonde rapidly rattled strange syllables through sleek painted lips. A young couple on a couch looked up from their newspapers, riveted by her words.

On the screen was footage of a corpse—a young woman, thin and bruised. She lay with her neck at an impossible angle and the camera zoomed in on a blue wound on her neck.

They would never show anything that graphic on American TV, Betsy thought.

The couple looked at each other, then at Betsy, and then back at the TV. The young man took his partner's hand in his and squeezed it.

"*Rozumite Anglichsky?*" Betsy said. "Can you tell me what she is talking about?"

The woman gave her a terrified look. Then she pronounced a word with a strong Slovak accent.

"Vahm-peer-uh."

"Vampire?"

The woman nodded three times.

"Monster. Assassin three woman. Other woman take away."

"Take away?"

"Kidnap," said an Englishman in an armchair, snapping his newspaper closed. "Here's the story in English."

He got up and gave Betsy the paper.

SINISTER CLUES TO ASSASSIN'S IDENTITY

Another woman was found dead early this morning on the outskirts of Bratislava. Ivona Dravikova was last seen at Nightclub Raucous Scandal, known for its late night scene, drunken stag parties for foreign tourists, and reported heavy drug use among its patrons.

Dravikova reportedly frequented the nightclub on a regular basis. Witnesses say she was chatting with a tall dark-haired man at about 1 A.M. She left the club at about 1:45, according to a source who declined to be identified.

Her neck was broken and she had bruises on her throat. A deep puncture wound was found on the left side of her throat.

This is the third such murder in the last four months in the Bratislava area. In addition, at least four other women have gone missing after frequenting one of the many bars in the locale.

"My God," Betsy said, under her breath. "The killer must be insane."

"With a fetish for drug addicts," said the man who had given her the paper.

"Excuse me, but how do you know that?"

"I'm on assignment from Scotland Yard. I'm working on this case. Two British nationals are among the missing girls." He extended his hand. "George Whitehall."

Betsy shook his hand. She felt her fingers tremble in his firm grip. Jet lag, she thought.

"I'm Dr. Betsy Path," she said. She nodded to the Slovak couple on the couch, including them in her introduction. "I'm a psychoanalyst in Colorado."

"Then you know about insanity," said Whitehall. "It seems most of these girls are Goth-Punk types, looking for exotic adventures and cheap fixes for their drug habits. And they seem to have found more than they bargained for."

"He works with Scotland Yard," said Betsy. "I think we should try to cooperate with him."

"What do you mean?" John offered her a bottle of water from the minibar. "He's looking for wayward girls, drug addicts who have disappeared. What does that have to do with your mother?"

Betsy sat down on the bed and opened the bottle. "Voda Dobra" the label read. The hotel probably charged a fortune for it, but she was desperately thirsty and had not checked the Internet yet to see if water in Slovakia was potable. She had been too young to worry about such things when she last visited the country.

"But he must have some connections here. Let's face it—I'm not sure how we are going to go about finding a lost American when we don't speak the language. I don't even know where she was staying."

John sighed. "Sure, why not? Talk to Sherlock Holmes down there, if he is still around. Ask him to lunch, if you want. I'm famished, aren't you?"

Betsy stood up from the bed, making the springs squeak. She gave her ex a weary smile and a kiss on the cheek.

"I'm going down," she said. "To see if I can find him."

"Then I'm coming, too," said John.

The Slovak waitress set down three tall mugs of frothy-headed beer.

"*Dobre chut!*" she said, with a friendly jerk of her chin.

"*Dakiyiem,*" said Betsy, managing to smile. "She just wished us good health."

"*Dakiyiem,*" called John, to the waitress's retreating back.

"You say your mother disappeared a week ago?" asked Detective Whitehall. "Without a trace?"

"We don't know where she was staying. Her last e-mail said she was going to Piestany from Bratislava to see the ruins of a castle that belonged to Countess Bathory."

Detective Whitehall put his fork down, a big bite of roast pork and sauerkraut speared on its tines. He pressed the white napkin to his lips.

"Countess Bathory?"

"Yes, my mother was working on a book, a sort of historical treatise on the woman."

"Quite a bloody subject."

"Are you familiar with her?"

Whitehall stuffed the large forkful of food in his mouth. Betsy wondered if he had done it on purpose to delay his response. He swallowed and took a long draught of beer.

"Yes. I am familiar with the legend of Countess Bathory."

"You say legend," said John. "So the stories of killing hundreds of women aren't true?"

"Oh, that part is true, all right. She was a murderer, and a vicious one at that. The number of victims may have been exaggerated—it seems that her legend was popularized by King Matthias and the Habsburg clan. The king wanted desperately to get his hands on her land and to smear the Bathory name."

"Why?"

"The seventeenth-century Bathorys—especially the Countess's nephew Gabor, King of Transylvania—detested the Habsburgs. The Habsburgs couldn't defend the frontier against the Ottomans, so it was left in the hands of the Bathorys and other wealthy Hungarian lords to stop the invaders. The Hungarians were largely Protestant and saw no advantage in keeping the Habsburg alliance."

"You seem to know a lot about the Bathorys," said John, sipping his beer. "Is their history a hobby for you or is there a reason for your research?"

The detective straightened. He looked into John's eyes, then at Betsy.

"There have been a number of murders reported both in Bratislava and in the Piestany area. One theory we have is that all this bloody business is tied somehow to the legend of Countess Bathory."

"Why would that be?" asked Betsy.

"Ask any Slovak if he knows the legend of Countess Bathory. There is not a Slovak alive who cannot recount the tale. The horror has seeped into the unconscious mind of the entire country."

Betsy regarded him, her lips parted. *Unconscious mind?*

"There may be a nutcase out there who is sucking blood from the girls' veins, mimicking the act of a vampire," continued the detective. "Or perhaps simply letting the victims bleed to death by slitting the jugular vein. The girls are almost drained dry when their bodies are found."

Betsy covered her mouth in shock.

A group of Czech tourists on holiday laughed at the table next to them. The incongruous sound made Betsy jump.

Chapter 44

The dwarf Fizko escorted Janos to the castle. The horsemaster studied his fishlike eyes, the flecks of spit that collected in the corners of his mouth. *An idiot,* he thought.

A sudden stench stopped Janos in his tracks as the walked by the castle garden.

"My God! What is that?"

Fizko stared blankly at Janos.

"The stink . . . it smells of dead animal!"

"Oh," said Fizko, wagging his big head. "That is the rotting carcass of a horse. It is buried in the garden to fertilize the vegetables."

Janos stopped.

"What are you talking about? The horses are under my care, no horse has died in these weeks!"

"Countess Bathory said it is a horse," Fizko said, stubbornly. "That is what it is. Come along, you will be late. She will beat me."

A wooden door studded with iron knobs the size of a man's fist opened as they approached. Janos was ushered into a hall ablaze with scores of torches and hundreds of candles, flickering in crystal chandeliers.

Countess Bathory stood before him, her hair pulled back by a pearl-studded headdress. Her white linen sleeves puffed around her arms, her bodice was encrusted with gold embroidery. She wore a white silk apron—indicating her status as Hungarian nobility—over a crimson velvet dress.

"Please, come in, *Pan* Szilvasi," she said. "I am eager for you to meet my houseguest and apprentice, the Countess Zichy of Ecsed."

Janos bowed deeply. He was stunned once again by the Countess's white marble complexion and piercing amber eyes. Erzsebet's lips were stained red with berry juice, her dark auburn hair glossed with ambergris oil. The roots of her eyelashes were darkened with Turkish kohl.

She looked decades younger than Janos knew her to be.

The Countess offered her arm for Janos to escort her. He took her arm tentatively, knowing this was usually an honor reserved for noblemen.

He had a secret he was anxious to share with her, but he knew he had to wait. The right moment would come.

As they walked, Janos heard the stiff rustle of the Countess's garments. A heavy floral scent rose from the fabric of her skirt. He noticed the delicacy of her wrist, tiny boned like the skeleton of a bird.

Countess Zichy of Ecsed was waiting in the anteroom of the dining room. She was dressed in a white apron over a Venetian silk dress.

"Countess Zichy, may I present my horsemaster, Janos Szilvasi."

The Countess did not curtsy, but extended a limp hand toward Szilvasi.

"It is an honor," he murmured, kissing the girl's hand.

She arched an eyebrow at his kiss, saying nothing. Janos noticed how she withdrew her hand hastily from his lips.

"We shall dine immediately," said Countess Bathory. She entered the dining room without further conversation, expecting her guests to follow.

"Whatever is that foul stench?" whispered Countess Zichy to Szilvasi. "It smells of putrid meat!"

Countess Bathory looked over her shoulder to see that her guests followed. Janos did not answer the young noblewoman's question.

Despite the opulent table, the fine Bohemian crystal, and the wines from Hungary and Italy, Janos could not enjoy himself. The glint that flickered in the Countess's eyes as she observed her guests was deeply unsettling.

"I trust you have found my handmaiden knowledgeable and efficient," said Countess Bathory to the Countess Zichy, taking a sip of Tuscan wine.

"She has obviously trained under your skilled hand," said the younger woman. She raised her chin. "You are much too generous to share her."

Erzsebet met the girl's eyes.

"Is there a problem, Countess Zichy?"

"A problem? Certainly not. It is just that—"

"Please go on."

"May I ask how she became so hideously deformed?"

Janos's swallowed his wine clumsily, but he said nothing. *Zuzana! She must be speaking of Zuzana.*

Erzsebet flicked her eyes at him and then back to Countess Zichy.

"She contracted the pox as a young girl. I took pity on her."

Countess Zichy dabbed her mouth with an embroidered napkin. "You are indeed the kindest noblewoman in Hungary. For she is ugly as an ogre."

The Countess's tinkling laugh filled the great dining hall.

Janos's fingers tightened. He cleared his throat, hiding his hands in his lap.

"Yes, quite hideous," agreed the Countess. She toyed with her silver knife. "But Zuzana serves her purpose dutifully and well. Those who serve me well are rewarded."

The clink of silver against fine porcelain was heartless to Janos's burning ears. He grasped his knife like a weapon, staring at his meat.

"And you, Horsemaster," said Countess Zichy. "Tell me of the— stables. Surely Countess Bathory has the finest horses in all Hungary. Was not your husband the King's Master of the Horse, Countess?"

"He served King Matthias in many capacities in the wars against the Ottomans, including financing the royal armies. Master of the Horse was just one of his titles," the Countess said, frowning slightly. "But the Black Bey is the title he liked the most. It was given to him by the Ottomans, for there was no man they feared more in battle than Ferenc Nadasdy."

"Count Nadasdy, Master of the Horse?" said Janos. "Indeed? Just as I am."

"You are a horsemaster to me," said the Countess quickly. "Not the same at all."

"But my father is the horsemaster to King Matthias's white stallions. Was not the white stallion I ride bred from one of the Habsburg royal studs?"

The Countess raised her glass to her lips. She swallowed a sip of wine before she answered. "And how do you know this?"

"The white horses of the royal stables are renowned, brought from Andalusia in Spain. His lineage is obvious." He paused a moment. "Or perhaps the stallion told me himself, along with many other secrets of Čachtice Castle."

Countess Bathory's eyes flew to meet his. A black fly lit on her cheek and she swatted it away savagely.

"I jest, Countess—forgive me. And now for my news, Countesses, if I may," said Szilvasi, sensing an advantage.

"News?"

"Yes. News I have been saving to share with you at this magnificent dinner."

"What news?"

Janos cleared his throat, anticipating the Countess's reaction.

"Good fortune has blessed the Szilvasi family, if you will forgive my boasting. King Matthias has knighted my father. He was given a fiefdom near Vienna."

"Knighted? Your father?" said Countess Zichy, her face brightening. She clapped her hands in the air. "What wonderful news for you, Horsemaster! The King must be highly appreciative of your father's service."

The Countess said nothing, but a shadow passed over her face.

"Yes, my father is now nobility. And a great ally of our good King."

Countess Bathory put down her fork. She glared at Janos.

"I correspond with my father constantly. He is always eager to hear about the conditions of the horses," said Janos. "And about your health, Countess Bathory."

He smiled and finally took a sip of his red wine, smacking his lips in appreciation. "Your grapes draw good flavor from such rocky soil, Countess," he said. "Who would think fruit would thrive here in the stony-cold wilderness?"

He knew the Countess understood. As the son of a nobleman—the close friend of the King—Janos was now untouchable. He would survive.

Another pair of flies buzzed about his head. They lighted on Countess Bathory's neck and cheek. She swatted them away.

"Curious there should be flies at this time of the year," said Janos. "There have been several hard frosts and snow. To have the vermin at the Christmas season is rare indeed."

Bathory gave him a chilly stare.

"There was a horse who died—one of the old nags the farmers drive to market. We buried it in the vegetable garden as fertilizer—a grave mistake, I realize now. The flies are born in the heat and rot of the carcass," she said. She paused a moment, then pressed a hand to her white forehead with sudden urgency.

"You must excuse me. I feel a headache coming on."

The footmen attending the table helped her from her chair. She disappeared, walking awkwardly into the great hall of Čachtice Castle.

Chapter 45

Grace was reading a leather-bound edition of *The Moon and Six-pence* when she heard the click of the lock. She looked up eagerly, hoping to see Draska. It had been days since she had seen the girl. Cool air rushed in from the drafty halls. The icy air gave her goose bumps and recognizing her visitor made her heart sink.

The Count greeted Grace with a curt bow.

"Good morning, *Pani* Path. I trust you slept well?"

Grace clenched her jaw so hard that her teeth hurt. She looked around the room for something to hurl at her captor. The book was slim, not enough heft. She wanted something breakable that would splinter into shards across his forehead.

"How dare you keep up this charade of politeness, you lunatic!"

The Count smirked. "Courtesy and good manners have always been a charade, my dear Dr. Path."

"Just what is it that you think my daughter has?" Grace asked, slamming the book down on the desk.

"Mind the book, Madam. It is a first edition."

"I am tired of all this secrecy. My daughter must be mad with worry."

The Count walked over and picked up the abused novel. He placed it back on the bookshelf. Before he turned around, he said, "What if I were to tell you that she was in Slovakia at this very moment?"

"You lie!"

Count Bathory turned around, his lips set in what might be taken for a smile.

"Madam, you insult me. It is true. I have a contact who keeps me informed—most discreetly, of course—when certain individuals' passports are registered. Your daughter has arrived in Slovakia."

Grace was swept by waves of emotion. First happiness—then worry—then dread. She refused to give the Count the satisfaction of a response.

"I do not know where she is yet," he continued smoothly. "But I have contacts in other places. It should not take long to track her down."

Grace looked at his pleasant smile. It chilled her to the bone.

"May I remind you: All she has to do is to cooperate. Why would I want to hurt her?" He closed the door gently behind him. The key clicked in the lock.

Chapter 46

The cell phone ringing woke Betsy from a dead sleep. She gasped, looking about the strange room, not recognizing her surroundings. Her heart thumped as she fumbled for the phone.

"Hello? Hello?"

"Betsy, it is Luis. Ringo is fine," he said before she could ask. "Your house is fine. But I have someone here who wants to talk to you. Very important."

"What? Who?"

"Hey, Betsy, it's me. I made Luis call you, he won't give me your number. But I had to call you. It's not about me, it's—"

"Daisy? Why are you calling me?" she said, sitting up in bed. She glanced at her watch. It was 10 in the morning. "What time is it there?"

"Two A.M. It took me all this time to convince Luis to call you. Betsy . . . there were men in the cemetery. They were . . . I'm sorry I don't know how to tell you."

"What?"

"They were digging up your father's grave."

"*What?*"

"We called the police and they scared them off. But I think they were looking for something."

Betsy realized she had started to cry.

"Oh, my God! How . . . Why . . . Why were you there?"

"I'm sorry, Betsy."

"Who? Who did this?"

"I don't know. There were three men. Two digging and one watching. They spoke this really weird language. I don't know what it was—"

"You called the police?"

"Yes, right away."

Betsy raked her fingers through her hair. "This is my cell phone number. If you hear anything, rumors, anything—"

"I'll call immediately. Absolutely."

"And . . . thank you, Daisy. Thank you."

Betsy hung up the phone. She dialed John's room. "Please come over, something's happened."

Then she whispered, "I need you."

Chapter 47

"If she had a headache," whispered Zuzana, walking beside Janos in the dark hall, "it could be a symptom of the falling disease. Of course she had to excuse herself. Within minutes she might fall into a fit."

"The falling disease?" said Janos.

Zuzana nodded. "It is a trait of the Bathory family. Something must have upset her deeply to bring it on. She has not suffered an episode in several years. The servants who accompanied her from Ecsed to Sarvar said it was much worse when she was younger. The Countess had frequent tantrums and fits when she was a young child—kicking, biting her tongue, her eyes rolling up into her head."

"There is evil in her blood," said Janos. "Evil in the Bathory blood."

Zuzana nodded. "Her nephew Gabor . . ."

"The Nero of Transylvania?" said Janos, his eyes narrowing in disgust.

"Yes, so you have heard the rumors at Sarvar Castle. Not one but two children conceived with his own sister, Anna. He is obsessed with the Bathory bloodline."

"Pah! The Bathory blood!" snorted Janos. "The siblings both should be congratulated on keeping the stock utterly pure."

"The Countess's mad aunt, Klara, practiced the black arts and sought lovers in the streets and alleys of Vienna. Woman or man, rich or poor, it made no difference. She had hundreds of lovers. But her fate was dark—she was raped by an entire garrison of Turks, and then smothered with a pillow."

"Good riddance."

Zuzana looked over her shoulder. "One more," she whispered. "The Countess boasts of an ancestor from two hundred years ago. Vlad the Impaler."

Janos narrowed his eyes. "The Impaler?"

Zuzana nodded. "The Countess is quite proud of him. She calls him the bloody defender of Transylvania. They say he impaled his enemies on spikes, to terrify the Ottomans, his enemies, and any of his servants who displeased him. A spike piercing their buttocks, emerging through the head."

"Why would she be proud of such an ancestor?"

Zuzana shook her head.

Janos rubbed his hands together, stroking the side of his left hand with his right thumb. "It is uncanny how Countess Bathory emulates her ancestor," he mused.

Zuzana focused on a milky scar at the root of his little finger.

"My father told me the family has been mad for centuries," she said. "*Az alma nem esik messze a fájától.*"

The apple doesn't fall far from the tree.

Chapter 48

Betsy and John filed a report with the police in Bratislava and contacted the American Embassy one more time before it closed for the Christmas holiday. But after that, they were too tired to do anything more than to go back to the hotel. They sat in her room, both a little dazed.

"I'm too exhausted even to sleep," Betsy said.

"I hear you," John said yawning. "Try to read a bit. I bet you'll nod off."

"Might as well check my e-mail," she said, grateful for the hotel internet access. She opened her computer and let it whir into consciousness.

She checked her e-mail. Nothing new. Then she Googled Daisy's blog.

After a while, John came and looked over her shoulder. "Does she talk about analysis on the blog?" he asked.

"It's weird," Betsy said. "It's as if she was doing her own self-analysis . . . using *The Red Book* illustrations as a stimulus."

"Kind of like you would do."

"I have never used *The Red Book* with any of my patients. Why would I?"

"Seems like one of your intuitive methods, that's all," said John shrugging. "Don't get all defensive. It sounded ingenious."

Her back stiffened. "What do you mean 'defensive'?"

"I just meant that you were always searching for innovative—unique?—ways to reach your patients. I meant it as a compliment."

She pushed her chair back, screeching on the tile floor, and folded her arms across her stomach.

"I didn't bring out *The Red Book*. She did."

"Maybe she had a flash of intuition herself."

Betsy frowned and looked at him standing there—palms turned out wide, the body language of a man who had nothing to hide.

She drew in a deep breath and forced herself to relax. Her face, her shoulders . . . her back. "Sorry, I am just on the edge. Would you mind if I slept through dinner?"

John studied her.

"Betsy, is there something—anything you want to tell me?"

Betsy looked out the window at the snow falling on the slate rooftops of Old Town.

"When I went to New York to see *The Red Book* display—you know, 'The Red Book Dialogues.' And—"

"And what?"

"There was a tarot card reader. Everyone in the audience pulled a card—I—well, this is stupid."

"No, come on. Tell me. I want to know."

"I drew a really disturbing card. The Nine of Swords. It had a picture of a young woman, a girl really, sitting up in bed crying. Over her head hung nine swords that continued off the card, so you couldn't see their points."

"What did the tarot card reader say?"

"She said that there were family secrets, things that I was about to discover. A tragedy—and—"

Betsy stopped, cupping her face in her hands.

"I'm afraid, John. My mother—is she the tragedy? Is that what it meant? And what family secrets?"

"Oh, Betsy—" said John, kneeling beside her chair. He pulled her to his shoulder. "Shh," he said, stroking her head.

"But—"

"You know how I feel about all this psychic stuff. It's a bunch of baloney. Somebody else must have pulled the same card in the audience, and his or her mother didn't disappear. It's all chance. It doesn't mean anything."

"A woman came up to me and said the Nine of Swords was known as the Lord of Cruelty."

"So what? It's all baloney, you know that! Look, I think you're overwrought. You have jet lag, you're worried about your mother. And then that English detective told you about the killer vampire, it fueled your imagination. It doesn't have anything to do with your mother."

Betsy wiped her eyes with the back of her hand.

"OK. You're right. I think I'm going to take a sleeping pill. I've been having nightmares. Vampires. And a woman made of stone. They're Jungian archetypes, but still—they're so real. It seemed like a memory more than a dream."

"Hey, Bets, it's OK," he said, pulling her close. "You've been through a hell of a lot. You want me to stay the night with you?"

Betsy sniffed back her tears. She kissed him on the lips. Tenderly, but not lingering.

"Sometimes I do. But we both know it would be a mistake."

"I didn't mean that—I meant to watch over you."

"Thank you," she said, getting up from the chair. She hugged him close, then let him go.

Chapter 49

Grace slept on a rollaway bed—more than reasonably comfortable, it was made up each night and folded up each morning by a silent chambermaid. She tried rudimentary Slovak with the woman, but the maid did not register even a flicker of comprehension. She just nodded courteously and went about her business, tucking in the sheets and fluffing up the down pillows.

Night was when Grace fell apart. She pulled the lavender-scented sheets close to her face, breathing in the clean scent. There was something about the incongruous luxury that made her sob uncontrollably.

One night she thought she heard an echo of her sobs. She stopped herself in midgasp and listened. The ebbing silence of the great hall and many empty corridors of the castle was all she heard.

Then came another cry—from outside the castle. She stumbled out of bed, the sheet wrapping around her leg and tripping her. She grabbed her glasses and settled them on her nose.

In the glare of the outside floodlight, she saw three figures.

A girl, this one dark-haired, screamed and sobbed as she struggled against two men dragging her toward the building and then out of sight.

Later that night, Grace woke to find herself sobbing, her pillow wet with tears. She had dreamed about her dead husband.

Grace hadn't dreamed since the night before Betsy was born.

In her dream, Ceslav was sitting beside her, his hand on her cheek, telling her something. His eyes were desperate, wanting her to comprehend.

What was it? Something about a patient. In Vienna, years ago, when he worked at some exclusive institution for lunatics.

The most frightening terror in the world was not ghosts, or monsters, not vampires, or any of that nonsense. The most terrifying creature in the world is a madman.

In her dream her husband shook her, saying, *Don't you remember? Don't you remember?*

She started crying because she didn't know what she was supposed to remember. And the kind man who had never said a harsh word to her when he was alive had seized her shoulders in her dream, making her head rock.

A far-off scream carried in on a gust of wind, and then was swallowed in the silence of the castle.

Chapter 50

The cold winds of December roared through Vienna, tearing slate shingles from the roofs, smashing them on the ice-glistened cobblestones.

King Matthias strode the halls of the Hofburg Palace, a caged lion. The click of his boots ricocheted off the vaulted ceilings and the stone walls lined with portraits of the King's Habsburg ancestors.

Matthias had received a letter from Cluj, seat of the Diet of Transylvania.

"Your Majesty, I beg leave to speak," said Bishop Melchior Klesl, entering the hall.

"Speak!"

"Your people should see you in church worshipping during the advent season," the bishop pleaded.

"Which people? The blood-thirsty Catholics or the rebelling Protestants?"

Melchior Klesl sighed. "Habsburgs have always been Catholic, your Majesty. The Mother Church holds the Crown in great esteem as defender of the Faith."

"My father refused last rites from the Catholic Church. I think I shall do the same," said the King bitterly. "Most of my subjects are Protestants in the Hungarian Lands."

Melchior Klesl looked at the scroll of vellum in King Matthias's hand.

"Bad news, Your Majesty?"

Matthias exhaled noisily, flapping the letter in the air.

"The swine Gabor Bathory is plotting against me with the Sultan. He has invaded Wallachia, expanding his kingdom. Fool!"

"Wallachia! What claim could he possibly have to those lands?"

"Bathory claims Wallachia is part of Transylvania and under the ancient Order of the Dragon," spat the King. "Groundless nonsense. Treason! He claims Vlad Tepes as a distant cousin."

"Vlad Tepes! The order of Dracula?" Melchior Klesl shook his head, as a draft blew in through the leaded glass. He drew his robes tighter around him. "The Bathorys have spawned a viper's nest of villains and cold-blooded murderers. It is easy to imagine Gabor is actually proud of his ancestry, rather than ashamed of it."

"Bah!" said the King. "The Ottomans will play with Gabor like a cat enjoys a mouse's scurrying. Then they will strike him down, installing an infidel of their choice as Voivode. They will knock once more on the gates of Vienna."

"Your Majesty, surely Gabor doesn't think he can hold Wallachia?"

Matthias swept up the parchment letter from Transylvania. He flapped it in the air with a vengeance.

"Gabor has executed his general, Boldizsár Kornis, in the public square to show his absolute power. My sources tell me there was a plot to assassinate Bathory in his bed, but the assassin lost heart."

"General Kornis's plan?"

King Matthias raised his chin, affirming. Tense ropes of muscle stood out in his neck.

"Bathory took the general's wife to his bed, as he had done with any number of other loyal officers' wives, making cuckolds of his loyal men. Komis had had enough of the despotic fool."

Melchior Klesl scowled.

"Barbaric Transylvanian, who gives his own sister bastards."

"His rutting does not concern me nearly as much as his political ambition," said Matthias. "He means to rule all Europe, under the Bathory banner. The man who penned this letter tells me that Gabor sent a delegation to Constantinople to confer with the Sultan. He is planning on invading Poland, to secure it for the Ottomans. The scurrilous swine!"

The bishop scowled, twisting the jeweled rings on his big-knuckled hands. "In hopes that the Sultan will name him Voivode of all the Eastern lands?"

"Of course. And he has assured the Calvinists that their religion shall be propagated throughout the Eastern empire."

The bishop balked. "Surely your report must be mistaken. The Bathorys wouldn't risk their fortunes for religion!"

"Domination is Gabor's religion. The whole cursed family is mad with power. Power and lust. Even the Sultan calls Gabor the 'Deli,' the madman." King Matthias clenched his hand in a fist. "Gabor Bathory means to unite Moldavia, Wallachia, Poland, and Transylvania in opposition to the Habsburg Crown."

The King stopped. He hunched his shoulders.

"Bathory's empire will be larger than our own if he succeeds. He will be as powerful as Vlad Tepes once was."

Chapter 51

The Countess ordered Brona the cook to prepare special meals for Countess Zichy.

"She is painfully thin and pale," said the Countess. "She has no flesh on her bones, her body is nothing but sticks covered in skin."

"They do not know good nourishment in the Eastern lands."

The Countess's face tightened in rage. She slapped the cook hard across the face. "What do you know of my country, you thick-headed idiot!"

"Yes, Madam. Forgive me, Countess," said Brona, managing a clumsy curtsey that made her bones creak. The imprint of Countess Bathory's hand blossomed red on her cheek and chin.

"Bah, you ignorant peasant! Heed me, Cook. Prepare tasty treats that will whet her appetite. Feed her butter cakes and meat, the choicest cuts. Give her cheeses and thick cream, pastries and jams."

"Yes, Countess."

"Your cuisine must be like a magic spell—she must be coaxed to eat, then eat more and more."

"Yes, of course, Countess. It will be a pleasure to turn out special dainties for your guest. I will try my best."

"And Cook, never dare speak ill of the Eastern frontiers and

Transylvania again," said the Countess, her voice ominous. "Do you understand?"

When Brona was dismissed, Countess Bathory muttered, "If the girl has no vitality in her veins, she is no use at all to me."

She glanced in her mirror and saw Zuzana waiting silently.

"Why are you skulking about like a thief? Brush my hair!"

Chapter 52

Nightfall comes early in the Rockies in December. It was pitch black by the time Daisy reached Carbondale.

Her mother had forced her to eat dinner before she left.

She still had the taste of sun-dried tomato brioche and watermelon chutney in her mouth when she knocked on the lavender door of the little Victorian on Main Street.

"All right, Funeral Girl," said Luis, opening the door. Ringo nudged past Luis's trunk-like leg, rushing to Daisy. He spun in circles barking and wagging his tail furiously.

Daisy knelt down to pet him and he licked her face over and over again.

"Good to see you before midnight, even if you are still dressed in black," Luis said, yawning. "Why don't you give up that witch look and wear some color? My mom can find you a nice fiesta dress—"

"Yeah, yeah. Enough, Luis," she said, with a dismissive wave of her hand. "I wanted to meet you here for another reason."

"*Entra,*" he said. "Come in and tell me."

Ringo clung to her side as she walked into the living room of the Victorian house.

"So what do you want?"

"You know that burglar? I don't think he was looking for money."

215

"So?"

She told him about what had happened in the cemetery. "Those guys were looking for something in the coffin. No chance there was any money in there. They were looking for something else."

Luis crossed his thick arms across his chest. "That's Doctora Betsy's business."

"Yeah, but Betsy isn't here. What if we could help her somehow?"

"What do you mean?"

"What if we could find whatever those guys were looking for? And like—hide it away some place else, where they could never find it. Because chances are, they'll be back."

Luis grunted. "If they do, I have my *cuchillo*."

"Yeah, but Luis! Even with a knife, you could get hurt. What if these guys have guns? And what if all three of them come at once?"

"Ringo and I can take 'em."

Ringo wagged his tail.

"Be realistic—"

"Hey! Look at who is telling me to be realistic. You dress like a witch every day. You more real than I am?"

Daisy squinted at him. "You are not being helpful, Luis."

"I'm here to protect this house from anyone who wants to take something from Betsy. Even you."

"But it's not to hurt her, don't you see! It's to protect her—"

"No. You leave her stuff alone. Come have a *cerveza* with me, witch girl. I know a place they don't ask for ID."

"You don't have to spend more than an hour with him," Daisy pleaded into her cell phone. Someone flushed the toilet next to her, nearly drowning out the voice on the line.

"It's like a colossal fav for me—yes, you can take *The Red Book* home for the weekend, I promise. Yes, I will interview you on my blog. Just—"

A silence.

"Jaz! You are terrific. Yes, we're there now. See you in about forty minutes?"

Daisy snapped her cell phone shut and left the ladies' room. She imagined the sensation Jaz would make when she entered. She was a Latina Goth, but she wore tight-fitting red clothes—slinky and sexy. She always had high heels with her in her bag, even in the winter, taking off her snow boots and putting on the black dagger stilettos once she got inside.

Luis would go crazy over her. The thought made Daisy smile, her tooth glinting.

The bar was dark, and the sour smell of old beer permeated the air. There were little linoleum-topped tables set in front of two musicians with electric guitars. A Latina waitress, with big hoop earrings and a flouncy orange blouse, sauntered up to their table. Her silver bracelets jangled as she placed two cans of Coke in front of them.

"*Tu especialidad, Luison,*" she said, eyeing Daisy. "Hey—it's Christmas! You still celebrating Halloween?"

The waitress put her hand on her hips, throwing back her head and laughing. The gold hoop earrings glittered under the fluorescent lights.

"No, as a matter of fact," said Daisy, narrowing her eyes. "Are you still celebrating Cinco de Mayo? Nice costume, girl."

The waitress's smile vanished.

"Ok, *chicas. Basta,*" said Luis. "*Gracias,* Lupe. *Gracias.*"

The waitress stomped off, cursing under her breath in rapid-fire Spanish. Daisy only caught the word "*Puta.*"

"I didn't order a Coke," said Daisy.

"And that ain't one. *Pruebala.*"

Her taste buds anticipated the sweetness of a soft drink. The stinging bite of tequila made her smile.

"Very cool. Like *mucho.*"

"Yeah, Lupe is *una amiga.* She didn't mean nothing bad about your funeral clothes."

"Cinco de Mayo is a nice day, too," said Daisy, settling back into her chair smiling. She tipped up her Coke can. Luis turned to listen to the band, making the wooden chair squeak under his weight.

Daisy glanced at the time on her cell phone.

Thirty minutes to go. Daisy was running out of time. She knew Jasmin wouldn't stay at the bar with Luis all night—she always had other plans.

Luis had left lights on in the little Victorian house. It made it difficult for Daisy to prowl about without being seen as she searched for an unlocked window.

Carbondale was in the Christmas spirit, rowdy and raucous. Despite the cold she could hear loud voices on Main Street, laughter and shouts, people on their way to restaurants or bars.

She walked across the frozen grass, her boots crunching over patches of hard snow. What was she going to look for? Something worth breaking into a house. Something worth digging up a grave. Grave robbing. The idea sounded Goth—the reality in the cemetery had made her shiver. She had no idea what might make someone do that. But she felt certain she'd know it when she saw it. She'd feel it.

All she knew was she had to get into the house.

She had forgotten her gloves. The cold slick glass and frosty chipped paint of the window frames bit at her fingers. She pushed up hard, grunting, trying every window she could find. Her bare hands came away covered in paint chips. Everything was locked up tight.

Damn, she whispered. She thought hard where a spare key might be hidden. Not under the old hemp mat, not under the flowerpots outside the door. Not nailed around the corner, or in a fake stone hide-a-key.

Then Daisy nearly tripped over the cellar doors, which were covered in snow. They were the old-fashioned kind that were at a shallow angle to the ground, opening up to what had been a root cellar in the mining days.

Daisy brushed away the snow to expose the metal handles. She tugged at the door and it opened, breaking a seal of frost. She pulled her headlamp from her backpack and went down the old wooden stairs.

There was a wet earthy smell inside. The cellar was packed floor to ceiling with boxes, old furniture, a brass coat stand. Daisy picked her way through the maze, until the beam of her headlamp fell on cement stairs leading up to the main floor of the house.

She heard the savage bark of Ringo on the other side of the door.

"It's OK, Ringo. Good dog," she said.

Ringo quieted and then began a series of joyous yelps.

She opened the door and emerged in a hallway, a lamp lit on a desk. No papers or files here. Ringo thumped his tail. He whined until she scratched him behind the ears.

Daisy walked into the front room, Betsy's office. The file drawers were locked. She checked the pad beside the telephone. Only a few words jotted there, "embassy" in big letters with a long distance phone number. She bent close to the pad and shone her headlamp on a scrawled word.

"Disappearance," she read aloud.

Also, "Dean in Chicago," with another phone number.

She ripped the page from the pad and stuffed it in her pocket.

It was something, but not what she was looking for. And with a sinking feeling, she looked at her watch. Jaz wasn't going to stick around very long, twenty minutes more, maybe.

Daisy took one more look at the darkened study where Betsy worked with her patients. She sighed, remembering the day she first really talked with her therapist. Her light fell on the two leather chairs, facing each other. A sadness emanated from them, empty and silent.

Ringo jangled his tags. He pressed his wet nose into the palm of her hand. She smiled down at him.

He was part of that first day, too. The first breakthrough she had with Betsy.

When she found her voice.

Her gaze fell on the shelf of books, most of them rare first editions in German. Her headlamp lit on the cloth cover of the book she had touched and almost pulled out that day.

She walked over and touched her fingertips to its spine. It, unlike the others, was not leather bound.

We used to have a first edition, Betsy had said.

It translates to Synchronicity . . .

Daisy's fingers gripped the spine of the book, pulling it out from among the others.

As she removed the book, the beam of her headlamp fell on a dark shape behind the row of books.

She set down Jung's book and pulled out several of the rare editions, uncovering what lay behind.

It was an oblong shape, wrapped in black velvet that absorbed the light. Inside the wrapping was a slim book. She unwrapped it carefully. It was old. The title was almost worn away, but she recognized the first words. "Synchronizität, Akausalität . . ." And behind it, she realized, was another book, even older.

She opened the second book. It smelled musty. Stiff creamy pages with a list of incomprehensible words in a language she did not understand. "Margareten, Barbora, Adela, Malenka," followed by words that all ended in "ova."

They were names, she realized.

Ringo whined, startling her. She whirled around.

An envelope fell out of the book, landing on the oak floor. She bent to pick it up. It was sealed and addressed to Dr. Elizabeth Path.

Daisy rewrapped both books and the envelope in the velvet and slipped the package carefully into her backpack. Glancing at her watch, she muttered an obscenity.

"Good dog, Ringo," she said. "Stay here. Luis will be back soon to let you out."

Daisy hurried back to the cellar and out of the house. She crossed the street, seeing a black car's headlights flick on.

She could not make out the faces in the car. But she knew she was being watched.

Chapter 53

B etsy wiped her eyes with her knuckle.

"You are tired," said John. "And jet-lagged. It's after midnight, Betsy. Try to sleep."

"It's staring at this computer screen. It dries out my eyes," she said. John looked over her shoulder, seeing a Visa card display with Dr. Grace Path's e-mail.

Betsy typed in "Rudolf II."

"Crap," she muttered.

She tried "Matthias." Then "Matthias 1608." "1608 Matthias."

"Shit," she said a little louder, twirling her hair around and around her finger.

"Just give up," said John. "There are thousands of combinations for a password. The statistical significance of finding—"

"Just *don't*, John. Don't!" she warned.

Betsy stared at the computer screen

"Does Esztergom have a *z* in it?"

John checked the guidebook. "After the *s*—why?"

The fall of Esztergom in 1543 was a significant battle that her mother always taught in her Eastern European classes. Betsy typed "Esztergom1543," hit Return and shouted, "Bingo!" as the computer screen changed from the log-in screen to a list of credit card expenditures in the days before her mother's disappearance.

The last charge had been for a meal in Piestany, Slovakia.

"She was in Piestany. That was the last time she used the card."

"That's the spa town. Pretty pricey for your mom—"

"Maybe she was staying somewhere near there and went out for a meal. Or maybe there's a B & B."

John was already on his computer.

Trip Advisor suggested just two bed-and-breakfasts in the area. He dialed his cell phone.

"*Dobre Den, Penzione Trematin.*"

"Hello, do you speak English?"

"A little. How may I help you?"

"We are trying to find an American woman. She may have been staying in your hotel. Her name is Dr. Grace Path."

"Are you the police?"

"Why do you say that?" asked John, motioning to Betsy.

"The American lady no come back. All her things—we put them in the suitcases and they wait for her here. We had to rent the room."

"She was staying there?"

"Yes. I made her reservations for a dinner at Hotel Thermia Spa Restaurant in Piestany. She never came back."

Chapter 54

"Dean Cox's office."

"Um. Hello. I'd like to speak to the dean, please."

"May I ask who is calling?" said a woman's voice.

"This is . . . Mary Jones. I was a student in Dr. Path's class last semester."

There was a pause on the line.

"I am sorry. I was expecting another call. The office is closed until next term. Please call after January tenth."

"Well, then I guess I'll be raising hell to the Foundation Board. My uncle is a major donor, and has been a member—"

The woman interrupted her.

"Maybe I can help you. The dean is on another line."

"Well—I want to contest a grade. I'm really pissed. And my dad is a big-time donor to the university."

"I see."

"I've left messages for Dr. Path, but she hasn't returned my calls."

"Dr. Path is . . . on leave and unavailable at this time."

"OK. So what I do about this grade? I mean I kept my exams and everything. I can prove that I didn't fail this class—I got a ninety-five on the final! And—and I've transferred to a different school. These are on my transcripts and now I don't have the credits—"

"These are matters you will have to take up with Dr. Path and the dean."

"If I can't speak to either one of them, how the hell do I—"

"I can send you a link to the paperwork required to file to contest a grade."

"When is Dr. Path supposed to be back?"

"She . . . she is researching a book in Slovakia. We don't expect her back until next term."

"Slovakia?"

"I am sorry, Ms. Jones. We can't discuss this—"

"Hey! I'm the one has an *F* on my transcripts."

"Please file the paperwork and the dean will review the matter. Which class was this?"

Daisy ended the call. She flipped open her laptop, opened a browser window, and typed in search terms.

SLOVAKIA. GRACE PATH, UNIVERSITY OF CHICAGO.

As an afterthought she added AMAZON.COM.

The search produced two books by Dr. Grace Path: *THE REIGN OF MATTHIAS II, EMPEROR OF THE HOLY ROMAN EMPIRE. TWO BROTHERS, TWO EMPERORS: RUDOLF II AND MATTHIAS II.*

There was one pre-order book: THIS BOOK HAS NOT BEEN PUBLISHED: *PORTRAIT OF A MADWOMAN: COUNTESS ERZSEBET BATHORY OF ROYAL HUNGARY.*

On the cover was the portrait of a pale-faced woman with a high, slightly bulging forehead. Her hair was held back in a headdress and her face was framed by a ruffled collar.

"Madwoman?" whispered Daisy.

FROM THE PUBLISHERS: DR. GRACE PATH, KNOWN FOR HER SCHOLARLY RESEARCH AND EXPERTISE IN THE REIGN OF MATTHIAS II, EMPEROR OF THE HOLY ROMAN EMPIRE, EXPLORES NEW TERRITORY IN THIS COMPELLING BOOK, EXPLORING BOTH

Daisy's black fingernails clicked against the computer keys. U.S. Embassy. Slovakia. She scribbled down the number and e-mail address.

"Bratislava," she murmured. "Where the hell is that?" She typed "Google maps" into the browser and, moments later, Bratislava popped into focus.

She dialed 411 and waited.

"Hi. How do I dial direct to Bratislava, Slovakia, from the U.S?"

"Yes. This is the daughter of Dr. Grace Path," Daisy lied, working hard to make her voice sound more mature. "I need—"

"I've told you before, Ms. Path," said an irritated male voice on the other end of the line. "We have no further information about the disappearance of your mother. Your report has been filed and all other inquiries will have to be made to the Bratislava police—"

"Wait? You—she's missing?"

"Excuse me," said the man, losing the edge in his voice. "You did say you were Dr. Path's daughter. Is this Elizabeth?"

All right, asshole, thought Daisy, her lip catching on her canine as she smiled.

"No. I'm—her other daughter. Mary. I had no idea my mother had been formally classified as missing."

"You should contact your sister."

"I—I've tried. I—can't get through to her on her cell. I've called and called. I am distraught with worry. I—"

"You might try her at her hotel."

"She didn't give me the address. Only that something was wrong—"

"Just a moment. Hotel Arcadia is the listing I have for her."

"Thank you. I'll call them immediately."

"Please know that the ambassador is looking into the matter. And if your sister locates your mother, she should call us immediately so that we can close the file. Good luck."

Daisy pressed the END button on her cell phone. She narrowed her eyes, thinking.

Chapter 55

Betsy's computer pinged, signaling an incoming e-mail. She frowned at the UK address, a username that she did not recognize.

DEAR DR. PATH,

I AM AN EDITOR-AT-LARGE FOR THE PSYCHOLOGY TODAY PUBLICATION. I HAVE BEEN TRAVELING AND WAS NOT PRESENT WHEN MY COLLEAGUES SENT THEIR CORRESPONDENCE TO YOU, CONCERNING YOUR WORK WITH SCHIZOPHRENIA, EMPLOYING FREE ASSOCIATION WITH THE RED BOOK PLATES.

HAVE YOU CONSIDERED EMPLOYING PLATE 34, WITH THE HIGH MOUNTAIN, WHICH COULD APPEAR INSURMOUNTABLE TO A PATIENT, ESPECIALLY DURING A FUGUE EPISODE? IT WOULD BE INTRIGUING TO SEE HOW THE PATIENT REACTS 4-6 HOURS (FROM P.) AFTER A ROBUST DOSE OF CLOZAPRINE, WITH THE CHALLENGE OF LOCATING THE WINDING ROAD TOWARD REALITY.

MOST IMPORTANTLY, IT IS PARAMOUNT THAT THE PATIENT REALIZES HE IS NOT ALONE. THERE ARE MANY OTHERS WHO SUFFER DELUSIONS AND NEED HELP.

Betsy became aware of the warmth of John's breath on her neck as he hovered, reading over her shoulder. Her skin prickled.

"Let me guess—" said John. "There is no plate thirty-four show-ing a mountain."

"No. No, there isn't."

"So she's—what? Four to six hours? *P* stands for 'probability'?" said John. "What does probability have to do in the syntax of the letter?"

"It's not *p* for probability, John. It's a capital *P*. Piestany. She must have had on her watch and timed the trip, even if she didn't know where she was going."

"Piestany?"

"John! She was kidnapped, like those girls. They disappeared from Bratislava and Piestany!"

Betsy stood up and ran her hand through her hair. Then she caught a fistful of it, twisting it violently as she thought.

"Four to six hours. East or west, north or south?"

"Let me get a map," said John, sitting down at her computer. He clicked on Piestany and slid the map into a wide focus, scanning the topography for high mountains.

"How is she getting these messages to us? There must be someone helping her," said Betsy.

"Look! The only big mountains lie east—the Tatras. Three thou-sand meters. That's—what? Ten thousand feet."

Betsy sat beside him. She leaned over to peer at the screen. His breath smelled of peppermint gum.

"Can I see something?" she said, taking the computer from him.

Betsy clicked on a tourist site for the Tatras advertising skiing and hiking. "A castle with a high wall in the Tatras. Not much to go on."

"The mountains are pretty remote," said John. "There might not be too many castles."

"And we're looking for one that is still inhabited. That's some-thing." Betsy tapped the screen. "What about the last bit. 'There are others who suffer.' What do you think she means by that?"

John took a deep breath. Betsy waited for the warm scent of pep-permint when he exhaled.

"I think there may be other kidnap victims," he said.

Chapter 56

One advantage of being a weird kid of a rich divorced couple— Daisy had her own Visa card. Gold, of course. Without wasting any time thinking about whether it was a good idea, she bought an airline ticket to Bratislava via Denver-Frankfurt as soon as she finished talking to the embassy.

She wondered if she'd have to tell her mother about the trip. Maybe she could just go. Leave a note saying she would be back in a week or two. And school . . . well, it would still be there when she got back. It was winter break now anyway. Besides, kids on ski teams disappeared for weeks at a time, and the teachers posted all their assignments on the high school website. She could keep up—if she wanted to.

Daisy did a search for weather forecasts in Slovakia.

"Wow. Cold over there, too." She was going to need woolen sweaters and jeans, warm socks, and her black boots. She rummaged around in her desk drawer to find her passport, from the trip to France she had made with her mother.

When her mother got home from playing tennis at the Aspen Club that morning, Daisy took a deep breath and jumped right into it.

"Mom, do you know where Bratislava is?"

"Is this your homework? Google it."

"Well, no. I'm going there for New Year's."

"You're what?"

"I'm flying to Bratislava. It's the capital of Slovakia."

"What do you mean, you're flying?"

"Well. I could go tomorrow, but there is a flight from Denver tonight to Frankfurt—"

"You know that's not what I meant. It's Christmas Eve, God damn it! What makes you think you can just fly off to Europe? And why Slovakia?"

"It's complicated, Mother. But it's something I have to do."

"Daisy Hart! You are NOT going to—whatever crazy place you said."

"Yes, I am. I am going to Bratislava. Mother, I have to—Betsy is in danger, I can feel it!"

"Betsy? You are—what? Is Betsy in Bacalava?"

"Bratislava, Mother. BRA-TA-SLAV-A! She is in terrible danger. I can feel it in my . . . bones! My skin! My whole body is throbbing with this fear."

"Oh, my God," her mother said, covering her mouth with her hand. "You are totally insane. I'm calling your father."

"I don't care."

"He'll cancel your credit card."

"He'd better not. I'll starve."

"You'll be right here. You won't starve. Don't be irrational."

Daisy stomped up the stairs. Her mother was already calling her father. She didn't care.

But she was relieved when he didn't answer.

Her suitcase was a carry-on. She packed her Goth essentials: white makeup, heavy black eyeliner, black lipstick, vintage necklaces. Enough underwear, socks, and sweaters to get her through a week. Then she could do laundry.

And of course both her phones—her black iPhone and the ruby-red cell phone from her father. If her father cancelled her credit card, she could do without food. But not without communication.

Chapter 57

There was a light rap on the door of the study.

"Come in, Heinrich. Tell me. What have you found in the Path house?"

"Nothing, Count Bathory," said a blond man. The pupils of his eyes were pinpoints, the irises sparkled an iridescent blue, a glacial lake. "We tore the house apart, looking," he said. "We could not return after the police were called."

"And the grave? Did his widow bury the ledger with him, Heinrich? That would indicate she wants no part of the proposed project."

"There was no sign of the ledger," said Heinrich, his voice barely concealing his disgust. Heinrich flexed his knuckles, remembering the cold night at the cemetery. The Count had sent him on this mad errand, digging at the frozen ground with an ice axe and shovel. When the red-and-blue police car lights illuminated the cemetery, Heinrich and his men had run.

"I think she knows nothing of this, yes?" said Heinrich. "The ledger?"

The Count lifted his glass of cognac to his lips. "It appears so. But she is an intelligent woman. Perhaps she knows very well where it is. She may be lying to me."

"So you think the daughter has the ledger?"

"I believe that is more likely. I understand that the father and daughter were very close," said the Count. His right eyelid began to twitch.

Heinrich fixed his eyes on the Count, watching.

"So you have nothing at all to report?" the Count said.

Heinrich shrugged. He did not like the Count's dismissive tone. "One observation. There is a girl, an adolescent. She is a Goth, dressed in black with a crucifix around her neck. We saw her enter the house the night we left."

"Enter the Path house?"

"Yes. She opened a cellar door, buried under the snow. She spent about a half hour inside. We were going to follow her but were wary of the police. The Path house is right on Main Street. The police already had a description of us."

"Did she find anything?"

"We could not tell. She wore a long coat, down to her ankles—she could have hidden the book. She walked to a bar. When she left, she walked down Main Street again accompanied by a very big boy, Mexican-looking. He waited with her for a bus to Aspen."

The Count puckered his lips, as if tasting something sour.

"She would have no idea what importance the ledger plays," he said. "I wonder what she was looking for?"

"Perhaps her own records. We have seen her on other occasions enter the Path house for appointments. She is often accompanied by her mother."

The Count took a long draught of cognac, musing this idea.

"You might be right. Psychiatric records hold an enormous fascination for the patient. She most likely wanted to read what her therapist had written about her."

The Count pressed his fingertips together, forming a temple. He pressed it against his forehead.

"I want you to find out who she is," he said at last. "What connection she has to Betsy Path. I want to know everything about her. Find out her name and trace her phone, her e-mail—"

"Why do you think she is so important?" said Heinrich. "To use so much effort to trace her."

"I do not want anything to thwart our forthcoming night games," said the Count.

"She is just a teenage girl."

"I have believe she is more," said the Count. "This girl was at the Path house. Too much synchronicity. There is a connection."

"A lot of hours will go into this search, Count. It will not be easy—"

"Did you hear me, Heinrich? Do it!"

Heinrich lowered his eyes to the floor.

"This week marks the four-hundredth anniversary of Countess Bathory's arrest," said the Count. "I will not have anything go wrong."

"Yes, Count."

"We shall have all our—guests—participate in the night games, to honor my illustrious ancestor. While the rest of the world keeps spinning through its mediocre course, we will celebrate with passion. We will feel the pulse of life, consecrate ourselves with it."

Heinrich watched the Count's eye twitch.

"We shall wait for the Countess to return!"

The Count felt his servant's cold stare fixed on him. "What, Heinrich?"

"I said nothing."

"It is not your words. I feel a sense of discontent. Am I right?"

"I serve you and only you, Master."

The Count plunged his head into his open hands.

"Count Bathory. Are you well?"

"Leave me, Heinrich," he said, his face still buried in his hands. "I feel a spell coming on."

Chapter 58

Countess Bathory lay on her bed, her lips foamed with spittle, her breath rattling in her lungs. She did not note the presence of Hedvika, who attended her throughout the night, or the chambermaids who regularly sponged her body, keeping their mistress clean and presentable as befitted her nobility.

Erzsebet Bathory's mind was filled with sights and sounds from long before, when she was a nine-year-old child and a gypsy band had presented themselves at Castle Ecsed.

"They are performers," explained her young nurse as she brushed Erzsebet's long auburn hair with a boar-bristled brush. The nurse had a gentle hand, for she had been warned of the little girl's temper.

"They beg to entertain your noble parents this evening. There is a dwarf and men who juggle. A minstrel sings and there is a shadow puppet show."

The little girl Erzsebet clapped her hands, her lace cuffs fluttering. She turned to her nurse, her face bright with childish joy.

"Will my father allow them to entertain us?" she asked. "He is so solemn and stern."

"I think your mother is so weary with sadness, he will engage them," said the nurse. The servant turned away from her young charge, hiding her face.

Erzsebet knew the nurse was crying, thinking of how Erzsebet's two older sisters had been murdered in the peasant riots. Erzsebet and the old nurse had hidden high in a tree and watched her sisters being raped and murdered.

Later, when peace was restored, her father had taken the young girl to see the peasants tortured and killed. Her mother was too ill with grief to attend.

"Watch them suffer, Erzsebet. Watch your sisters' murderers suffer," her father said, through his clenched teeth. "They shall suffer on earth before they burn in eternal hell."

Erzsebet stared hard at the men: so terrifying before, so fearful and harmless now. She fingered the stiff fabric of her father's coat sleeve.

"Rejoice in their suffering, my daughter," he said, his face cold as stone. "Rejoice!"

As the men's private parts were torn off with white-hot tongs, the little girl opened her legs and urinated. Then she fell to the ground, writhing, her body contorting.

When she came back to the world, her mother stroked her head.

"You have the Bathory disease," she murmured, stroking her child's hair away from her damp temples. "Your noble blood carries both honor and curse."

Erzsebet had pushed the memory away. Now there was to be juggling and dancing, puppet shows and bawdy jokes that made the adults laugh. There would be wild boar and wine, sweet cakes and honey.

The puppet show was the best. Erzsebet sat with her older brother Istavan, watching the antics of a woodcutter and his donkey. The donkey brayed and the woodcutter kicked him. But the donkey was stubborn and soon got the best of the woodcutter, spilling his load of sticks and kicking his master in the arse.

Erzsebet loved the puppets and begged for more. Istavan declared he was too old for children's stories and stomped off to brood and drink wine.

"Ask your mother for a penny," whispered the woodcutter's voice, when Istavan had left. "Then we will entertain you all night long without tiring."

"I cannot touch money," said Erzsebet. "My father will pay you."

"This is for me and the donkey," said the gypsy behind the screen. "Or tell me where your mother hides her money."

"My mother leaves no money in the castle but for the cook to buy food and wine on market days."

"So in the kitchen?"

"Play more. I want to hear the donkey bray."

"First I must rest," said the gypsy, climbing out from behind the screen. "I am fatigued from the long journey to Ecsed. May I have a jug of water?"

"Ask a maid," sniffed the young aristocrat. "I am not a servant."

"Forgive me, young Countess. I will go to the kitchen and find a jug of water. Then I will return with more tales of braying donkey."

But the gypsy did not return. Erzsebet swiveled her head at the commotion coming from the kitchen.

"Red-handed! The gypsy stole a thaler from the kitchen jug!" cried the cook. She chased the scoundrel out of her kitchen, all the time pounding his back with a stick of firewood.

"Help, help! Catch the thief," she shrieked.

Erzsebet heard no more stories of the donkey and the woodcutter. The next day, the gypsy puppeteer was sewn inside a dead horse, the man's filthy head gasping, tongue fat with thirst. He cried for water as flies accumulated on his bloody wounds, laying their eggs.

Erzsebet's father took her by the hand, and led her to watch the dying gypsy. Above the roaring buzz of flies, Count Bathory pointed his chin in disgust to the half-dead thief.

"Water," mumbled the puppeteer. "Have mercy!"

Count Bathory scowled, pushing his daughter closer to the wretched man.

"Behold, daughter, what becomes anyone who betrays a Bathory."

Within two days the puppeteer was dead, rotting inside the maggot-laden guts of the horse.

Chapter 59

The letter from his father that Janos had received at Čachtice Castle contained news about more than just the knighthood.

> The Palatine Count Gyorgy Thurzo wishes to meet with you. He asks you to wait at the Plow tavern the afternoon of the twenty-fourth. A messenger will meet you there. Make sure that you are not followed, my son. Count Thurzo wishes to discuss serious matters of the Crown.

Janos told Guard Kovach that a cousin from Sarvar Castle was stopping briefly at the thermal springs of Piestany to water and rest his horse. He said he was going to visit and would be back in the evening.

At the Plow, the stable boy, scratching fleabites on his ankles, took Janos's horse to the corral behind the stone building.

A mist of sour beer and cheap wine enveloped Janos as he entered the tavern. That sour embrace battled the rich aroma of a savory goose roasting over the spit.

"What drink you?" asked the tavern keeper.

"Medovino," said Janos.

The big man grunted and nodded to a maid, who scurried about, tucking back a stray lock of hair under her kerchief. She ladled a good portion of the honey wine into a crockery jar and handed it to Janos.

She looked at his face and took a quick sip of air.

"What is it?"

"I know you," she said. "You are the horsemaster at the castle. I work there sometimes, helping with the laundry."

Janos nodded.

"So we are both in the employ of the Countess," he said.

"Ah, but I will not spend a night there," whispered the girl, moving close to his ear. "You are the rider who brought Vida back to the village to the cunning woman!"

Janos looked around the tavern. He saw no one watching them. "Do you know Vida?"

"Yes. The poor girl still suffers from her wounds."

"She was poorly treated by the Countess," said Janos cautiously.

The girl looked over her shoulder before she spoke. "The Countess is a witch with the devil's own pastimes. Village girls have disappeared forever into the bowels of the castle."

Janos whispered to her over the rim of his mug. "Why do the girls work for her?"

The maid's eyes narrowed. "There is no other work for them. My uncle owns the tavern. He gives me food, I have a roof over my head. Not all are as fortunate as I."

Her eyes darted around the tavern. She bent close to Szilvasi's ear. "There is an iron maiden in the dungeon."

"What?"

"A brass coffin cast in the form of a woman. Filled with spikes. The Countess orders a servant girl to polish it. One of her witches opens it and then the others slam it shut with the girl inside, impaled. The ugly ones, Ilona Joo, Dorka, and the dwarf bring pans to collect the blood for the Countess's bath."

"Her bath?"

"It is the blood of virgins that keeps her skin so white and youthful. The dark stranger has encouraged her to—"

"Daneka!" shouted the innkeeper.

"I must go," she whispered.

Janos pressed his lips to the rough rim of the crockery jar. The wine was heavy and sweet, warming his throat and belly.

Other customers nodded to him, and he watched the diners tear into their portions of goose. They mopped up the yellow fat with chunks of coarse bread, and laughed into their jars of wine. Their laughter clashed with the image the tavern girl had just burned into his mind.

"Janos Szilvasi?" said a quiet voice.

Janos turned to see a young squire, dressed in the livery of a courtier. He wore a puffed cap of satin and leggings of thick black wool. His jacket was slashed with pleats, winking white silk against charcoal gray.

"Is your horse stabled near?" the squire said.

Janos nodded and looked for the servant girl. Instead, her uncle approached, his voice gruff. He asked for payment thrice as much as Janos expected.

As the tavern owner eyed the coin in his hand, he jerked his head for Janos to approach him.

"Forget you ever saw my niece," he warned, his eyes sliding to the courtier. "And pay no heed to whatever she may have said to you."

Chapter 60

The Palatine's castle near Piestany was not a fortress like Čachtice Castle—or like Gyorgy Thurzo's principal home, Orasky Hrad, which lay farther north along the Orava River, rising high out of a limestone cliff, its gray stone walls impenetrable. This much smaller residence in Piestany stood on a hillock, outside the town, encircled by great oak and ash trees. It was ringed with only one defensive wall, the crested banners of the Thurzo family flapping above the stone turret. The rooms within smelled of well-oiled wood and wealth. Rich dark silks and satins adorned long-nosed Thurzo ancestors staring down from portraits in gilded frames.

Count Thurzo sat in a chair, his fingertips tapping at the nail heads in the leather upholstery. When he heard the clop of horseshoes in the courtyard below, he rose and approached the window.

He is young, he thought, looking down at Janos. *Too young, perhaps.* He smiled. *Or maybe just young enough.*

Thurzo's eyes studied the white stallion Janos rode. Perfect confirmation—a warhorse. Strong muscles rippled under the gleaming coat. The stable boys led it off to the paddocks at a trot, struggling to control the steed.

A knock on the door.

"With permission," said a voice.

"Enter."

The courtier bowed deeply. "Janos Szilvasi," he announced.

"Count Thurzo," said Janos, walking into the room. He inclined his head stiffly but made no move to bow.

"You look like your grandfather," said the Count. "Do you know that he trained three of my personal mounts at the Battle of Esztergom?"

"Yes," said Janos. "I believe there were two mares and a stallion. The stallion was called Avenger, the mares . . ."

"Empress and Ottoman Challenge," said Count Thurzo, completing his sentence. "How do you know?"

"I rode all three, early in their training."

Thurzo pressed his lips in surprise, his chin rising.

"I am surprised a boy so young—what were you at the time?"

"Six, my Lord."

"Six years old? Allowed to ride such spirited horses, meant for—"

"Noblemen?"

Thurzo narrowed his eyes. "I was going to say 'battle.' Your grandfather obviously had great faith in your riding skills."

"He did."

"Hmm . . . well." The Count motioned for Janos to take a seat. "You may know that there have been reports of cruelty—*ne*, torture and murder within the walls of the castle."

Janos nodded. "Yes."

"Yes, you say. You have heard such stories? And do you have reason to believe them?"

Janos looked directly into the Count's eyes, rather than speak to the floor as an inferior should.

"The maidens whisper of cruelty, of disappearances. I have witnessed the wounds and suffering of a poor girl, her hands scorched with hot coins for having reached for food in the Countess's pantry."

"Ah, but that's punishment for stealing. Hardly the murder and mayhem that I describe."

"The girl was starving. The Countess purposely starved her to see her suffer."

"Yes. I know of the girl. But no court of law would consider her punishment unjust. She is a peasant, she is a thief."

"She was starving!"

"This is not my concern." The Count waved his hand in dismissal. "My interest is a certain noblewoman who was invited recently to Čachtice Castle. She is the first of several girls from noble families who have been extended invitations to winter at the castle."

"What is her name?"

"Countess Zichy of Ecsed," said Thurzo, watching Janos's face. "Do you know her?"

"I dined two nights ago with the lady, Palatine."

"You?" snorted Thurzo. "The countess invited her horsemaster to dine at her table?" He inclined his head. "But of course! Your father is to be knighted by the King next week. News travels quickly even in the wilds of the Carpathians."

Janos heard a horse whinny. He eyes flicked toward the window.

"I hope your stable boys can handle my stallion."

Thurzo grunted. Janos could tell by the pinched look on the Palatine's face that he did not like the interruption.

"How did the Countess Zichy look?"

"Rich and spoiled," said Janos. "She said ugly things about the Countess's handmaiden."

Thurzo nodded. He stroked his black beard playfully. "Ah, yes. Erzsebet's beast, my wife and I call her—what's her name?"

"She is not a beast!" shouted Janos, rising to his feet.

"Steady, boy. Do not forget to whom you speak," murmured Thurzo, not bothering to rise. He motioned the young man to sit once again, flicking his finger. "You do not want me as an enemy."

Janos sat slowly, but met the Count's eyes, refusing to look down.

"Let's get to business, shall we?" said Thurzo. "The two of us have a common foe, I believe—the Countess."

Janos said nothing, his shoulders still trembling in anger.

"If something untoward should befall the young Countess Zichy, King Matthias would be able to bring Erzsebet Bathory to trial. But only if she injures a noble."

"But what of the others? I have heard—"

"Yes, the pastor is compiling a list. It is said to contain almost a hundred peasant girls' names already. Surely he exaggerates. But whatever happened to them, it was no crime. Those girls were her personal property."

"They were human beings!" said Janos, his voice edged in anger.

Thurzo made a sound of disgust, wet and thick in his mouth.

"Do not be a fool, Szilvasi. Those women are expendable in the eyes of the law. But a countess, a lady of noble bloodlines, is not."

Janos looked away.

"If you truly want justice, you can stop the bloodshed. You can be my ally, Szilvasi."

"Ally?" said Janos, a bitter taste in his mouth.

"Yes," said Thurzo, leaning forward in his chair, making the wood creak.

"What do you need me to do?"

"I need you to report to me immediately if the Countess Zichy is injured or . . ."

"Or what?"

"Disappears."

"I can do that," said Janos.

"Good. Good," said Thurzo, stroking his bearded chin. "Now that you know the way, I will expect you to bring news here directly. Do not trust a messenger or try to write to me in Vienna. Countess Bathory has spies everywhere."

"I understand," said Janos, rising from his chair.

"One other thing," said Thurzo, escorting Janos to the door. "There are tales of a stranger dressed in black who visits Čachtice Castle. It could just be Carpathian folklore, these simple-minded peasants love to exaggerate. Some say it is the spirit of Count Vlad Tepes, Dracula himself, who visits the castle."

"The Impaler?"

"The great slayer of the Ottomans—and of peasant servants who offended him. I fear my cousin Countess Bathory takes him to be her mentor."

Thurzo noticed that Janos clenched his fists at his sides.

"He lived and died two centuries ago," Thurzo said, smiling. "I want to know who this visitor is. I do not believe in ghosts. Do you, Horsemaster?"

"With such a monstrosity in the living, there is no need for haunting spirits."

Thurzo opened the door. "It might interest you to know that Count Vlad Tepes is a distant cousin of Erzsebet. . . . Good journey, Szilvasi."

PART

-2-

Chapter 61

The taxi stopped at the Michalska Brana, the oldest gate in the walled city.

"I cannot go. Must walk. Too small, this street." The taxi driver shrugged.

Daisy gazed bleary-eyed at the tiny street, gleaming gray from the cold morning rain. A small sign read MICHALSKA BRANA BED AND BREAKFAST.

"OK. I can carry my bag. How much do I owe you?" She had sorted out the brightly colored euro bills she had withdrawn from an ATM in Frankfurt. It looked like Monopoly money to her. She let the eager driver draw out a few bills from her hand.

"Take something extra for Christmas," she said. He smiled, plucking another colored bill.

She rolled her suitcase over the bumpy cobblestones, staring up at the pastel colored buildings, decked with evergreen garlands. Twinkle lights glistened around the shop windows, and she heard carolers in the next street.

It's like a freakin' fairy tale, she thought. A cold, wet wind sliced against her back. She wrapped her scarf tight around her face and neck, glad for once she wasn't wearing her white Goth makeup, which she had taken off to prevent hassles with TSA at the airports.

"You will be staying for how many days?" asked the woman with bright purple hair.

Wow, Daisy thought. *Even the middle-aged women dye their hair freaky colors here.*

"Uh. I don't know. Can I just pay by the day? I don't know what my plans are yet."

"Yes, of course. It is low season and we have no reservations for your room. Stay as long as you like."

Daisy felt the jet lag sucking her into the floor. She looked around the Michalska Brana hotel. It had been recommended on Lonely Planet. And it was cheap enough.

It smelled of coffee and toast, mixed with the faint odor of cigarette smoke.

A glass elevator slipped down a glass shaft.

"Do you need help with your bags?" asked the clerk.

"No, no. I can handle it. Thanks. Oh, do you have Wi-Fi?"

The grape-haired woman's face brightened. "Of course. No password needed."

Daisy threw herself face first onto the stark whiteness of a down comforter. She drank in the clean, fresh aroma of the bed linen.

She propped herself up on her elbows, turning on her cell phone.

There were a series of frantic messages from her mother.

"Daisy? Where are you? Call me immediately! You didn't go to, to . . . wherever that was. Don't dare tell me you went there!"

Next new message.

"Daisy, this is your father calling. Your mother says you have run away to . . . Bratislava? I don't even know where Bratislava is—"

In the background, Morgan's voice: "It's the capital of Slovakia, Roger."

"Wherever. Damn it. Call me. Call me now!"

Next new message.

"Hey, it's Kyle. You weren't home when I came by. Your mother is totally flipped out. Give me a call or send me an e-mail so I know you are OK."

Next new message.

"Daisy, it's Morgan. Where are you? Mom has never been so worried in her life. What's in Slovakia that you would drop everything and go there? Call me. I can keep a secret—well, you know that already. Hey, and don't forget. I know exactly where you are. You've got Dad's GPS cell phone with you. Do you really think he isn't going to cut your allowance because you took that phone to fucking Slovakia?"

Next new message.

"Daisy, this is Betsy. Your mother used my emergency line at the answering service to call. She said you were talking about going to Bratislava. Is that possible? Call me immediately. You have my cell phone number."

Daisy collapsed onto the bed, the soft duvet enveloping her shoulders.

I could sleep for days, she thought.

She pressed speed dial and waited to hear Betsy's voice.

Chapter 62

As John drove up the snowy hill to the foot of Čachtice Castle, he glanced at Betsy. She stared out the window, watching the bare branches of the trees.

"You OK?" he said, reaching for her hand, his eyes on the rutted road.

She twisted her fingers in his.

"I don't know. I don't know anything anymore."

"We'll find her," John said, squeezing her hand.

"But what about this nutcase killing women and draining their blood?"

"The inspector said it was only young women. Your mom definitely does not qualify. She'd give anyone who approached her one of her professor looks over her glasses and scare the shit out of them."

"Who'd want to kidnap a sixty-five-year-old historian?" Betsy smacked the dashboard with an open hand.

John didn't answer. He parked the car alongside the road. The snow was too deep to continue driving.

They got out of the car and walked up the long hill to the snowy ruins of the castle. The wind whistled through the trees and over the tumbled stones, perched on a rocky cliff.

"What the fuck did we expect?" said Betsy, pulling her scarf tight around her neck. "This is only a ruined castle."

She shivered, staring at the tumbled walls. "It gives me the creeps."

Betsy's phone rang. She scanned the screen for the name.

"Great," she said, pushing her hair away from her ear. "That's all I need. . . . It's Daisy." She moved next to the one stone tower that remained of the old castle so she could hear.

Flipping the phone open, she asked, "Daisy! Where are you?"

"I'm in Bratislava. I came to warn you—"

"Warn me? Daisy! You are in Bratislava? What?"

Betsy rolled her eyes, looking at John for strength.

"You can handle it, Doc," he whispered.

Betsy nodded.

"Look, Daisy, we're traveling right now. But we'll be back in Bratislava in a few days. Just—just stay right there. Unless you want to fly back to Aspen and—"

"I didn't come all this way to just turn around again. Tell me where you are."

"No. No! This is my own affair. I appreciate your thinking I need protection. You know that's called transference, that you have transferred your feeling to me, and while it is normally a natural, good sign of thera—"

"Damn it! Don't talk to me like I'm on a couch. Someone is trying to hurt you. Someone dug up your dad's grave. They did! And they were searching your house."

"That is my business."

"I've got something that belongs to you, Betsy. I took it from your house. It's old and freaky, but maybe—"

"What? What were you doing in my house, Daisy Hart?"

John shot Betsy a look. Betsy shook her head, her jaw clenched.

"It was behind your books, on the bookshelf. Hidden way back—"

"My bookshelf? What were you doing rooting around in my—"

"It's complicated. Look, I just found it. OK? It's . . . I don't know, a notebook with a rotting red leather cover. It's got . . . maybe a list of names? Girls' names. I think it might be in Slovak. I Googled some of them. Some are Hungarian, most are Slovak."

"Daisy!"

John glanced over again. He knew that tone of voice. But Daisy kept going.

"I took the list. I mean . . . you can have it back and all. It just seemed like I should take it. I don't know, I—"

"Damn it! Daisy . . ."

"There are six hundred twelve names. I counted them. And it's freaking old. It's all yellow, like a bundle of dry leaves."

"Oh, God. Try not to damage it. Put it in a safe place—is there a safe in your room?"

"Yeah, I think so."

"Put it in there and lock it up. Promise me you will do that."

Why was this notebook hidden on the shelf? It must have valuable information—but a list of girls' names? Six hundred and twelve girls.

"Now listen to me, Daisy. John is with me, and watching out for me. OK? So I am protected. Now I'm worried about you."

"Don't be. I'll go lock up the names. Call me later, OK? I can't get my cell phone to work here."

Betsy drew an audible breath.

"Are you calling from a land line, Daisy?"

"Yeah. I tried to dial 01 and 011 but neither one works—"

"You need to hang up. Now! Do not call me except on your cell phone—"

"Like, is this phone tapped or something?"

"Just hang up. Stay there in the hotel until we get back. A few days. And Daisy—watch out. Be really cautious. Super alert. Promise?"

"You, too, Betsy. Hey, and Merry Christmas! Look, I didn't mean to cause trouble—"

Silence—a dropped call.

Betsy stared straight ahead, her eyes blurring with tears.

"Don't think about her right now, Bets. You need to focus on what we can do to find your mother."

"John—did you realize it's Christmas?"

He gave a short laugh and shook his head. "Merry Christmas," he said, reaching out to rub her neck. "We'll get through this, Bets. We'll find her."

Chapter 63

Daisy woke late in the afternoon. She looked around the simple room, eyes sticky with fatigue. Sleet streaked the windowpanes, blurring the view across the tiny street.

"What the fuck am I doing here?" she whispered. "Some Christmas!"

She struggled to the bathroom and splashed her face with cold water. Her naked face looked back at her, vulnerable and childlike. It had been a couple of years since she had gone without her daily white makeup.

She fumbled through her bag and brought out the white foundation. With savage sweeps of her fingertips, she covered the naked skin.

When she came downstairs, the receptionist looked startled. Then she smiled.

"You are Goth," she said, nodding her head. "Many Goths in Bratislava."

"Really?"

"Many, many. You see them. I can tell you names of bars that have Goth scene. You like?"

"Sure. I can't speak Slovak, though."

"Young people learn English in Bratislava. English to survive," she said, opening a map of the city. "OK. So. Are you lesbian?"

"What?"

The purple-haired woman shrugged. "I want to send you to the right bar. Straight or lesbian?"

"Straight," said Daisy in a loud voice, looking over her shoulder. "Like really straight."

"OK, OK," said the receptionist. "This is the one." Then a cloud of doubt crossed her face. "You must be very careful, though. Bars are safe, but do not leave with strangers."

Daisy sensed the woman's sudden anxiety.

"Why?"

"There was murder. Goth girl, like you. Last week."

Her cell phone rang, the ring tone "Riders on the Storm" by the Doors.

Daisy frowned at the number on the screen.

She pressed ANSWER. "What do you want, Morgan?"

"Where the hell are you?"

"Bratislava," she said, looking up at the pastel plastered ceiling of her hotel room. "Pretty cool. They like Goths here."

"Do you know Mom has called the FBI, Missing Persons, and Oprah?"

"Oprah?"

"She thought she might do a feature on runaway Goths. Maybe get some international attention. You know Mom."

"That's fucking freaky. I'm fine. And I told her where I was going."

"What are you doing there?"

"Following a hunch."

"You followed your shrink, right? Mom says she's there, too."

"So what?"

"So that's fucking weird. Patients don't follow their shrinks to strange foreign countries."

"Yeah, and you are really an authority on normal behavior. Daughters don't usually—"

"Don't say it!"

"Whatever. You are weirder than I could ever try to be, even as a Goth."

Daisy pressed the END CALL button hard, as if she were killing an insect under her fingertip.

Nightfall came earlier than Daisy expected. By 4:30 it was dark, and it was an ominous reminder that she had traveled to a distant land without a clear understanding of what she hoped to do.

Why had she come?

To protect Betsy. To battle some unseen force.

That seemed pretty lame now, as she lay staring at the ceiling of her hotel room.

No, it was the recurrent dream, the sense of foreboding. The castle and the woman in blood. In her dreams it made her heart jump in her chest, so she woke screaming.

Somehow this dream was connected with Betsy, Daisy just knew it. She couldn't shake that premonition, no matter how hard she tried. It haunted her, urging her on.

"I've got to get out," Daisy said, her voice strange in the empty room. She yanked her black coat from the armoire. The hangers jangled against each other.

Daisy walked to the corner where the taxi had let her off that morning. She didn't really feel like sightseeing—that wasn't a Goth thing, right? But the Michalska Brana Tower, rising above the ancient town gate, was spooky enough to make her want to explore whatever might lie inside.

But the door to the tower was locked. A sign said 9:00-17:00.

Daisy looked up and began walking backward, her head tilted up to see the top floor and the green patina of the cupola.

A fat raindrop splashed in her left eye. Then another down her neck.

It had started to rain again and she didn't have an umbrella. Umbrellas weren't something that Aspenites carried. She tightened her scarf around her neck.

Her boots splashed through the puddles and rivulets along the cobblestone street as she hurried back to her hotel. She gave the receptionist a wave as she waited for the glass elevator up to her room.

"Wet weather," said the woman. "But it may pass soon."

Staring out the window at the night sky, the idea that she had run away to Bratislava seemed absurd. She didn't even really know where Betsy was.

Daisy rubbed her misaligned tooth with her thumbnail. She stepped into the glass elevator.

"You are a total idiot," she whispered to herself.

She stepped out of the elevator and walked to her room. With a twist of the brass key, she let herself in. She flipped open her computer and opened her blog.

"OK, Goths. I'm going to check out some local bars here and nail down the Goth scene. Next entry will be a porthole into Eastern Europe's Freak World."

She shut down her computer and walked to the safe. She entered the code, looked inside, and when she was satisfied the cracking pages were still secure, she locked them up again.

The receptionist had told her that the bar opened at nine, but there wasn't much action until midnight. Daisy decided to take another look at the old town of Bratislava until the scene picked up. She had slept most of the day and felt not the slightest urge to go to bed.

The cold air slapped her face as she set foot on the cobblestone street. The rain had stopped and the wet wind carried the smells of wood fires, roasting chestnuts, and dampness. She drew another deep breath. The smell of grilled onions and sausages from the outdoor vendors made her mouth water.

First stop, sausage, she thought. *I'm starved.*

Floodlights made the buildings glow against the night sky and she marveled at the medley of colors. The pastel buildings were edged with filigreed trim, the shuttered windows a contrasting color. In the fairyland of whimsical houses, she wandered the winding streets, imagining past centuries.

From the enormous pink Archbishop's Palace to the original crumbling walls of the city, Daisy felt a pulse of history. The buildings were as real yet ethereal as the abandoned shell of a cicada, clinging to a tree branch, molded by the life it once held. She heard the ring of horseshoes against the cobblestones, smelled the malodorous gutters, saw the bright colors of the bishop's robes. She imagined the glint of the jewel-encrusted crown of the many Kings of Hungary and the Holy Roman Empire as one by one they were crowned at St. Martin's Cathedral.

Daisy clutched her guidebook, staring up to the illuminated buildings. A gloved hand touched her back.

"Have you seen the view from Michalska Brana, the main gate?"

Daisy whirled around, her black coat swinging against the legs of a silver-haired man dressed quite formally. He had a dark gray overcoat and immaculately shined shoes. He gestured with his cane.

"You should see it. A magnificent sight, especially at night."

"Is the tower open? I think it closed at five. I missed it."

"Ah, yes, for tourists that is the case," said the distinguished man. She noticed, as he smiled, that his teeth were long and white. "But there are those who have special privileges. You should not miss the opportunity to see the whole of Stare Mesto—the Old Town—from the height of the tower. It is a once-in-a-lifetime experience."

Daisy sensed danger in this elderly man—a shiver of apprehension rocketed up her spine.

And she liked it.

Like Little Red Riding Hood, she thought. Man, look at those teeth. Maybe they're dentures, she thought. People that old don't have such white teeth, unless they're movie stars.

Yet she liked the jolting tingle she felt, to discover what mystery lay ahead. *A once-in-a-lifetime experience*. It was better than staring at the ceiling in her hotel room.

"Allow me to introduce myself. I am Pavol Kovac."

"I'm . . . Violet Jones. Nice to meet you."

"How charming. You were named for a flower," said the stranger.

Daisy lips met in a thin line.

"You know, Violet, I could accompany you to the tower. I have the key, thanks to contributions I have made to the city of Bratislava over the years."

"You do? I mean, you really have a key?"

"Of course, I am a benefactor of the reconstruction of Stare Mesto."

"You must have made some awesome donation."

"Yes," he said. "Come this way. I will show you."

The lights bathed the tower rising over the arched gate. The round copper copula, green with age, stabbed the night sky.

"Come this way," said Daisy's companion. "We must enter the side door."

The corridor was pitch black. Daisy heard the scuttle of mice.

"Let me lead the way," said the stranger, pulling a small flashlight from his overcoat pocket.

Climbing the stairs, they passed exhibits of armor and weapons throughout the ages. Every floor was dedicated to warfare, weapons, and instruments of torture from the Dark Ages to the nineteenth century.

Daisy pulled out her own headlamp, focusing the beam on a huge metal structure in the form of a woman.

She stopped in her tracks.

"What is that?"

"Ah, you have found her!" her companion said, directing the flashlight beam at the monstrosity. "That, my dear, is an iron maiden, one of the most vicious tools of torture of the sixteenth and seventeenth centuries."

He flashed the beam on the wrought copper face of the maiden. Then he hooked his bony fingers around the edges of cover, pulling it open.

Daisy's headlight beam illuminated the dozens of sharp spikes within. She approached the maiden and ran her finger across one of the spikes. It tore at her glove.

"If a prisoner is to be—dispatched," he said, "he or she would be thrust inside, against the spikes, and then the front of the maiden slammed shut."

"Oh my God," whispered Daisy. In the silence she heard the muffled sound of footsteps far below.

The stranger stared at her.

"Why are you looking at me like that?" she asked.

"Why do you wear black clothes and paint your skin white?"

"What? Because I like it," said Daisy. "Why do you wear a black cape and look like Dracula?"

The stranger laughed. The throaty sound made her jump as it ricocheted around the tower. Pigeons roosting in the windowsills launched themselves into the darkness, their wings scraping the windows. The stranger led the way up the last flight of stairs.

"Here we are," he said, opening the door to the balcony that encircled the base of the cupola. "For you, my charming night companion."

He gestured grandly at the sight of Stare Mesto, its buildings and fountains illuminated in pools of light.

Daisy drank in the sight, the ancient buildings clustered in twisting cobblestone streets. The gray stone cathedral of St. Martin's, a massive presence. From this vantage point, she could see almost all of the old city.

She listened intently. The only sound was the dripping of the rain gutters. It was late and there were few passersby at this end of town. Most of the action now was in the nightclubs and bars outside the walls of the Stare Mesto. Then she heard a burst of laughter and conversation from the street far below.

Daisy gazed down at a small cluster of young people who were approaching the gate. She noticed they stopped talking as soon as they entered the tunnel through the Michalska Gate. She craned her neck, looking down to watch them emerge from the other side. Her view was partially blocked by the stone supporting the balcony.

"Why did they stop talking?" she asked.

"It is a superstition," the stranger said. "They must be students. It is said if a student speaks when passing through the Michalska Gate, he will fail his exams. The Slovakians are very superstitious."

"Are you?" asked Daisy.

"I am Hungarian," he answered. Daisy noticed the skin puckered around his mouth when he spoke. His lips pulled back, exposing his teeth.

She stared at them in the darkness. *What a set of choppers.*

"There is a great difference between Hungarians and Slovaks, the Conquerors and the Conquered."

Daisy was about to ask him about the difference, when his knees buckled.

"Oh, oh!" said the stranger, leaning against the wall. He breathed heavily.

"Are you all right?" asked Daisy.

"Forgive me, my dear. I have to admit I am feeling a bit woozy from the climb."

"Let me help you—"

"No, no. I will descend and wait for you at the bottom of the stairs."

"I'll go with you—" said Daisy.

"No, that's not necessary. You must have a few moments to admire the beauty of the city. I will be at the door when you come down. Please do not worry about me."

He disappeared through the door, closing it behind him before she could protest.

Then she heard the turn of the lock.

"What the fuck?" she said. She turned her headlight beam on the door handle, and pushed down hard. The door was locked.

"You crazy bastard!" she said. "Hey, let me out of here!"

Daisy pulled at the door, then kicked it furiously. She heard the slap of footsteps on the wet street below her. The white-haired man had emerged. He was speaking to a large blond man. They both strode back to the entrance of the tower.

She knew she had only minutes to act.

Chapter 64

Janos's eyes adjusted slowly to the darkness. The air in the church was laced with mildew. There was no art adorning the stone walls. The only focus of the splintered pews was the simple altar and its pair of flickering candles.

A man in black clerical robes knelt in the front pew. He rose to his feet.

"Merry Christmas."

"Ah, I suppose it is past midnight. Merry Christmas to you, Father."

"May I help you, my son?" he said. "I am Pastor Ponikenusz."

"I am Janos Szilvasi, horsemaster to Countess Bathory."

A shadow crossed the pastor's face.

"I see," said Ponikenusz, extending his hand. Janos noticed the stiff formality in the handshake.

"I have come to speak with you." Janos leaned close to the pastor's ear. "But our conversation must be private. I am a friend of Vida's."

Ponikenusz's eyes brightened in the darkness. He studied Janos's face carefully.

"I remember now," he said, nodding. "You are the one who delivered her to the cunning woman."

"The girl was mad with pain."

"I am pleased you have come to the house of the Lord. There is no more private place to speak. We have no knaves hiding in chapels or spies in dark corners. Our humble church has nothing but this one room for the faithful. Sit, my son. Please."

"I have spoken to Count Thurzo," said Szilvasi. "He has told me that you have buried the bodies of scores of girls."

"Yes, this is God's own truth. But I have told the Countess I shall not continue to do so."

"Were they murdered?"

Ponikenusz moistened his lips. "What interest do you have in their deaths, Horsemaster?"

"I will not knowingly serve a murderess, Father. I will seek justice."

Pastor Ponikenusz bowed his head. "Yes," he said at last, "they were murdered." He looked directly into Szilvasi's eyes in the half-light. "There is no doubt. Brutally tortured, their bodies mutilated, God bless their innocent souls."

"Tortured. And then she sent them to be interred in the church yard?"

"With full church rites. She insisted on that. Making up lies about their deaths when all one has to do is examine them to see the truth. Devoid of blood, drained through their open veins. I bless their souls, but now I have refused to allow our cemetery to be the repository of her diabolical cruelty."

Janos cast his eyes about the simple church, which was cold and gloomy. The wax of the crude candles gave off an acrid smell.

"Diabolical?"

"The Countess Bathory enjoys the suffering of others. Those who escape alive bring stories of naked girls whipped, their private parts burned, their breasts bitten by the Countess herself, as if she were a rabid dog."

Janos thought of Zuzana.

"You have great courage to challenge the Countess," said Janos.

"I am a servant of God," said Ponikenusz. "I cannot condone the deeds of a murderess. I must protect the lives and souls of the faithful. That is why I approached the Palatine Thurzo and have written our King."

Janos extended his hand to the priest.

"Then we are brothers in this common purpose—to bring her murderous deeds to the light of justice."

"The Countess shall most certainly be judged before God," said the pastor, looking past Janos's shoulder to the cross on the altar. "It is earthly justice I doubt."

Chapter 65

race sighed, tears leaving a wet trail down her face.

From her calculations, today must be Christmas. Betsy must be worried sick. A flicker of a memory shot through her mind, that disastrous Christmas in Carbondale when she had gotten so drunk on plum brandy. The first Christmas after her husband died.

No. Was murdered. He was murdered. And now would this madman murder her?

Why had she not been suspicious that night in the hotel in Piestany?

She shook her head, remembering the night she was kidnapped.

The Hotel Thermia dining room was opulent, hung with chandeliers that glittered in the mirrors. She had been seated in the front of the room, looking out the floor-to-ceiling windows to the lit garden beyond.

She had ordered garlic soup, a Slovak specialty, to take the chill from her bones. She had spent the day walking the ruins of Čachtice Castle, comparing her seventeenth-century sketch to the rocky remains. The wind was bitter, and the stones glinted with frost. The footing was treacherous. She had seen only five other visitors in the course of the day, hidden in mufflers and overcoats. They snapped a few photos and hurried back down the steep path to get out of the wind.

There inside the Hotel Thermia it was warm, even if cavernous. She nodded to the waitress, who took her order.

"I would like the *diviak lesny*—wild boar?—in sour cherry sauce," said Grace, suddenly famished.

The Slovak girl smiled at the American woman's attempt to speak in her native language.

"*Dobre*," she said, writing down the order. Then she wound her way through the many tables, which were crowded with overweight Germans, Arabs, Russians, and Hasidic Jews who had come to Piestany to take the waters.

When the waitress returned, she set a flute of champagne on the table.

"I didn't order this," said Grace.

"No, the man at table there did," said the waitress inclining her head to the left discreetly. "In . . . *smoking* . . .?"

"Tuxedo," Grace corrected.

Grace turned to see the gray-haired man rise from the table. She wanted to find her glasses so she could see him more clearly. He accepted a winter cape from the waiter, buttoned the clasp, and took a silver-tipped cane.

He bowed low to Grace, in an exaggerated, old-fashioned manner.

Grace dipped her head in acknowledgement and mouthed, "Thank you."

"Tell me who he is," she whispered to the waitress.

"All I know is that he is a count. From Hungary, I think, but his Slovak is perfect. He dines here a few times a year."

The man left, turning his caped back on the women watching him.

After feasting on wild boar, buttered potatoes, and caraway-spiked cabbage, Grace refused dessert. The half bottle of Zumberg Cabernet had gone straight to her head, accompanied by the champagne sent by the stranger.

She drank strong black coffee, lingering over the cup. The laws for DUI in Slovakia were stiff and she had to remember the way back to the pension.

When she finally felt clear-headed, she rose, staring at the table where she had seen the stranger. A cold finger touched the base of her spine.

It was raining hard outside when the valet brought her the rented car. Wet leaves plastered the windshield. The valet made a desultory attempt to clear them off.

She took off into the driving rain, across the bridge from the island toward the village of Moravany Nad Vahom.

Then she felt steel against her temple.

"Drive carefully, Dr. Path, or you will kill us both."

The car swerved, making the gun barrel knock against her head. She regained control, looking straight ahead. Her knuckles clenched white on the steering wheel.

"What do you want?" she said. "You can have my purse."

"Oh, no, that will not please my master at all, I am afraid. Turn right at the end of the bridge. There is a car waiting for you."

Chapter 66

She must be here, you fool!" shouted the Count. "She was locked out on the balcony. I locked the door there myself!"

"I swear to you she has disappeared, Count Bathory. Come and see for yourself."

The Count struggled up the stairs, breathing hard at the second climb that night.

His servant, a blond man with large shoulders, walked behind him. When they reached the top floor, the servant unlocked the door to the balcony.

The lights on the buildings of Stare Mesto had been extinguished. Now the only light came from street lamps and a few shop windows.

"Jiri, this door has been locked the whole time?"

"Yes, Count. I swear to you."

The Count lifted his lip in a snarl, exposing his long teeth. He directed the beam of his flashlight on the platform that ringed the turret.

"You go this way, I will go the other. She has to be here. Be ready."

They walked in opposite directions, two shafts of light slicing the dark night.

Invisible but terrifyingly close, Daisy covered her face with the black sleeves of her Goth gown. The dress had made the climb difficult, but now she was glad to have the dark cloth to cover her too-white face. She had already ripped her dress to make a rope of black crepe to secure her as she climbed off the balcony and behind the supporting stones of the underlying platform.

She pressed her body as close as she could to the cold, wet stones.

"Fool!" said the Count.

"She has disappeared," muttered Jiri. "She is a witch!"

"Shut up, incompetent Slovak moron," said the Count, striking his cane against the servant's leg. "Call the driver."

Daisy only heard gibberish, *Slovak, maybe?* Unintelligible. The voices faded as the men circled the tower one more time. She huddled under her black coat, blinking sudden snowflakes from her eyes. She threaded the twisted length of crepe fabric through the wrought-iron bars, hoisting herself up, her boots braced against the stucco, until she felt the rim of the platform against her soles.

She soundlessly straddled the iron railing as easily as mounting a horse. She slid silently over it, and pulled off her boots. In her stocking feet, she crept to the open door. As the two men played their lights over the ground below, she made her way quickly and silently down the circular staircase and out the ground-level door into the darkness of the shadows of Michalska Gate. She pressed herself against the wall as a black limousine drove to the door of the turret.

The license plate gleamed just feet in front her as the taillights shone red and the chauffeur left the car idling.

The EU symbol of a ring of gold stars orbited above the white "SK" for "Slovakia." The license plate was PP—586.

Daisy's shaking hand had trouble getting the key to turn in the lock of the hotel's front door.

The receptionist opened the door, bleary-eyed from watching a soccer match on television.

"There is trick to it," he said as he opened the bolt and let her in. "You have to turn it twice counterclockwise, not once. I think it is different from American locks, no?"

He smiled at the girl, but then quickly registered the fear in her eyes. Tucked under her arm she carried her leather boots that dripped onto her soggy overcoat. Her woolen stockings were torn and muddied.

"Are you all right, Miss?"

"What does 'PP' stand for in a license plate?" she gasped.

"'PP'? I think it is Poprad, near the border with Poland. The High Tatra Mountains," said the clerk. "Did you get hit by a car?"

"No," she muttered. "It just missed me."

Chapter 67

Draska woke to a strong smell of ammonia. She covered her nose in disgust, opening her swollen eyes as best she could.

The woman in the barred cell next to her squatted over a plastic bucket, urinating.

"Where am I?" Draska muttered. Her mouth tasted like dry cotton, her tongue thick. Her head ached, pounding at her temples. The air was dank.

"Ah, you are awake at last," said the woman, urine still splashing into the filthy bucket. "We thought they had drugged you to death. You've been unconscious for days."

"How long—where am I?" Draska struggled out from under a blanket on a soiled mattress. She tried to focus her eyes in the dim light, the room illuminated only by burning torches.

"We don't know," whispered the woman, as she pulled up her dirty leggings. "We don't know where we are. Or why. All we know is that ghoulish men and women bring us food and water. We hear screaming, pleas for help."

"What?"

"It's true," said a voice with an English accent. "Please speak in English, I can't understand but a little Slovak."

"Why we here?" Draska tried to find words in the foreign tongue.

"We are all kidnapped in Bratislava. At night, near nightclubs or bars."

Draska pulled her dirty blue hair from her eyes so she could see better. She already knew much more than she wanted to know.

The English woman added, "There is a white-haired freak called Count Bathory who questions us. Where did they kidnap you?"

Draska shook her head, trying to clear the drugged confusion.

"From above. I worked for Count Bathory."

The other girls jumped away from the bars, staring at her in horror.

Chapter 68

Zuzana came upon Janos at the river below the castle. He was wrapped in a thick woolen blanket, motionless. Frost had collected on his hair, coloring it white, as if he had aged overnight.

"Janos! Are you—"

He did not answer, his open eyes did not blink. The white stallion stood motionless at his side.

"Wake up, Janos. Wake up!" she said, shaking the immobile figure. Her face creased in terror.

She shook him hard. He did not respond, his eyes staring blindly at the moving water.

The horse reached out with its soft muzzle, nudging him.

Janos blinked. He looked up at Zuzana, with no recognition in his eyes.

"Janos! Are you ill?" she asked, her hands frantically moving over his face, trying to bring it back to life. "Do you have the falling disease?" She wanted to scream.

"No, no. Do not worry," he whispered, his voice still sounding far away. "I am . . . listening."

"You will die of cold. Look at the ice on your hair, your eyebrows. How long have you been here?"

Janos looked around slowly at the frozen edge of the River Vah, the light reflecting off its surface.

"Perhaps—all night?"

"We must get you to the castle at once! You are as cold as a graveyard bone."

"I am all right," he said, rousing himself slowly from his position.

"What are you doing here?"

He looked at her eyes, stormy blue in worry. "I needed to think."

"Think by the warmth of a fire, you fool!"

"Too many distractions. It is difficult to explain."

"It is madness, that's all."

"No, Zuzana. The world is a torrent of madness, I need to hear beyond. I have had these spells since I was a child. They are normal and healing for me."

The stallion nuzzled his neck.

"Must you be so alone that you risk freezing to death?'

"I was not alone. I was with my horse."

Chapter 69

Palatine Thurzo was brought before King Matthias, who was seated in an enormous high-backed chair, playing chess with Counselor Klesl. The King looked up, annoyed.

"You look hard traveled, Count Thurzo," he said, surveying him. "What matter keeps you away from Court?"

Klesl stood up, bowing to the king, and moved a few paces back.

"I have been overseeing business in upper Hungary," responded Thurzo. "And meeting with commanders on the Ottoman Front. I wanted to see with my own eyes what progress the royal army has made. I will give you a full report tomorrow."

The King grunted. "And naturally you would have taken lodging in the Bathory family castles behind the front lines?"

"Your Majesty, they are my relatives—my wife's cousins, aunts, and uncles. And mine. Of course I would enjoy their hospitality."

"Perhaps you had time to meet with family members in your travels. How did they embrace the news of a murderess staining the Bathory name?"

"Your Majesty?"

"Thurzo!" the King shouted, pounding his fist on the oak armrest. "Are you loyal to me or to your Bathory relatives?"

"I am forever loyal, steadfast and true to the Habsburg crown," said Thurzo, bowing low and fingering his velvet cap in his hand.

"Yet, Thurzo, you do not convince me that your devotions are not divided. I ask you again. What say the Bathorys of Erzsebet's murderous ways?"

"They beg you send our cousin to a convent," said Thurzo, lowering his eyes before the King. "She would spend the rest of her days behind the church's walls."

"Ah. Of course, a convent," sniffed the King. "An ironic place for the remaining years of a Calvinist-turned-Lutheran countess. She will never be heard of again, and her riches would remain in the Bathory family, except for a handsome dowry paid to the Catholic Church."

Thurzo touched his beard, and then dropped his hand to his side.

"The family pleads with you, King Matthias, to keep the secret of her vicious bloodletting. If the common people learn there is truth to the rumors, we will have peasant uprisings as we did forty years ago. Our family—*your* allies—will be in danger. Your political and military strength on the Hungarian Ottoman front will be compromised."

"Do you not think the Countess should be tried for her blood crimes?"

"Let the family convince her to enter a convent, I beg you, Your Majesty."

"NO!" roared the King, slashing the air with his bejeweled hand. "Neither I, nor any Habsburg, shall be blackmailed by the Bathory family!"

"Your Majesty!"

"Gabor Bathory betrays the Crown and bargains with the devil himself in Constantinople. Loyal servants have reported two envoys have been sent to the Sultan on Gabor's behalf!"

"Gabor is indeed a Bathory, but he does not represent—"

"No, Thurzo. Hear me: You shall apprehend the Countess and bring proof of her crimes to me. She shall be tried before Parliament.

The Bathory name shall be a curse word in the mouth of generations to come. Bring me proof!"

"My Lord—the girls who have disappeared or died are servants. Lawful conduct—"

"No," said the King, looking again at the chessboard. He made a swift move, capturing Klesl's knight. His frown eased in satisfaction. He turned to Count Thurzo, knowing that the Count was very much aware of what the King was about to tell him.

"My distinguished Palatine . . . the Countess has made a fatal move. She invites daughters of impoverished noblemen to Čachtice. Should she lay a finger on those girls, the House of Bathory will fall. As King and defender of the law, I shall see that Erzsebet Bathory is tried and beheaded."

And that, thought the King, *is how the game is played.*

Chapter 70

Daisy, a blanket wrapped around her damp shoulders, accepted the clerk's offer of *slivovica*—Slovak plum brandy—and sipped it slowly. She tried to stop her body from trembling.

"Let me escort you to your room," said the clerk. He flipped up a sign at the desk that read I WILL RETURN MOMENTARILY. "You should take a hot shower. I can bring you food, yes?"

"No. No, thank you. I just want to rest."

The man pressed the button for the glass elevator.

"I am so sorry, *Slecna*. We have so little crime here. But now, with this killer loose, it is not safe for any girl."

He took her room key and unlocked the door. He snapped on the lights and gasped.

"Holy shit!" said Daisy.

The room had been torn apart, ransacked. The mattress was flipped over, her clothes strewn across the floor. Her empty backpack was tossed in a corner.

Daisy shook uncontrollably, her teeth chattering.

"I will call the police immediately," said the clerk. "You will stay next door, take hot shower now. I will pack up your belongings and deliver them. Put on chain. Do not open the door for anyone."

He muttered something in Slovak, switching off the lights. He hurried down the stairs to get a key to the vacant room.

Daisy stared out the window at the falling rain. Then she remembered the ledger in the safe. She entered the code.

It was still there.

Chapter 71

HOTEL THERMIA
PIESTANY SPA ISLAND, SLOVAKIA
DECEMBER 25, 2010

The Hotel Thermia restaurant manager, Ludomir Mylnar, called the waitress Dalena into his wood-paneled office and explained the situation in rapid Slovak. Betsy noticed how the woman threw anxious glances toward the manager and picked at her cuticles.

"This American woman, she is your mother?" asked the young woman in English.

"Yes," said Betsy, her eyes stinging with tears.

Dalena's face softened.

"Please tell me anything you can remember about that night," said Betsy, wiping her eyes. "You and the valet were the last people to see her."

"Yes, I want to help," said Dalena, looking at Betsy and then to the hotel manager. "She ate alone, at a table in front, looking out to garden. She was kind, she spoke a little Slovak. She had gray hair."

"Yes," said Betsy.

"She left a good tip."

"She would."

"And I remember. She was sent glass of champagne."

"By whom?" said Betsy.

Dalena looked up at the manager. He nodded for her to continue.

"Count Bathory."

Betsy froze. "*Bathory?*"

"Yes," said the manager. "He is man of great wealth who takes the waters here. Bathorys have come for cures at Piestany for centuries."

"Centuries?"

"Even Countess Erzsebet Bathory would take the cure. Her attendants set up tents by the hot springs of the River Vah. She would spend weeks here, bathing and purging. It's part of the history of Piestany."

"And this Count Bathory? Who is he?"

"Some say he is direct descendant. The Count has been coming here since he was little boy, I am told. He is elderly gentleman now."

"Why would he buy my mother champagne?"

"She is an attractive woman, no?" said the manager.

Betsy shrugged.

John offered. "Yes, for a woman her age. Quite intelligent and lively."

"Perhaps he was making—gesture to the lady," said Mylnar.

"Did he leave with her?"

"No. He left before," said Dalena. "I remember him gesturing farewell with his cane."

"And the valet brought the car around for her?" asked John.

"Yes. We have checked," said the manager. "She tipped the valet. He remembers her distinctly."

"Did anyone follow her?" asked Betsy.

"No one knows," said Mylnar.

"Where does this Count Bathory live?" asked John.

The manager looked uncomfortable.

"You must have a billing address, right?" asked John. "Telephone number?"

"We cannot divulge that information," said Mylnar.

"You don't understand," said Betsy. "My mother has disappeared! She was probably kidnapped!"

"There is no reason to think that because a gentleman buys a lady a drink, that he is guilty of kidnap. She left alone."

"Yes, but her car was found abandoned just over the bridge. Someone—"

"I am sorry, Madam. I cannot discuss the personal information of a guest."

John rose from his chair. "I don't think you understand. If you don't give us this information now, we will get it through the police and with the help of the American Embassy. That would bring a lot of unwanted publicity to Hotel Thermia."

The manager jutted out his chin. "I repeat. I cannot divulge this information about one of our guests."

Betsy closed her eyes, composing herself, then she stood.

"I thank you, Mr. Mylnar," she said, "for your cooperation, at least as far as my mother's last meal with you. And especially you, Miss," she added, nodding to the waitress.

The waitress stared down at the carpet.

"I think you can expect a visit from Detective Whitehall, who is working with the Bratislava police," said John. "I believe Count Bathory's whereabouts will be of great interest to them."

John opened the door for Betsy, who hurried out into the hall, her face covered with her spread fingers. He knew she would not want anyone to see her cry.

Mylnar tugged at John's sleeve.

"I didn't want to alarm the lady's daughter," said the manager. "But you aren't the first to inquire about Dr. Grace Path. A tall blond man with blue eyes was asking about her a week before."

"An American man? A Slovak?"

"No, he had a distinct Hungarian accent. He asked if I know the whereabouts of Dr. Path, that he was a research associate from Budapest. I told him I had never heard of the lady but would he like to leave a note for her in case she should come to the spa or restaurant."

"He smiled at me. A smile that chilled my bones. 'No message,' he said. 'I will find her.'"

John was digging for the rental car key in his pocket when Betsy's phone rang.

"It's Daisy," she said.

"That's all you need," said John, looking back across the parking lot to the illuminated entrance of the Hotel Thermia Spa and Restaurant. Snow blew, intermittently obscuring the building.

"Get in the car," said John. "I'll start the heater up."

Betsy listened in horror as Daisy told her about the stranger and being locked in the tower, how the room had been ransacked, but the ledger was safe.

"Daisy!" said Betsy, her words rushing. "Are you all right?"

"Yes. Just dirty and banged up from climbing. You got my e-mail, right? I was cold, like totally shivering. But the hot shower helped a little."

"You were probably in shock."

"I'm OK."

"Can't you—could you promise me to stay in the hotel until we get back?"

"And when is that? I can't just sit in a hotel room rotting away. And I want to catch that dick who locked me out on the tower."

"NO!"

"What do you mean, no?"

"I mean—"

John grabbed the phone from Betsy.

"Daisy, you are going to have to believe Betsy. The strange old man who tried to trap you is a lunatic—and deadly."

"Well, he is not going to keep me locked in a bedroom in Bratislava for days. He is just an old looney-tunes with pearly whites. Besides—

I can go without my Goth makeup, put my hair in a hat, no one will—"

"What did you say he looked like?"

"He's an old guy with a cape, white hair."

"Did he have a cane? A silver-tipped cane?"

"Yeah! How did you know?"

"Just stay inside the hotel, Daisy. That 'old guy' could be more dangerous than you can imagine."

Chapter 72

Janos was racked by a high fever. Convulsions shook his body. He lay delirious as the fever consumed his body, seized his mind.

"Oh, Janos," murmured Zuzana into his ear. Erno Kovach had sent for her in the dead of night, thinking a woman's touch might heal. After all, it had been Zuzana who had run for help, begging Guard Kovach to send a wagon to bring the delirious horsemaster back to the castle.

Zuzana sat beside Janos's barrack cot all night. She rinsed her linen rag in a bucket of icy water, mopping his sweating forehead. Her hands were red with the cold.

"I told you that the river mists would freeze your blood and make you sick," she whispered. "But you had to listen to the voices."

She got the stable boys to help her and together they carried Janos to the barrack's kitchen. Despite the burning heat of his fever, she knew he needed the warmth of the fire to fight the river chill that had attacked him.

Janos groaned, writhing on the straw pallet by the fire. His fists clenched and unclenched. Then he roared, throwing his head back against the rag-stuffed pillow, as if wrestling an invisible demon.

"Stand back, *Slecna*! He has the river devils within him," said the cook, pulling her away. "The spirits come out at night in the mists, preying on the soul of a good man. Sure as do the witches."

"I will not stand back," Zuzana said, shaking the cook's hand off her arm. She wet her towel and mopped again at Janos's sweating brow, as he heaved ragged breaths. "He is my childhood friend!"

The cook grumbled and cursed but went back to his iron cauldron. He watched from the corner of his eye as the young woman with the poxed face soothed the delirious man.

Maybe the demons will leave her be, frightened by her pitted face, he thought. *Anyone as ugly as that has no fear of witches.*

An hour later, he handed her an earthen bowl filled with meat broth to spoon-feed her patient. Zuzana nodded her head at his kindness.

"You are indeed a good friend of the horsemaster," said the cook.

She did not seem as homely as before. The light of the fire played a strange trick, coloring her face rosy and glowing.

It is her soul that shines through, thought the cook. He chastised himself for his earlier judgment.

"The horsemaster is blessed to have you at his side," said the cook. "And I am an old fool."

When the Countess learned of the horsemaster's illness that morning, she insisted he be moved out of the barracks and inside the castle to a proper bedchamber.

"His father is a nobleman. I shall not have it rumored at court in Vienna that he has died of negligence at Čachtice Castle. Make up a bedroom for him, one that has a window that opens to sunlight."

Zuzana curtsied and said she would make the arrangements.

"He should not be moved away from the smell of horses," said the cook, when he heard of the plan. "He has a connection with them that is deep and unearthly."

Zuzana stared at him, but this time she did not berate the wiry man for his superstitions.

"Cut a lock of hair from the mane of his white stallion, Cook. I will tuck it under his pillow."

The cook smiled, exposing his crooked teeth. He picked up a sharp knife and headed next door into the stables.

Countess Bathory instructed Brona to make rich broths of bone marrow and root vegetables to give him strength, tea of birch bark to relieve the fever. Zuzana put stones, warm from the fire, into his bed, to warm his body when he shook with cold.

Janos screamed in his nightmares, sweating heavily, rolling violently, as he fought the demons of his fever.

Zuzana gnawed at her fingernails until they bled. She thought of her own fever as a child, the fever and illness that had left its pox scars over her body. What terrors did he wrestle?

That night the fever returned with a vengeance. She was terrified that he would be lost before sunrise. She plucked the strands of the white horse's mane from under his pillow and forced them into his clenched hands.

"Take strength from the moon horse," she whispered. "Take it!"

But instead of quieting her patient, the coarse touch of the horse-hair made him rabid with anger.

"You shall be defeated!" he croaked, his voice hoarse with phlegm. "Your evil soul shall be imprisoned in the stone of your wickedness! You shall be haunted by those you have murdered!"

"Be still, Janos. Be still," crooned Zuzana, holding his forehead to calm its thrashing. She watched the cords of his neck, the clenched jaw. His cries pierced the night.

"What does he say?" said a voice in the shadows.

Zuzana froze. It was the Countess. Her gown rustled as she approached the bed.

"He is feverish, his words make no sense," Zuzana said, standing at attention. *Please do not speak again, Janos. Be still, I beg of you!*

"Sometimes the fevers bring the truth bubbling forth as a mountain spring," the Countess said, her amber eyes cold as jewels. "I asked, what does he say?"

"I cannot make out exactly," said Zuzana, avoiding her mistress's stare.

"Answer me!" Erzsebet raised her hand high to strike the obstinate maiden.

"You shall be encased in stone, the stones that have witnessed your wickedness!" shouted Janos.

"Stones?" the Countess said, lowering her hand. Her black eyebrows arched high over her white face. "How strange."

"He battles demons, Countess."

A flash of fear crossed Bathory's face, as she looked down at the feverish horsemaster. "Stone? Encased in stone?"

"I fear he feels the weight of death upon his chest," said Zuzana, wiping his brow with a wet rag. "Pray, pay no attention—"

"Sharp bones and stony residue! A mortal hell! The eternal prison!" Janos shouted, his lips flecked with foam.

The Countess's face blanched and she pressed a linen handkerchief to her mouth. She flicked her eyes to her handmaiden.

Zuzana saw fear in her eyes like blazing flames.

"Say nothing of this, ever. I command you! He is indeed insane with fever," the Countess said, gathering her skirts. Her quick movements stirred the air, guttering the candle at Janos's bedside.

Chapter 73

After a long interview with the police—supplemented with sandwiches and hot soup the clerk brought up from the restaurant next door—Daisy had fallen into a deep sleep. When she awoke it was past eleven o'clock. She looked restlessly around the four walls of the hotel room.

I can't stay here. I've got to get out of this place.

The incident with the old guy had freaked her out and the last thing she wanted to do was be alone. She had to find some kindred spirits.

Finally, an hour after midnight, Daisy slipped out of the pension, locking the door behind her. She pulled her hood up against the falling snow. She brought along both phones—her own and the one her father had given her—and clicked on the GPS, marking her destination. With a Google Map printout in hand, she navigated through the edge of Stare Mesto toward the modern urban center of Bratislava.

She crossed through the short, dark tunnel of the Michalska Brana Bridge to Zamocnicka Street, where the tires of hurrying cars turned the snow to dirty slush. Nightclub Raucous Scandal was a twenty-minute walk from Michalska Brana, and passing headlights illuminated a different universe. Gone was the fairytale world of

Stare Mesto: the pastel buildings, cobblestone streets, pretty shuttered windows, and old streetlamps of wrought iron.

The streets were asphalt, neon lights screamed. Graffiti in bold colors were scrawled over gray buildings. Young people in hip clothes with boots and trench coats filled the sidewalks. Prostitutes lined the streets, their stiletto heels spiking the dirty ice. A few homeless people slept huddled in the entrances to apartment buildings, their dirty rags and old sleeping bags wrapped tight around their bodies. Police cars prowled, slowing down to monitor groups of pedestrians on the snow-dusted sidewalks.

Punk hair colors—garish blues, purples, and reds—were more common here than her own jet-black Goth hair. Men and women wore a lot of leather, spiked dog collars, or crucifixes that swung on their necks as they stomped down the stairs to the basement club. Several men and women sported Mohawk cuts.

A man with bleached yellow hair, dressed in biker leathers, sat on an orange stool, taking money in his tattooed fist.

"How much?" Daisy asked.

The man smiled, flashing a silver tooth, a glint in his eye. He touched her cheek with his hand, spiraled in a black-and-green snake tattoo.

"For you, Beauty, it's free."

Daisy shied away from his snaked hand but nodded her thanks.

"Go on, shy one," laughed the bouncer.

Daisy made her way to the bar, pressing against leather-clad bodies.

"A beer," she shouted over the Slovak chatter, clashing cymbals, drum beat, and electric guitars.

Several Goths lifted their heads at her English. One girl with streaked red-and-pink hair motioned to her.

"You are American? American Goth?"

"Yes," Daisy said, lifting the frothy beer to her lips. She breathed in the tobacco smoke and the smell of beer that permeated the sticky floorboards. "I wanted to see the Goth scene in Bratislava."

"Ah!" said the girl. "See!" She gestured with a wide sweep of her arm. "We are a happy people."

The two young men with her laughed at her English. A blonde girl, several years younger, said nothing.

"Welcome, American Goth Girl. What is your name?"

"Daisy. Like the flower."

"Ah, I am Jarmila. This is Ignac and Jarak. And my little sister, Lubena."

There was a small stage at the front of the club, where a band banged out "Crazy Goth Girl."

She hides in the shadows

Her clothes are in tatters

A frenzy of pale arms rose in the air, writhing, bracelets jangling, undulating with the music like current-swept coral. A dark-haired singer in leather and spikes strutted the small stage, the microphone pressed to his lips. The guitars on either side of him whined. Daisy noticed the girls' waving hands had fingers bent in the sign of horns.

"Larson. The singer. They love him," nodded Jarmila. "He is mobbed after the show."

Gotta watch your heart

She'll tear it apart

The screaming of the crowd made it difficult to follow the words of the song. Daisy cupped her ear, trying to hear the final verse. But cheering and howls made it nearly impossible. She could make out the collective voice of the crowd: *Crazy Goth Girl.*

Larson whipped off his sunglasses, finishing the song. A screech of feedback made the crowd cover their ears, screaming and cheering. The singer shook his hair from his eyes and looked at the group by the bar. He held up the mike, his black leather gloves cut away at the fingers.

"For luscious Goth girls who like to dress in black!" He pointed at Daisy.

She smiled back at him, canine tooth glinting. The singer feigned a swoon, grasping at his heart.

"I dig that tooth, girl," he said. "Bury it in my neck tonight."

Lubena scowled at Daisy.

"He speaks English," said Daisy.

"They are Scandinavian," said Jarmila. "We have a lot of nationalities here."

The blonde little sister said something in Slovak. She frowned at Daisy.

"My little sister wants to know why you are here."

"I told you already," said Daisy.

The girl stared at her. Daisy stared back until the girl looked away.

Chapter 74

It was near 4 A.M. when the band finally finished. Daisy took a final sip of beer and bid Jarmila, Ignac, and Jarak good-bye. Lubena was not with them.

"Come back tonight again," Jarmila called.

"Then we have breakfast together," yelled Ignac. "I will fry sausages."

It was sleeting now, slowly changing to snow. Daisy pinched her woolen hood close to her chin.

She jumped as she felt a hand on her shoulder.

"Sorry! Didn't mean to scare you. Larson would like you to join him." It was the drummer from the band.

Daisy peeked out at him from under her hood. "OK," she said. "Why not?"

She squinted through the snow and started toward a limo parked just in front of the club. The windshield was streaked with sleet and slush and she could not make out the figures in the car.

With one swipe of the wiper she thought she recognized a figure inside. A silver-haired man was talking to the driver, his pale skin sickly in the muted light of the back street. She stopped in her tracks.

"Not that one!" said the drummer, steering her away by the arm. "We are not 'limo' band." He pointed to a dark van, scrawled with what looked like graffiti. "That's us."

He led her to the van and pulled the door open. A cloud of sweet smoke poured out into the night. Daisy swished the sleet from her crepe dress and climbed in.

"Hey, Gothic Girl," said the lead guitarist, sucking on a pipeful of hash. "You have captured Larson's heart. But you are a baby, aren't you?" Smoke gushed from his mouth, and the drummer grabbed for the pipe.

In the very back of the van sat Larson, glassy-eyed. He patted the seat next to him. Daisy crawled back and sat next to him.

"Ah, but you are even more delicious close up. What's your name?"

"Daisy Hart."

"Heart! Yes, you are my heart, Gothic Girl."

"Not that kind of—"

"Daisy? Like the flower?" said the bass guitarist from the seat in front of her. "That's cool."

"Want a toke, Daisy my Heart?" asked Larson. "We have some coke if you'd rather."

"I'm good."

"You're American, right? What are you doing here?"

"I'm—well, it's complicated."

"Of course, of course," said Larson, his leather jacket squeaking as he slid his arm across the leather upholstery above her. "I expect nothing less."

"Hey, can you—tell me who is in that limousine?"

"In front of us?"

"Yeah. I thought I glimpsed someone I knew."

The lead guitarist blew a lungful of smoke out in a coughing fit. Everyone laughed.

"He's just an old man," said Larson. "He hangs out in that limo after gigs when we play here. Sometimes he gets girls to go in. Maybe they think it is us, that they are going to hang out with the band."

"He never gets out of the car. But his flunkies do," said the lead guitarist. "They bring him girls. Usually they are really wasted."

Daisy looked out through the sleet to see Lubena walking with a man in his twenties, dressed in black leather. He gestured to the limo, and the door opened. Daisy could see the withered hand and a gold ring, and a flash of a silver-tipped cane.

Then she focused on the license plate: PP—586

"Shit!" she said. "That's him!"

"What's the matter, Goth Girl?"

"That guy tried to kidnap me! He's fucking insane!" She scrambled out of the seat.

"Are you serious? That old man?"

"Let me out!"

The door flew open and Daisy bolted out. She pounded on the limo's windows.

"Get out of there, Lubena!"

Lubena pressed her hand against the window, her fingers spread out against the glass. She was mouthing something, screaming. Her eyes were wide in terror.

The limo's engine roared to life.

Daisy started kicking the door with her heavy boots. A second later Larson and the drummer jumped on the trunk, fists pounding the rear window. The bass guitarist threw himself across the windshield.

Daisy ran to the front of the car, pulled out her cell phone, and snapped a picture of the license plate. Then, with a flash of inspiration, she yanked at the metal, forcing the red cell phone between the license and the car's grill.

"Let the girl out!" screamed Larson.

A hand reached out the driver's window, holding a pistol. There was a sharp report, a single shot, and the bass player screamed, clutching his arm. He tumbled off the car as it lurched into reverse, knocking Daisy off her feet. Blood streaked the wet pavement.

Larson went sprawling as the limo sped forward, barely swerving to miss the injured bass player and Daisy.

"Are you all right?" she asked the wounded man. "Jesus, he shot you!"

The bass player moaned, clutching his arm.

"Alex is shot!" shouted the drummer. "Get an ambulance."

Daisy scrambled to her feet, running back to Larson. "Are you OK?"

"Who is that freak?"

"That's what I want to know. He just kidnapped that girl."

Larson looked at her, dazed from his hard fall to the asphalt. He put his hand out, grasping her fingers.

"Look, Daisy! You are bleeding, too."

Daisy looked at her fingers, split open from prying the license plate loose. She searched the wet asphalt as she knelt by Larson. The cell phone wasn't there, it hadn't been jarred loose.

"I'm OK," Daisy said, and she smiled grimly.

It was time to call her sister. She had the GPS tracking information.

Chapter 75

BRATISLAVA, SLOVAKIA
DECEMBER 26, 2010

The cell phone connection was not good in the little café, one of the few still open in the early morning hours before dawn. Daisy was distracted by the echo of her own voice as she told John about the kidnapping of Lubena.

"Bathory? Daisy, are you sure it was Bathory?"

"Absolutely. A guy got shot by this weird fucker."

John exhaled.

"Betsy never wanted to put you into danger. You chose to follow her."

"Our destinies are intertwined."

"Oh, horseshit, Daisy," said John. "Stop saying that! That's putting Betsy in a compromising position."

"What is she saying, John?"

John shook his head at Betsy, scowling.

"We want you to stay in the pension. We want you safe."

"Well, that's not going to happen. I've got a tracer on that limo."

"What?"

"I stuck my other cell phone—the one my dad gave me, with the GPS—behind the license plate. I'm going to track that fucker wherever he goes. And I am going to turn it over to the police. He put a man in the hospital a few hours ago."

"No. No, you can't do that, Daisy."

"Why the hell not? He kidnapped a girl—"

"Because—" John looked at Betsy. "Because it will put Betsy's mother in danger."

"John!"

"I have to tell her."

"Hey, tell Betsy not to worry," said Daisy. "Tell her I already know that her mom's been reported missing at the American Embassy. And I know she is publishing a book on Countess Bathory—"

"How did—"

"If you want the GPS information, I'll give it to you," said Daisy. "They're headed north."

"Where?" said John.

"How do I know? They're still traveling. But if you want to know where they finally stop, and you don't want the police involved, let me help you. I can meet up with you or I'm going by myself. I know they're probably headed for Poprad Presov. That's up on the border of Poland. I can fly there. Poprad Tatry airport. But there's not another flight until the day after tomorrow. I'd get in at 2:00 in the afternoon."

There was silence on the phone line. Then John finally spoke.

"We'll pick you up at the airport," he said. "We'll make our way up north."

Daisy smiled, her cheekbones touching the iPhone's screen.

"See you there. Tell Betsy we're all in this together."

John sighed. "I don't think that's what she needs to hear right now."

Chapter 76

The highway was icy and snow-blown. Huge snowplows burrowed through, plowing a path that John could follow. The storm had let up and a majestic range of mountains rose high on the horizon.

"Gorgeous," murmured John. "Not the Rockies, but certainly beautiful. Saw-toothed."

Betsy pressed her lips together tight, leaving them bloodless.

"Never realized they had mountains like this in Eastern Europe," said John. "I hear the skiing is pretty good—"

"I don't give a flying fuck about the skiing!" shouted Betsy, exploding.

"OK, OK! Calm down."

They passed a red-roofed hotel, built in the spa fashion of a century ago. Steam rose from its thermal pools.

John sighed. "You know, we could—"

"You can drive a little faster now," said Betsy, her back tensing. "It isn't snowing that hard."

"Daisy won't be here until the day after tomorrow," said John. "What's the hurry?"

"My mother! That's the hurry. Daisy could text coordinates to us, couldn't she?"

John shot her a look.

"It wouldn't make any difference, Bets. We really need to take a day to rest up. You are going to eat something, relax, and take a sleeping pill. You haven't slept in days."

"The hell I am! I can't sleep. My mother is probably being held captive by that lunatic—"

"She may be, but you are so damned tired you're about to crash. What kind of clear thinking can you muster up when you can't see straight? You aren't thinking logically. Let's take a day—"

"NO!" she shouted. Then, "Watch out!"

The red brake lights of the snowplow flashed.

John braked as gently as he could, trying not to skid. Ahead were red flares and a roadblock. Several people in dark jackets milled around. One figure approached their car.

John lowered the window and a police officer with an ice-crusted scarf wrapped around his neck bent his head to speak to them.

"We speak English," said John.

"Ah, Americans? OK," said the police officer. "You no go here. Avalanche. Road closed."

"How long?" asked Betsy, her face pinched with anxiety.

"Long?" he said, shaking his head.

John tried.

"Road open tonight? Tomorrow?"

"One day. Two day maybe. Big avalanche."

"Thank you," said John.

"Hotel Thermia. Good food," said the police officer, patting his down-padded tummy like a big bear. "You stay one, two day. Open road."

"Thanks again," said John. The police officer waved, warding off traffic as John turned the car around.

When he looked at Betsy, she had her head in her hands, sobbing.

John had the restaurant send up two bowls of goulash. He set the tray on the table beside the bed where Betsy lay covered in an eiderdown duvet, her eyes swollen and red.

He sat down beside her.

"It will do you good to eat something," John said, stroking her wet hair, fresh from the shower. "And a day of rest will make you think more clearly. Neither of us has any idea what we are up against."

"A monster," said Betsy. "We are up against a fucking monster."

John kept stroking her hair.

"You know that, right?" said Betsy. She propped herself up on her elbow to look at him. The sleeve of the white spa robe slid down her arm.

John sighed, glancing out the window at the starlit night. He knew the jagged Tatra Mountains were there in the darkness.

"Yes. We might be. I want to protect you. You need to sleep. You need to make rational decisions."

Betsy looked into his eyes. She smiled sadly.

"I've never been very good at that, have I, John?"

He didn't answer, but continued caressing her hair.

"I chased you out of my life," she said.

"We were both awfully young, Betsy."

"But I did. I slammed the door on our marriage," she said, putting a hand over his. "I never gave it a chance."

"Your mother was damned angry when we got married. I don't think she ever liked me."

"That's not true. She told me one Christmas after my dad died that she really thought you kept me level-headed. I hated her for it."

They both laughed.

"Here," said John. "Sit up and eat some of the goulash before it gets cold. You need some nourishment."

Betsy nodded and pulled herself to a sitting position against the carved headboard. John placed the warm bowl in her hand.

"Dad used to make goulash when I was little," she said, dipping her spoon in the thick stew. "With lots of paprika."

John dug into his bowl. "I remember. It was wonderful after a ski day."

Betsy tasted, closing her eyes. "This reminds me of his."

She ate silently, each spoonful a memory of her family. John set down his own bowl. He rummaged in his suitcase and pulled out an orange plastic medicine bottle. He shook a pill into his hand.

"Take this, Betsy. Lorazapam."

Betsy stared at the pill.

"You might as well. You need a good night's sleep, sweetheart. Nothing is going happen tomorrow. The road is closed. Daisy gets in to Poprad in two days. Come on."

Betsy looked up at his pleading eyes. She held out her hand.

"Good girl. You'll feel better and think more clearly after a night's sleep. Maybe a good day's sleep."

She set down her empty bowl, nodding her head once. He handed her a plastic water bottle to wash down the pill.

"Will you sleep with me?" asked Betsy, searching his eyes. "I'm scared, John. Like I never have been before."

"I thought you'd never ask," he said.

She shook her head. "You know. Just next to me. Hold me."

He started to unbutton his shirt. There was tenderness in his smile.

"I know," he said. "I know."

Chapter 77

HOFBURG PALACE
VIENNA
DECEMBER 27, 1610

Pastor Ponikenusz hated to travel by horseback, but the message from Zuzana was so dire he had no choice. He had to ride to Vienna. The clergyman of a poor parish could not afford to travel in a coach, wasting the precious thalers of his congregation.

He had borrowed a horse from the livery in Piestany and followed a coach bound for Vienna. The rain and sleet froze on his woolen cape. He shivered, dressed in woolen garments that his congregation had donated over the years, including scratchy leggings that, while warm, bit into his skin as his legs rubbed against the leather of the saddle.

The horse followed the coach, never veering—it was hardly necessary to touch the reins. Ponikenusz's manhood was shaken and pinched beyond Ottoman torture by the time the sun rose over the city of Vienna.

The pastor nearly fell off his horse at the castle gates.

"Count Thurzo has commanded me to present myself before the King."

The guards laughed at the bedraggled clergyman. "At least Catholic priests arrive by coach!"

The guards admitted the poor man to the castle. The footman insisted he bathe and don clean clothes before admitting him to court.

Ponikenusz sighed his gratitude as a bath was drawn for him. But he did not linger a second longer than he had to, for time was essential, a matter of life and death.

"I have come to warn Your Majesty that the Countess Bathory continues her cruel murders and torture."

"Why is it that you come instead of Janos Szilvasi? I was told by Count Thurzo he would make the next report."

"Szilvasi is taken ill. I do not know that he has survived the night. The Countess's handmaiden nurses him within the castle."

The King sat up straight.

"My horsemaster's son is within her castle walls? Ill and vulnerable?"

"He and the Countess Zichy," said Ponikenusz. "But indeed, all the other common maidens who have disapp—"

"Countess Zichy? How fares she?" said the King, his face creased with concern.

"The handmaiden Zuzana says she has disappeared. She went to Countess Zichy's chamber to prepare her toilette, and the young noblewoman was missing."

"Send word to Palatine Thurzo immediately!" roared the King.

"Your Majesty, Palatine Thurzo gathers his witnesses as we speak. I sent word to him, and with your permission, he will arrest her at once."

"By God's grace at last!" shouted the King. He stabbed his finger at Ponikenusz.

"You, clergyman—ride back this night to Čachtice. You shall be witness to Countess Bathory's arrest!"

Chapter 78

Draska feigned sleep as the fuchsia-haired Ona approached, carrying a silver pitcher and a crystal goblet.

"Draska," she whispered. "Draska. *Prosím!* Wake up!"

Draska opened her eyes. Ona's eyes glowed in the dim light.

"Why am I here?"

"You will become one of us."

"What do you mean?" Draska pulled herself up to her knees, her hands on the bars of her cell. "Let me out of here!"

"You don't understand—you are shown great mercy. You betrayed the Count. He knows of your treachery, Draska."

"What—"

Ona set the goblet and pitcher on the stone floor. She reached through the bars and grasped the prisoner's arm.

Draska trembled at her touch.

"You will become one of us."

Ona motioned her chin toward the pitcher and goblet. She released Draska's arm, reached down, and lifted the goblet.

"This is your salvation, Draska," she said.

Draska reached through the bars and grabbed the glass. Perhaps she could use it as a weapon.

"Does my mother ask where I am?" she asked.

"We told her you went to visit your cousin in London. The traitor with whom you betrayed the master."

Draska's heart skipped a beat. She looked at the silver pitcher as Ona lifted it. It was engraved with a filigreed "EB" in raised roses and thorns.

Ona tilted the pitcher side to side, cocking her ear at the slosh of liquid. Her eyes shone, black and luminous.

"What is it?" asked Draska.

"You will see. You will learn to crave it."

A shiver of apprehension slid up Draska's spine.

"God curse you! What is it?"

Ona poured the liquid, thick and red, into the goblet in Draska's outstretched hand. The tang of alcohol stung her nose. A heady, rich red wine.

Draska pulled the glass back through the bars.

She sniffed, detecting another odor.

It smelled metallic.

"Drink," urged Ona.

"What is this?" She tilted the glass, examining the wine. Darker threads swirled through the liquid. The torchlight flickered in the depths of the cut glass.

"It is nourishment. It is the essence of life."

The color drained from Draska's face. "It is blood. Blood and wine," she whispered, her voice trembling.

"Drink it! You will starve if you do not drink it. You will die!"

"I cannot drink blood! You are all insane!"

"Shut up! You fool! You do not know what I risk by initiating you—"

The sound of approaching footsteps interrupted her. Ona stood up from her crouch, looking over her shoulder.

"See what you have done!" she hissed.

Two phantom-pale men approached.

"You are not to talk to her," said one of them.

"I was—"

"Shut up. She is not of the Bathory line."

"She has lived all her life in the castle. But she refuses to drink."

One of the men, with a crewcut and nose ring, sneered at Draska. "Good. Let the traitor die."

The other man, his eye twitching, nodded. "Starve her."

"Better yet—she can be harvested."

The men turned away, laughing. Ona shook her head, giving Draska a look of pity and disgust. Then she snatched the goblet away and followed the men into the darkness.

The Count stared at the portrait of Countess Bathory, mesmerized. Her flawless skin shone polished as a white marble statue. Dark brows arched haughtily over amber eyes. Her dark red hair was swept up, revealing her shell-like ears. Ears that were dainty, belying her power and cruelty.

"Why do you forsake me, Countess?" he asked the painting.

His henchmen had stolen the portrait from the Čachtice village museum decades ago. It now hung in the mahogany-paneled study where he often spent his evenings. His servants had grown accustomed to the Count's murmurings directed to the likeness of his ancestor.

The Count sighed, staring into the depths of his glass of red wine. It was a rich ruby Margaux, a heady vintage. He swirled his glass, making the wine lick the higher reaches of the goblet.

"I have created a world in your image," he said. "I have killed the one man who threatened to reveal my secrets in order that I might serve you unobstructed. There is no one to stand in our way now."

Then he pinched up his face as he thought about the missing ledger.

"Why do you not appear, my lady? This is your celebration."

He took a long draught of his wine.

"I beg of you, return to your rightful place among those who worship you. I have dedicated my life to your memory."

His lips curled in a cruel smile.

"I think you will be pleased when you see what we have planned."

Chapter 79

Vida heard that Ponikenusz had left for Vienna. The chatter in the tavern was that he left trailing the night coach in order to address the King.

"They say that Janos Szilvasi is near death with a fever," said the barkeeper.

"Who nurses him?" said a bearded patron, taking a deep draught of his beer.

"They say it is the poxed one who sits by his bedside. The Countess has taken him into the castle."

"She will kill him!" said another patron, a dog curled at his feet.

The barkeeper shook his head and wiped a dirty rag across a table.

"Her tastes are for women's blood, not men's."

Not if she thinks he is an informant to the King, thought Vida, throwing her woolen shawl over her shoulders.

She pulled the iron ring on the heavy wooden door. A cold wind lacerated her ankles as she hurried out.

Aloyz brought Vida to the scullery, knocking at the splintered door. He had thrown a dark blanket over the girl's head and shoulders so she wouldn't be recognized until she was safe among the women she trusted.

Hedvika, as always, had accompanied the Countess to the dungeon to play the nightly games.

"Vida!" exclaimed the other maidens. "How we have missed you!"

"But do you dare return?" asked one. "The mistress will punish you—"

"She will take you to the dungeon," whispered another. "Countess Zichy has—"

"What's all this?" growled a voice.

The women stopped breathing.

In the doorway stood Brona the cook, wooden ladle in her hand.

The girls stood in front of Vida, trying to hide her from view.

"Get away," Brona said, swatting them with her ladle. "You think I don't know a dear daughter has returned? Come here, child."

She embraced Vida, then stepped back. "Let me see your hands, girl."

Vida opened her palms. The young girl's face flinched with pain.

The wounds had scarred to thick pink and white flaps of skin, edged in black char. Only a little pus oozed from them. The cunning woman's remedies had saved her hands.

"I will take you myself to Szilvasi and Zuzana. The rest of you stay here," Brona said. Then she shot a look at the knot of girls, their faces drawn with fear.

"Warn us if you hear the Countess emerge from the dungeon. And," Brona said looking them over one by one, "if anyone betrays this child, I will poison your food, I swear by all that is holy."

Chapter 80

The cook's candle spilled a pool of light in the dark hall, as she led Vida up a turret stairway, then stopped and rapped her heavy knuckles against a door.

It opened a crack, just enough for Vida to see white bed sheets and then a sliver of a scarred face at the wedge of the open door.

"Vida!" gasped Zuzana, opening the door wide. She set her candle on the table and went to hug her friend.

Brona smiled, watching the two young women, but her smile vanished as she saw the fevered Janos clawing the air with his outstretched fingers.

"NO!" he screamed. "Leave her alone!"

Vida stared as Brona rushed in, her skirts flying.

The cook caught the horsemaster's flailing hand in midair.

"Just as I thought," she said, kissing the fevered man's hand. "See the scar beside his little finger."

Zuzana gaped at the cook, who cradled the hand of her sick friend. "His mother said he caught it in a well rope."

"Bolt the door," Brona whispered. She said nothing until the plank was slid across the door.

"No rope did this," Brona said, spitting out the words in excitement. She wiped her mouth with the back of her hand. "It was cut with a knife—"

"What? Why would she—" said Zuzana

"He is a Taltos. I am sure of it," said the cook.

"What?" asked Vida. "What makes you say that?"

"That scar," said Brona. "He had a sixth finger. His mother must have cut it off. They would have killed him if they'd found it."

Zuzana studied Janos's hand in hers. She rubbed her fingertip over the scarred edge of flesh at the outside of his his little finger.

"Killed him?" said Zuzana

"The Bathorys," whispered Brona. "The King. They all fear the power of the Taltos."

Vida shook her head. "That scar doesn't prove—"

The cook dismissed her objection with a wave of her thick hand. "His talent with horses, how he whispers to them. Listen, it is a vision he sees now in his fevered head."

"What?" said Zuzana.

"He has come to save us," said the cook, glancing at the suffering man. "It is he who will defeat the Countess."

Vida and Zuzana stared at the young horsemaster.

"How can he possibly help now?" whispered Zuzana, folding his waving hand into her own, bringing it to her lips, then lowering it, nestling the scarred hand against his heaving chest as if returning a baby bird to a nest. "He's dying."

Chapter 81

Draska's mother, Mathilde, the castle cook, banged her fist against the Count's chamber door. The delicate wood, painted with Venetian motifs, flexed under the assault.

"I know you are in there!" she bellowed. She rattled the brass handle. "Open the door or I am calling the police. Now!"

Ivan, one of the Count's manservants, opened the door. He stared at the cook, menace burning in his eyes.

"Stand aside," Mathilde said, her broad hips pushing past him.

Ivan grabbed her meaty arm, digging his thin fingers deep into her flesh.

"He cannot be disturbed now."

Mathilde wrestled her arm away from him.

"Then you cannot stop me from calling the police. My daughter is not with her cousin in London—that was all a dirty lie!"

"Mathilde, Mathilde," cooed a voice from within the recesses of the bedchamber.

"Count Bathory? I must see you at once."

"Enter, my dear. Enter. It is not often I entertain my family's most loyal servant in my boudoir."

The Count wore a crimson satin smoking jacket. He balanced a stack of newspapers on his lap.

"Come, sit down Mathilde."

"I didn't come to sit, Count Bathory. My daughter is missing and I was purposely given false information about her whereabouts."

"Oh, really? How's that? I am often left out of the loop with the household comings and goings."

"Ivan here came to tell me that Draska was called away immediately, that she had traveled to London—"

"Oh, yes," Ivan insisted, "Draska told me about a cousin being very ill."

Mathilde pressed her lips together tightly. Her nostrils flared. "Her cousin is fine. Draska never went to London. I want to know where she is."

The Count shifted the papers on his knees, his veins showing through the pale skin on his hands. He frowned.

"Mathilde, I do not like your tone of voice. How should I know what happened to Draska? She is a teenager and adolescents are less than responsible, should we say—they say one thing—"

"My daughter is very responsible. She would never have left—"

"I told you. I do not know what has happened to her," the Count said coldly. "I think you should return to the kitchen immediately, Mathilde."

Mathilde saw the Count's eyes change, as if a cloud had passed over, his countenance turning dark and menacing.

"You have clearly forgotten your position in this household," snapped the Count. He lifted a newspaper from the stack, ignoring the servant. His eyes scanned the headlines.

Ivan led the cook out the bedroom door, locking it behind her. The Count called his manservant to his side.

"See that she does not have access to the telephone. Do not let her out of the castle."

"She will cause trouble, Master—"

The Count hissed, rising up like a cobra. His sudden leap from the chair belied his age. Ivan backed away, cowering, his hands raised over his neck and face.

"Silence!" ordered the Count, his eyes lit with fury. "I will take care of her."

Chapter 82

Two horse-drawn coaches clattered to a stop at Count Thurzo's residence in Pressburg. Coming from different directions, they arrived at the same moment, their wheels cutting dark slices in the snow, digging deep to the cobblestone below.

Torches smoking in their gloved hands, guards hurried out to greet the travelers. The light leapt as the weary passengers climbed out into the night.

In the first carriage, Emerich Megyery, tutor and guardian of Countess Bathory's son Pal, had traveled two days from Sarvar. He had written Count Thurzo that he had urgent news of Erzsebet's transgressions but would only deliver the information personally.

As Megyery looked to the second coach, he recognized the other visitor.

It was Miklos Zrynyi, husband of Anna Nadasdy-Bathory, the Countess's eldest daughter.

In the warmth of the great room, Megyery closed his eyes, sipping the strong mulled wine. The long coach ride from Sarvar—wheels jolting along the rutted winter road—had left him aching and deeply fatigued. The urgency of the news he brought the Palatine had forced him to the Hungarian capital in breakneck haste.

Famished from the journey, he ate heartily of the midnight breakfast of roast pork and paprika-spiced sausages, laced with saffron and savory with fat.

Megyery knew that he would need the stamina to face Thurzo.

Miklos Zrynyi spoke first.

"Count Thurzo, Palatine of Royal Hungary and good cousin: Hear my grievance, as I swear upon all that is holy, it is the truth."

"Speak, Count Zryni. You will find a willing ear and trusted confidante of our King, Matthias."

Zryni collected his thoughts, inhaling deeply.

"Last Easter, I accompanied my wife to see her mother, Countess Bathory, at Čachtice Castle. The day following Holy Sunday I indulged in a hunt for wild boar. After the hunt, I dismounted and left my horse in the care of a Čachtice stable boy."

"The horsemaster Szilvasi was not present?"

Zryni shook his head, bewildered by Thurzo's interruption.

"No, Count. It was a stable boy who took my mount. I whistled to my hunting dogs, accounting for all but one: my favorite bitch, Zora. She did not heed me. Indeed I could not find her anywhere.

"I walked the castle walls calling for her, until I came to the vegetable gardens. The soil had been newly tilled for planting. Great clods of earth had been overturned—there I found Zora digging.

"When she still refused to come to me, I struck out through the plowed earth, waving my riding crop. Instead of cowering, she growled at me. She was gnawing jealously on something—a bone, its rancid meat still clinging. I struck my dog's back with the riding crop. As she slunk away cowering, I bent closer to inspect her filthy treasure.

"It was a human leg, a girl's, her laced shoe still attached to her rotting foot."

The scribe's quill scratched wildly at the parchment. Thurzo steepled his outstretched fingers, placing his fingertips to his forehead.

Megyery and Zrynyi exchanged guarded looks. Neither was sure of Thurzo's reaction. The information they brought could determine their futures in the labyrinth of political power surrounding the Hungarian Parliament, the Palatine, the Bathorys, and the Habsburg King.

At last, Thurzo spoke. "And what did you do, having found this . . . corpse in the kitchen garden?"

"I told my wife to pack at once, that I would never set foot in the castle again."

Count Thurzo listened, nodding to his scribe as he dipped his pen in the inkwell. "And your verdict, Zrynyi?"

The young man looked at the fire. Thurzo could see his jaw working in the yellow light. "As we discussed a month ago, I agree with my kinsmen that the Countess should be sent secretly to Varanno to enter a nunnery."

"Our King does not allow this option," said Thurzo. "My question is whether you will join me in witnessing her crimes and assist in her immediate arrest."

Zrynyi answered at once, the knots in his shoulders unknitting in relief. He saw a reciprocal loosening of muscles in the tense Megyery. "I will, my Lord, with all my heart. I am faithful to the Habsburg Crown."

Thurzo nodded. He turned to Megyery. "I do not need to ask where you stand, sir. Your animosity toward Countess Bathory is well-known, Megyery the Red."

"Only fed and fattened with hearty years of horrific evidence, my Lord. Ferenc Nadasdy left his heir in my charge. I am the sworn protector and guardian of Pal of Nad—"

"I know your situation, Megyery. And I am well aware of the brutal stories the peasants of Sarvar recount of Countess Bathory. Also of her bitter animosity toward you. We shall not travel those old roads. What new information do you bring?"

Megyery wrinkled his brow, registering the Palatine's impatience. He wet his lips with his tongue.

"A peasant came to me—formally to Pal, but he being a mere twelve years of age—"

"Continue without embellishment. Get to the meat of the subject."

"The peasant came with a grievance. He had journeyed the many miles from Čachtice, his face drawn in exhaustion, but his eyes bright with fury. He said that a certain maiden, who was in the employ of Countess Bathory, was his betrothed. He had warned her not to accept work at Čachtice Castle, but she had no choice. Her situation was one of the most dire poverty.

"Her job included fetching buckets of river water each day from below the walls of the castle. The lad would wait for her to whisper endearments as she filled her buckets.

"One day she did not appear. Nor the next day. But the following day, another maiden came down from the castle, the two buckets in her hands. She told the boy that his fiancée had disappeared.

"My scribe took the complaint, as I heard it. I have the document here."

He produced a parchment from his leather satchel. A servant accepted it and carried it to the Palatine's hands.

Thurzo glanced at the letter. "The light is poor," he grumbled. "Tell me of its contents."

"I heard the young man's story. He was met by Kovach, the head guard of Čachtice, at the castle gates, the man turned the wretched boy away, saying that the girl left of her own accord in the middle of the night. A slattern, he called her. 'You are well rid of such a harlot.'

"The boy knew the guard was lying. He had listened to the tales of strange disappearances of scores of girls. It is said that no one in Čachtice or the surrounding areas will dare work for Countess

Bathory now. Her witches scour the countryside for new victims, maidens in far-off villages who have not heard of the mayhem of Čachtice Castle. And even there, word of her evil has spread. She is called the Beast of Čachtice by the villagers.

"He collected the names of girls who had gone missing in the past decade, never to return to their homes. Girls who were in the employ of Countess Bathory.

"In the letter you will find scores of names of brave men and women who will testify against the Countess if she is brought to trial."

Thurzo looked down at the letter in his hand. His lip curled up in disgust.

"This very night, I have received word from Vienna," said Thurzo. "Countess Bathory holds Countess Zichy prisoner."

The two men gasped.

Count Thurzo sipped from his goblet.

"Gentlemen," he said. "To protect the Bathory interests, it must be us—her kinsmen—who make the arrest. The Countess will fall under my jurisdiction as Palatine—I can arrange to deal with her on terms that will be favorable to her heirs. I propose the two of you accompany me to Čachtice. We leave at once."

Chapter 83

Maybe she missed the plane," said John, watching the last of the passengers come down the stairs from the little prop plane. "Great—"

"That's her!" said Betsy, gripping his arm. "In the black coat."

John squinted, seeing a girl with her hair tucked up under a woolen cap. Wearing no makeup.

"She looks so—innocent," he said. "Are you sure that's her?"

"Absolutely," said Betsy.

When she spotted them, Daisy's lips stretched in a smile.

"I'm so glad to see you," she said. "I know—I know I shouldn't be here."

Betsy pulled her close in an embrace. She rocked her patient in her arms, refusing to let go. "Thank God. You're safe!"

John took Daisy's rolling bag. Then he reached for her backpack.

"Wait, I've brought the papers I found. Let me get them out."

"They can wait—"

"No, John," said Betsy, touching him lightly on the shoulder. "I want to see them."

Daisy knelt on the rough carpet and slid a red plastic folder from the zip pocket.

"I tried to protect it," she said. "It looks really old."

Betsy took the folder. The warped edges of the pages were brown as toast. "I remember my mother taking me to university libraries to see primary sources. Vellum like this was used several hundred years ago."

"And this," said Daisy, handing her the envelope. "It's addressed to you. I didn't open it, honest."

"Thank you," said Betsy. She studied it for a moment, then closed her eyes. "It's my father's handwriting," she whispered.

Daisy thought about another letter she had seen once . . . lying on Morgan's pillow . . . the cramped scrawl of her father's handwriting.

John watched Daisy's face turn rigid.

"Excuse me," Daisy's voice was suddenly harsh. "I've got to go to the ladies' room."

She hurried away.

"What's with her?" said John.

"Maybe she's airsick," said Betsy. "It was a little plane. She probably got bounced around."

John shrugged, unconvinced. He watched Betsy's eyes drift, gazing up to the right, trying to recall something.

"What did I say before she bolted off for the restroom?" she asked.

"You were talking about the letter."

"What did I say, exactly?"

"You said, 'It's my father's handwriting.'"

Betsy bit her lip. "Stay here."

She put the red plastic folder and envelope into John's hands. She ran for the bathroom.

As she pushed open the swinging door, Betsy heard a retching sound and the terrifying rasp of a gag. Two Slovak women were knocking hard on the aluminum door of the stall.

"*Prosim*," said Betsy, pushing past them. She pounded on the door. "Daisy, let me in."

"Go . . . away. It's something . . . I ate."

"No it isn't," said Betsy. "It's something you are remembering."

A strangled sound filled the restroom. Betsy dropped to her hands and knees and crawled under the stall door.

Daisy could not protest. Her face was blotched both red and white. Her hand was stretched over her throat, her eyes wide in terror. She was on her knees on the tile floor. Betsy knelt next to her, supporting her torso.

"A thread of air, just a thread. Slipping into your lungs. Follow it."

"I . . . can't—"

"Follow it. Only a thread. It could slide down anything. It has. It enters your lungs. Let it out. In . . . let it out."

Daisy nodded.

"See it, Daisy. Visualize it. Slipping in, coming out. A blue thread, a soft blue. Follow it in, follow it out."

Daisy closed her eyes, listening to the voice of her therapist.

Between gasps, she offered two words, her eyes pressed tight.

"My father."

John rapped on the restroom door.

He stuck his head in.

"Betsy? Is she all right?"

"We're getting there. I'll be out in a few minutes. Just hold on."

Ten minutes later, Betsy came out of the restroom. She stopped at the water fountain.

"What's happened to her?" asked John, watching Betsy wipe the cold water off her chin.

"Repressed memories. Something bad about her father."

"Jesus," said John.

When Daisy came out twenty minutes later, her eyes were outlined in black kohl, her face plastered white in heavy makeup.

A little boy drinking at the water fountain stared up at her. He ran, grasping for his mother's hand. The woman took him in her arms, comforting him.

"Daisy has on her war paint," whispered John. "Watch out."

Her dark stained lips pressed together, a hard slash across her face.

"I'm ready now," she said. "Let's go find that asshole."

Daisy gave John and Betsy the tracking information from Morgan, leaning over the front seat, following Betsy's highlighter on the map of Slovakia.

"Last thing she told me was that they were heading toward the Polish border. Take the D1, then we turn north in twenty kilometers toward the mountains."

"OK."

Betsy rubbed her forehead. *The rise in elevation must be giving me a headache*, she thought. But Aspen's altitude was eight thousand feet; she shouldn't have any problem.

Then she remembered the envelope Daisy had given her. She pulled it from her bag and opened it carefully, working not to tear her father's writing.

Pulling out the pages inside, she recognized the format immediately. It was a psychological report on a patient.

Case Study Report: Count Vilm os Bathory.
Attending Physician: Ceslav Path

Count Vilmos Bathory was admitted to the asylum on March 15, 1972. He was 32 years of age at the time. His family insisted he be institutionalized because "he was a danger to the family and others," harboring delusions of sadistic powers—including vampirism. He was arrested after biting a fourteen-year-old cousin on the neck, inflicting wounds that required hospitalization.

Count Bathory was an attractive, athletic man, standing 1.9 meters, and possessing a powerful yet slender physique. During the first few months, he had to be restrained in a vest to keep him from physically assaulting his attendants. As a precaution, he was restrained during psychiatric treatments as well.

The patient was at first unwilling to speak or eat. He would not maintain eye contact with his doctor or anyone on the hospital staff. He remained silent and withdrawn for approximately two weeks, while losing over 10 kilograms of weight.

On April 1, he finally did speak to an attendant. He agreed to eat only if he were given raw meat. After discussion amongst staff psychiatrists, the patient's request was granted. The consensus was that nourishment in some form was imperative to the Count's physical health.

Attending Physician observed the Count eating. He eschewed the knife and fork, instead gnawing like an animal at the raw beefsteak served to him. He later licked the blood from his hands, apparently relishing the taste.

After several meals of raw meat, the patient regained his original strength and vigor. He then demanded to be served the "juice" of pressed raw meat, claiming that another noble—the Princess Sissy of Austria—survived on such a diet for years.

Dr. Path negotiated a compromise with the patient. If the Count would participate in therapy and agree to take supplemental vitamins, he would be granted the special dietary request.

"Morgan's last message said the transmitter hasn't moved for over thirty minutes," said Daisy.

Betsy raised her eyes from the report. She had another page to read.

"They may have stopped for food," she said.

"No, I don't think they would chance that, not with a kidnapped girl in the car. I bet they've reached their destination," said John.

"It's about . . . fifty miles from here," said Daisy, reading her sister's text. "And Morgan thinks they may have stopped for good."

Betsy craned her neck, looking back at Daisy.

"Why is your sister suddenly helping you?" she asked. "I thought you hated each other."

Daisy stared back at her.

"I never said that," she answered, shaking her head.

Betsy remembered that Daisy knew nothing about Morgan's visit to her Carbondale office. She turned back around in her seat, staring out the windshield at the craggy mountains rising before them.

Chapter 84

They had been driving for two hours with little conversation. The radio played mostly American music, interrupted by energetic, incomprehensible blasts of Slovak.

Daisy pointed out the many castles built up on craggy promontories. "How did they build straight up from the rock like that?"

"Ottoman slaves captured in the wars," answered Betsy. "At least that's what my mother told me about one castle. I remember her telling me the story when I was a little girl."

Betsy closed her eyes, her face crumpling. John took one hand off the steering wheel, and stroked her wet cheek.

Betsy bit her lip, taking a deep breath. "The Hungarians threw the slaves into a pit to die the moment they placed the last stone."

John switched off the radio with a savage twist of his wrist. He didn't understand a word and the music was mostly tunes from the nineties that made him nostalgic.

And unreasonably sad.

The snow fell wet on the windshield, fat goose feathers of white. John peered through the driving snow. Betsy reached over and massaged the back of his neck.

He sighed, relaxing at her touch.

"So you guys are lovers, right?" said Daisy.

Betsy dropped her hand. She twisted around in the front seat.

"Hardly. We are old friends. Not that it is any of your business, Daisy Hart."

Daisy snorted, rocking back into the upholstered car seat.

"Ha! You are such a liar, Betsy. You two have been so totally carnal—"

"Daisy, that's enough," said John, his hands a death grip on the steering wheel.

Daisy stared out the window at the passing countryside, dusted white with snow.

"Why don't you two live together?"

"Daisy," said Betsy. Then she forced a laugh, dry and brittle. "We are diametrically different. We share no common ground."

John said nothing. He rubbed the sore spot in his neck, the place Betsy had touched.

"So what's wrong with that? Yin and Yang, right? As long as you have balance."

"We aren't . . . suited for each other," said Betsy, looking out at the white countryside through the passenger window.

John threw her a glance.

"That's not what John thinks," said Daisy. "I see the way that vein in his neck throbs when he looks at you—"

"What vein?" said John, the flat of his hand reaching for his neck. "That's nonsense."

"Well, look at her, John. And Betsy, watch that vein start pulsing."

John frowned, staring straight ahead through the windshield.

"I am not going to look at her. If you haven't noticed, I am driving on some pretty slippery roads in bad weather."

"We Goths are intuitive," said Daisy, tapping Betsy on the shoulder and leaning forward to whisper in her ear. "He's totally into you."

Chapter 85

The Countess Bathory sat on a wooden throne, her heavy gown billowing over her feet. A dark shawl was draped around her neck to protect her from the bitter cold. Snow whitened the courtyard, and the breath of the frightened women before her erupted in billows of vapor.

"Strip them!" commanded the Countess. "Let the games begin!"

Two handmaidens, girls lured by Ilona Joo from destitute hovels in the countryside to serve at the castle, crossed their arms against their breasts and begged for mercy. Brutal hands snatched at their garments, stripping the buttons and ripping the sashes, until they stood naked in front of the Countess, their skin scratched raw by clawing nails.

"What tedious sport," complained the Countess, examining their white flesh, puckered with cold. "Can you not make them suffer for their sins?"

Ilona Joo pushed one girl headfirst into the snow. Hedvika made the other lie face up, staring blindly at the sky of the open courtyard, and then grabbed a bucket of icy water and threw it over both girls. One screamed. The other only mewed, her body racked with spasms, her forearms clutched tight around her naked breasts.

Frozen in the snow beyond them lay the white body of a girl who no longer struggled. The girls stared at her in terror.

Then a fourth young woman was brought to the courtyard. She stood tall, with a presence that unnerved even the most experienced servants of Countess Bathory. They backed away from her fiery glare.

As the guards loosened their grip on her arms, Countess Zichy of Ecsed stared in disdain despite her terror, displaying an aristocratic manner unlike any of the girls used before in the night games.

"I am a countess," she shouted. "Keep your beastly hands away from me, or your families and their villages will be burned. There will be no safe haven from my father's revenge!"

"Pay her no heed," said Countess Bathory. "Go on. Strip her of her garments."

"You know my family—and the King—will punish you for this," said the young Countess. Her contemptuous scorn chased away Fizko's hands. He fumbled in front of her, bowing.

"*I said strip her!*" screamed Bathory, shaking with rage at her servant's hesitation.

Ilona Joo stepped forward, flanked by Hedvika. Together they tried to unbutton the garments, but the Countess Zichy scratched at their eyes.

"Seize her," ordered Countess Bathory. "Tear the clothes from her back."

The two servants stared in wonder at the sumptuous garments: brocaded silk and wool. The fineness of the cloth unnerved them.

The Countess Bathory made a growling sound, deep in her throat, and Hedvika reached out, grabbing the Countess Zichy's gown at the cleavage with her big peasant hand and tugging hard.

A shriek of shredding cloth filled the courtyard, pearls pinging on the ice. The sound emboldened other hands that snatched now at the gown, ripping the fine garments from the girl's body. Their peasant eyes bulged and mouths twisted in pleasure as they uncovered the naked flesh of the noblewoman.

She stood, a white statue, nude in the snow.

"Douse her with cold water," said the Countess. "Make her suffer for refusing to obey me."

A greasy-haired woman with a fiendish smile threw a bucket of ice-cold water on the shivering girl.

"NO!" the victim cried, her courage and pride dissolving. "What have I done to deserve this?"

A smile broke the stony countenance of Countess Bathory.

"Push her into the snow," she commanded. "Roll her about until she chatters and her tongue is silent. Pack her mouth with snow, I say!"

Ilona Joo pressed wet snow into the young noblewoman's mouth. The girl gagged, fighting the maid's beefy fingers.

Hedvika pushed aside the two other girls, their lips blue and puckered, coated in ice. She roughly pushed the young countess to the ground and, together with Ilona Joo, rolled her over and over in the snow.

Countess Bathory threw her head back in ecstasy. Before her lay one dead servant girl and three naked women, all dying, their skin pale and tender as rose petals in the snow.

Chapter 86

Foothills of the Tatra Mountains
Border of Slovakia and Poland
December 28, 2010

As John drove, Betsy continued to read.

During the course of treatment—a period of two years—Bathory confided his dreams to his therapist. The patient regularly dreamed of his ancestor, the Countess Erzsebet Bathory—a notorious sadist and murderer of hundreds of young women. The patient described the brutal torture and sadistic pleasure of watching innocent women die. Count Bathory became noticeably excited at the description. He displayed physical signs of sexual arousal: penile erection, glittering eyes, and increased swallowing of saliva.

Attending Physician initiated questioning, asking why Bathory so delighted in the suffering of women. The patient drew back his lips, snarling like a wolf. He refused to answer any more questions or participate in any further therapy.

Attending Physician ordered the dietician to stop the feedings of blood, which Bathory continued to insist on referring to as "pressed meat juice." Bathory reacted violently to this change in diet, exhibiting signs of acute withdrawal, much as a heroin addict would manifest if suddenly deprived of drugs.

In the hours that followed, the patient collapsed in the corner of his room, shaking with spasms.

John put his hand on Betsy's arm. He could see she was so engrossed in reading that she hadn't looked up to see where they were.

"There it is," he said.

Betsy saw a dark-turreted castle rising before them. On one side extended a vast garden, encircled by a black iron-spiked fence. The other side was built flush with the edge of a rocky cliff. A murder of crows swooped and circled, their harsh cries echoing down.

"Oh my God!" gasped Daisy, looking up from her iPhone. "It's the castle from my dreams!"

John parked the car in a wooded pullout.

"Let's reconnoiter," he said, setting the parking brake. "We need to figure out how to get inside the gates. And it'll be dark in a few hours."

John and Betsy both got out of the car. Daisy didn't move.

"Go on without me. I'll be fine," she said.

"Daisy!" said Betsy. "That madman tried to kidnap you in the tower. We're not going to leave you here alone."

"Look, I've got to call Morgan."

"I don't—"

"I've got to talk to Morgan. Privately. It's really important. I told you we haven't really talked with each other in years. I've got to ask her some things while she's still talking to me."

Betsy hesitated.

"Important things, Betsy," Daisy pleaded.

"Come on," said John. "Daisy, sit in the front and blast the horn if anyone comes near."

Betsy nodded. She dug a finger under her glove, scratching at the palm of her hand. "Don't move, don't go anywhere, promise?"

Daisy nodded, catching the worry in Betsy's eyes. "I promise."

"And lock the doors."

"OK, OK!" Daisy turned back to the tiny screen.

John and Betsy walked along the edge of the woods, trying to stay out of sight.

John went a little ahead in the shadow of a rocky knoll. He suddenly jumped backward.

"Shit," he muttered.

"What?"

He lifted up one foot and stared at his shoe. It was covered in mud, despite the patches of hard snow and dirty ice on the cold ground.

"It's all wet here," he said. He looked at a rivulet carving through the mud and moss.

Betsy traced the source of the water to a seeping hole in the rocks. She brushed aside the tangle of dead vines and heard the rush of water.

"It must be an underground spring," she said, "for the water not to be frozen. Slovakia is riddled with caverns and thermal springs."

"Well, my foot is freezing," said John. "This water isn't hot at all, I promise you."

Betsy wasn't listening. She was staring beyond him.

"What is it?" John turned to look. A pond, silver with ice, stretched out about fifty yards from them.

The snow had stopped and white mist rose steaming from the water. Ice clung to the bare branches of the weeping willows. Frost outlined the bark eyes of the birch trees, staring solemnly.

The frozen world glittered as the sun's rays filtered through the steam coming off the water in gently moving waves, ghosts gliding over the pond.

"I—think I am having déjà vu," Betsy whispered. "I have seen this place before, I swear I have."

"It looks like a Christmas postcard, it's beautiful," said John. He put his arm around her.

Betsy nodded, gliding into his arms. She thought how well she fit against his chest, his arms wrapped around her. She closed her eyes, letting herself be comforted.

When she opened her eyes again, her attention was riveted elsewhere. In the dusk, a scrap of white against the iron-spike fence caught her eye. She moved out of John's embrace.

"Stay away from the fence!" whispered John. "They probably have a video camera."

But Betsy had already scrambled up the swell of the hill. As she got to the fence, she realized that what she had seen was a sheet of paper. She jumped up to reach it.

Her eyes were riveted on the paper, the edges flapping in the wind.

At the last instant, she sensed danger. A pack of German shepherds, trained guard dogs, silent in their approach, snapped at her grasping hands, punching their muzzles and bared teeth through the iron bars. One caught her ski jacket between his teeth, pulling her closer. Two others snapped at her head.

John shouted at them, rushing the fence. He banged his fist on the first dog's muzzle, dislodging his grip on her jacket.

Betsy fell back, collapsing in the snow. She clutched the scrap of paper in her fist.

"Jesus, Betsy!"

The dogs still snarled through the fence, baring long white teeth.

John sat down beside her, panting. He glanced at what she had in her hand, a photocopied picture. Beneath the picture was written, The Return of The Macabre Court of Countess Erzsebet Bathory, the Blood Countess. The photo was circled in red, a diagonal slash running across the image.

"Someone else must be suspicious of the Count," said Betsy, her voice low.

John leaned over her shoulder and studied the picture, a black-and-white copy of a painting of a vicious scene. In a snowy courtyard, white-kerchiefed peasant women—servants—surrounded several naked women who were dead or dying in the savage cold. One victim was held upright by three of the servants, who grasped her arms as her body sagged, trying to surrender to death and collapse into the snow. Horror on her face, her mouth open in a scream, trying, even as she died, to cross her white arms over her naked breasts.

Another lay prone, propped up on her elbows, pleading for her life with the last of her strength as one of the peasant women hurled a bucket of water at her.

Two others lay in the snow, either dying or dead, no longer struggling to cover their nakedness.

Around the courtyard, a handful of men and other women looked on, warmly dressed, their faces contorted with spite and hatred.

And, on a wooden throne, an imperious figure, dressed in layers of brocade and swathed in a black shawl, leaned back in satisfaction, relishing the sight.

"It's like Detective Whitehall said, 'Countess Bathory is in the subconscious of every Slovak,'" said John. He tapped his finger on the grainy photocopy of a painting. "What an evil bitch."

"It is more than that," said Betsy. "It is the most disturbing depiction of sadism I have ever seen."

"She's really getting off on it," observed John. "Look how she is leaning back in her chair, looking like it's Christmas morning."

"Like she's about to climax," said Betsy, studying her face. "The artist got it right. And not just her. Look at the vicious pleasure in the tormentors' eyes."

"That one with the bucket of water," said John. "And the men watching. See the gleam in their eyes."

Betsy was silent, so John continued.

"I had a photography professor once who said that if you want to capture the truth of a catastrophe, turn your back on it and photograph the emotion in the eyes and faces of the onlookers. That's the story."

Betsy nodded, her fingers cautiously tracing the savage glee of the perpetrators, the onlookers. And especially Countess Bathory.

"Freud would say that this is the id—the beast within—breaking through the barriers of the ego and especially the super-ego."

"I don't know if I've ever heard you citing Freud."

"For this case, he's dead-on."

They both stared at the black-and-white picture.

"That's a scene that would make any normal, well-adjusted human being shiver with despair. But . . ." Betsy hesitated.

"But what?"

"If a mentally unstable mind—a psychotic sadist or killer—were to see this, he or she could actually be inspired."

"Betsy! Come on—"

"No, I mean it. This painting would appeal to a very dark, twisted mind, someone who would want to emulate this kind of torture."

"Betsy, no. It's a warning. Look at the slash through the image. Someone is challenging the Bathory legend."

John stretched out his arms and pulled Betsy to his chest. She nestled briefly against the soft wool, haunted by the image.

Daisy's black curtain of hair fell on either side of her face as she hunched over her iPhone. She had not received any updates from Morgan in the last hour. She scrolled through dozens of messages in her in-box.

Morgan has always been erratic, she thought. She bit her hand.

Erratic? The understatement of a lifetime. Why should I be surprised—

Daisy rehearsed the conversation in her mind, her lips moving silently. This had waited too long and it was tearing a hole in her. Somehow right now, with everything so crazy, so out of control, this was suddenly the moment when she could. The moment when she had to. Just say it all and be done with it.

I found the letter on your pillow, Morgan. A gushy, pornographic love letter, in his handwriting.

Oh, yeah—I read it. And then I puked my guts up.

Mother thought it was food poisoning. I started choking, trying to tell her.

How could I tell her? What her own daughter had done—it would have killed her. That her husband was a psycho leech, and her daughter was screwing him?

When we got home from the ER, you both were gone. You and him.

Daisy remembered that she had promised to move to the driver's seat so she could blast the horn. She sighed, rolling her eyes. She closed her computer, shoving it into her backpack.

That whole big lie about making a clean break for Mother's sake, Dad filing divorce papers from Florida. Leaving me with the mess. You telling Mother that it was better to go live with Dad because of "personality differences." And that he was tutoring you for the college boards.

Right! It would break her heart. How can I ever tell anyone the truth? You both make me sick.

Daisy hooked her finger under the door lock, clicking it open. She slid across the backseat, lining her foot up to step out of the car, moving to the front seat. Her eyes were riveted on the iPhone screen. Three bars, she thought, good enough reception to reach Morgan.

She took her right hand off the door and dialed.

The car door wrenched open. Strong arms grabbed her. A bony hand clamped over her mouth as she was dragged out of the car.

Her cell phone clattered to the floor.

"Daisy?" said her sister's voice. "I'm in Warsaw. My plane—"

Daisy looked up and saw two white-faced men in black, one with a syringe. He plunged the hypodermic needle into her arm.

"Daisy, can you hear me?"

Chapter 87

The late afternoon wind kicked up snowy gusts as Betsy and John made their way back to the car. Whirlwinds of white obscured their vision, ice crystals stung their eyes.

Cresting the hill, Betsy saw the silver gleam of window glass. She halted in midstride, squinting.

"Look!" she said, pointing, and she ran down the icy slope, sliding with each step.

"Daisy! Daisy!"

The door of the car was wide open. The snow was trampled flat.

"Daisy? Daisy!" The pitch of her voice matched the shriek of the wind.

"He's kidnapped her, John!"

John looked at the tangle of footprints, the skid of boot heels. He ran, following the trail in the snow. About thirty yards away, he saw the wheel marks of a vehicle where it had been parked, and then turned around again. The tire tracks led back toward the castle gate.

"What are you looking at?" said a voice, through the wind. The English was accented in Slovak.

John turned around and saw an old man walking a dog, who sniffed the snow.

"Did you see a car come this way?" he asked.

"You did not answer my question. Why do I answer yours?" said the man, whistling for his dog. He pulled his scarf tighter around his neck as the wind blew.

"I'm sorry. I think my friend has been kidnapped. I think these are the car tracks."

The man stared at John with faded blue eyes. "She has come back to haunt us all," he said. "You cannot kill the devil."

"What?"

"Do you have car? I will take you to someone who maybe can help you."

"My name is Bartos Jelen," said the man, sliding across the backseat, pulling the dog in after him. The smell of wet dog filled the car.

"There is evil in that castle," he said. "All of us in village have felt it for years. Some post warnings around fence, but the police pull down."

"We saw one. A scene of torture. In the snow—"

"Yes. There were dozens posted, but the police destroy them. They missed that one."

"It's pretty brutal—"

"Istvan Csok painted realistic portrait. Original is at National Gallery in Budapest."

"What do you know about the castle?" said John.

The elderly man pulled off his cap. His gray hair stood up in all directions.

"I know nothing. I feel," he said, thumping his chest with his fist. "I have stared into eyes of the Count. Light does not return. He is Bathory—what more do I need to know?"

John looked quickly at Betsy in the passenger seat. Her face was pinched in anguish.

"Forgive us, I know you want to help. But we need to go to the police, Mr. Jelen," said John. "Our friend may be in danger."

"Ah! You think I am addled old man," he said, nodding his grizzled head. "Listen to me. Police here will do you no good. He pays them to turn blind eye."

"I'll call our ambassador. They'll have no choice but—"

"Ambassador! How long will that take? Your friend is dead by then. No, I take you to a woman who will help you. She knows the castle. She too is an enemy of the Count."

Chapter 88

I do not trust Thurzo," said the King, inspecting a map on curling parchment. The winter light illuminated the inked borders of Habsburg Hungary and the ever-encroaching Ottoman territories.

Bishop Melchior Klesl stood at attention, listening.

King Matthias slammed his hand down on the map in disgust.

"Will he really arrest his own cousin?"

His voice echoed off the white plaster walls of the vast palace room. Melchior Klesl imagined the crystal chandeliers chiming in a frenzy, to the point of shattering, at the rising thunder of the Monarch's voice.

This King is happiest in a military tent, camping near his soldiers, thought Klesl. *He is not suited to life in a palace.*

Melchior Klesl bowed. "Indeed, Your Majesty. I fear your instincts are correct."

"They share the same blood, Thurzo and the Countess. The same miserable Bathory blood!" spat the King. "Would that I could blot it from my kingdom, every drop!"

The Bishop of Vienna closed his eyes, gathering his thoughts.

"If you will permit me to speak, Your Majesty. I have the same concerns about Gyorgy Thurzo."

"Well? Speak!"

Melchior Klesl looked down at the King's fine leather riding boots, gleaming even in the dim light of winter. The King would ride his white Andalusian mare around the Hofburg gardens and through the streets of Vienna within the hour, despite the cold weather.

Klesl doubted it would improve his dark mood.

"As you say, Your Majesty, Thurzo hesitates. He may not have enough evidence. But there may be something else keeping him from arresting Countess Bathory."

Matthias frowned. His index fingers massaged his temples, where his head throbbed.

"If I may," said Melchior Klesl, "I believe Thurzo fears Gabor Bathory, especially now that he has the support of the Ottoman Sultan. Gyorgy Thurzo plays both sides: the Habsburg Crown and the Bathory family."

"The rogue! If Thurzo does not arrest her soon, I will ride to Čachtice and do it myself!"

Outside the Hofburg palace, there was a clanging of bells. The sweet voices of Christmas carolers filled the air, as the Viennese celebrated the Christmas season leading up to the Epiphany.

Melchior Klesl raised his chin, listening. "Even if Thurzo arrests the Countess immediately, it will be weeks before the Hungarian judges in Pressburg will hear her testimony. They will not reconvene until the second week of January."

"Precisely why he has stalled arresting her," growled the King. "A New Year's present to the entire Bathory family!"

Chapter 89

HIGH TATRA MOUNTAINS
SLOVAKIA
DECEMBER 28, 2010

Pan Jelen leaned forward from the back seat, pointing to a brightly painted house at the edge of the village. The dog wagged his tail, pressing up between the front seats, trying to see ahead.

"This is my house," said Jelen. "My house guest is the woman who can help you."

"Mr. Jelen, we really have—" John began.

"No," said Betsy, touching his arm. "Let's see who he is talking about."

"But—"

"We won't spend but five minutes," she whispered.

A big woman with graying hair stood at the door. She was dressed in a heavy overcoat and about to put a knit hat on her head.

She said something in Slovak to Jelen, ignoring the guests.

"May I present Mathilde Kuchar," said Jelen, unhooking the leash from the dog's collar. "She is the cook up at the castle. She escaped through an underground passage below the kitchen floor, fleeing Count Bathory."

Mathilde nodded, but did not extend her hand. She spoke again in Slovak, her face creasing in agitation.

Betsy listened. She turned to John, translating. "She says she had to leave. Her life was in danger."

Mathilde and Jelen stopped talking, staring at her. Mathilde's black eyes studied Betsy, a flash of interest crossing the cook's face.

Mathilde nodded, a curt movement of her chin.

"You speak Slovak," Jelen said. "So few do."

"Only a little. Just a few words, simple conversation."

Jelen spoke rapidly to Mathilde now, so fast that Betsy could not follow. But even John could make out the word "Bathory."

Mathilde's face crumpled as if she were going to cry. But then she drew up, a hard determination smoothing her skin. She took Betsy's hand in hers.

"Come," she said. She flicked her eyes at John. "But not him. Only you."

"What?" said Betsy, looking at John.

"You can't just go off with a woman you can barely communicate with," said John. "You don't know her at all!"

"Her family has lived in the castle for generations. She knows a way underground into the dungeon."

"So what? How do you know you can trust her? What if the Count sees you?"

"I don't know why, but I trust her. She told me there is a warren of underground tunnels the Bathorys used as escape routes. Every castle in the region had them—"

"Then I want to go, too."

"She won't take you. I tried, she just won't."

"What—because I don't speak Slovak?"

"She said she saw something in my face, something she recognized. But for whatever reason, she's not letting you come with us."

"Betsy—do you know how dangerous this is? What if the tunnel caves in? What if you get lost?"

"What if my mother is murdered while I am sitting on my hands? Do you think I could live with that?"

"Betsy—"

"What do we do? Wait until the American Embassy gets off their bureaucratic asses and starts investigating? You think that is really going to happen? Mom will be dead, if she isn't already—"

Betsy's face pinched up, red. Tears welled in her eyes, spilling down her cheeks. She swiped at them with her knuckle. She would not permit them, not now.

"Come on, Betsy," said John, pulling her to his shoulder. "I'm just trying to reason with you. What if something happens to you?"

"I promise—I promise I won't act on impulse. I promise you! But I'll go crazy and never forgive myself if I don't try.

"And Daisy," she said, covering her swelling eyes. "She thought she was protecting me, the little idiot. I've got to find her, John. I have to!"

John took a deep breath, exhaling in a long sigh.

"OK, Betsy. OK."

Betsy followed Mathilde through the labyrinth of pitch-black tunnels. Motes of dust swirled in the glow of her headlamp.

"How do you know your way through here?" she whispered, speaking Slovak.

The older woman looked over her shoulder. "Old secret. My family work for Bathory many generations. I play here, child with brothers. They . . . find caves."

"But—" said Betsy, stopping to into a side tunnel.

The big woman seized Betsy's arm.

"Not go that way!" she hissed. "You fall."

"What?"

"Water. Ice cave. Danger. Very danger."

She gripped Betsy's wrist, pulling her ahead. They stopped in front of a sagging wooden door, rotted with age. In the close quarters, Betsy could smell cooking grease mixed with sweat emanating from the cook's scalp.

"There—tunnel go up, dungeon. My daughter, Draska, there, I think. Your friend?"

Betsy drew a breath. "Daisy."

Mathilde nodded, biting her lips. Her hand rested on the splintered door.

"If Count Bathory sees us," said Betsy, "he will kill your daughter and my friend. And both of us."

"So," said the cook, her slanted eyes glinting in the light. "He must not see. You go through caves, then door to dungeon. Come. I show."

Before they went through the rotting door, the cook motioned for Betsy to turn off her headlamp.

"But we can't see anything," Betsy whispered.

The cold, dank space was not simply dark, but as if any trace of light had been sucked out, leaving a textured inkiness.

"You do not need to see," said the cook. "Later, you turn on again. Not now. We feel. We hear."

Betsy nodded. It seemed she had heard these words before.

"This old escape way from castle. Bathory, many enemy."

The cook kept looking over her shoulder in the direction of the rotted door. The darkness wrapped itself around Betsy, and she shuddered.

"I take you more ahead now. But then, you see. Tunnel fall down long, long years ago. Rocks very close. I could go when little girl. Not now. I escape through kitchen tunnel. Bigger, but they guard now."

The darkness grew even tighter. And colder.

"But you can go. Possible, I think."

Possible, thought Betsy. *All I have is "possible."*

"We push door, slow. Door make noise. We put mouth water there. Very, very old."

Betsy could hear the big woman gather the juices from the back of her mouth, spitting copiously where she felt the hinge under her fingers.

Chapter 90

KRAKOW AIRPORT, POLAND
DECEMBER 28, 2010

Morgan's flight reached Krakow in the late afternoon. She waited in a slow customs and immigration line, clenching and unclenching her fists, blinking in the harsh florescent lights.

The yawning official straightened his posture when he caught sight of the auburn beauty approaching his window.

"So little luggage," he said, with a thrust of his unshaven chin. He eyed the orange priority tag on her one small bag that could double as a backpack. Compact enough to carry on, but she had checked it.

"You no stay in Poland long time?"

"No," she said, her eyes trained on his hands.

"Poland beautiful. We appreciate beautiful American girls."

"Are you going to stamp my passport or not?" she snapped, her green eyes blazing at him now.

He hesitated, taken aback at the fierce glitter in her eyes. He flicked through her passport pages.

He stamped her passport and handed it back to her.

"Smile, pretty girl," he said.

A stony expression was her only answer. He motioned quickly to the next person in line.

She walked out to the pink slice of sunset peeking through gray clouds. The wet cold slapped her face. She zipped her down coat tight around her throat.

Passing cars churned up dirty snow, spraying the curb with black slush. She rolled her bag to the taxi stand, where a half-dozen cab drivers jostled each other, seeing the girl in a long, black coat, one who clearly had money.

"Taxi?" they shouted. With no other customer in sight, the cabbies were wolves ready to pounce.

She stared at the pack of cabbies, her vision still blurry from the long flight. They huddled bearlike under their overcoats, woolen scarves coiled around their necks, unshaven faces bristly, leather shoes scuffed and splotched with slush.

"How much to hire you to drive to Poprad, Slovakia?" she said to no one in particular.

"Fifteen hundred zloty!" shouted one.

"Twelve hundred—"

"One thousand zloty!"

The cabbies pressed in tight around her. She caught the smell of body odor and tobacco and wrinkled her nose in disgust.

"Look, Miss. Clean car, fast, very fast," begged one cabbie, his hat folded in his chapped hands. "Only nine hundred zloty. Include gas, everything."

"Show me your car."

Chapter 91

John sat in the car, watching the snow accumulate on the trees. He flicked on the wiper blades every few minutes to keep a clear view of the castle, bathed in light.

Why wouldn't the big woman let him go with them? What if she was luring Betsy into a trap? Maybe she had lied about her missing daughter.

But Betsy had been adamant. So sure. Damn it! He should have insisted, forced her to go to the police.

Why hadn't they done something rational? Betsy's damn hunches. Her irrationality had ruined their marriage. Why had he relented this time, knowing how dangerous the scheme was?

A ping on Betsy's iPhone interrupted his brooding.

He looked over his shoulder and closed his eyes. Prying into e-mail was not something he normally did.

Damn it. Nothing was normal now. He touched the screen with his finger, opening the e-mail.

DEAR DR. PATH,

PLEASE ALLOW ME TO INTRODUCE MYSELF. I AM DR. ANDREW SIMONOFF, A PRACTICING ANALYTICAL PSYCHO-THERAPIST HERE IN PALM BEACH, FLORIDA, AND GRADUATE OF THE C.G. JUNG INSTITUTE IN NEW YORK.

I have been working with a young patient for the last three years. Her name will not be mentioned in this letter but she is the sister of one of your patients. I shall refer to your patient only by her initials: DH. My patient will be identified by the initial M.

You must realize that only extraordinary circumstances—and concern for the health and welfare of our patients—would lead me to write to you.

In short, my patient has disappeared and I fear for her safety. According to her stepfather, she left their house in Palm Beach yesterday evening and has not returned.

He received notification of a charge on his credit card for an airline ticket to Krakow, Poland.

The stepfather is distraught, and perhaps with good reason. M.'s behavior has been erratic of late and her sudden departure indicates a mental struggle that has been ongoing for at least the past three years of therapy.

I believe that she may be trying to find her sister in Eastern Europe. Her stepfather reports that she was tracking your patient via a GPS device. That device has also disappeared from the house.

If you should encounter M., you should be aware of a few psychological factors that may protect you, your patient, and my patient.

She can become enraged to a point of violence. This includes episodes in which she can do harm to herself and others. Because of a deep-rooted trauma, M.'s behavior is unpredictable. She was institutionalized for three months and subsequently released to her stepfather's custody.

I have not experienced any of these episodes, but I have reviewed her records. Apparently she attacked

AND INJURED THREE FEMALE WARD NURSES IN A LOCKED FA-
CILITY AND A 6'3" WARD GUARD DURING ONE OF HER EPI-
SODES. ALL THIS DESPITE HER RELATIVELY LIGHT PHYSICAL
FRAME AND BODY WEIGHT.

I WAS CERTAIN SHE WAS MAKING STEADY PROGRESS, AND
WE WERE ON A PRECIPICE OF PSYCHOLOGICAL DISCOVERY.
NOW, HOWEVER, I SHUDDER TO THINK OF HER FACING THAT
PRECIPICE ALONE, WITHOUT PSYCHIATRIC HELP.

PLEASE CONTACT ME AT ONCE SHOULD YOU ENCOUNTER HER.
I HAVE NO ETHICAL COMMITMENT THAT REQUIRES ME TO SHARE
OUR CORRESPONDENCE WITH HER *STEPFATHER* ESPECIALLY IF
YOU SHOULD ASK ME TO KEEP THIS INFORMATION PRIVATE.

I THINK I MIGHT HELP YOU UNDERSTAND THE DEPTH AND
SYMPTOMS OF HER TRAUMA, WHICH MAY BE USEFUL TO YOU
SHOULD YOU OR YOUR PATIENT ENCOUNTER HER IN SLOVAKIA.

M. HAS JUST TURNED TWENTY-ONE AND IS AN ADULT. I
DON'T BELIEVE SHE WOULD WANT HER *STEPFATHER* TO KNOW
HER WHEREABOUTS NOW.

SINCERELY YOURS,
A.D. SIMONOFF, MA, PhD

John swallowed hard. He slid his finger across the screen, opening
contacts. He scrolled down the list to the bottom.

The phone took about thirty seconds to begin ringing. A man's
voice answered.

"Detective Whitehall?" John said.

An hour later, snow covered the windows of the car. Blasts of wind
swirled it away again, leaving behind transparent beads of ice, frozen
diamonds adhering to the windshield.

Daisy's phone pinged, making John jump. An incoming e-mail.

What the hell, thought John, rubbing his forehead. *I've already pried into Betsy's e-mail.*

He flicked on the overhead light and twisted around, looking around for the phone. An iPhone in a dark purple leather case studded with medieval axes lay on the floor of the backseat.

John reached over the seat to retrieve it. He scrolled down the pages of unopened e-mails. A lot was spam, websites for Goth wear, makeup, jewelry, Goth music, movies, and chatrooms.

The most recent incoming e-mail, the one that had caught his attention with its alert, was from Kyle, Snowboard Dude.

HEY, DAISY!

RN'T U EVEN COMING HOME FOR NEW YEARS? I'M OVER THE EDGE WORRIED ABOUT YOU!

WILL U BE BACK FOR THE X-GAMES IN JANUARY? I WANT U IN MY CORNER, GOTH GIRL. GET YOUR BUTT BACK HERE. SERIOUSLY. I'VE GOT A NEW SNOWBOARD—IT FLIES LIKE A ROCKET. IT'S KEVLAR—BULLETPROOF VEST STUFF.

U MADE THE FRONT PAGE OF THE ASPEN TIMES. "ASPEN GOTH GIRL VANISHES IN THIN AIR."

OK NOW I'M SUPREMELY WORRIED.

THAT WAS A WILD DREAM ABOUT THE WITCH TORTURING THE WOMEN IN THE SNOW. WHAT'S UP WITH THAT? YR SHRINK WOULD HAVE A PARTY WITH THAT 1.

YR SISTER MORGAN CONTACTED ME THRU YR BLOG—DID YOU SEE? I DIDN'T EVEN KNOW YOU HAD A SISTER. SHE GAVE ME HER E-MAIL. THEN SHE CALLED ME.

SHE SAID I SHOULD CONTACT HER IMMEDIATELY IF I HEAR ANYTHING FROM YOU. SHOULD I TRUST HER? SHE SOUNDED KIND OF WEIRD.

Morgan told me she had the SAME dream as you posted. "Daisy's in great danger." She said she would intervene. WTF?? Intervene?

Yr sister totally freaked me out, BUT what can I do to help u? I don't even know where u r!!

Kyle's phone number was in Daisy's list of contacts and John called it, looking out the ice-encrusted windshield at the pinkish gray clouds beyond the castle, giving a ghostly hue to the falling snow.

Nightfall descended swiftly in winter in northern Slovakia.

Kyle answered on the first ring.

"God, Daisy!"

John cleared his throat.

"No, I'm sorry. I'm—a friend, calling on her phone."

"What kind of friend?" said Kyle, wary. "A friend who rips off her phone?"

"A real friend. I'm her therapist's husband. Former husband."

"What are you doing with her phone, dude?"

"OK, listen. She left the phone in her backpack in our car. I think that Daisy may have been kidnapped—"

"Kidnapped. Ah, shit!"

John heard the boy's voice crack.

"Hang on. Don't panic. I need your help. Betsy's gone to look for her, but we're in the dark."

"Where are you?"

"Slovakia. On the Polish border."

"Jesus! That's where she said she'd be. She gave me coordinates in case she didn't come back—"

"Who?"

"Daisy's sister, Morgan."

John stared at the creeping growth of an icicle on the passenger window. It was thin and sharp, a dagger.

"Wait. Morgan said she's coming here?" "M" from the therapist's report must be Morgan, he realized.

"She said something about destiny. 'My sister's destiny is forever my own.' She said it like two or three times. I thought she was totally wasted."

Through the ice on the windshield, the gray stone castle looked distorted in the distance warped like a fun house mirror.

"Do you think she's really coming here?"

"I don't know," said Kyle. "She was kind of—cold and vague on the phone. Like she was making a pronouncement."

Silence.

"So why did you call me?"

"In case you had heard from Daisy," said John. "To see if you had any information that could help us—"

"Last word from her was on her blog, posted for all her friends. No e-mails, no calls."

"What's the name of her blog?"

"Aspen Goth Girl."

"I'll find her, Kyle," John promised. He heard a snuffling sound on the line.

"Is she going to be OK?"

"I—I hope so," said John. "Sure," he added.

He tried to ignore the feeling that he was lying to the boy.

Chapter 92

ČACHTICE CASTLE
DECEMBER 28, 1610

His eyes flew open, showing white rings of terror. His fingers grasped the sheet, and he sat up gasping for breath. He stared at the crucifix on the opposite wall.

Zuzana jumped back, spilling the jug of water she was holding.

"Where am I?" he croaked.

"Oh, Janos, Janos!" she cried, setting down the earthen pitcher and embracing him. The candlelight flickered, making their shadows dance on the plastered walls.

"Where am I?" His breath came in harsh gasps.

"Janos, calm yourself. You are within Čachtice Castle. The Countess insisted you be nursed under her roof."

"Where—where is she?"

"I do not know. I have been by your side all along. I—"

Vida entered, bringing a bowl of soup on a tray.

"Janos!" she whispered, closing the door behind her. "The fever has broken!"

Janos stared, his eyes unfocused.

"Where is the Countess this minute?" he repeated. "I smelt the burnt bone of evil, even in my sleep."

Zuzana and Vida exchanged looks. He was still haunted by the fever.

Vida shuddered. "The brazen witch tortures young women now above the dungeon. She has been in the east courtyard, laughing as women freeze to death begging for mercy."

"Are they there now?"

"No, the guards have thrown their frozen bodies over the walls, after draining them of blood. The night wolves will devour them and carry off their bones."

Janos raised himself in bed, his trembling elbow barely supporting him.

"Tell Aloyz to ready my horse. I must ride to Vienna," he said.

"Janos, you are too weak," said Zuzana. "You could never make the journey."

"I must tell the King. I do not trust Count Thurzo. She should have been arrested by now!"

"You must let us help," Zuzana insisted. "I can ride. You know I can."

Janos stared at her. A memory flashed of the little girl who galloped her pony in the hillside meadows of Esztergom.

"I know the way to Vienna," she said; she was not going to back down. "I traveled many times with the Countess."

"Of course you can ride, but not the white stallion," he said. "You must dress as a man, ride as a man. But the bandits along the road, the Ottoman armies—"

"I will avoid them. I have young ears and eyes. Give me a fleet-footed horse."

He smiled. He saw the excitement in her eyes, the chance to gallop a horse in the wind and rain. To escape Čachtice Castle forever.

Then his face drained of color. He fell back onto the pillows, closing his eyes.

"You must rest, or the fever will return," Zuzana said, taking his hand. "Vida, send word that Aloyz should come stealthily through the kitchen entrance and see his master. He is to bring his riding clothes."

Janos nodded, fighting to open his eyes. He struggled to gather his wits.

Zuzana searched in the bedclothes and found the lock of white mane. She placed it in Janos's hand, which was moist with sweat.

He stared at the talisman. He curled his fingers tight around it, closing his eyes.

"But Vida, you and I must find the ledger," he said. "With the pages as evidence, the Countess will be damned for all eternity."

Chapter 93

ČACHTICE CASTLE
DECEMBER 28, 1610

The Countess's retinue was roused from their sleep.

"Get up! Get up!" said Hedvika, slapping a switch across the slumbering servants.

The groggy handmaidens threw back their bedclothes, their eyes wide in alarm. They broke the ice on the surface of the washbasins, splashing their faces to dispel the slow wit of their sleep.

"Make haste for the Countess's departure!"

Torches burned in the Countess's dressing chamber. The maidens sorted the gowns and aprons on broad plank tables. The wrinkles in the silks and linens were smoothed by attentive hands, two women working in tandem to place each garment in a cedarwood chest.

"Bring all of my best clothes," commanded the Countess, sweeping into the room. "I will be in royal company. And my warmest furs. The winds of Transylvania in winter are cold-toothed."

The ladies trembled at her description, fearing for their own lives. "Which of us will accompany her?" they whispered. "Why does she seek refuge in such a savage land?"

"Have the coaches packed and ready for my departure."

"When do we depart, Countess?" asked Hedvika, pushing back a stray lock of hair from her face.

"When you hear the cats scream, that is the hour," replied the Countess. "Soon. But first I must bathe—and find pleasure."

She walked to the looking glass, touching a hand to her face.

"I cannot let him see me so old and tired."

Chapter 94

The stable boys threw back the dark cloth that covered the black carriage. Frost gleamed on the veneer of lacquered wood and the Bathory shield—red wolf's teeth—emblazoned on the coach door.

Guard Kovach had enlisted Aloyz and his stable boys to carry the Countess's trunks and boxes from the castle. Guards kept a wary eye on their progress, watching that swift fingers didn't dig into the treasures.

"Should I harness the horses now?" asked Aloyz.

"Not yet. Keep them groomed and at the ready," said Kovach.

"What a pity if the Countess travels the roads at New Year," said Aloyz. "It is a bad omen, I have heard."

Kovach cuffed the boy's head.

"Shut your ignorant mouth," he said, turning away. Aloyz watched the other guards' tense faces.

The smallest boy, Halek, carried a birch chest clutched to his chest. He looked down at the knotted eyes in the white wood. They stared back, unblinking.

His foot slipped on the hoarfrost of the stone floor.

"No!" he cried, his cargo launching from his arms.

The chest belched out its contents, metal ringing on the rock.

The white stallion reared in his stall, his hooves tearing at the air.

Aloyz stared at the objects strewn across the stable floor.

In the torchlight, the blades of sharp knives glittered. Needles as thick as his little finger littered the stones. Scissors, their blades brown with dried blood. Pincers black with char gaped wide-mouthed.

"What meaning is this?" asked a voice.

Aloyz recognized the barracks cook, who, like the stable boys, stood wild-eyed in horror. "She takes these tools in travel? What wicked occupation does she practice?"

"Keep silence!" snapped Kovach, whirling around to face the cook. "If you value your life, you will forget what you see, all of you!"

"Blindness, you demand!" said the cook, spitting on the cold, dirty stones. "I have turned a deaf ear to gossip, but now I see murder spread out at my feet!"

Chapter 95

High Tatra Mountains
Slovakia
December 28, 2010

Night had snuffed out the pink glow on the horizon. In the beam of the taxi's headlights, the curtain of falling snow mesmerized the Polish driver.

"You have friends or family here in Tatras?" he asked. He had not spoken to his strange passenger since they crossed the border of Slovakia.

Morgan hesitated. "Yes."

He waited for more, but there was only silence.

The driver shrugged, resolving not to try to communicate further. He had a sour taste in his mouth. He almost wished he hadn't taken the fare.

He thought of his family and warm grog and smoked kielbasa at home. A smile crept across his face.

He felt the green eyes staring at him from the blackness of the backseat. His smile vanished. His hands tightened around the steering wheel as he drove through the storm.

Suddenly, after what seemed like an endless silence, Morgan gave a barrage of directions.

"Turn left and go uphill three kilometers. Turn right at the church with two steeples. . . . Look for a private entrance, a gate. Maybe a guardhouse."

The driver did as he was told, squinting against the gusts of snow, swirling across the narrow roads.

"This is it?" he said at last. He pointed to a black spiked gate, ten feet high, with a guardhouse beside it. A guard emerged from the dark, a flashlight in hand.

The taxi driver noticed a black holster on his hip, even from a distance.

"Let me out here," said Morgan. "Don't go any further."

"But, *Slecna*," he protested. "Let me drive you to the door. The storm—"

"Let me out here! Stop!"

The driver jammed on his brakes, skidding. Morgan dug through her purse and stuffed his hand with euros.

The driver snapped on the cab light, counting the cash.

"It's all there," she muttered. "And then some. To help you forget you ever saw me."

She slammed the car door and heaved her backpack on her shoulder, walking away from the taxi.

The driver watched her red hair speckle with snow as she trudged toward the guardhouse.

Chapter 96

Downstairs, the kitchen was in an uproar. Brona stood in the midst of the chaos, her face beaded with sweat from the blazing hearth. She and her scullery maids were readying plum-wine cakes, roasted chickens, stuffed goose, and clove-studded hams—enough to last the long, cold journey to Transylvania.

"What doings are these to depart in the middle of the night?" the cook growled to Hedvika. "How can I roast the fowl in such haste without scorching? The fire is newborn and the hot flames char the skin."

"It is the Countess's wish to depart at once," said Hedvika. "It is not your position to question her decision. Make haste!"

Brona muttered, giving the big maiden the evil eye.

"Do not forget to pack cheeses and butter," added Hedvika, turning her back on the cook. "And the jars of goose fat. We will keep it warm by the heat of the coach brazier."

While Brona and Hedvika sparred, Janos and Vida crept down the hall into the Countess's bedchamber.

The room was in disarray, the bed covers awry from the rush of packing. Heavy chests still gaped open.

"Her writing desk," whispered Vida. "Hurry!"

"Stand watch," said Janos.

He rifled through her drawers: blotting papers, sharpened quills, pen knives. He pushed aside sticks of red sealing wax and bronze stamps embossed with the Bathory wolves' teeth, encircled by a dragon eating his own tail.

Stacks of letters were tied up in scarlet ribbons. He saw the Bathory seal broken open on a parchment, folded into perfect quarters. He unfolded it quickly and read: "My Beloved: I have found her. Your Cousin and Servant, Gabor."

"Hurry!" whispered Vida.

He jiggled the last drawer. It was locked.

He pulled out the short, sturdy knife he used to trim reins and hooves.

Vida looked at him, terrified.

"You will scar the wood!" she said.

He shook his head, sliding the blade carefully into the gap at the top of the drawer. He wedged the blade down gently, springing the lock.

As the velvet-lined drawer yielded to his hand, he gasped in horror.

Inside, he saw locks of hair, tied in ribbons. Dozens of bundles in an array of colors, some strands dull with age, others still glossy.

He snatched his hand away as if he had touched a viper.

"Someone is coming!"

The shadows in the corridors obscured the approaching figure. Vida, knowing that Janos had not found the ledger, emerged and stood blocking the chamber door.

"What are you doing here?" demanded a voice.

It was Brona, her palms open in astonishment.

"Did I not tell you to stay hidden?"

"I bade her to accompany me," said Janos. "Come inside, Brona."

The big woman crossed the threshold. Janos closed the door silently behind her.

"What are you doing?"

"I am searching for the Countess's ledger. The book that holds the names of her victims."

Brona stared back, her eyes glinting in horror at the words. "Victims? She is—a murderer?"

"There is no question. Have you not wondered at the disappearance of so many maidens?"

"She punishes them, I know. She burns their hands, whips them. A cruel mistress—Vida—"

"Brona, no," said Janos, his hand on her shoulder. "She *murders* them."

Brona shook her big head, the words working their way into her brain.

"No," she muttered, though she knew in her heart it was true. Brona knew she was dull-witted; her late husband had often told her so. But she realized she had known the truth about the Countess all along. She had refused to admit it, even to herself. Now she was forced to face the truth, and it was shattering.

With her peasant knowledge of local herbs and cookery, she had won a place long ago in the Nadasdy household, as had her mother before her.

Now she looked down at her cook's hands, fire-scorched, callused, and worn. These hands had given sustenance, warm soups and scraps of roasted meats, to hundreds of girls. She had fed them like so many geese, her pockets full of corn.

"There is a book, a record of her crimes penned in her own hand," said Janos, watching her. "We need it as evidence."

Brona licked her lips and then set her jaw, as tight as bulldog's on a bone. "She is not so stupid as to leave something so valuable lying about. If she has such a book, it will be on her person, always."

She remembered the orphan girl Paula, a scullery maid. The girl had been sent to Brona's kitchen when she was only eleven. She worked scouring the blackened pots with ash, fat, and water. The girl worked night and day at Brona's side and soon became the cook's pet.

One day little Paula did not show up at the kitchens. Brona had searched the castle grounds and Čachtice Castle for days, looking for the girl.

At last Brona had broken down and cried, holding her head in her hands.

"Why are you weeping?" demanded the Countess, sweeping into the kitchens unannounced.

"I cannot find the orphan girl, my scullery maid," said Brona. "She has disappeared. Countess, I am so worried."

Erzsebet's eyes lit up.

"Ah, yes. And that girl's name was?"

"Paula."

"I need the surname as well."

Brona's forehead wrinkled.

"Paula Cerveny."

The Countess nodded, drawing a bound vellum book from her apron pocket. She flipped through the pages.

"Cerveny," she said. "I only recalled the name Paula. Quite slight, inappropriately weak. Blonde. Thank you, Brona."

She slipped the book back into her pocket, leaving the cook bewildered.

Now Brona understood, and her sorrow and guilt turned to rage. Her sooty fingernails dug into the palm of her hand.

"I will get the book for you," she said. "And may she burn in eternal hell, as Christ is my witness."

She made the sign of the cross, closing her eyes. She lumbered out of the Countess's bedroom, her big shoulders heaving.

Chapter 97

The guards brought in their struggling prisoner. She twisted violently in their arms.

They pushed her into an overstuffed armchair and stood on either side of her. One drew a gun, looking at his master.

"Why are you here, little witch girl? Why do you stick your nose into my business?" said the Count. "You are a constant annoyance."

He poured himself a glass of red wine, swirling the stem as he observed the contents. He smiled in satisfaction.

"You disappeared from the tower, into thin air. Now you have followed me."

Daisy said nothing.

"Perhaps you are indeed a witch. How did you find me? What do you want?"

"You kidnapped a girl in Bratislava, at the nightclub," said Daisy, raising her rope-bound hands. She could barely keep her eyes open, the men had injected her with some soporific drug. Still, her anger boiled, giving her stamina. "Let her go."

The Count studied her face, her white makeup streaked with dirt. He chuckled, though his eyes had a menacing glint.

"My dear, you are certainly in no position to make demands. Perhaps you are a circus clown with your white makeup, yes? Not a witch at all, just a silly clown."

"And who do you think you are?" said Daisy. "Count Dracula?"

The Count pressed his lips to the rim of the crystal glass, taking a sip.

When he met Daisy's eyes, his own were hardened, the light extinguished. "You are a fool, witch girl! Amusing with your black funeral clothes and white corpse makeup. You intrigue me. But still . . . a fool."

The Count saw a glint from the open neck of her woolen coat. The left corner of his lip curled up, twitching.

"Remove the—"

Daisy followed his eyes. Her cuffed hands reached up and she touched the crucifix on her neck.

"This?"

"Take it off, I said!"

"What's it to you?"

"Take it off!"

Daisy stared back at him. "*You* take it off. How am I supposed to do anything with my hands cuffed, dickhead?"

The Count let out a scream, so anguished and shrill that Daisy ducked her head between her shoulders like a turtle. The two men who had kidnapped her stepped forward.

"Give her the full dose," the Count said, between clenched teeth. "Dress her for the games. And remove that damned cross."

"Yes, Master."

They turned, one grabbing her from behind.

"Keep your goddamn hands off me!" Daisy ordered.

The last thing she remembered were thick fingers snapping the chain on her neck, and the little crucifix falling to the floor.

The Count stared at the fire. The witch girl had unsettled him. He still felt the inquisitive stares of his subordinates, astonished at her insult.

Who do you think you are, Count Dracula?

She would regret that. Oh, yes.

The shrill beeping of an alarm cut the silence. Bathory turned away from the fire and walked toward the screens showing the surveillance cameras.

On the monitor showing the castle gates, Count Bathory saw a girl, auburn hair blowing across her face. She squinted hard against the wind, but he knew that face.

He knew that face!

He shot a look at the portrait of the Countess and back at the monitor screen.

A vein pulsed erratically in his forehead. He pressed his fingertips to the cool skin as his eyes closed, his lips moving silently.

Chapter 98

Betsy shone her light up at the stream of trickling water. The liquid sheen disappeared into a small hole in the rock, past the splintered remains of timbers. There was a cluster of bats roosting at the entrance, rubbery wings crisscrossed around their faces in slumber.

"Here," the cook whispered. "Way to cave, tunnel. To castle."

Mathilde was barely able to stand on the slippery rock. Her labored breath sent puffs of vapor, illuminated in the beam of her flashlight.

"Ano," grunted the cook. "Yes. I think. Maybe. Yes. You go there." She shook her head. "But I cannot. As child—yes—but now—" She gestured to her wide girth.

"No, it's OK. I can," said Betsy.

"Be care. There are holes, different places from dungeon. Down, down, down. You fall, you die. Stay this path. No turn. At end, door. Wood."

Betsy scanned the rocky walls with her headlamp, looking for footholds. She planned her route up to the hole where the water emerged.

"I think I can do it," she said.

There were only about five moves to climb the rocky wall before she could reach the opening. She was wearing her winter hiking boots, and she had climbed pitches a lot tougher than this one.

The treacherous part was the slick rock. Not quite ice, but slippery all the same. Her foot slipped twice when she was trying for a toehold, but she always had two hands supporting herself and the other foot squarely positioned.

When she reached the rotten timbers and the narrow opening, she nodded to Mathilde below her, sending a bobbing flash across the cave floor.

Now the entry.

Betsy approached the bats with caution. She had no alternative but to crawl under them. The opening was barely two feet tall, which meant squirming beneath the creatures.

She thought about rabies. She remembered stories about bats entangling in women's hair.

Were those stories real or only myths? Myths, she told herself. To frighten children and fools.

She snapped off her headlight to avoid startling the bats.

In the darkness, she suddenly felt the weight of the small ledger in her front pocket. It would interfere with her climbing, pulling her weight across the rocky tunnel.

Betsy pulled it out of her pocket, the plastic rustling. She slipped it into a zippered compartment against the small of her back.

She did not know where she was crawling to, or how far she had to go. She did not know what other creatures might inhabit the cave. Snakes? She remembered a story her father had told her about a viper biting a woodcutter in Slovakia. Had he died? Do snakes live so far underground?

Only if there were rats.

Her fingers splayed out tentatively, inching blindly along the wet rock.

Above her she heard the rustle of movement.

Bats used echoes, didn't they? Did they sense her movement beneath them?

She heard another rustle. She crawled ahead, trying to move past the bats as quickly as possible.

Suddenly there was a high-pitched cheeping sound and a fluttering roar. She snapped on her light to see scores and scores of bats coming toward her, making a mass exodus from the cave.

She ducked flat, her interlaced fingers across her head, her hands clasped tight against her ears.

A few deep breaths later, Betsy inched ahead in the darkness, pushing her fingertips forward, feeling her way through the cold, wet tunnel. Her bare hands tasted the edges of the jutting rocks and ledges.

A faint mineral smell evoked a memory of a tomb she had visited in Egypt many years ago with her father.

Her father.

She could not think of him now. He could not help her. He was dead.

In the tight space, the only trace of life was her own body and the smell of her sweat, sharp and acrid.

She flashed her headlamp on at long intervals, relying on her sense of touch rather than sight. She could not risk anyone seeing the light when she finally reached the dungeon. The passage squeezed her tightly, then widened and released her, then squeezed tight again and tighter yet. *Push your right shoulder through, twist your head, pull your torso on through the hole in the stone,* she told herself over and over. She used muscles long untested, moving more like a serpent than a human.

She flashed on her light, trying to negotiate the impossibly tight tunnel. With her face pressed against the gray-red rock, she could feel the edges of the raised veins that meandered through the stone. She was climbing now, the passage angling upward. She used the deep muscles of her back, shoulders, and arms to pull herself up. She snapped off the light, pushing on.

The blackness enveloped her, a dense velvet hood. The darkness took on a dimension of its own, becoming much more than the absence of light. Texture and depth forced her to look harder—further—into the inky distance.

Her eyes strained to see further.

She saw flashes of colors, drifting twigs and spots ascending and descending, a carnival of motion. She could feel her heart pound against her rib cage.

No. She could hear it.

She saw red. Flowing red. She jerked back her right hand in horror, the slickness of the rock suddenly sinister. She stopped, paralyzed, watching the pulsing tide surround her.

A figure gestured from the corner of her eye. She jerked her head around to see.

Her right foot slipped. The sudden jolt pulled her right hand from its hold. Loose rock rattled down beneath her, echoing through the blackness.

Her left hand and foot strained, as the right side of her body searched blindly for purchase, her knees and hips banging hard against the rock.

She pressed her eyes shut. The colors extinguished, her toe struck a ledge. With her right hand pressed flat against the wall of the cave, she slid her weight up. In her blindness she felt her way.

A vision flashed, of the blind worms and eyeless fish living deep in caves and on the floor of the ocean.

She did not want to open her eyes. Even with her eyes closed, she could still see the contours of rock, the cave itself.

She thought of John and his logic. The way his eyes would open wide as he assessed a problem. She inched her way forward, eyes shut tight.

There were voices. A steady conversation, just beyond her hearing.

No. There were no voices. The murmuring was her mind searching desperately to fill the absolute silence.

The murmurs continued. She strained to find words.

Her rip-proof jacket—her favorite for skiing in the trees—protected her skin from the rock. A bulge in her zipped back pocket had twisted around, pressing against her side.

She thought about taking it out, leaving it behind. No, this book of girls' names was somehow important. Her father had hidden it behind his most beloved book. She twisted her jacket around so she didn't feel the pressure. Now she felt the hard lump of her pocket-knife against her upper thigh.

She shifted her jacket again.

She wriggled wormlike through a level passage, an endless journey. Dust from fallen rock made her cough. She could not risk letting anyone hear her approaching.

She tied her bandana over her nose and mouth.

She choked back phlegm, not allowing herself to cough. Her chest tightened with the effort.

The rocks were smoother now, like the polished rocks in a river. To her cut and bruised hands, they felt like jewels.

A smell made her stop. A foul, human stench.

She opened her eyes.

She could see light, only a few feet above through the cracks in a wooden panel. She stopped, listening.

From the other side of the door, she could hear moans.

Chapter 99

BATHORY CASTLE DUNGEON

HIGH TATRA MOUNTAINS, SLOVAKIA

DECEMBER 28, 2010

Stand up," said a woman's voice.

Daisy slumped on the carpet, against the foot of the bed. She struggled to open her eyes, rubbing her arm where the man had inserted the needle.

"I said stand up!" cried a woman with fuchsia hair.

Daisy rolled to her knees. The woman grasped her forearm and yanked her to her feet. She plastered Daisy's face with cold cream. With a towel, she removed the white makeup with quick, hard strokes.

"You must dress. Put on shift. Put on gown. No sleeping!"

The woman ripped off Daisy's clothes. Daisy spun clumsily on her feet as her garments were stripped.

"You! Pay attention. Put on shift."

"Who are you?" Daisy mumbled. "What's a shift?"

"We no have time. Put on shift. Put on gown, stockings, shoes."

Daisy stared at the woman, not comprehending. Ona pulled the shift over her head.

"Sit down," said Ona. "Put on stockings."

"Stockings?" said Daisy. "I don't wear stockings."

Daisy's eye wandered to a table with fruit arranged on a platter.

"I'm hungry," she said.

"Good," said Ona. "Put on stockings, you get food. Do not, and I will whip you."

"Whip me?" said Daisy.

What the fuck?

Ona smiled, her lips stretching a cold thin line across her face.

"I am very good with whip. You shall see. You must dress quickly. Soon you will not be able, when drug begins."

"OK, OK," said Daisy. "Whatever. Give me the stockings."

"Good," said Ona. "When dressed, meet other girls."

"Just put her in the corridor," said a guard. "The Count will want her soon."

A man supported Daisy by her elbow, steering her toward a barred door. She stumbled, the drug affecting her motor coordination.

He pushed her through the door, swung it closed, and locked it behind her.

"Make some friends," he called, laughing.

Daisy, dressed in seventeenth-century garments, approached a barred cell in front of her. Her steps were unsteady. She pulled a red apple from her sleeve, looked at it with puzzlement, and handed it to the filthy prisoner's grasping hands.

"Who are you?" asked Draska, biting savagely into the apple. She shook in spasms as she chewed her first food in days.

Daisy frowned, looking down at her white lace apron. She rubbed the starched linen between her fingertips, shaking her head.

Draska noticed a thin streak of white makeup at the girl's jawline.

"I—" said Daisy. "I know a way out of here."

"But you no have key," said Draska. "How can I follow?"

Daisy stared at her blankly. She gave no reply.

"What is your name?"

"She will kill you if you show terror," Daisy said. "She feeds on terror. And on blood."

"Who? She?" said Draska, swallowing the last of the apple.

"Countess Bathory."

"Count Bathory. Is man!" corrected Draska.

Daisy's confused look warned Draska that something was not right with the strange girl with the dyed black hair.

Daisy shook her head and walked aimlessly to the next cell.

"How did you get out?" asked a British voice. "Or are you one of them?"

"Get help!" hissed another voice. "You are the girl from the night-club! It's me, Lubena. For God's sake, help us!"

Daisy's eyes studied the steel bars. She touched them gingerly with her fingertips. "They are different," she muttered. "The cages—they have changed."

"She is as crazy as the rest of them," muttered the English girl, starting to cry. "Look at her eyes."

Chapter 100

BATHORY CASTLE
HIGH TATRA MOUNTAINS, SLOVAKIA
DECEMBER 29, 2010

Go away, now!" commanded the guard. "It is past midnight. I am warning—"

"Stop!" cried the Count's voice on the intercom. "I am sending a car to the gate to fetch my guest. Miss—?"

"Morgan."

"*Slecna* Morgan, do you have a surname?"

"Morgan will do," she snapped. "Do you have my sister in here?"

Silence. Morgan heard the ice crystals pelt the window of the guardhouse, rattling the glass.

"Perhaps you should come and see for yourself, my dear," he said at last.

"Run," whispered the guard, his hot breath in her ear. "Run away while you still can. You don't know—"

A black limousine appeared, its tires crunching the icy crust. Big wet flakes of snow were illuminated in the headlights.

The driver with white hair—but a young face, she noted—opened the door. He bowed, low and stately.

The guard reluctantly opened the gate.

Morgan threw back her hair with a toss of her head, heaving her backpack higher on her shoulder and stepping into the backseat of the limousine as if she had been waiting for it all her life.

Chapter 101

The rider set off just before dawn. Aloyz alerted the sentries that the horsemaster needed to leave on urgent business.

The gate was opened and the bay mare trotted down the rocky path toward the main road northeast of Čachtice. Aloyz watched as rider and horse disappeared into the thick bank of fog below, gleaming an eerie silver in the moonlight.

In the blaze of dawn, Zuzana was able to canter her horse, the road flattening and following the Vah River. The cold air stung her skin. She breathed in the salty warm scent of the horse. The smell comforted her in the cold mist.

She had gone only a few hours from the castle when she came upon a troop of soldiers, watering their horses in the river. She spied the double-headed eagle insignia of the Habsburgs, flapping yellow, black, and red over the tents.

Her mare whinnied at the scent of the horses and in an instant a mounted scout galloped out of the dark woods. He overtook her on the road, before she could react.

"Stop! Who goes?"

Zuzana's heart thumped. If she spoke, he would know her gender instantly.

The scout pulled his horse alongside her. A rough hand snatched back the hood from her face. Her face was splattered with mud from the rutted road, but he could see her blue eyes sparkling with defiance.

"What do we have here!" he crowed. "A maiden riding astride?"

"Let me go," she answered. "I have urgent business with the King."

She drew her sleeve across her face, wiping away the mud.

The scout dropped his hand from her hood, seeing her pocked face.

"The King?" he gasped. "A poxed witch to see a Habsburg?"

"Pray, let me continue on my way!"

The scout's face loosened further in astonishment, his jaw dropping.

"Where do you come from?"

"Čachtice Castle."

"We ride there this very day. These men are Count Thurzo's party."

"Count Thurzo? The Palatine?"

"I dare not say more. I will accompany you to his tent," said the scout. "But cover your face with your hood so you don't draw attention from the troops. They may take you to be an evil omen."

Count Thurzo was washing his face in a stream when the scout approached him. He squinted at the sound of footsteps, blinking away droplets of water from his eyes.

"What have you got there?" said the Count rising.

"A maiden who says she is from Čachtice Castle," said the guard. "She brings news from Janos Szilvasi."

The Palatine accepted a towel from his servant and wiped his faced dry.

"How do I know she is not a spy, attending the Countess?"

Zuzana drew back her hood and leaned forward in the saddle where the Palatine could see her clearly.

He gasped. "It's you. Countess Bathory's little monster!"

Zuzana stared back at him.

"You remember me, Count Thurzo," she said. Her mare moved restlessly. Zuzana reined her in, swinging the horse's head back to face the Palatine. "I come in the name of horsemaster Janos Szilvasi, who lies ill in Čachtice Castle."

"Why does he send you on this mission?"

"Because my absence would not raise as much suspicion. Because I can ride. And I know a way you can enter Čachtice Castle without laying siege, for her guards will fight to the death to keep you out."

"I have the King's soldiers here!" the Count snorted. "Bathory's men will not hold out for long."

"And she will disappear into the warren of tunnels beneath her castle, never to be found. You will not bear witness to her crimes. The Countess will take refuge. She will find an ally. Perhaps the strange visitor they call the Dark One. He wears a Bathory ring."

Count Thurzo clenched his fists at his sides. A flush of red colored his damp face.

"The Dark One? You say he wears the Bathory ring?"

"Yes."

"There is only one Bathory as cruel as she—Gabor of Transylvania. If she flees to him, no one, not even the King, can stop her."

The Count considered the money, soldiers, and resources Gabor would amass with Erzsebet's alliance. Sarvar, Kerestur, Leka, Ecsed, Wallachia, Transylvania, possibly even Poland.

The Ottomans. Gabor had sent his emissaries to Stamboul.

"Then you must take her by surprise," said Zuzana. "Tonight."

Count Thurzo nodded slowly, studying the glint of her eyes. Chips of the bluest sapphire.

"Choose a small party from your men. A small band of soldiers. I will guide you. Stealth is your ally.

"Then you will catch the Countess in the act of murder."

Chapter 102

BATHORY CASTLE

HIGH TATRA MOUNTAINS, SLOVAKIA

DECEMBER 29, 2010

The driver escorted Morgan to the drawing room. She shook the snow from her hair, a cascade of auburn locks swirling about her shoulders.

"Such a late night visit," said the Count. "From a beautiful stranger. Still I feel we have met before."

"You have my sister here," said Morgan. "I want to see her immediately. She is coming home with me."

"What?"

"You have kidnapped Daisy Hart. You are to release her immediately or a contact in the United States will send the coordinates of this location to the FBI and the CIA. And the American ambassador in Bratislava. Got it?"

"Sit down," said the Count, reaching for a chair himself. "I do not understand."

"Did I stutter?" said Morgan. "What's not clear?" She reached for her backpack and pulled out a pack of cigarettes. She lit one and extinguished the match with an agitated wave of her hand.

"*You*—you are related to the witch girl?"

"Goth," said Morgan, blowing out a plume of smoke. "She likes to be called Goth."

"But—you are—nothing like her."

"What does that matter to you?"

Morgan felt the presence of the driver still close to her side. He looked tense, shifting his weight from side to side.

She looked up at him.

"And they will arrest you, too, Mr. Chauffeur. As an accomplice."

"Bartos, you can leave us now," said the Count. He stood unsteadily and walked over to the crystal decanter.

The chauffeur hesitated, watching the count's wooden motions.

Bathory poured himself another glass of wine. He drained it with one tip. An ugly grimace seized his face, twisting his features.

He is insane, thought Morgan.

Glass shattered as the Count hurled the empty goblet at the stone fireplace.

Morgan shielded her eyes from the flying shards.

The Count's eyes wandered unfocused about the room. His gaze stopped on a portrait on the wall, a small, ancient rendering of Countess Bathory.

He cocked his head, listening.

A strange smile spread across his face. He looked at Morgan again with an intense stare.

"Of course," he said, though he didn't seem to be speaking to her. "I had forgotten. Of course."

"Of course, what?" said Morgan.

He waved his hand, dismissing her words. The motion was like erasing a chalkboard.

"Wait. Bartos—inform the attendants we will have one more guest at tonight's games, a very special lady indeed. And bring"—he arched one eyebrow—"a welcoming draught, for the beautiful lady.

"She seems to have forgotten herself. We will help her to remember her former glory."

Chapter 103

Brona ground cloves and cinnamon in a stone bowl. She sprinkled the mixture into the warming wine.

She poured the mulled wine into the Countess's goblet. Then she thought again of the murdered girls. Her hand tightened around the goblet.

"The mistress is distressed," said a crying servant girl as she rushed into the kitchen. "She asks again for her wine at once. She is in an evil temper. She pinched my arm. Look."

A reddish-blue welt spread across the girl's upper arm.

"I'll serve the mistress myself," Brona said, as the maid started to take the tray away.

"But—"

Brona put on a fresh apron. She tidied the linen cloth on the tray.

The Countess looked up from her needlework.

"Brona," she said. "What brings you out of the kitchens?"

"To better serve you, Countess," she said, bowing. "I so rarely have the honor of seeing you."

The Countess's eyebrow arched.

"You are not a handmaiden, Cook! You smell of onions and garlic. See that you stay in the kitchens where you belong."

Brona set the tray on a little table beside the Countess. It was so dark in the room she could not understand how her mistress could see the needle.

"Since you are so eager to talk with me," the Countess said, taking the goblet in her hand, "tell me why you are spending such an exorbitant amount on flour. We cannot afford such—"

Brona bumped the Countess's outstretched hand.

The wine sloshed from the goblet, splashing red on the white apron that covered the Countess's gown.

"You clumsy peasant cow!" said the Countess, leaping up. "Look what you have done."

Brona snatched the linen napkin from the tray and doused it with water from a jug.

"Mistress, forgive me! Let me take the stain off immediately before it sets."

She began soaking the Countess's apron with water, blotting the stain with the napkin.

"You clumsy fool! This gown is Venetian silk!"

Brona spread out the apron to its full width, lifting it clear of the silken gown.

"You fool!"

"Forgive me, Countess, but I must remove your apron before it soils your dress."

She untied the apron, helping her mistress out of the garment.

Her hand dug into the pocket of the apron, extracting the ledger. She shoved it into the pocket of her own apron.

"Oh! Look at your shoes. And the hem of your dress."

Brona dropped to her knees, blotting at the Countess's clothes.

"Never mind!" screamed the Countess. She plucked up the needle from her embroidery and plunged it into the cook's scalp.

She gave it a savage twist.

Brona screamed, her big hands flying to her head.

"I shall change my garment," said the Countess, twisting the needle. "Send the laundress to my bedchamber at once!"

Chapter 104

Vida took the ledger from the cook, who kept her hand clasped over her head in pain.

"Let me attend to it," said Vida, her gentle hands touching the wound.

"Oaaaw!" Brona moaned.

"The gash is bad. I will dress it."

"No," said Brona. "You must give the book to Janos and leave this castle immediately. The Countess will murder you! Go now!"

Vida placed the ledger in her apron pocket. She looked out through the leaded windows. Through the warped glass, she saw the figure of the horsemaster, striding toward the stables in the moonlight.

"Hurry!" said Brona.

Vida raced down the stairs. She stood panting at the doorway, looking for any sign of the Countess or one of her wicked faithful. She dashed across the courtyard toward Janos.

"Here, take this!"

"Vida!" Janos said, looking around, frantically. "You risk your life—"

"Take it," she said, shoving the ledger into his hands. "I am leaving this evil place."

She reached up and kissed his lips. Before he could respond, she ran toward the gates, her footfalls echoing across the cobblestones.

Janos felt a chill. He whirled around, searching the windows of the castle in the moonlight.

Someone was watching.

Chapter 105

Zuzana told Count Thurzo about a passageway, a secret entry from the mountainside above Visnove, the tiny hamlet at the edge of the river.

"If you approach from the village of Čachtice, one of her spies would be sure to alert her. There are many passages and tunnels through the caverns below the castle, but I shall show you one through which your soldiers can pass."

"Are you sure of the passageway?" said Thurzo, as he rode beside the girl.

"I could find my way blind through the darkness," she answered.

Doricza, a plump, fair-haired maiden from the Croatian countryside, had never imagined such quantities of food and drink as weighed down the noble table of Countess Bathory. There were strange fruits, exotic spheres of yellow that gave off an intoxicating smell and freshness, unlike anything she had ever seen. A rounder cousin of the fruit, bright orange, remained partially eaten. Its spiraling rind—alternately white and gold—lay coiled like a Christmas ribbon.

But the most precious among the treasures were the golden pears. Mounded high on a silver plate, the delicate fruit tantalized her. They stood untouched, for the Countess had little appetite.

Soon the fat flies would cover them, thought Doricza. Her heart-shaped face quivered. Despite the December cold, those black spots of pestilence, the eternal plague of Čachtice Castle would swarm. Oblivious to the rhythm of nature, the filthy creatures would rub their greedy legs at their banquet, rotting on the linen-spread table.

Doricza gazed sadly at the tower of gold fruit.

Her hand reached out, snatching the top pear. She stuffed it in her apron pocket, hurrying to the kitchen before Brona noticed her absence.

Chapter 106

As Count Bathory descended, he was greeted by the cold, wet air of the dungeon.

"Show me the prisoners," he said through the barred door to a skeleton-thin guard.

The guard unlocked the door, bowing. Bathory's face was rigid, an ugly twist in his lips. The guard shrank back.

The fetid smells of rancid urine and feces assaulted the Count's nose. He drew his wrist over his nostrils.

"Clean up these girls at once! Bathe and dress them properly, scent them with lemon verbena. They must be fed, their eyes bright."

Two prisoners—girls whom the others had assessed as insane— shrank back in the dark shadows of their cells, like beaten dogs. They recognized the voice, and it made them tremble.

The newer girls—ones who did not know better—called out to him.

"Yes, a bath! A meal. Oh God, feed me!"

"Help me, sir! Help me—"

"Silence, you whores!" he shouted. He swung his cane hard against the bars, smacking imploring hands.

He stopped in front of Draska's cell. Something caught his eye on the floor, just within the bars.

"What is this?" he said, stooping to pick it up. Then he found another and another.

"Apple pips? You have been eating apples?"

Draska hung her head, looking at him through her dirty blue hair.

"Answer me! You stole an apple!"

"How could I steal anything, Count Bathory? You locked me—"

"YOU STOLE AN APPLE!"

Draska shrank back in the corner of her cell.

"He's completely mad—" whispered the English girl.

"You will pay for your dirty sin tonight, girl!" shouted the Count. "You shall all pay for your filthy habits!"

He turned and swept out the door, his black cape flowing behind him.

PART

-3-

Chapter 107

race sat up, knocking her head hard against the sofa's wooden armrest, the sound of the double lock, a key turning in the door, waking her from a fitful sleep. With one hand she fumbled for her glasses, the other hand wrapping around the brass lamp at her bedside.

She considered its weight in her hand. If the Count attacked her, she would not die without a fight.

She thought of her husband. A fight to the death, she swore to herself.

The Count had been acting more and more erratically. Something had deeply agitated him. If he were to have a full-blown psychotic episode, she would not survive his violence. She remembered Ceslav's words: *Nothing is more frightening than an insane mind. Nothing.*

The brass handle moved down and the door pushed open. A flashlight appeared, its beam dodging around the room, searching for her.

She snapped on the lamp, its hefty weight still gripped tight in her hand.

"Who is it? What do you want?"

A tall, white-haired man nodded to her. He was young, the hair belying his age.

"*Pani.* Please to turn light off."

"No. Who are you? What do you want?"

"I am Bartos, Count's chauffeur. I come to help you."

"Help me?" said Grace. She adjusted her glasses on her nose. "I don't believe you. Why would you help me?"

"Because I want—'clemency'?" he whispered, approaching her.

She backed up, raising the lamp higher. "What are you talking about?"

"Clemency," he repeated. "I look word up in dictionary. I want to talk to Slovak authorities, tell Count's crimes."

"So go ahead and tell them. What do you need me for?"

"You witness. I help you escape, you tell judge I good man, not like Count. We talk to American ambassador. Clemency."

Grace said nothing. She wondered how anyone could be considered innocent who was in Count Bathory's employ.

"Let me help you," he said. "Put down lamp. Someone can see it. Count kill many girls tonight."

Grace heard the sound of glass shattering and angry words shouted, echoing through the corridors of the castle. She thought of Draska.

She snapped off the light, plunging the room into darkness.

Grace followed behind the chauffeur through the castle halls. He stooped low, looking over the curving marble banister.

She heard a woman's voice. She raised her head enough to see a swirl of dark red hair, and a woman slapping and clawing at her captors.

"Get your fucking hands off me!"

Not Draska, she thought. An American.

What was an American doing here?

As the men pulled the girl away down the hall, the chauffeur waved her to follow him down the stairs.

He did not see the figure in the shadows, watching.

Betsy lay in wait, hidden deep in the darkness of the tunnel. Long minutes elapsed.

She was crouched below a wooden door. The tunnel had leveled off to a space perhaps three feet deep. Enough room for her to relax and try to imagine what would happen next, what she could do.

She wedged her face tight against the wood, slimy in the damp. Through a crack between the boards, she could see there was no one in the room.

Betsy could hear the shuffle of feet. She heard the soft moan of a girl, somewhere in the near distance.

She closed her eyes, pressing her eyelids tight together.

Grace stared into the trunk of the car, paralyzed with fear. She had an appalling fear of tight places.

The trunk smelled of rancid urine.

"Get in!" the chauffeur whispered, his voice hoarse.

"Look at me," she said. "Look me in the eye, damn it!"

His eyes were frantic like a wild-eyed horse.

"You must take me out of here the second we pass the gates. You must promise!"

"Not until main highway. Then, I promise, lady. Now—in!"

"Where are you going, Dr. Path?" said a voice. "You must remain for tonight's entertainment. I insist. "

Grace jumped.

When she turned, she saw a puff of smoke in the cool, wet air, and heard the ear-shattering roar of a gunshot. The Count stared straight ahead at his target, the pistol still in his hand.

Two men grabbed her arms, dragging her back toward the castle.

The chauffeur fell dead, a small crimson hole in his forehead.

Chapter 108

In the dark of night, Count Thurzo's men assembled at the mouth of the cave. The King's scout had intercepted Thurzo's party along the road. The Habsburg rider accompanied an exhausted pastor, barely able to sit his horse.

"We will take the Countess by surprise," Thurzo had told the King's men. "Megyery the Red and Miklos Zrynyi will accompany me along with ten men. You and the pastor can come with us to see justice done. The rest of the troops are to circle around to the entrance of the castle. We will let them in the main gate once we have arrested the Countess."

Thurzo turned to Zuzana. "You are certain this corridor leads directly to the dungeon?"

"Yes, it is part of the labyrinth. There are other entries, but this is one where a man can stoop, not crawl on his belly."

Thurzo thought about the girl crawling like a worm through the dark tunnels. The commander of the troops had accompanied the small band this far, and now he held the Count's horse as Thurzo dismounted.

As the Count started to enter the cave, Zuzana stepped in front of him, blocking his way. "Let me go ahead, Count Thurzo. If the

407

Countess learns you are approaching, she will flee. If I go first, I can draw her attention."

And her wrath, thought Thurzo. He opened his mouth to refuse her offer but saw the burning glint in her eye, despite the dim light.

"We will let you have only a few moments, no more," he said, giving her a curt bow. "I admire your courage, *Slecna* Zuzana."

"Always keep your right hand pressed against the wall. That way you cannot lose your way. Follow the wall until you see the stone stairs. The door is fitted with sharp spikes. You will hear the screams before you reach it, I fear."

She drew her cloak tighter around her shoulders. "Come quietly," she said, disappearing into the darkness.

Thurzo turned to his captain. "We are ready to proceed. Return to your men and lead them around to the main road. Be careful to stay well out of sight. Give us an hour. I want to gather enough evidence to convince the tribunal of her treachery."

Hers and all the Bathorys, he thought bitterly. For if he did not present sufficient evidence to condemn the entire family, Gabor would retain his full power and find reason to attack Habsburg Hungary and even Vienna itself.

Thurzo realized the treacherous line he walked. He must bring enough evidence against the Countess to sentence her, dissuading Gabor from his quest for the crown. But he must also be careful not to produce so much damning evidence that the Habsburgs and their subjects turned against the entire Bathory family.

"Until midnight," Thurzo said, dismissing the rest of the troops.

The commander headed down the hillside toward the road below, trailing the Count's horse behind his own.

Hedvika pulled the screaming girl by her hair. She shoved her to the Countess's feet.

"What's this?" said Erzsebet, regarding the plump maiden.

Hedvika produced a bruised pear from her pocket. "I found this in her apron."

The Countess's eyes narrowed. She turned to the sobbing girl.

"How dare you betray me!" Erzsebet's voice was low, dripping with menace. "I take you from a filthy hovel, and you repay me by stealing?"

"Mistress," pleaded Doricza. "It was only one piece of fruit, and the flies were lighting on them. They had stood untouched since Christmas Eve—"

"Silence!"

Ilona Joo and Dorka crept out of the shadows, like stray cats.

"Take her to the dungeon. She will pay dearly for her crime against me!"

The two descended upon the girl, but it took Hedvika's strong arm and wrenching pull on the girl's long hair to drag Doricza to the dungeon.

As the screams diminished in the distance, Erzsebet thought of Darvulia. Incantations, omens, dreams—and the spells the witch had taught her.

She heard the cats squall in the turrets, screaming like wounded human infants.

I can feel their approach, she thought. *I must depart. Just one bath, one last glorious rejuvenation before he sees me. This maiden will serve me well.*

Darvulia, how could you desert me when I need your magic?

A draft blew down the hall. She felt the chill of the night storm, the wind haunting the corridor.

She thought of the incantation the witch Darvulia had taught her. She repeated it now.

Thou little cloud, protect Erzsebet; I am in peril. Send thy ninety cats, let them hasten to bite the heart of King Matthias and of my cousin Thurzo, the Palatine! Let them tear apart the heart of Megyery the Red.

The wind twisted the heavy brocade draperies.

"Oh, Dark One. I come to you," she said. "Only let me bathe myself in youth and feed my heart upon the terror of this maiden."

Chapter 109

A silk gown lay on the canopied bed.

Morgan rubbed the fine material between her fingers. It was deep crimson and black, and the exquisite weave of the fabric felt like cool water. Next to the gown lay a black apron.

And a huge ruffled collar.

This is ridiculous, Morgan thought. *My head will look like a centerpiece on a Thanksgiving table.*

A fuchsia-haired servant entered the chamber to help her dress.

"Take off bra," she said. "Put on slip."

"Go to hell," said Morgan firmly. She gave the servant a chilling stare.

"We have little time. Count becomes angry. Take off bra."

"No," said Morgan. "I will not." Her body stiffened, her fists clenched.

Ona watched the American's woman's face harden. If she snatched at her bra, there would be a fight, an ugly one. The girl had long sharp nails, and the look of a tiger.

Ona handed her the embroidered chemise and linen shift.

She had picked enough battles for one day.

Morgan slipped on the chemise and shift. When Ona turned to reach for the dress, Morgan dug a finger into her bra, touching the warm metal.

She smiled.

Chapter 110

Betsy clicked off her headlamp and was plunged into darkness. She placed her hand on the rusty iron handle of the door. With a deep breath, she pushed down the handle. When nothing happened, she set her left shoulder against the door and heaved forward.

With a shriek of corroded hinges, the door gave way. She stopped, listening for voices.

Please, please, let there be no one in the room.

The door was behind a heavy tapestry, hidden from view. Her fingertips ran across the rough backing of the tapestry, feeling her way to its edge. At last she saw the flickering light of the torches.

Her eyes blinked in the erratic light.

Thank God. No one's here.

But they will be back.

Brown stains marked the stones, splatters on the wall. Betsy focused her attention on what to do next, not on what took place in the past.

She crouched in the shadows. A table stood in the middle of the room, raised on a wooden dais. A linen lace tablecloth covered the surface. A mahogany lectern, exquisitely carved centuries before, stood on the table.

She saw strange metal objects—farm tools?—set out on a long table alongside the dais.

Betsy searched the room carefully before daring to venture out. She crept hunched low to the long table. There she saw fire-blackened tongs, pinchers, a pitchfork. All sorts of crystalline glassware lay beside the tools. One looked like a decanter for wine.

An ancient leather satchel tied up with a cord lay on the far corner of the table. There was a silver spoon, two more fine crystalline decanters, and a strange gold funnel, with a plastic molding covering the stem.

On the floor was a tub made of granite, with a long plastic hose running from the drain. Ugly brown stains had discolored the gray stone.

She looked quickly away, climbed the dais to look at the tome on the lectern. It was not an old book, its creamy pages were new and modern.

Betsy blinked, focusing her eyes.

It can't be, she told herself. She looked again.

It was *The Red Book*.

She scanned the pages. A passage was highlighted in red.

The task is to give birth to the old in a new time. The soul of humanity is like the great wheel of the zodiac that rolls along the way. . .There is no part of the wheel that does not come around again.

The Red Book *as sinister?* she thought.

She heard her father's voice.

A knife in the hands of a good man can cut bread to feed his family. A knife in the hands of malevolent man is a weapon. Anything can be good or evil, Betsy. Everything is neutral, assigned a value only in the hands of the holder.

Betsy stared at the book as her father's words continued in her head:

Even the best analysis can fail. You must understand this, Betsy. Along the tortured journey through a man's or woman's mind, there are those who are lost forever. You must learn to protect yourself from tumbling into their abyss.

For ultimately we are connected.

The sound of footsteps sent Betsy scrambling back behind the tapestry.

Betsy peered out beyond the edge of the weaving. Her position was steeped in shadows, for the torches were in the far corner of the room. Only when a flame leapt was her wall illuminated for brief seconds.

A young woman in an antique silk gown entered slowly, escorted by an elegant white-haired man with a walking stick. Something in his exaggerated paleness, the grace of his posture, reminded Betsy of someone she once knew.

Betsy saw the glint of the silver-tipped walking stick. And she remembered.

She had been a very young girl, bored with adults talking about Austro-Hungarian history, dates, papers and books they had published. He had called her to him, away from the crowd. He sat in the shadows of a room filled with paintings of Ottoman-Hungarian battles.

He showed her his carved walking stick, with a silver dragon with ruby eyes. She sat on his knee. He shifted her weight.

That left knee hurts me, he had said. *That is why I walk with a stick.*

He whispered he was a distant cousin and glad to make her acquaintance. He let her play with the dragon.

The bright rubies glared at her.

Betsy remembered the shocked look on her mother's face when she came rushing to sweep her child off the man's lap. The scent of fear on her skin. Betsy had never forgotten the stranger, but her mother and father refused to speak about him.

Don't talk to strangers, was all her father had said. *And never, ever talk to that man again.*

Betsy looked again at the woman in the silk gown, a huge white lace collar extending under her chin, a stiff square panel.

The woman's skin was pallid, her eyes made up in an elaborate fashion. She walked in a wooden gait. Perhaps she was drugged.

Her hair was a shining auburn.

The woman stopped, gazing at a portrait of Erzsebet Bathory, one Betsy had seen over and over on the internet.

The young woman's hand drifted up to her cheek. The Count watched her intently. He smiled, reaching for her hand.

Betsy stared. She recognized the red-haired woman.

Chapter 111

Janos buried the ledger deep in the straw, in the corner where the white stallion was stabled. He knew that no one would dare enter. The horse was tamed to his hands alone; even Aloyz stayed away from this corner of the stable.

"What did she give you?" demanded a voice in the shadows.

Janos recognized the voice immediately. "Who?"

Guard Kovach stepped toward him. He had a dagger in his hand. "We stopped her at the gate," he said. "I saw you."

"She is innocent, Kovach. Let her go."

"It is out of my hands, Horsemaster. The Countess will determine her fate. Or perhaps she will leave it to the Dark One in Transylvania."

Janos swallowed hard.

Kovach smiled. "Now give it to me."

Janos stared at him through the darkness. The captain's silhouette appeared enormous against the lime-washed wall, a giant exaggerated by the torchlight beyond Janos. Dagger in hand.

"Give it to me!"

Janos thought of the girls' murders. He thought of Vida, risking her life. Then he remembered Zuzana, who should, even now, be bringing Thurzo to Čachtice.

"No."

"You Hungarian fool!"

Kovach lunged. Janos leapt aside, looking around desperately for a weapon. There was nothing.

"You betray the Countess!" growled Kovach.

"And you betray God!"

Kovach slashed at Janos, catching his upper arm. Blood soaked the linen tunic, but he dodged the second thrust. There was no escape—Kovach positioned himself at the stable door.

He closed on Janos, walking quietly, slowly.

The dagger glinted in the torchlight.

Janos ran to the far side of the horse. He touched the stallion's neck, his lips moving silently. The skin on the horse's flank quivered, his ears flattened.

Kovach crept closer, his fist tightening around the knife. He had worked Janos into a corner of the box stall. There was no escape.

"In the name of the Countess—" said Kovach.

A shrill whinny rang through the night air. The horse whirled his head around. He seized the guard's arm with his long teeth, his powerful jaws crushing the bone.

Kovach screamed.

The white stallion reared, snapping his rope. His iron-shod feet flashed out at the captain, knocking him to the ground.

Janos turned away, clutching his wounded arm. He heard Kovach's scream cut short as the stallion's hooves shattered his skull.

Chapter 112

John saw headlights illuminating the iron grillwork of the gate.

Three police cars raced up the road, red-and-blue lights flashing. Two police officers bounded out of the car, guns drawn.

The castle guard took out his cell phone. He spoke rapidly and then set the phone down, as the police approached with guns pointed.

One police officer began questioning the guard.

Another car drove up. John recognized one of the passengers who jumped out of the car.

"Detective Whitehall!" he shouted.

John stared at the butler's preternaturally blue eyes.

"No, I am sorry," the butler repeated. With his blond pomaded hair slicked back, he managed to look surly even as he confronted the Bratislava authorities.

John looked around the room. The fire was lit, the hearth deep with glowing embers. On a small table near the fireplace stood a decanter of red wine. He saw a splash of liquid on what must be a treasure—a very old tapestry of a slain dragon.

He touched the stain. It was still wet. He brought his fingers to his nose—wine. On the floor a shard of glass twinkled.

"The Count is not in residence. I believe he is in Bratislava," said the blue-eyed man, unblinking.

"You liar!" said John.

"We have reason to believe that he is indeed in residence," said Detective Whitehall, glancing at John. "We will wait to see him."

"Wait?" said John. "We can't wait. He has kidnapped at least three women. He has a friend of mine hidden somewhere in the castle."

"I will assume that you will produce proof of this 'kidnapping,'" said the butler, his voice cool and controlled. "Otherwise you wouldn't dare enter this house."

"We have the license plate seen at the scene of a kidnapping," said Detective Whitehall. "We have been tracking this car for two days now."

"I am sorry, I don't think I am aware of your . . . jurisdiction?" said the butler.

"Detective Whitehall, from Scotland Yard."

"Scotland Yard? That certainly does not give you the right to slander my employer, a Hungarian citizen of nobility. I shall call the embassy at once."

"I am in charge of this investigation," said a burly police officer. "I am a captain in the Bratislava division of the Slovakian National Police. I require your complete cooperation."

"This will not be good for delicate Hungarian-Slovak relations," said the butler, a thinly veiled threat. "Please convey this to your president. He knows Count Bathory, of course."

The police captain grunted.

"So," said the butler, raising his chin. "You have a license plate number. Witnesses often misread license plates, as I am sure you are aware. You have no subpoena. And I tell you the Count is not at home."

"We can search—can't we?" asked John.

The police officer approached him, saying in a quiet voice, "These castles have many secret doors and passageways. We need him to be more cooperative."

"You have no real evidence, no subpoena," said the butler. "I shall have to ask you to please leave at once."

John pushed past the police officer. Raw anger propelled him forward.

He heard a crunch under his boot.

John looked down. It was Daisy's crucifix, broken on the floor.

Chapter 113

The Count escorted Morgan to a high-backed chair on the dais. Two skeletal men stood on either side of her, dark pools under their eyes like bruises against the white of their skin.

Peering around the border of the tapestry, Betsy watched the tableau from the corner of the room.

"Call off the ghouls," Morgan said, slurring her words.

She's drugged, Betsy thought.

"No, I think it would be best if they were at your side," said the Count. "Be a good girl now and don't interfere, or we will have to tie you to the chair. Most undignified. Especially unfitting for the role you will play tonight."

He called to the woman attendant, beyond Betsy's field of sight.

"Bring in Dr. Path now," he said.

Betsy held her breath as her mother was led in, shackled. A fuchsia-haired woman set her down in a heavy wooden chair with leather straps on the armrest. Betsy heard the rip of Velcro as the attendant opened the straps and closed them again around her mother's forearms.

"Good evening, Dr. Path," said the Count. "Welcome to the four-hundredth anniversary of the Countess's arrest. We will proceed with the night festivities."

He turned away from her and walked to the lace-covered table. Betsy watched him touch the objects there, one by one, in deep reverence. The decanter, the golden funnel. He unwound the cord and opened the leather satchel. He held up a gleaming blade. Then another. He smiled.

He touched the silver spoon. Finally he stroked *The Red Book* with an open palm. His fingertips lingered on Jung's words.

"That's *The Red Book*," said Morgan, blinking hard to clear her head.

"Ah! You know Jung's masterpiece?"

"Why? Why do you have it?"

"It is the journey of the soul. The diary of a madman, not afraid of darkness. I am not afraid either, I embrace it. I shall paint my own masterpiece in blood."

Then he frowned. He touched the spoon again.

"Akos, Andras—" He said something in Hungarian to the two men guarding Morgan.

They both glanced at the red-haired young woman, then left her. They closed the door quietly behind them.

"Why did you send them away?" mumbled Morgan.

"Do not worry, my beauty," said the Count. "Relax. Tonight you must simply enjoy."

Grace struggled against her leather fetters, saying nothing.

The Count walked to the opposite wall from Betsy's hiding place, which was also covered in ancient tapestries. He lifted the corner of the hanging next to the portrait of Countess Bathory, uncovering a safe set into the stone.

He punched in a combination, swung the safe open, and withdrew an ornate ebony and ivory box.

Betsy watched as he brought the box to the table. He opened the box, dipped the silver spoon into it and brought it out, filled with white powder. He took a knife and leveled the powder perfectly. He dropped the contents into the large decanter.

"What's that?" asked Grace. "What are you putting in there?"

"Uncontrollable desire," he answered and laughed quietly. "No, no, I jest," he said, regarding her intent stare. He snapped the lid closed on the box. "What we will add tonight is ambrosia. This is merely a dash of spice."

Morgan started to rise from her chair, unsteadily.

"NO!" he snapped. His hand shot out, covering the box. "Stay there, or you will be punished."

Grace's eyes narrowed to slits. "You drug them," she said. "What is it? Heroin? Their teeth, eyes—"

The Count turned on her. "Don't say another word, Dr. Path. I warn you—"

"They're all addicts. That's why they're so pale and thin. They're addicts, not vampires!"

The Count strode over to her, seething. He slapped her face.

Betsy started to lunge from behind the tapestry. Something stopped her.

"Shut up!" shouted the Count. "They live on blood—they cannot live without it!"

"You want a cult of vampires," Grace said, slowly. "But they're just a bunch of crazed junkies!"

The creases in his brow deepened. He stared at the imprint of his hand blossoming on her cheek.

"You total shit!" screamed Morgan. "You just hit a helpless old lady!"

"My Countess . . ." he started, turning to Morgan. "Do not listen to her. I have created a perfect world in the image of you."

"I'm not her," said Morgan, shaking her head. "That psychotic Countess. *You* are psychotic."

His eyes flew open. "Oh, my darling. Do not say that. I worship you!"

He tried to take her hand. She snatched it away.

"Get away from me."

A wild light danced in his eyes. His cheek twitched.

"Look, I bring you pleasure." He barked orders into an intercom. "You will see. I will amuse you thoroughly. I have followed your ways—"

"Go to hell, you creepy bastard!"

Bathory stared at her silently. His scowl returned. The wild light died.

"Of course," he said. "For an instant I thought you were really her."

"Think again, asshole."

The two guards reentered. Count Bathory barked an order in Hungarian. Andros picked up a length of rope hanging on a steel spike, jutting from the wall.

"You will be tied now, my Lady. I will not tolerate any more interference," said Bathory.

The guards seized her, securing her arms to the heavy chair. Morgan struggled against their grasp.

A girl was marched in, her hands bound, her face preternaturally pale, as if she had never seen the sun.

"Ona, bring the girl here."

"Daisy!" Morgan screamed, still wrestling against the men and the rope.

Daisy stared at her sister without a flicker of recognition.

"You've drugged her, too. Daisy!"

Count Bathory's face twisted in a smile.

"Yes, but the drug she has is ever so much stronger than yours. Yours is meant to relax, nothing more. Hers is—well, she has been in a different dimension, I would say."

"Daisy! It's Morgan. Daisy!"

Again, a blank stare.

But slowly, a flicker of recognition grew. In the recesses of her mind, a dim memory.

It was the voice that pulled Daisy from her dreams. A voice that had called to her before, when evil had stalked her years ago. Morgan had intervened.

This is true evil, thought Daisy, *not like the things I thought I experienced in the cemetery or a Ouiji session or a haunted house.*

As a Goth she had played at daring the dark side. Her black clothes and the corpse paint on her face paid tribute to what was beyond mortality, to the spirit world. Her Goth ways were a nod to a dimension far beyond the petty cares of life in the twenty-first century. Daisy was intrigued by the shadows, pulled by the tide of mysticism.

That world had called to her, ever since her parents divorced.

No. Ever since her father's visits to the girls' bedrooms.

Daisy's throat tightened. She began to gag.

"She's choking!" screamed Morgan.

The Count looked at Daisy, his mouth puckered.

"The drug has never had that effect before," he said. He studied the gasping victim with a clinical eye.

"Daisy!" whispered Morgan, her voice soothing despite her fear. "It's all right. I'm here, baby sister. No one will hurt you."

Daisy closed her eyes, her chest heaving.

The darkness enveloped her again, soothing.

Goth. She had welcomed that thrill. She had sought dark tales and magical rites. It was a game. She plunged deep into the pool of shadows, forgetting everything else. The taste of darkness, so rich— she savored its opium.

To forget, the most perfect gift.

But now she knew that unfathomable evil lurked this side of the netherworld. Here in her realm, in this world, a psychotic stranger raged with a madness that summoned the bloodiest nightmares.

This was no tale from a dusty book. This insanity was real, lethal.

And somehow her sister had penetrated this world, just as she did the other nightmare.

"Do not worry. This drug will not last much longer. Potent but a short duration," said Bathory, observing Daisy's eyes.

The Count studied Daisy, tapping his walking stick on the rock floor. After a moment, he gestured with the cane and the guards pushed her down into an iron chair, bolted into the rock. They bound her arms and legs to the metal.

The Count opened the ancient leather case. He picked up a blade. "Do not move," he said. "It will go easier . . . for now. Andras!"

Andras hurried with a white porcelain tray. He placed it under Daisy's wrist.

Count Bathory looked once more at Morgan.

"For you, my lady," he said, bowing stiffly

He sliced the white skin of Daisy's wrist with a deft cock of his wrist. Blood splattered into the tray.

"You sick fuck!" shouted Morgan. She twisted, struggling against her ropes. "You monster, leave her alone!"

As Betsy watched, her breath felt trapped deep in her lungs. She forced herself to breathe.

She remembered her father warning her.

Swear to me you will never treat delusional patients. Never!

But why, Papa?

A patient in his past had haunted him, was all he said. This patient was the reason he had fled Europe for good. He refused to tell her any more.

There is ugliness in the world I will never relive, was all he would say. *It is best left buried.*

What kind of Jungian are you, Papa?

The Count laughed as the blood collected, pooling in the ceramic tray.

"Does this not amuse you? Oh, I see. Not yet."

Betsy gathered herself to leap into the room, then she stopped.

Her instinct was to run to help her patient, to free her mother and Morgan. But she could feel John's presence by her shoulder whispering, *Wait! Think, first.*

She stayed behind the tapestry in the darkness, trying to collect her thoughts. Anguish burned her throat. But to show herself now was certain suicide. What could she accomplish?

Betsy caught a whiff of blood, the odor of copper coins. This madman had kidnapped these two girls, her own mother. He was torturing Daisy—an innocent girl who had tried to protect her.

Betsy had spent her life working on the side of sanity, trying to preserve human dignity in the face of madness. But this was more than madness. This was evil. This could not be cured. It could only be killed.

Extinguished.

Her mouth twisted with hatred, with rage. The tendons of her neck stood out as she clenched her teeth. She felt a fire deep within her, an instinct to strike, to kill this man who threatened those she loved.

You are the other, her father had said. *The unspeakable thoughts, the basest desires, the unfathomable horror. All of this is part of you as much as you deny it. It is your shadow.*

When you realize that, you will indeed be a Jungian. What decisions you make, given the ugly face of your shadow, is who you are.

Remember: Nothing human is alien to me.

The sour taste in the back of her mouth gave her the urge to spit. She choked back the bile and watched, her left cheek twitching.

She remembered the ledger, zipped in the back pocket of her jacket. The names of all those girls.

The Count motioned and Ona applied a tourniquet to Daisy's arm. Then she bandaged the wound, using butterfly adhesives. Her practiced hands indicated that the sinister chore was a familiar one.

Using the golden funnel, the Count carefully poured the blood from the tray into the crystal decanter.

He swirled the blood around, watching the red liquid in delight.

He walked toward Morgan.

"Get away from me," she snarled. "Get away! Leave me alone!" Daisy's voice cried, small and distant.

"Get away!" Daisy said. "Run! Don't let him touch you!"

Standing before Morgan, the Count recited from *The Red Book*.

"The task is to give birth to the old in a new time. The soul of humanity is like the great wheel of the zodiac that rolls along the way—"

He swirled the blood again in the decanter. A dark sheen clung to the glass.

"Everything that comes up in a constant movement from below to the heights was already there. There is no part of the wheel that does not come around again."

Blasphemy. The Red Book *interpreted as evil*, thought Betsy.

Daisy gave a small cry and fainted, her head lolling as she slumped in the chair.

Betsy swallowed, her tongue sticking to the roof of her mouth. She had to act—but again John's voice told her she had to wait.

Ona knelt beside Daisy.

"Little witch," she ordered. "Wake!"

She slapped the girl's pale cheeks, trying to bring her back to consciousness.

Daisy's eyes flickered open.

She's still alive, thought Betsy. *But she could die of shock.*

The door of the dungeon swung open. A dark-haired servant stood at the opening, speaking quickly in Hungarian.

The Count's face turned stony. He issued an order. Akos left, casting a pointed look over his shoulder at Andras, who stayed behind.

"Some unfortunate business threatens to interrupt our pleasure," said the Count. He turned to Morgan. "But the night games will continue as planned. Precisely as you practiced them four hundred years ago, my Countess."

Chapter 114

Zuzana hurried through the dark underground corridor, her fingers trailing against the rocky wall. She carried no candle but ran blindly, her skirt flying behind her.

A cold draft of air curled around her ears, neck, and shoulders as she reached the juncture of tunnels. She saw torchlight at the end of the tunnel, heard the murmur of voices. She dropped back, behind fallen rubble.

Suddenly from the dungeon, the corridors, and the castle above came the scream of a baby. Then another, and another.

Zuzana froze. Could the Countess be torturing infants?

Then she recognized the sound. Every cat in the castle howled, the weird cacophony unbearable.

What could it mean?

Zuzana searched for amber eyes in the darkness. She was barely able to breathe; the cats' screeching flooded her ears.

"The servant girl Vida was found, running for the gate," said a man's voice. "She has been captured. She was seen giving something to the horsemaster."

"The horsemaster?" It was Hedvika's voice.

"Captain Kovach has gone to retrieve whatever she gave him. He should be here momentarily. Also, *Slecna* Zuzana cannot be found."

"She and Vida—"

"Captain told me to notify the Countess at once."

"Consider her notified," said a voice behind Zuzana. A cold hand clutched her forearm in the darkness, the grip tightening hard against the bone.

"Guard!" shouted the Countess, yanking at Zuzana's arm, pushing her forward. "Here is our traitor!"

Zuzana jerked away and began to run. The riding boots she wore were too large for her. She stumbled, fell, and scrambled back up.

The first guard seized her. Two more followed with torches.

"Fool," said the Countess, out of breath. She slapped Zuzana hard across the face. "Did you think I do not know these corridors better than you? You and your clumsy, clattering boots. Why are you dressed this way?" The Countess pulled her close. "You smell of horse sweat. Where would you be riding at this time of night?"

Zuzana did not answer.

"Hold her!" Bathory said, her jaw set in anger. "Take off her coat, bring the torch."

The guards pulled the cloak from the girl.

"I've always wondered if there remained anything beautiful beyond your eyes. In your eyes, I see your brother. On your skin, I see death. But what lies hidden beneath your bodice?"

Countess Bathory's hand flashed out, ripping Zuzana's bodice, exposing her white, perfect breasts.

Bathory raked her nails deep into the girl's flesh.

Zuzana howled in pain. She fell back into the guard's arms, blood streaming down her breasts.

The Countess sneered at the girl writhing in the guard's arms.

"Your dear brother. You shall join him in death."

Entering the dungeons, Thurzo's men came across Doricza's body first. The Croatian girl had been stabbed, the Palatine could see that. But she also been cudgeled savagely, her flesh a bloody pulp. Her body had been dragged into the shadows of the tunnel.

Gyorgy Thurzo bent down over the girl's corpse, removing his glove. His hand touched her face.

"By God, she is still warm," he whispered to the pastor. The pastor began praying, his lips moving silently.

Thurzo strode along the rocky corridor, the others behind him, to the entrance of the upper dungeon. There he saw a young girl—not more than sixteen—also dead on the floor. Their footsteps clattered, descending into the bowels of the earth.

He heard the muffled screams of girls somewhere close. He raced down the rock steps nearly impaling himself on a door fitted with spikes. He swung the door open and saw the Countess herself.

She was seated on a stool, a dead girl's body at her feet. She screwed up her bloody face, her eyes squinting to see.

"Who goes there? You shall pay for your intrusion!"

"Not so," Count Thurzo roared. "This is not one of your servants but the Palatine Prince of Hungary who stands before you and has come in the name of the King to bring justice to these accursed walls!"

Countess Bathory stared back. Her blood-drenched hand touched her face, and she looked down at her victim.

The rest of Thurzo's party pressed into the fetid room. Beads of water clung to the rocky walls, the dampness accentuating the stench of death.

"Countess Bathory, you are arrested for the crime of murder, by order of King Matthias."

Two guards seized the Countess by the arms.

Fizko, Dorka, and Ilona Joo stumbled up the stairs, their hands tied. Guards prodded them ahead at the point of a pike.

Thurzo looked around the chamber. There were three girls, all tied and gagged. As the pastor cut their bonds, they wept uncontrollably in his arms, like small children.

"Where is Zuzana?" the clergyman asked.

"She was not tortured long, Father," said a black-haired girl, still clinging desperately to him. "She broke loose from the guard and ran. She did not suffer long, I swear it."

She pointed to a great dark hole in the ground. The pastor could hear the echo of rushing water, deep below.

Janos ran down the stone steps. He stood panting at the scene. The blood-smeared Countess. The dead girl at her feet. The sobbing girls standing to one side. Thurzo's men staring wide-eyed, their faces white with disgust and horror.

The Countess looked at Janos in disdain, raising an eyebrow on her flawless, pale brow.

"Are you looking for your little friend, Horsemaster?" said the Countess, her voice icy. "Because if you are, it is too late."

"What have you—"

"Look for her in my carp ponds, I believe that's where the water flows. Her body will feed my fish well."

"You—"

"We shall have fat carp come springtime. I must invite you to dine again."

Her skirts made a swishing sound as the guard dragged her up the stairs.

Chapter 115

Bathory Castle
High Tatra Mountains, Slovakia
December 29, 2010

John clutched the broken crucifix in his hand.

"This belongs to Daisy Hart," he said. "She disappeared today, just beyond the gates of this castle."

The butler looked at the cross. John could smell the sweat emanating from the servant's wool jacket.

John watched the man look away.

"Where is she?" he shouted. "Tell us!"

The police officer picked up his cell phone. He dialed a number, spoke briefly, waited. Moments elapsed. Finally, the policeman nodded his head. He locked eyes with the Hungarian butler.

"We have permission to continue the search," said the officer. "From the highest authority. I suggest you cooperate from now on, Mr.—"

"Gellert. Heinrich Gellert."

"Show us the lower floors of the castle, *Pan* Gellert. Now!"

Chapter 116

A guard pounded on the thick oak door. Andras slid the bolts and opened the door. He and the guard spoke briefly in hushed voices.

The Count ignored the men.

Andras looked one last time at the Count and slipped out the door, following the guard into the darkness beyond. Ona put down the candlestick and hurried after them.

The Count roared—an inhuman sound. The candlelight guttered in a draft from somewhere deep in the castle. It caught the Count's eye, distracted him for a moment from his rage.

He closed the iron door and slid the bolt shut. Grace glanced toward Morgan and back to the Count again.

He walked toward the candle, hypnotized. He bent down, picking it up from the floor. He lifted the crystal decanter from the table and swirled the blood again. He turned to Morgan. "Watch, my Mistress! I shall bring back joyous light to your eyes!"

Now! Betsy thought. She surged out of the trapdoor and threw herself at the Count. His bad knee crumpled and he screamed with pain as he fell heavily to the floor, his head hitting the stones. He lay suddenly still and silent.

Betsy screamed, "Mom! I'm coming!

At least she is safe for the time being.

Breathing heavily, Betsy took her pocketknife from her jacket and cut through the ropes holding Morgan to the chair.

Morgan didn't react. She didn't look at Betsy. Her eyes were riveted on the Count and his victim, her sister.

Morgan's fingers dug into her bodice and pulled out an object.

The thin, sharp blade of a switchblade sliced the air.

Betsy didn't see the Count struggle back to his feet, blood running down his face from a cut above his eye, where his head had hit the stone floor. He stared at Betsy, his eyes transfixed on her face.

Then he turned toward Daisy.

"Whore!" the Count shouted, lunging for Daisy's throat. "This is all your fault! You shall be punished in the name of Countess Bathory."

"Get off of her!" screamed Morgan, charging toward him.

The Count twisted in time to fend off her attack. He held up one hand, protecting his face. The other grabbed for Morgan's arm.

He pulled her down on top of him. They both wrestled for the knife. Bathory managed to get a tenuous grasp on the hilt.

Morgan grabbed his wrist, the blade twisting in his hand.

Bathory wrenched the knife from Morgan's grasp, but she rolled on her side and swung her knees up, striking the Count hard in the crotch.

He screamed, losing his grasp of the knife. She snatched it from him with the deft move of a street fighter.

Morgan plunged the switchblade between his ribs. She pulled out the knife. She stood above her victim, panting.

The Count lay very still. Morgan hovered over him.

He suddenly lashed out, knocking the knife from her hand. It clattered across the floor.

He spoke as he raised himself to his knees. His eyes blinked wide in astonishment.

"You betray me, Mistress," the Count said, staring at Morgan. "Have I not dedicated my life to you, Countess?"

He caught sight of Betsy, just behind her.

"And you, my cousin? I knew I would see you again, but not like this. Not here—"

"I am not your cousin," said Betsy. She stood warily, wondering if Morgan had inflicted a mortal injury.

He crumpled again to the floor, his hand pressed against his ribs. He curled up in a fetal position.

Keeping an eye on the Count, Betsy cut the ropes that held Daisy to the chair.

"Hurry," Betsy said. "Get help!" Daisy stood up, unsteady for a moment, then she stumbled out the door into the corridor and up the winding stairs.

Betsy turned back to Morgan, who stared blankly. A bloody wound blossomed on her sleeve, soaking the silk.

"Morgan! You're hurt."

Betsy untied the red bandana around her neck.

The blood was pumping fast, too fast for the small bandana. She dropped it on the floor, her fingers flying to undo the bow on Morgan's apron. She wound the material tightly around the wound, securing the ties. She kept one eye on the Count as she worked.

"I tried to protect her. I always protected her, my little sister," Morgan mumbled. "I would never let him touch her."

"I know," said Betsy. "Morgan, I know. Be still now."

"It wasn't right," said Morgan, shaking her head. "I told him so. They are related by blood. I told him to take me instead. We're not related, not really, you know." Her voice was empty. "And I loved him. Once."

"It's all right now, Morgan," said Betsy, pulling off the girl's red-stained lace collar.

Morgan's clammy skin and distant stare betrayed symptoms of shock.

A gurgle rattled in the Count's throat. Betsy turned.

"You are the last of the true line, Dr. Elizabeth Path," said the Count, his voice hollow and rasping. He was on his knees on the stone floor. "The Countess's daughter, whom Gabor tracked down in Transylvania. She was your ancestor. They planned to raise her together, he and the Countess, to be their legacy. The most deadly of us all."

"You are insane," muttered Betsy.

The Count watched his blood pool. He appeared not to hear her.

"After the Countess's death, after Gabor's death, destiny turned. The girl was forgotten, except for her Bathory name. Your father knew—"

The Count's breath was ragged.

"Your father betrayed us all," he said.

"My . . . father?" Betsy shot a look at her mother, tied and gagged. She needed to untie her, but she was suddenly too tired to move.

Instead her fingers fumbled with the zipper of her back pocket. She pulled out the ledger.

"What did my father have to do with this?" said Betsy, scrambling to her feet.

"Ah!" gasped the Count. "So he did find it after all."

"What is this?" said Betsy, shaking the small book at him. "What does it have to do with my father?"

"My dear. That is why I had to kill him."

Grace twisted hard in the chair, her feet thumping the stone floor. Her eyes were wide and white. She shook her head violently.

Betsy stared back at the Count. She zipped the book back into her pocket, her hands moving mechanically.

"You? You killed my father?"

Betsy could hear the thud of her mother's shoes, her heels beating against the stone. A warning.

But the mention of her father pulled Betsy toward the man crouched on the floor.

"What are you talk—"

The Count snatched her ankle and brought her down. Morgan's switchblade was in his hand.

Betsy struggled and kicked at the knife. "No, this isn't for you," he cried, surging to his feet. The knife clattered to the floor. "Bathorys die encased in stone, for eternity."

With the strength of a lunatic, he dragged her by the leg toward the shadows of the room. A large opening loomed black in the corner. She felt the cold air, heard rushing water in the darkness below.

"This is how a true Bathory dies," said the Count, rolling her off the edge. "Buried in the rock."

John heard Daisy's voice in the corridor below. He pushed past the butler, Whitehall, and the police officers, clattering down the stairs.

"Daisy! Where are you?"

"Down here!" she screamed. "Help us!"

Her voice trailed off. She had returned to the dungeon.

Daisy saw that Morgan was soaked in even more blood than before. Her hands were slick and crimson, her face splattered.

And the Count had disappeared.

Morgan's eyes had a haunted look.

"He's gone," was all she said. Then she was silent.

Daisy touched her sister's cheek. She put her arms around Morgan, rocking her against her shoulder.

"It's all right, Morgan, it's all right. You saved me again. Let me take care of you."

Morgan stared glassy-eyed past Daisy's shoulder.

Just steps behind Daisy, John rushed in.

"Where's Betsy? Is she here?"

Daisy stood up. "No! She was here, John. When I ran to unlock the door. She couldn't have left—she—"

They stared at Morgan. She flicked her eyes at the dark opening in the corner of the dungeon.

"Oh, my God" John said, running.

John threw himself on his stomach at the edge of the precipice. A cold draft of air chilled his face.

"Betsy! Betsy!" he called.

All he heard was his own voice echoing back, and the rush of distant water.

From the corner of the room, John heard sobs. He twisted around to see two policemen cutting the ropes and setting Grace free.

"Oh, John," she said, stumbling toward him. "My Betsy!"

Chapter 117

The icy-cold water was beginning to numb the searing pain in her shoulder, but Betsy knew her situation was life-threatening. She had landed on a rock and she could feel the jagged edge of her broken collarbone just beneath her skin. For a moment, she closed her eyes and relived the terror of her fall and the moments after, as she slid down the rocks and into the eddying pool of the underground spring—and then the horror of watching another falling body blot out the light far above her, the echoing screams filling the dark space and stopping abruptly as the body hit, head-first, skull splitting against the stone.

She opened her eyes and looked again, just to be certain. Yes. The Count lay motionless, eyes wide-open, Morgan's knife sticking out of his neck, buried handle-deep.

Even through her pain, Betsy felt a grim satisfaction. Morgan had protected her sister. And in a moment of sudden clarity, her own life hanging in the balance, Betsy's analyst mind solved a problem. She understood what Morgan had been talking about just moments before—and she knew how Morgan had protected her little sister years ago.

440

Betsy screamed for help, but no answer came. The tug of the icy current weakened her, and she knew it would soon carry her away.

The water no longer felt cold. It burned, a scorching heat. As she clung to the rock, she felt as if her mind was already drifting with the current, floating gently away into a dream.

As her fingers finally lost their grip, she heard a shout.

"Betsy! Betsy!"

In her dream, it was John's voice.

We could have been happy.

She let it go—along with everything else she remembered about her life—and as the stream swirled her away, she heard her father's voice in her mind again. *Nothing human is alien to me.*

Chapter 118

BATHORY CASTLE DUNGEON

HIGH TATRA MOUNTAINS, SLOVAKIA

DECEMBER 29, 2010

Grace sobbed as she clung to John.

"John! Betsy—he pushed her—"

John held her tight enough to feel her heart beating.

"There is an underground river," he said. "I can hear it."

The police were questioning half a dozen girls they had freed from the dungeons. John broke in.

"Are any of you from here?"

"I am," said Draska.

He pointed at the dark opening. "Where does this river go?"

Draska shook her head. "I do not know. Waters come out of rock everywhere."

John looked at Grace, then Daisy.

"Daisy, can you look after Grace—this is Betsy's mother."

John stopped. Daisy's face was taut, haunted with grief.

"Are you OK?" John asked.

"Go, John. I'll look after her, I promise."

"You are Betsy's mother?" said Daisy.

Grace covered her eyes with her hands, crying silently.

"Then you have to find her."

Grace didn't answer.

Daisy gently pulled Grace's hands away from her eyes.

"You can, you know."

"Leave me alone, please."

"I can't do that. Time is running out."

"You are as insane as the rest of them. There is nothing I can do now."

"Yes, there is. I had dreams that led me here. But I never dreamed the ending." Daisy searched Grace's eyes. "There's a piece missing, and I think you have it. You know the ending. Don't you?"

"I don't have any information," Grace said, fighting her sobs. She turned away. "Leave me alone."

Daisy looked down at her bandaged wrist. She winced with grief, her stray tooth exposed.

"Are you ready to live with the fact that your daughter is dead?"

Grace snapped her head around, outraged.

"You are cruel!"

"No, I'm not. I think you have the answer, and you're not sharing it. *The Red Book* says we are all connected," said Daisy. "The collective unconscious, pooled universal knowledge—"

"Shut up! You're making no sense!"

"You have the missing piece of the puzzle, I know it!" Daisy shouted at her.

"You are delusional. The blood loss. I'm not like my daughter. I'm not like my husband. I don't dream. And I am not a Bathory."

"Neither am I," Daisy said. "But you are her mother, she came here searching for you. There has to be a connection, I know it."

"You know nothing about me."

"Please, Grace, help me! Come with me. Please?" Daisy began to tremble, her teeth chattering.

"This girl is in shock!" said Grace, but no one heard her, except Draska.

"For your daughter's sake!" pleaded Daisy.

Daisy took Grace's arm and led her to the edge of the pit. Grace shuddered when she heard the rush of the river below.

"Think," said Daisy. "No, don't think. Remember. Where does this river flow?"

"I don't know. How could I—"

"Have you ever dreamed of a river? A river flowing beneath rocks?"

"Go away!" Grace said, turning away from her. "Don't touch me."

Draska watched Grace walk away from Daisy.

The Slovak girl approached Grace, putting a comforting hand on her shoulder.

"Listen to her," she said. "She is trying to help."

Grace lifted her face from her hands, looking at the girl who had risked her life to send a message to her daughter. Draska's breath was sour with fear and adrenaline.

"You try now. Yes?" asked Draska. "For daughter?"

Daisy took Grace's hand in hers. She pressed it gently but urgently.

"You love your daughter," Daisy whispered. "I do, too. Please try. Please?"

Grace closed her eyes. She nodded.

"Come outside," said Draska. "Come. We help you."

The two girls took Grace gently by the arms, helping her to the door of the dungeon.

"You can't leave," said a police officer. "We have to question Dr. Path. We must get a statement."

"She has to find her daughter. Now!" said Daisy.

The police officer raised his eyebrow. "The woman who fell into the underground river? There is no—"

Grace looked at the man, her face crumpling.

"You really don't want to complete that sentence," said Daisy, her teeth clenched, exposing her canine tooth.

"No," said the police commander, motioning the officer away. "I will accompany them. Let me get you coats. Come, Dr. Path," he said offering his arm. "Come upstairs, please."

PART
-4-

Chapter 119

John stood, paralyzed by uncertainty, ice crystals forming in his hair. In the gray predawn light he could see the tall iron fence and his rented car beyond the gate.

"Come in," called a policeman who had taken over the guard-house. "Come in and rest."

"I can't. I have to find her—"

"Hot coffee," said the policeman. "Help you think."

The Slovak led John into the guardhouse. "Here, drink," he said.

John nodded, accepting the cup. His hands moved with the jerky stiffness of a puppet.

The policeman pointed. "They come."

John saw two figures emerge from the castle entry. Then a third, much larger. He recognized Daisy, then Grace. Then the National Police Captain.

"They're trying to find her," he murmured.

"But—there is no track," said the policeman. "How can they find body with no—"

John turned, shaking with emotion.

"I am sorry—" said the guard, putting his hand on John's shoulder. "But chance of survival—"

John said nothing. He just stared into the milky gray light. Tears welling in his eyes, he left the guardhouse, staggering blindly after them.

Grace fought through the deep snow. The pale light exposed earlier tracks, but she did not notice them. She walked almost without seeing, searching without looking, stumbling with a blind certainty toward a place she knew from the one and only dream she had ever remembered. The dream she had told her husband so many years ago, the night before Betsy was born.

And then she was there. The frozen pond. A graceful place, the boughs of the weeping willows coated with ice and snow. It was dawn, and the rosy glow of the sun burned through the remaining clouds, a mist of vapor rising from the silver surface of the pond.

A few ducks paddled between broken patches of ice. They plunged their heads under the water, looking for food. At the edge of the pond a river flowed over rocks polished smooth from millennia of rushing water.

She felt a swell of sorrow. She knew this place. She remembered this spot where she had never been. It was not a happy memory.

"Here," she murmured.

She struggled to the frozen shore where the river met the ponds.

The white, perfect form of a woman lay face up beneath the ice.

Chapter 120

Somewhere in the castle above, a bell tolled a mournful early-morning hour as Janos was lowered into the ice cave on a rope, clutching a burning torch, ignoring the pain in his wounded arm. Thurzo's men fed the slack slowly as he descended.

The rippling formation of the walls were a wolf's mouth closing around him, undulating and raw. Diamonds of light glittered. Ice crystals sparkled. Milky white sheets of ice shimmered in the torch-light.

He winced, seeing the brown blood staining rocks below. Zuzana was not the first to fall into the abyss. He thought of all the families who had searched in vain for their beloved daughters.

They lay here, hidden in an icy tomb.

The air was much colder, blowing over the coursing water carving through the blue-white ice. Mighty columns gleamed in his torch-light. Hanging chandeliers of ice arched to meet with sharp pillars thrusting up from the cave floor.

And below this glittering beauty, strewn across the rocks, lay the bodies of girls, like broken porcelain dolls, ghostly pale and coated in ice. Their frozen features sparkled, stars shimmering from their translucent skin. In these depths, there were no wolves to ravage their flesh, no rats to gnaw their bones. They were perfectly preserved.

Merciful death had kissed them with peace, their tortured faces relaxed at last.

Janos forced himself to close his eyes to the girls long dead. He had to find Zuzana.

She was not here among the dead.

He followed the course of the river threading through the cavern. He picked his way along the frozen shore.

He held his torch high, the ceilings of the cavern now not a wolf's mouth, but the smooth vaulted arches of a cathedral.

His lips moved in silent prayer, not daring to speak in the holy silence of the underground. Spirits—far more ancient than mankind—dwelled here, amid the rock, water, and ice.

As the cave descended less steeply, the river moved more and more slowly. The rush against the stone was muted, the water undecided whether to freeze and join with the icy shelf or to slice its course onward.

Janos walked on. His torch flickered once, twice. Then it was gone. He was plunged into darkness. He closed his eyes and followed the sound of the cold-blooded waters.

As time wore on, he heard the water change its heartbeat, moving more rapidly. He opened his eyes to see light playing off long white icicles, the savage teeth of the wolf guarding the way to a small opening—and, beyond that, the glint of the rising sun.

At last he fought his way through the opening and looked down to the river spilling out into a series of ponds. The branches of the weeping willows bowed low in reverence to winter's reign.

It was there he found Zuzana, staring wide-eyed to the rosy dawn, her body lodged under a thick sheet of clear ice.

Chapter 121

Daisy stared at Betsy's body, beneath the ice. She stood paralyzed at the sight.

"Daisy!" shouted a voice. "Grace!"

John hurried toward them, stumbling through the snow, fighting through the drifts.

Wide-eyed in horror, neither woman spoke as he reached them.

He looked down and saw Betsy and, without thinking, he lunged.

He crashed through the ice, embraced her freezing body, and pulled her from the pool. Her face had turned a pale blue, mottled in white.

What is the chance of surviving more than thirty minutes in icy water—what is the probability?

Probability. Chance, margin of error. Statistics—his identity, his life—all that was his enemy now, logic his foe.

She was dead. He knew it. Here was the proof, the blue-white flesh, the open eyes.

"No!" he roared, falling to his knees. "No!"

He bent over her, his open palm cradling her head. He placed his lips over her open mouth.

He breathed hard. Breath after warming breath.

He heard Daisy's boots crunching next to him as she knelt in the snow.

She crossed her palms, pushing rhythmically against Betsy's chest. Tears streamed down Daisy's face, but she said nothing. Her anguished eyes sought John's.

John and Daisy worked silently, blinking dumbly in the glow of sunrise.

Grace watched them.

She gazed out over the frozen pond, remembering her dream.

Detective Whitehall found the three Americans poised over the body. He led the ambulance medics to the scene.

As the Slovaks pulled the desperate man and girl away, Whitehall turned. He looked out over the pond, the icicles on the weeping willows splintering the glow of dawn.

The medics allowed John to accompany them in the ambulance. As a matter of protocol, they kept up the artificial respiration for the duration of the ride.

John held Betsy's frozen hand, squeezing it rhythmically as if it were her heart.

"Live," he whispered. "Live. Against all probability, damn it! Live."

He cried silently into her frozen hand.

He felt a flicker, a slight curling of her finger.

"She moved her hand!" he shouted. "She moved!"

The medics looked at each other, and then to the face of the foreigner.

"No, she could not. She is—"

"No, listen to me! She did it again. Look!"

He cradled her hand like a bird in his cupped palms. Her fingers moved tentatively, searching for his.

One of the medics placed a stethoscope against her breast. He stared into the air, listening blindly.

His face lit up.

"Yes, yes. Very little. Heart."

Chapter 122

ozens of soldiers searched Čachtice Castle. They overturned mattresses, searched wells, dug up shallow graves.

Count Thurzo had every servant within the walls of the castle brought to him, one by one, in the great hall, to give testimony. He sat at a great oaken table along with his scribe, with Miklos Zrynyi and Emerich Megyery as witnesses.

A guard accompanied Janos Szilvasi to the door.

"Horsemaster Szilvasi," said Count Thurzo. "Please enter."

The pond ice had left deep gouges in Janos's hands where he had fought the frozen water to free Zuzana's body. He wore rags wrapped around his fingers.

"Your friend Zuzana provided us entry," said Thurzo. He hesitated as he noticed the torment in the young man's eyes. "She was a brave woman."

Janos reached in his tunic, fumbling. He withdrew the vellum ledger, shaking the bits of straw free from the pages.

The young horsemaster stared directly at the noblemen before him. "I have read these pages. There are six hundred twelve names. Girls the Countess murdered. She gives descriptions of each. And whether they provided her good sport."

Miklos Zrynyi gasped. "Six hundred twelve?"

"Did you not suspect, Count Zrynyi?" said Janos, narrowing his eyes at the Countess's son-in-law. "How could you be so blind for so many years? How could you tolerate the stench—"

"Enough, Szilvasi," snapped Count Thurzo. He stretched out his hand to receive the ledger. "Your evidence and written testimony will be used in court. I plan to assemble the judges immediately in Bytca."

"Bytca?" said Janos. "Your castle? Will she not be tried by the Pressburg courts? Or in Vienna by the crown?"

Thurzo stroked his beard. "No. I want to have the Countess tried immediately. The courts will not reconvene until after Epiphany."

"But—"

"Horsemaster, you have been useful. Now I must ask you to leave."

Janos stared into Thurzo's dark eyes. He saw a flash of anger.

"Guards, please escort the horsemaster to the stables. He may select any horse he chooses to ride. Then see him through the gates of Čachtice."

Janos set his jaw, facing Count Thurzo. "You will see that justice is served. Zuzana gave her life—"

"Take him away!" shouted Thurzo.

Janos threw off the hands of the guard who tried to seize him by the arm. He walked out the doorway, never looking back at the Count.

"Six hundred and twelve victims?" whispered Count Zrynyi. "If this ledger ever gets in the King's hands, he will certainly seize all the Countess's lands! He will make all Bathorys pay for her sins, leaving us paupers!"

"The ledger will never reach the King," muttered Count Thurzo. He turned the ring on his finger, round and round, thinking.

"The horsemaster knows that," he said at last. "Good sirs, there is such a thing as too much evidence."

Thurzo gave a stern look to the scribe, who nodded. He set his quill down.

Count Thurzo opened a leather pouch. He slid the ledger in among other documents.

"This ledger belongs to the Bathory family. It shall remain as part of our records, not for the eyes of judges or kings."

Chapter 123

Gabor Bathory rode out, his eye searching for coaches approaching from Royal Hungary. He pulled back the black hood on his cloak, his Bathory ring glinting gold in the setting sun.

Her advance scout had ridden hard day and night to bring word that the Countess would take refuge in his castle, swearing her loyalty to him in his quest.

"Did she receive any tidings that warned of her arrest?" asked the Prince of Transylvania. "Why did she choose to leave Čachtice now, on the cusp of the New Year?"

The scout shivered, knowing full well that the spirits ruled the midnight skies as one year gave birth to the next.

"No, she had no evidence," replied the scout, wiping salty sweat from his eyes. "She had a premonition, a dream that the end was near. The howling of cats."

Gabor's face went rigid. He wasted no time in assembling his troops. With his cousin's vast wealth and the prominent names of Nadasdy and Bathory, he would take Poland.

Then Vienna.

But he needed his Cousin Erzsebet's power—her wealth, lands, and strategic castles.

Hours passed. His scouts were sent far ahead to escort the Countess's entourage. Gabor's ear anticipated the cursing of drivers, the clatter of hoofbeats, the clanging of pots and pans.

There was only silence. Then the howls of wolves, echoing across the dark woods. A low fog rolled up from the south, clinging to the mountainside.

Gabor's amber eyes scanned the horizon. Skeletal branches of birch trees etched against the backdrop of snow, stretching for miles.

If she did not appear, he would send the girl away. A bastard daughter of the Countess would no longer be an asset.

A gust of wind roared in from the southwest, blowing ice and snow in ghostly forms, chasing each other across the valley below.

He turned his horse back toward the mountains of Transylvania, a black hooded figure disappearing into the mists.

Epilogue

Aspen Farmers' Market
September 24, 2011

There is no more glorious time in the Roaring Fork Valley than late September. The aspen leaves turn gold, setting the mountains aflame with color with every breeze. Snow dusts the peaks, powdering the gray, rugged rock. Locals make bets on whether all the ski slopes will open on time.

Silver glints on the water of the Roaring Fork River, rippling through the valley, winding around huge boulders and wader-clad fisherman. Red-tailed hawks soar and dive in the cobalt skies, playing the wind currents flowing over the mountains. The solemn spruce trees, their shadows stretched long and ominous, hint at the winter to come.

Daisy and Morgan walked together, inspecting the bright apples at the Aspen Farmers' Market on East Hopkins Avenue. The smell of roasting green chiles wafted through the streets, making the mountain air smell more like Santa Fe than a Colorado ski town.

Betsy spotted them in the crowd. Daisy held an apple by the stem, twirling it in front of her sister's eyes. They both laughed at some private joke. Morgan reached out, resting her hand on Daisy's wrist, a gesture of affection.

Sunlight sparkled on Daisy's canine tooth as she smiled.

"Her mother told me that she had braces at six," Betsy told John. "Apparently she had fully formed teeth at birth."

"That's freakish."

"It happens, I guess. That last wild tooth came in when she was twelve. She refused to have it straightened."

"You want to go over and say hi?" he asked.

She gazed at the sisters. "No, let's leave them alone. We'll see them this afternoon at the wedding."

"It's good to see them doing so well," said John.

They watched the two sisters raise a hand in greeting as Daisy called to a blond teenager in a baseball cap at a vegetable stall.

Kyle loped over to them, slinging his arm around Daisy.

"Your mom, too," said John. "I've never seen her look so happy."

"She just got a royalty check," said Betsy, laughing. "The book's doing better than she ever dreamed."

John took her hand. "The Countess is finally doing some good."

"And she got a letter from the bank. The Bathory Reparation Trust is getting contributions from all over. More than she expected. Mom thought giving half of her royalties might be most of the money, but she was amazed how many Bathory relatives want to purge the stain of the Countess from their name."

"Can you blame them?"

"At least the descendants of the victims will have some retribution for the horrors their ancestors suffered. Not a bad legacy for my dad. It's the best memorial he could ever have."

John pulled Betsy against him, cupping her chin with the palm of his hand. He tilted her head up gently, looking into her eyes.

"Ready to change your name back to Bathory?"

"I'll always be a Path, John," she teased. "Even after the ceremony."

They watched as the two sisters drifted off into the crowd arm in arm.

Betsy took John's arm, and they wandered over to the basket of apples.

"I'll take this one," said Betsy, picking up the apple Daisy had touched. John reached for his wallet, taking out a dollar. The farmer nodded, digging in her apron for change.

"Take a bite," said Betsy, rubbing the fruit on her red flannel shirt. She held the apple up to his mouth.

He closed his hand over hers and bit hard into the apple.

"You have always led me into temptation, Elizabeth Path. I have never been able to resist."

She smiled, biting into the other half.

HISTORICAL NOTE

According to historical record, Erzsebet Bathory was arrested on December 29, 1610. Her trial took place on January 2, 1611, at Bytca, the ancestral home of Count Gyorgy Thurzo.

The decision to hold the trial in Bytca, instead of Vienna or Pressburg, was rumored to have been made to save face for the Bathory family and to settle the affair quickly. The Hungarian Parliament was recessed for the Christmas season, and Count Thurzo deemed Countess Bathory's case to be urgent.

According to trial transcripts cited in Raymond McNally's *Dracula Was a Woman*, the following entry describes the fate of the Countess's accomplices, Ilona Joo and Dorka.

> . . . as the foremost perpetrators of this great blood crime, and in accordance with the lawful punishment for murderers, to have all the fingers on their hands, which they used as instruments in so much torture and butchering and which they dipped in the blood of Christians, torn out by the public executioner with a pair of red-hot pincers; thereafter they shall be thrown alive on the fire.
>
> As for Fizko (Janos Uujvary), because of his youthful age and complicity in fewer crimes, we sentence him to decapitation. His body, drained of blood, should then be reunited with his fellow accomplices, where we wish him to be burned.

Critical testimony came from Bathory's many servants. One witness in the trials was Jakub—also referred to as Janos—Szilvasi, who claimed to have a ledger written in the Countess's own hand, listing the young women murdered, and details about them, such as, "She was too small and provided no sport."

The Countess Erzsebet Bathory was not allowed to appear at her own trial. She was sentenced in absentia.

Countess Bathory's punishment was to be immured in her own castle: Stone masons sealed up a tiny cell where she would spend the last of her days. There were two ventilation hatches and only a small slit in the stone where she could receive food and water. She was confined to this cold castle prison until her death.

For two years—1611 to 1613—she predicted that her cousin Gabor, Prince of Transylvania, would avenge her incarceration and come to her rescue.

Gabor Bathory's fortunes reversed after the incarceration of Countess Bathory. No longer seeing Gabor as an asset, the Ottomans pushed him out of Wallachia and Moldavia. The Sultan then set his sights on Transylvania itself. Gabor Bathory was assassinated on October 27, 1613. No further historical record exists for Erzsebet's illegitimate daughter, who disappeared into Transylvania the day after her birth.

King Matthias decreed that the name Erzsebet Bathory would never be uttered again within the Holy Roman Empire.

Countess Erzsebet Bathory protested her innocence until her death. She died on August 14, 1614, "without crucifix or light."

ACKNOWLEDGMENTS

Carl Jung's psychoanalytic methods and *The Red Book* were a springboard for this novel. Jung's perspective on mental illness, psychology, and synchronicity helped me look for interconnections among characters, past and present. I felt I was looking through a long tunnel of mirrors reflecting into each other, a sense of eternity. (Fun stuff for a writer.)

Thank you forever, Andy Stone, my husband and first editor. Your own lyrical writing sets a high standard for me. I always feel you are sitting on my shoulder, Mr. Editor. (Sometimes I have to brush you off while writing and say, "Hey! Give me a break!")

My eternal gratitude to screenwriter and acquisition editor Lindsay Guzzardo for "discovering" me. Lindsay was not only an acquisition editor but a hands-on developmental editor. She worked with fierce dedication on edits and overseeing revisions.

Melody Guy gave me guidance I cherish as I worked through extensive rewrites. She really believed in this novel. I was lucky to have two great editors to oversee such an ambitious book.

In addition, Terry Goodman, senior editor at Amazon, and editor Alison Dasho oversaw every facet of the publication of this novel. Thank you, Terry and Alison, for taking me under your wing.

Copyeditor Paul Thomason kept me honest with his own research and fact-checking. Thank you for your thorough and extensive work, Paul. . . . Especially with the mind-boggling task of keeping track of dates and the timeline for the two plots (and subplots) set four hundred years apart!

My gratitude to Lelia Mander for her work on this manuscript.

Jackie Ball made excellent suggestions as well. I loved the formatting throughout the book.

Amazon author-team. You are the best. Special thanks to Jessica Poore, Susan Stockman, Nikki Sprinkle, Gracie Doyle, and all the others who have worked so hard on my behalf.

Deborah Schneider, agent extraordinaire—this is the book that led me back to you (or you back to me?) after a nearly two-decade absence. Thank you for sending me that lightning-quick e-mail and signing me once again with Gelfman Schneider.

Speaking of Gelfman Schneider, thank you to Victoria Marini and Cathy Gleason for all your support.

Gratitude to my agents Betsy Robbins, Sophie Baker, and Claire Nozieres at Curtis Brown in London. Thank you for enabling me to share my work with readers in many languages.

Lala Barbosa helped me by letting me have a perspective into the Aspen High Goth world during the time frame of the novel. (She is the most cheerful, friendly Goth I know!)

To my readers: Sarah Kennedy Flug, Ted and Nancy Kuhn, John and Susan Boslough, thank you for your reading and encouragement. I remember those vivacious dinner parties, each of us describing our novels, screenplays, and acting.

Lucia Caretto, my eagle-eyed reader. Thank you for your friendship. Our afternoons together chatting in Spanish and Italian keep my brain sharp(er)!

Anne Fitzgibbon Shusterman, Ann English, and Michael Cleverly—your belief in me decades ago nourished my bruised ego over the twenty-seven years it took to publish a book.

Deep gratitude for those editors and agents through the years who took the time to write me thoughtful rejection letters and make personal phone calls. Your encouragement was crucial to my eventual success.

I am grateful to the Aspen Writers' Foundation for your support through the years. (It has been surreal to be on stage after being in the audience for over thirty years!)

Thank you to Doctors Brano and Eva Branislav. The first Slovakian ambassador to the United States, Lichardus Branislav, assured me that Countess Bathory's crimes of terror had not been forgotten among the Slovaks. Her infamy is essentially part of the Slovakian collective unconscious.

To my beloved parents, Cdr. Frederick R. Lafferty and Elizabeth Vissering Lafferty, who taught me to love books, travel, people, and languages—and for supporting my great love of horses. I love you both dearly and forever.

To Col. James R. Spurrier who brought horses and polo into my life at an early age. That flame burns bright, even in my writing.

Bud Heatley taught me much that I know about doctoring horses and a light hand on the reins. I'll never forget you.

My sister, Nancy Elisha, who taught me to read and write before kindergarten. She used to tell me stories when I was a little girl . . . now it's my turn to be the storyteller, big sister. . . .

BIBLIOGRAPHY

In writing this novel, I relied on many research books, including:

Infamous Lady: The True Story of Countess Erzsébet Báthory, by Kimberly L. Craft

Bathory: Memoir of a Countess, by A. Mordeaux

The Bloody Countess: The Atrocities of Erzsebet Bathory, by Valentine Penrose

Dracula Was a Woman: In Search of the Blood Countess of Transylvania, by Raymond T. McNally

Memories, Dreams, Reflections, by C. G. Jung, Aniela Jaffe, Clara Winston, and Richard Winston

Man and His Symbols, by Carl Gustav Jung

The Red Book, by C. G. Jung, Sonu Shamdasani, Mark Kyburz, and John Peck

Jung on Synchronicity and the Paranormal, by C. G. Jung and Roderick Main

The I-Ching or Book of Changes by Richard Wilhelm, Cary F. Baynes, Hellmut Wilhelm and C. G. Jung

The Book Of Symbols: Reflections On Archetypal Images, by Archive for Research in Archetypal Symbolism and ARAS

Synchronicity: An Acausal Connecting Principle. (From Vol. 8., Collected Works of C. G. Jung)

The Archetypes and The Collective Unconscious (Collected Works of C. G. Jung, Vol. 9, Part 1)

The Portable Jung, by Carl G. Jung and R.F.C. Hull

ABOUT THE AUTHOR

NORAFELLER.COM

The daughter of a naval commander, Linda Lafferty attended fourteen different schools growing up, ultimately graduating from the University of Colorado with a master's degree and a PhD in education. Her peripatetic childhood nourished a lifelong love of travel, and she studied abroad in England, France, Mexico, and Spain. Her uncle introduced her to the sport of polo when she was just ten years old, and she enjoys playing to this day. She also competed on the Lancaster University Riding Team in England in stadium jumping, cross country, and dressage. A veteran school educator, she taught at Aspen High School for years. She lives in Colorado.